STARTED

MW00805884

For two men taken far too soon.
Kesler Casimir, my best friend,
And one of the greatest influences and role models I
have ever known. He always believed in Kojiro,
and in me.
Madison Meyer, the incredible artist who penned
the image on the following page, who always
challenged me intellectually, pushed me to
do and be better, and never shied from rebuking me
when I deserved it,
as a friend should.

This one, gentlemen, is for you.

-KOJIRO-

希
望

Khalil Barnett

BookLocker
Trenton, Georgia

Paperback ISBN: 978-1-958878-09-5
Hardcover ISBN: 978-1-958878-10-1
Ebook ISBN: 979-8-88531-373-5

Published by BookLocker.com, Inc., Trenton, Georgia.

Printed on acid-free paper.

The characters and events in this book are fictitious. Any similarity to real persons, living or dead, is coincidental and not intended by the author.

BookLocker.com, Inc.
2022

First Edition

Library of Congress Cataloguing in Publication Data
Barnett, Khalil
Kojiro by Khalil Barnett
Library of Congress Control Number: 2022920498

BOOK I:
THE SERPENT AND THE SHEPHERD

"Your thoughts are the voice of God. But which God, how many, and to what end?"

-Xiao Xiao Chen, from The Bodhisattvas
of a world reality adjacent.

THE MARX FAMILY CAME FROM OLD MONEY, but their stately, 10,676 square foot Mediterranean-style mega mansion was built the same year their only son Coletrane was born. **Coletrane Thelonious Marx**, his name was the result of a disagreement between mother and father. Both huge fans of the revolutionary jazz movement of the '60s, they wanted to name their only son after one of the pioneers at the front of that renaissance. Adaeze, his mother, wanted to name him after the saxophonist John William Coletrane. And Vincent, his father, wanted to name him after Thelonious Monk, the improvisational pianist who was the second most recorded jazz composer after Duke Ellington. In the end, they settled on both.

Vincent was an architect by trade, so he designed it himself. It was one of the luxurious Isles of Osprey homes in Dr. Phillips, Florida.

The towering masterpiece was situated on a .94 acre lot with 145' waterfrontage, lush landscapes, custom siren fountains made of marble and granite. There was a circular stone paved driveway that wrapped around to a courtyard parking pad with two garages that connected to an enormous botanical garden engirdled in a thicket of looming poinciana trees.

On the other side of the property was an oak canopy herald to a labyrinth hedge maze where in the center of which stood a twelve foot jadeite statue of a horse-bound feudal warrior with his <u>unsheathed</u> sword pointed up at the sky, the horse balanced upright on its hind legs.

All of this, it was just the iceberg tip of grandeur that made up the lives of Vincent and Adaeze, a life that Coletrane would inherit as a birthright but never enjoy as a man. For the kind of reasons that inundate a life in chronic stupefaction, irreparable.

Vincent's grandfather, Ndulue Obasi Marx, was owner of one of the first small oil exploration companies in Nigeria in the 1920s. Being almost clairvoyant when it came to business, he made non-commercial findings in Akata before selling his company to a consortium of Shell in '37 at the start of the big petroleum boom when it was still possible for a small oil man to make a huge bid on profits before the larger oil companies swallowed up everyone. He took his money and got into the shipping and railroad business where he amassed enough wealth to create a legacy to span generations, enabling his grandson Vincent to attend the best schools, get the right prestigious degrees, and know all the right families to make forging a career in architecture a relatively easy trajectory. This also enabled Vincent to only work as an architect part-time and devote most of his energy and resources to his true passions; archeology and history.

The resplendent garden belonged to Adaeze, and was not an ostentatious addition to the property but a vocational passion of her own. She employed a team of botanists who developed herbal medicinals and restoratives that were distributed to dispensaries in poor communities and allotted for free to people who could not afford fancy drugs through the cold, corporate pharmaceutical system.

This was a philanthropic effort that spanned across the entire state of Florida. Because unlike Vincent, Adaeze did not come from money. She was Afro-Caribbean from the Windrush generation, and her family migrated to the United Kingdom some-time after World War II, around the same time that Adebowale was making his millions in the 40s. Adaeze's grandparents gained citizenship in the UK under the British Nationality Act of 1948 during the time that the British government was in a state of recovery from the great losses of the war and encouraging immigration from the former countries of the Commonwealth of Nations. Her mother Vea met and married Emilio De Silva, a white European toy maker who had his own modest shop, but the family barely made ends meet and so Adaeze, her brothers and sisters, all grew up poor. She married into wealth shortly after meeting Vincent, but the knowledge of seeing friends and family suffer and die for lack of access to proper medicines when needed was written into her DNA. As a child she had both Vea and Emilio, as well as three brothers and two sisters. But by the time she was an adult, her nuclear family had dwindled to just her and her father.

By the time that Coletrane was eleven years old, in 1986, Adaeze's botanical company, **Anexity Works**, had spanned beyond the state of Florida and had franchises in Louisiana, Georgia, Arkansas, Virginia, New York, and Maine -so far. Vincent on the public stage became world renowned in the field of architecture, but was considered an eccentric Indiana Jones type collector for his work in archeology. He was also a tenured professor of history at the University of Central Florida.

So, <u>Central Florida</u>, though <u>a very red and very racist</u> area, had gotten used to (or at least tolerated) the idea of Black Wealth and Excellence being deep-rooted in the polestar of the community.

Coletrane always had a front row seat to this, especially during the fundraiser parties that his parents would throw right there on the property. People from all over the world would attend; doctors, lawyers, senators, big business tycoons, etc. People would come to watch Cirque du Soleil-like performances on the open lakeview acres of grass, they'd eat at the outdoor kitchen where famous chefs would prepare lavish dishes, and under the towering hand-painted ceiling and beyond the grand foyer, so many important bourgeois people would mingle on the imported Italian marble floors of the seemingly endless lower layer of the Marx's colossal home.

On the night of one such party, during, in fact, Coletrane's eleventh birthday weekend, the boy was upstairs in his bedroom and hanging out with his best friend Marcus.

Vincent, like son like father, was also removed from the party while Adaeze carried the task on her own of entertaining guests. He was down in the gallery and past a private entrance, hidden away with *his* friend, Jeremiah Cross, in a wing of the house that was used as an archeological trophy room and library that boasted custom wood cabinetry from floor to ceiling and a liquor cabinet made of Mozambique ebony that, on its top surface, held an agate bust of Ibrahim Frantz Fanon.

Coletrane and Marcus, they were working on a school homework assignment together. Vincent and Jeremiah, they were checking out one of Vincent's most recent archeological finds: **an eight foot tall statue of a man with African features, standing in _contrapposto_, in a hooded robe with his empty arms open as if they were holding something of considerable size and weight. Only, whatever those stone hands were holding was not present.**

"Not quite up to the Polykleitos cannon, this one," Cross said, playing unimpressed. But Vincent was used to this little ruse. This was their game, after all. Cross was one of the upper 1% industrialists exploring the big business and innovation opportunities of Silicon Valley. He was a media proprietor and entrepreneur that would eventually become the founder and CEO of a multi-national technology company called **Rain Forest**. He had only a passing interest in archeology, beyond, that is, his investments in Vincent's *hobby*.

"Perhaps,' Vincent walked around the statue, talking to Cross over his shoulder, who sort of loitered like a semi-curious sloth. "But the discipline is fully _disengo_, as were all of his works."

Vincent was a tall man, naturally strong in musculature and bearing the athleticism of his Nigerian genes. But Cross, with his bald head and perpetual three day shadow beard, was of average height and had never been much of an athlete. He grew up rich and pampered in Toronto and came to the states to begin venturing in business on a ten million dollar "loan" from his father Galen. But, after being awakened to the importance of heath when Galen dropped dead suddenly from a heart attack the previous year, Cross took up jogging though and yoga, not to mention was fast developing a passion of his own for archery.

Still, he had something of a *small man complex* when in the presence of Vincent, who, nonetheless, was older than him by at least a decade. This subconscious complex of his, it made Cross always bring a subtle air of competitiveness to their somewhat tenuous though oddly firm camaraderie. They were the contradiction of a ship at sea being tossed in the waves of a storm.

So, Cross sighed when Vincent mentioned that, *disengo.*

"Judas Ulehla," he said knowingly, a statement shaped like a question.

"Yep. Correct," Vincent didn't bother trying to hide his enthusiasm.

Cross took a sip of the scotch in the highball he was holding.

"Your Ulehla supposedly precedes Michelangelo by at least 700 years, yet somehow he is aware of the disengo discipline?"

Vincent smiled,

"My friend, it isn't academia. Not in essence, really. Still, if you'll humor me, it remains uncertain when or even how long ago Ulehla lived. Of the two other statues of his that I've found, what is different about this one?"

"A pop-quiz? After I've been drinking?"

"This one is easy."

At the same time, in a bedroom on the other side of the estate, Coletrane was similarly regaling his friend Marcus with charismatic musings.

"It came to me in a dream,' he said, looking up and remembering, "There were lights coming out of darkness. Like completely pitch black, except for the lights. Twentysomething..

Twenty-seven of them, I think... Yeah! Twenty-seven! Telling me a story. And also, I think, a warning. I woke up real fast because I couldn't breathe!"

Marcus looked at him quizzically, tilting his head.

"What? How does that help us with our project, man? It's due Monday and tonight is Saturday?"

"It's called inspiration."

"But why twenty-seven?"

"Huh?"

"Twenty-seven. Why twenty-seven lights?"

"I don't know."

"What? Come on, man!"

"Look. It'll be a piece of cake,' Coletrane told his protesting friend, who hated school work on the weekends and, in general, math. 'We can act like we're making our own *Dungeons & Dragons* game."

"You said the same thing last week, Train," Marcus countered, pouting.

The boys were in pajamas. It was a sleepover, a rare thing. But exceptions are made during Coletrane's birthday weekends, and already at eleven he'd gotten pretty good at the art of manipulation. For instance, he was allowed to exploit the influence his parents had on the private school he attended and wear his hair long and wild. His mixed heritage made it billowy when worn in the style of an afro, but for school his mother would usually braid it. Today however, this weekend, it was as wild and loose as ever. Tossing about his head like a chrysanthemum or a bushel of coffee brown cotton.

Marcus' American Black family was originally from Georgia. His father, Leonard Green, boxed when he was young, founded three record labels and made a fortune in investments. But Leonard's brother, Jackson, owned a barbershop chain in Florida. So, the boy was always clean cut. He'd taken after his father by forming an interest in boxing already at the young age of twelve, so he was already tired of school.

This is where, once again, Coletrane's powers of manipulation would kick in.

"The report has to be on the power of mythologies and how they influence the world," Coletrane reasoned, his excitement and imagination growing. "We can make it about a warrior that faces the warning from the dream!"

"But what's the warning?"

"I don't know."

"You don't know that either?!'

"Hey,' Coletrane argued, "Inspiration doesn't have to make sense. My dad says that all the time. It don't gotta make sense. All it's gotta do is push you forward."

"We're gonna get an F, man," Marcus groaned.

"We are not getting an F."

Coletrane got up and walked to the window, pacing with the bearing and confidence of a general. His bedroom window was facing the estate's boat dock out on the lake behind the house, so he looked out beyond the water and at the trees made black in the night time light. This is how he formed the idea.

"Let's do this. **Let's create a samurai**. Let's give him a history, a legend, everything."

And then he turned to face Marcus, to put a point on his seriousness, his enthusiasm,

"Let's make it as though he really lived."

Vincent's trophy room was a sight to behold. It was an enormous depository of collected munitions from every era of war, paintings and murals bearing imagery of fire breathing leviathans, Cain and Abel at each other's throats, Krishna from the Hindu faith, Jesus with bleeding holes in his hands, etc. There were, besides the new one that Vincent and Cross were examining, two other deific statues (one a woman, the other a man) by the sculptor Ulehla -ancient, ascetic, each bearing aesthetics seemingly representative of a different sculpting epoch.

Cross sighed.

"You are determined, it would seem, to piss off your investors. Namely, me. What have the grants been for? To study this... mysterious Judas Ulehla, or to solve the riddle of Abraham's cube of 3?"

"We already know the cube of three, Jeremiah," Vincent paced while pontificating. "The number of New Testament books. King Ben-hadad's betrayal of Ahab. The fall of 27,000 Aphek footmen. King Azariah's governance of God's people in the 27th year of Jeroboam II!"

"You are being coy, old friend. You claimed to, specifically, be able to locate the true location of the fabled cave of Hebron. And that in the place of Abraham's Sarah was instead an element more valuable than gold and all the world's oil combined."

"We are on the cusp of it all, if only you would entertain my theories of Ulehla! The so-called *cave of Hebron* is hidden and misnamed on purpose, by Ulehla's design. Consider how he got his own name! He was a descendent of King Zimri, ruler with the shortest recorded reign of Judah. And these three statues, the only ones attributed to Ulehla.."

"Attributed by you," Cross countered, slyly.

"Combined," Vincent pronounced, segueing on Cross' interruption, "they are a clue. We're not looking for a mystery behind the cube of three at all. We're looking for three itself, these three. Look at them, Jerry!"

"Don't call me Jerry, damnit!" Cross winced, shaking his head, "I told you how much I hate that!"

"Look – at – them! And drink your drink."

Cross sighed again, walked over by the statues to give them a look up close. Still nursing the highball in his right hand, he took spectacles from his shirt pocket with his left and put them on. Vincent, he went over to the Mozambique liquor cabinet to fix a drink of his own, three fingers of scotch whiskey. Cross scanned each one of the Ulehla statues through squinting eyes despite the lenses making the gesture unnecessary. Then he looked back at the new statue. Vincent was next to it with his arms folded, a smug grin on his face. He was wrist rotating the highball to slightly slosh around its mahogany contents. Cross rolled his eyes.

"Vincent, must you stand there looking so self-satisfied?"

"It's part of the fun," Vincent took a sip of his drink.

"Out with it, man. What is different about this one? What is the big revelation?"

"Isn't it obvious?" Vincent asked, turning to face the statue and gesturing in emphasis to the statue's arms. "He's holding something. Or at least, was."

At this point Vincent strolled over to Cross and tapped glasses with him.

"Perhaps he is praying that you don't get sued."

"Haha,' Vincent exclaimed, springing to buoyancy, "It is not debatable. Let me show you."

There was a bronze Egyptian-style etagere bookcase set against a wall between two standing, gold-plated Iron Maidens. Three glass shelves connected the etagere pillars, but the only thing on them, at the top and centered, was a large leather-bound book with an onyx, oval-shaped stone on its center and a golden buckle latch closure over its dense stack of no less than 700 wood-pulp pages. The book had a medieval appearance and was heavy, but Vincent, after putting down his drink, lifted it with ease and brought it over to a Babylon round table made of gray and white marble, setting the heavy book down and blowing on it lightly to lift a coat of dust off its surface.

Cross joined him at the table.

"Another find?" Cross asked.

"My divers found the Ulehla sculpture coordinates northeast of Bermuda, 350 miles below the middle of the Atlantic. It was cargo in the ruins of a sunken Azores ship, circa 1427. This book is what the statue was holding."

"What?" Cross near chuckled, expecting the punchline to a joke that he knew by Vincent's tone would never arrive. "How is that even possible?" he continued. "Either I've had too much to drink this evening, or you have."

"Neither. The book was stone upon delivery, and part of the statue. Only when I set up the statue in here did the book become, well, this. A live book resting in stone arms as if on fancy shrine. You're the first I've shown it."

Cross gave Vincent a quizzing look. But before he could voice another retort, Vincent said, "I have proof."

That's when Jeramiah sighed, saying, "Vincent, one could describe your obsession as a form of anthropological violence."

"Nothing so violent as robbing graves to lard the exhibits of colonial museums."

Before Cross could respond with the obligatory *touché*, Vincent turned and walked back over to the etagere to retrieve a manila folder.

Walking the envelope back over to Cross, he said, "My manservant Poole was with them on the trip. He took photos from the harbor and faxed them in."

Vincent pulled six photos from the envelop, all different angles of the statue taken from the dock and up on the ship bay. The book in hand, solid stone.

"It happened overnight, Jeremiah," Vincent whispered, saying Cross' first name as he only did when imparting something of considerable gravity, "I've shown you this because it confirms what I've been saying for years, and helps piece together the mystery of Ulehla. How does a statue sculpted no sooner than 1621 finds its way into the cargo of a sunken 1427 ship captained by Goncalo Velho?! It corresponds to the Theosophy texts that I studied in Tibet. It confirms the Visuddhimagga, the Patisambhidamagga, the-"

"Don't say it out loud," Cross cut him off, shaking his head. But Vincent was already too deep into the moment.

"It confirms, or at least implies, the existence of manomāyakāya."

Cross sighed and shut his eyes, moved away from Vincent who was so into his reverie that he didn't notice how much he'd invaded Cross' personal space by moving closer and closer on each word.

Cross gulped downed the last of his scotch.

"Tulpas, Vincent? I picked the wrong night to drink with you."

"A refill?"

"Of course."

What Cross didn't notice while thoroughly flabbergasted by the implications of the book magically turning real from stone, is that on the left arm of the Ulehla statue was a **glyph-like carving** embedded in the forearm. Vincent was aware of it however, and quite familiar with it -in fact. His son Coletrane had the exact image as a **birthmark in the same place on *his* arm**.

Across the water to the back of the house, far beyond the dock visible from Coletrane's bedroom window, were the blackened thicket of trees. Those trees, they were a coppice of bald cypress reaching out for miles. So dense that they appeared as one continuous body to the naked eye. They were especially ominous in the midnight lighting, under calm black skies that seemed to carry a warning on the air -a grievous admonition. This was long after the party had ended. All the guests had gone home, the boys were asleep in Coletrane's room. The manservant Poole had tended to all the evening affairs, Vincent and Adaeze were in the master wing amid the comfort of dreams that affluent people have cradled by the quiet lullaby of tranquil rest.

So, no one was consciously aware of the onyx crystal on the mysterious book housed in the trophy beginning to swirl with vibrancy, no one knew the coming consequences of Coletrane's earlier musings echoing in the universe.

"Imagine the greatest warrior to even fight with a katana, our man is much better than him. Better than any katana fighter that ever walked the earth, and burdened because of it."

"Burdened?" Marcus asked when they had this conversation much earlier that evening.

"Yes," Coletrane replied. "He'd have to be. For balance. My father told me, that is what makes us able to walk without falling over. The burden that balances our talent."

"Ok. Sure. Sounds cool."

"You bet!"

Over the wall of bald cypress hung a black and purple sky daubed with dim striates of gray clouds. Amidst them was the moon, full and bright. No one could see this if they'd been watching, but that moon's light began to blanch as it split in two -like a figure eight.

"He will be unstoppable, but troubled even beyond death. His weakness can be his emotions, and it will be his strength too. His passion. His love."
"That's corny."
"Shut up. It isn't."
"I'm kidding."
"No, you're not! Close your eyes and imagine it."
"Come on, man.."
"Do it! He is strong in a way that frightens him, but his great sword feeds him courage with its every kill. Peace only comes from his love, but that is taken from him."

Beyond the figure eight moon, beyond the trees, beyond Florida and the modern world itself, an impossible, forgotten history spans over three thousand miles of mountainous peaks, alpine foliage and cedar. There are beautiful rivers and snowcapped mountains in the distance. These sprout from nothingness, growing into existence under the watch of a midnight sky in feudal Japan.

Coletrane's voice, it doesn't follow; it **devises**. The purple heron, the dark and light morphs, the great egrets becoming physical and given life by a child's imagination stretched out across worlds. They come to life and coast on the winds, swooping here and there, as craters spanning miles and miles fill with sea water, as the mountains erect and reach into the sky, an august archipelago of deciduous broad-leaved forests, aerial grasslands of high ranging flora, Yabutsubaki and Shii trees further than the eye could see. Entire ecosystems of marine and land-bound wildlife fill the forests and rivers; a rich biodiversity of species coming to life in open and isolated habitats; terrestrial mammals, vascular plants, there were giant flying squirrels, macaque, red-backed vole, other heron of all types and colors, serow running in the fields, black woodpeckers excavating the bases of trees for dinner, and men and women building villages and families while never aware that they were less part of the natural world than from myth created by the imagination of a boy from the future.

"What about his final resting place?" Marcus asked, as those ecosystems of myth aged and coalesced not only with the past but, finally, the present.

And as Coletrane thought of his reply to Marcus' question, already the universe acquiesced. Coletrane's enthusiasm was thus that he didn't even feel, or at least was so engrossed that his conscious mind ignored it, **that the birthmark on his arm was slightly producing a burning sensation just below the surface of his skin**.

"You're right,' he replied, *"at some point he has to have died. His legend lives on, in the minds and hearts of the people around the world inspired by his stories."*

"Like an archetype," Marcus' enthusiasm was growing.

"Yep. Just like that."

"And that word has to be in the paper, man. We won't get an F using words like that."

"Dude, focus!"

And so, the universe did exactly that. In modern day Honshu, deep in the mountains of Takayama at a latitude of about 2,400 meters, in the icy hemisphere that was home to the ptarmigan, or "messengers of God", a bamboo bridge manifested out of this air, stretching out miles above a ferocious river and connecting to a narrow road cut into the side of a mountain and wrapping all the way around past several dangerous breaks in a deadly passageway that was herald to the black entrance of a cave barely visible beyond dense squalls of snow.

———

AT THREE OTHER POINTS IN THE WORLD, at the exactly the same time that the universe was creating an alternate past and an amalgamated present on the whim of Coletrane's potentially disastrous imagination, and at the exact same time that everyone in the Marx home was sleeping, there was an awakening -of The Immortal Watchers, or **Three Interstices** between Fact, Fiction, and Myth.

In Mahālangūr Himāl, at 8,848 meters, the earth's highest peak, she rose and was made entirely of golden red dust collected in human form. Her body was clothed in a hooded robe that looked exactly like the ones carved in the statues of Judas Ulehla. Her long hair never stayed the same texture or color, instead ever-flowing like a restless sea, and her skin under the robe was made bronze but her eyes took on the shape of crystals full of the golden red dust that was the stuff of her physical composition, the dust within those crystals ever swirling like monsoons -*storms that would swallow the memories of any who looked into them.* On her forehead manifest the Ulehla Glyph that Coletrane has as a birthmark, and through her mystic eyes she could see all the way to the terrible thing that would happen to Coletrane that night. **This was Zhrontese**. She would and could prevent it, but knew she should not yet intervene.

In Antarctica, a frozen point between the Dome Argus and the Dome Fuji, at 13,000 feet above sea level, microscopic particles of rhodium rise up from the land, enough of it to form the soul and solid casing of a human man. His skin takes on a graying color, but the rhodium solidifies into ebony crystals for his eyes. They swirl with the mysteries of the macrocosm, as his tall muscular body becomes covered in a hooded Ulehla cloak much like Zhrontese's. His head is bald and he bears the features of a man of African descent, and like the statue representing him in Vincent's trophy room, the man bore the Ulehla Glyph on his left forearm. **This one is Manthis**, and he can see all the way to Coletrane. He could prevent the regrettable thing that is going to happen, but knows to not intervene.

On the edge of the Tian Shan range and the Taklimakan Desert, there is a place called the Flaming Mountain. The hottest place on earth. From the surface at a temperature of 175 degrees Fahrenheit, brown dust rose up to form the pale white body of another man, lanky and menacing, his head as bald as Manthis' but with a much leaner, chiseled face. On it was a braided seventeen inch beard that was brown as his eyes, eyes that became andradite crystals holding the answers to all questions that could ever be asked by a sentient mind. Except for one, the question of why he didn't intervene against the frightful thing about to happen to Coletrane from the far distance of his perch. He too was clothed in a hooded robe, and the top part of his robe was open enough to reveal a large Ulehla Glyph at the center-most point of his sternum. **His name was Clymene**.

The Three Interstices, all aware of each other, watched from the great distance at the Marx home in Orlando, Florida.

It was just after 2am. There was a stillness that matched the calm of the lake, a misleading aura of a peace, safety. Young Coletrane would be the only one awakened by a sound that he didn't actually hear. Marcus was on the guest air-bed, lost in a dream. Down on the first level, tucked beneath the stairs, was the room where Poole slept. This was adjacent the wine cellar, the butler's pantry, and not far from the formal living room that held a two-sided gas fireplace that precipitously came alive with embers of blue fire that were cold instead of hot. This cold, it spread throughout the entire house.

Coletrane's mind was restless, now that he'd awakened. And he realized that he was a little hungry too. So, he got out of bed.

As soon as his bare feet touched the agar surface of the floor, he felt the unusual coolness and even made a mental note of how weird it was to be so cold on a night in May. He put on socks and walked carefully so as not to wake up Marcus as he went to his closet for a robe. Then he quietly opened his bedroom door and went out into the hall.

There, it was much colder and he could see his breath. Down the hall to the right was the master wing where his parents slept. The breath that he could see, it formed thin, translucent filaments that wafted in the direction of the master wing and caused a somewhat psychedelic reaction in Coletrane who could see what appeared to be a burrow of fog coaxing him to go towards it instead of downstairs to the kitchen.

For the rest of his life, he will regret having done so.

Each footfall towards his parents' bedroom, the fear in him grew simultaneous to the urge to take yet another step. When he finally made it to the door, after what seemed like hours crossing the short distance, his hand was almost ice when he reached for the doorknob. The door opened, however, on his own.

At that moment, as the door opened, the ancient book on the shelf inside the trophy room, its golden buckle latch unlocked and the onyx crystal on the front began to beat like a heart with a faint blue color emanating from its center. Then the cover flipped open, revealing to no eyes present that there was nothing written on the wood-pulp pages. Until now, as passages began to manifest on the first page and beyond -passages written in blood red, their meaning hidden behind the wall of an extinct language.

Many years later, Coletrane would realize that it wasn't external cold that he was feeling as he was entering his parents' bedroom, but, just like the moon reflects light from the sun rather than producing light itself, the cold was a chill happening inside of him. The icing over of his spirit, his hopes and dreams, every possibility of a normal life going frigid as herald to what he would never be able to unsee beyond that door.

He stepped inside, and the first thing he noticed was the blood. It looked black in the night, and it was everywhere. On the walls, the furniture, the ceiling fan. There were blood patterns on the panoramic windows that cast shadows into the room, creating the appearance of him stepping into an enormous, murder of blood-born Rorschach mosaics. That's when he saw his mother, Adaeze. *Plural.*

Her facedown upper torso was on the floor next to the left side of the bed, her lifeless arms reached out as if their last effort was an attempt to flee. The lower part of her body was still on the bed, entrails clearly exposed in a way that looked less human and more like gutted cattle. Coletrane's eyes didn't believe it, his voice was stuck in his throat, his body and mind were yet to catch up with what they were seeing. And before they did, a shadow moving at the right of his peripheral drew his attention away from one horror and onto the next.

It was his father Vincent exiting the lounge room. The man staggered backwards, alive -but his left arm was gone.

Vincent fell against the doorjamb on his right shoulder, the other half of his body covered in the tar-looking blood.

"Son," was the only word he could get out before the blade of a sword burst through his chest. This chucked him forward, all the way out of the lounge room with the sword still inside of him and its wielder, a black, almost seven foot tall specter, following. This specter moved incredibly fast, drawing the sword from Vincent's body and then slashing crosswise in a *yoko giri* cut that separated Vincent's head from the neck. The body fell forward and the head was tossed by the force over to where Coletrane was standing, some of the blood splattering onto the poor boy's face and robe.

This is when he could finally get out a word of his own,

"Dad?!" But though it felt inside like a scream, it came out as barely a whisper. His knees hitting the floor as he fell before his father's head made more noise than his voice. And even though his eyes were filling with tears and confusions, he could see when he looked up what was now calmly walking towards him.

The specter, like the way it got colder with Coletrane's every step towards his parents' door, the specter's every step towards him revealed more of what he was. It was like a translucent pneuma of dew solidifying as it got closer. The stepping parts became feet wearing rosewood geta elevated on two prongs. Above this were the drapes of black hakama, and above that were a red and gold kamishimo and over it a black sleeveless kataginu jacket.

Still a man of near seven feet in height, with broad shoulders and big hands, a belt around his waist carrying an onyx short sword and the empty scabbard to the blade he still held in his hand. By osmosis, Coletrane already knew that the shiny unsheathed sword was named **Hatsukoi**. And when the man was finally standing in front of him, not five feet away, he looked up into his bearded face. The long jet black hair on his head was not tied, and the eyes, Coletrane would never forget, the pupils each split and formed into figure-eights like the impossible moon did outside earlier at the outset of this brutal event.

That is when Coletrane gave him a name and said it out loud for the first time,

"Kojiro?"

The sound of it either hurt or offended the samurai, and so immediately upon hearing it -he raised the sword overhead in a blink and brought it down with a sideways slash across the boy's chest, a slash punctuated by a deafening scream!

COLETRANE THELONIOUS MARX, THE MAN, woke up with a start. The nightmare was a familiar one, but no matter how many times he would experience the memory, it would always be as if it were happening in real-time; it would hit him like a lightning strike.

His bare chest was drenched in sweat, and on the ace size bed with him were five sleeping women -all aspiring lingerie models, visiting from Brazil for an opportunity that only led to a rich man's bedroom. They were all naked, including Coletrane. The women were still experiencing exhaustion and mild nausea from the ayahuasca consumed during the previous night's sex session, so none of them were startled by Coletrane's violent awakening. There were still some traces of psychedelic color patterns as his eyes adjusted to the light, that and afterimages of furniture and the surrounding environment when he moved. But this was gone after just a few moments, kind of like the effects of the ayahuasca itself as well the sex from Coletrane's perspective. Both were addictions for him, not for pleasure but for reprieve, however brief, from the enduring consequences of his trauma.

Thirty-three years old, physically strong as if he hadn't aged a day beyond twenty-one, and built like an Olympian from a lifetime of martial arts and body building, he felt inside as if he were as brittle as a twig. When Coletrane stood, he was six foot two from the floor. His hair was still as bushy as it was when he was a child, but he wore it in a bun on the back of his head that was reminiscent of a sangtu top-knot. On his face he wore a wide though thin-cut beard. There were several tribal, dragon, wolf, and lion tattoos along his musculature, on his arms, back, and legs, but none covering the long scar across his chest from the night that he was almost killed by a demon.

Coletrane walked over by the windows, where his body was swathed in sunlight. That light was far warmer and welcome than the Rorschach patterns of blood in the cold setting of that fateful night which haunted him. He looked down and saw Poole in the grass by the doc, right at the crust of land before the calm seams of lake water.

Jonas Poole, the man was sixty-two years old and still lithe as a boy. He was doing a complicated series of tai chi forms, swaying between slow and fast depending on the demands of each transition. And he did this every morning, without fail. Coletrane (Poole agreed with Vincent and preferred to call him Thelonious), he used to practice every morning with Poole. Especially after the death of his parents. But despite how much he practiced or how adept he became, spiritual aspects of the discipline were never enough to quell the darkness inside of him. He preferred the violent martial arts for that purpose, though they still barely helped; Krav Maga, Escrima, Muay Thai, Bacom, Vale Tudo, Silat, and of course the way of the Japanese Sword. He was adept in each one of these; he was, for loss of a better description, a **prodigy of violence.**

Every one of Coletrane's teachers marveled at how quickly he picked up the techniques, as if possessed by a demon himself. As if supernatural! Some even encouraged Poole, who raised him after the brutal death of his parents, to try steering his focus away from the fighting arts entirely. But the wise man knew that Coletrane would hear nothing of it. This strengthened their relationship in ways that went far beyond friendship, far beyond the dynamics of mentor/student, and further, even, beyond the filial.

So, Coletrane watched his surrogate father performing kata -quietly envying the peace of it.

The large tattoo on Coletrane's back was of a Yamata no Orochi dragon in an epic battle with a powerfully built Anubis wielding a khopesh and kukri. This is the first thing one of the girl's focused on upon waking up, seeing Coletrane standing over by the panoramic windows.

He turned to her when he heard her sit up and stretch, and she smiled at his considerable girth before looking up at his face and saying,

"Good morning."

The word *morning* barely escaped her lips however before he replied,

"Why are you still here? Any of you, for that matter?"

———

AFTER THE GIRLS WERE GONE, Coletrane showered and got dressed. He was partial to tapered thin-knit turtleneck sweaters, and his favorite color was black. So, he wore one of those turtlenecks over black slacks and shoes.

The house was as quiet as a tomb as he walked through it, as it always was. Only he and Poole resided in it, and there were rarely any guests besides the brief visits from the many women who enabled Coletrane's addiction.

He made his way to the trophy room and went straight to where the book still was, rested on the etagere between the Iron Maidens. Opening the book, Coletrane felt the pages as if they were alive. Caressing each one and carefully flipping them over. What he saw was more confirmation than surprise; new chapters of the lost language in blood ink filling two dozen of the erstwhile blank pages, both sides.

This is when Poole walked up behind him carrying two warm coffee mugs, fresh steam rising from the rim.

"Happy birthday, Thelonious," he said, bringing Coletrane the coffee.

Poole was relatively short at 5'9, but appeared taller for his posture. He was bronze in skin, had friendly features on a pear shaped face, and always had a calm and patient way about himself. He was German by his father but Afro-Eurasian by his mother, who was a migrant from Jordan that met his father while he was in exile from the Luftwaffe. Poole spent much of his childhood on boats and at sea. So, Coletrane taking his time to turn away from the book to address him wasn't something that could ruffle his feathers.

"Thank you, Jonas," Coletrane finally said, turning from the book and taking the coffee that Poole handed him.

"You're troubled today. Not the demeanor I'd expect on the morning of your thirty-third."

Coletrane shrugged, walked over to the gallery of ancient weapons. Three full walls of them; blades, armor, shields, from many eras of war. Each piece had to be worth a fortune, belonging in museums, but instead were the showcase of an eccentric's collection.

To his back, Poole said,

"I've suggested it before but, perhaps it is time to stop using your parents' old room as your own. It isn't healthy."

"We are all dying a little bit each day. There is no such thing as healthy. Besides, look in the book."

Poole being every bit aware of the phenomenon of the book as well as the mysterious prophesies associated with it, was reluctant to do so. But did anyway.

"I see. So, you're having the nightmare again."

"Yes. Right on schedule. You know what that means."

"I do, indeed."

Coletrane then turned away from the weapons collection to face Poole, the gravity of the moment in his gaze and voice.

"The story is alive,' he rubbed the birthmark on his forearm, feeling this time the subtle burning sensation that was just underneath the surface. "Alive,' he repeated, 'but not well."

SUNRISE, HOUR OF THE HARE. DECEMBER 25TH IN A portion and time of feudal Japan that exists beyond the shadow of recorded history, this morning marking the death of one heartbroken warrior's soul.

Kojiro ko-Mitsu walks the murky halls of the catacomb leading into the Testing Dungeons of Lord Zsu Ch'an's Northern Province. His great sword, Hatsukoi, is already unsheathed and at his side, seething with the same rage that he felt.

Each of Kojiro's steps, heavy. And each carried him closer towards his dark destiny.

He was a man apart with the taste of death on his tongue.

Reaching the end of the hall, Kojiro came out into the open room putting his feet in blood dampened earth; where men's bodies were torn apart for the purposes of testing the quality of swords, punishing criminals, and hardening young boys that would rise to become Samurai.

There were sword racks and smiths. There were men cleaning up several bodies of the dead, collecting entrails, torsos, heads, limbs...

There were children carrying old, rusty blades that were too heavy for them. But these boys were burgeoning samurai, set to cut down criminals and vagrants being led on a chain-line entering through another of the chasm halls.

The undertaker, Izanagi, was exceptionally tall and large. A hardened giant at 6'4 carrying 240 pounds of solid muscle, and still there was fear in his eyes upon seeing Kojiro standing before him with so much rage in his face and posture.

"Izanagi," Kojiro called, surprisingly very quietly, 'a word with you, man."

Izanagi walked over, careful not to take his time with an angry samurai warrior of the pedigree of Kojiro ko-Mitsu, and yet he was tentative still. He was afraid that the warrior might cut him down with Hatsukoi.

"My lord," Izanagi answered with a grunt and bow.

Kojiro himself was tall at 6'1, but still he disappeared in the space of Izanagi. All Kojiro wore were black joba hakama pants, every solid muscle in his exposed upper body making him look a product of feral energy only half from the civilized world. He looked up at the towering giant and said,

"Tell me of the Nichiren sword, Hatsukoi, forged by the priest Nichi-O and wielded by the hand of Kojiro. What kind of blade is she known as?"

"A six body blade, my lord."

The tempered rage broke forth like a shattering mirror in his voice, Kojiro saying, "Then line me up seven condemned men!"

———

At the flooded meadows flanking the river Masaaki there were the great purple-gray herons that wade for shrimp and aquatic insects, showing off their morphing plumes and graceful balance on the water. Ittei was there, enjoying their presence. This humble warrior who dreamt of putting down the naginata of his family's honor in exchange for the less hostile arts of music and painting, played Shizu no Kyoku on his shakuhachi flute as an offering to nature. This while, not a mile east, his liege Kojiro ko-Mitsu was playing a far different song.

And somehow Ittei could sense it all, feeling, while he played, a conflict in the Universe telling him that this song would be the last happy song he'd play for at least some time.

Still he played on, sure it was important that he do so.

His mind stretched out in a way that made him feel like he was hovering above the atmosphere, looking down on and seeing all at once the majestic beauty of the surrounding vistas. The sprawling volcanic mountains over the horizon cast in the backdrop of the Masaaki. There was a bamboo thicket leading down an osculating path into the Zsu Ch'an palace, enveloped in an orchid marsh teeming with the twitters of insects attuning to Ittei's flute -a sound almost supernatural.

He was only somewhat aware of the presence invading his mind, or, rather, supplying his mind with its thoughts -a presence that very well could have been the source of his talents and the spirit in his chest...

He was only vaguely aware of it, but Ittei's mind was being invaded by the influence of an unknown and incredible being.

A goddess. The "supreme being", a spiritually inclined person would call her, drifting down into the atmosphere in the guise of invisible dew. He could not see her, but she could see him. And few would ever know, if any would ever discover, that **Astrid was no goddess at all.** Not in the traditional sense of the word. But, rather, an amnesiac visitor from another planet that, looking upon this world with… curiosity.

She watched Ittei sitting in a meditative posture, his legs folded, back upright, and arms balanced horizontal as he played his song. A strange thing to notice, but she liked the fitted groom of his Sangtu topknot hairstyle and could smell that it was dressed in cedar oil. His kimono was red silk and his oak wood naginata had a sheathed blade that reached out fourteen inches in a katana curve.

She wanted to touch the married warrior –his marital status obvious by the Sangtu- as her body began to solidify just over the trees to his left, but that wouldn't have been a good idea. Her pale blue skin would be far too hot to the touch, and would burn him to death before he even realized he was being touched. And if he saw her, her bright orange eyes, her blonde, brown, black hair, the golden glow of her body and skintight earth suit that were far too mythic and beautiful for his human mind to interpret, his vision would be inverted within moments –causing his mind to behold a flipside view of himself the extent of reveal powerful enough that his cerebral cortex would explode out of his head.

Such, apparently, is the nature of things. Creator and created are not supposed to meet on the surface of a living sphere.

So, she just watched him play, transmitting intuitively the instinct to sense the distress of Kojiro from a distance.

But Astrid kept her distance. And while still unaware of her, Ittei thought that the sensation he was feeling was the trees carrying a message over to him from the Province.

For some reason, he knew it was time to put away the flute and return home. It was upon Ittei's departure that Astrid would experience something quite new and peculiar.

Hovering in the sky, this place of her creation and invisible to her every subject, Astrid's mind was invaded by a splinter of thought that not only made her visible and tangible, but also robbed her of the focus necessary to maintain flight. She came crashing down fast and violently to the earth, her fall broken only by the many tree branches she hit on her way down.

When she finally hit the tussocky ground, Astrid was less in pain than she was subdued by a state of awe; on her skin were cuts and bruises from the fall, neither of which she'd ever experiences.

"How silly of me," she said to herself. "But…. how?"

This question was answered by her recollection of that which robbed her of focus, the image that made her fall:

> *In her mind she saw it, herself coming face to face with a spectral silhouette version of herself. A diaphanous outline of her contours, her eyes bright and golden, and in the space of her curves a cosmos; an air-siphoning space of blackness, and all light coming from a scatter or orbs. Three of those orbs were mini moons, two covering the space where her breasts would be and the third taking the place of her womb.*

"Interesting," she whispered.

———

A resplendent two mile imperial bridge leads into Lord Tzu Ch'an's Northern Province, where lies the entrance to his fortified Orchid Castle of exceptional beauty and architecture. The wooden and marble design, stone and white plastered walls were laced in the ancient Confucian gold of the Jesuit voyages.

It was a gold known for having been so entrenched in history that many thought its back-story just a myth to exaggerate the value of the gold that took on a strange luster, always shining impossibly. The Cosmetic Tower and the seventeen parapet Gates spanned their distance more than 2,000 meters around the inner moat, stood an incredible 100 yards tall –higher than the highest peak of the towering seven story castle.

The servant Dōken Yoshisada hurried on his way, tripping over himself and his bad leg as he went through the many corridors and up the winding staircase leading to the Cynosure Temple where he'd find Lord Tzu Ch'an doing his daily ritual; reading the classics.

This time, the Spring and Autumn Annals.

Tzu Ch'an's armed female guards, Yoko and Akiyama, were dressed like geisha and flanking either side of Lord Tzu Ch'an's Lotus Reading Bench that sat in the center of a solarium tier above which was a wide circular opening in the ceiling. A fall of cherry blossom petals danced down on him as he read, his attention suddenly averted by a commotion outside the room.

Yoko and Akiyama didn't move, but their five like-dressed sisters who were sitting on their knees along the back wall, their hands all at once gripped the shōtō blades in their laps.

The monks outside the hall tried to calm Yoshisada and keep him from entering the Temple, but Lord Tzu Ch'an beckoned them to let Yoshisada pass.

"Dōken, is it? The swordsmith Soden's son. Are you this eager to read?"

The Lord had a very amicable way of speaking, as if his life had washed away the instinct to urgency. He was a student of the earliest Shinto practices, even wrote extensively on the existence and influence of Kami, the deific spirit manifestations of our hidden selves, the anthropomorphic essences that play mythic roles in people's lives. Some of his writings have even made it into the bodhisattvas. And being a front-runner on the literature, art, and philosophies behind the **Dragon Kings legends**, he knew the importance of maintaining good chi when faced with the threat of bad news.

"My Lord,' Dōken blurted out, falling to his knees. "Izanagi sends news. With your permission, Lord Tzu Ch'an…"

"Proceed."

"It is Kojiro. He has left the province! He is going-.

"I know where he is going," Tzu Ch'an said, with grave acuity.

Dōken lead Lord Ch'an and his Geisha Guards into the Testing Dungeon where young boys were cleaning up the mess of seven men sliced in half at the torso. The red vexing charcoal mist that Hatsukoi emitted when in use was still clearing in the air, causing Dōken to cough and gag while Tzu Ch'an knew better to narrow his eyes and mind his breathing. He knew that the poisonous dust could become psychedelic to an untrained mind.

So, while careful with himself, the Lord took in the surroundings.

Izanagi bowed.

"This news, Lord Ch'an,' Dōken began, 'Does it not trouble you? Kojiro is gaikoku-jin, a fugitive! Outside the protection of your domain, he will be approached by the Bafuku Ashigaru for his past indiscretions."

"Calm yourself, Yoshisada. Kojiro can handle the feeble Ashigaru."

And then Tzu Ch'an considered, keeping his thoughts to himself. *What*, he wondered, *if he makes it to his destination? What consequences perhaps greater than those he seeks to avenge will befall him?*"

———

BY THE STABLES AT THE EAST GATE, KOJIRO was dressing his horse, Ayame, with the tools he'll need for the journey. Rouge, for one, in case he is slain. Apricots and peaches to eat, chestnuts, persimmons. Moshi, dried sardines, koi.

All would fit in a small enough tote bag he'd throw over the satchel for Hatsukoi and Jun, his onyx Lionbear short sword. He packed two kama and iron fans, kozuka blades, shuriken, and a golden Tzu Ch'an jutte, for good measure.

"I'm guessing my advice right now will fall on deaf ears," the familiar voice called to Kojiro's back. But the warrior wasn't in the mood for the wisdom of his friend.

"You're gonna give it anyway, Jubei," Kojiro said, not bothering to turn away from his personal ritual of cleaning Hatsukoi before mounting Ayame.

Jubei approached with that swagger of his, all 240 pounds of him coasting on air, it seemed, like a heron in flight.

He wore white hakama pants, wooden waraji sandals and leather chords cross-wrapping round his wheelbarrow arms until they collected as pugilist fist wraps. He was another tall man at 6'6, had a chonmage with the ponytail reaching out the top of his head like a black jade fountain. His splitting thirty pound broadsword was strapped to his back –heavy, for sure, to an ordinary man, but it might as well had been a small bag of rice to the powerful hero.

He had to look down to find his best friend's gaze.

"Kojiro, listen,' he began, the genuine sorrow in his voice, 'about Taya... I heard..."

"No," Kojiro cut him off, stern, quick, 'don't speak of it..."

A moment passed between them.

Hatsukoi, clean to a perfect luster, was now again sheathed and packed on Ayame. Three snowy egrets flew by going west. Probably heading towards the Great Willow Lake, Jubei thought, just catching them in his peripheral. Kojiro on the other hand couldn't help but notice the purple and white Sakura petals being carried over by the wind and scattering all around.

Beauty, in this moment, like an assault of knives.

"I am sorry, yuujin..." Jubei put a hand on Kojiro's shoulder. "Well... somehow I don't feel the new strength in this shoulder. I'm told Hatsukoi is now a six body blade."

"Seven."

"Impressive... What do you plan to do, man? You leave Tzu Ch'an's protection and you'll have to deal with Takauji and his Ashigaru at some point. That's a given. And I'm also told that ah... well, your old friend, Katsurou? The son of a bitch has been seen in these parts recently."

45

"Good then. Maybe we'll have fellowship on the way," the cool bitterness simmered under Kojiro's voice. He clenched Ayame's woolen reins, saying without turning to his friend,

"I will find it, Jubei… The answer to the one question that a man should never ask, but must ask still; by what means can I kill a God?"

Jubei narrowed his eyes. He understood that his friend was in pain, but had he gone mad too?

"Where?" he asked. "Where will you go?"

"Far West of here. Northwest, in fact. Deep in the mainland of Honshu. There is a temple hidden beyond the Valley of Swords called **The Tabernacle of the Thalatha**."

"The Thalatha?" Jubei was incredulous, for he knew the word. "Moths.. You would risk your life on a quest for moths?"

"It is not a quest for moths," Kojiro was annoyed.

"And the Valley of Swords, I've heard, is a myth. Or a metaphor for tall grass."

"Nothing written in the Bodhisattvas is myth or metaphor. Besides, my father saw it. He told me stories about both the Tabernacle and the Valley as a child. This is where I will find my answer."

Jubei sighed and shook his head. "You mean *we*."

Kojiro gave him a look.

"Of course, I am alerting the men and of course we are coming with you.

"Don't let me twist your arm about it," Kojiro said, flashing a rictus grin.

"Hahaha! How about this for an idea?! Let's each of us man this trip on our own two feet. Let Ayame stay and rest in safety. This isn't her fight, after all."

"Hmm. I wonder if she likes the sound of that."

They both observed Ayame. Of course, she'd rather stay and rest. It was clear as much by her eyes.

Kojiro sighed, a moment of playfulness between friends.

"It's settled then, fool."

CYNTHIA DEGRUY LIKED WAKING UP to the Lafayette morning news, despite its usual dour content. Every morning at 3:45AM, her eyes opening to the abstract resin pedestaled Bambara Chiwara mask looking at her from a perch on the nightstand next to her bed, Cynthia's television would come on as an alarm prompting her to the ritual of preparing for work. Disciplined and driven, she would never linger or oversleep. Her philosophy, in fact, was that far too much time in general was spent doing that; wasting away in a state unconsciousness, the average human being spending 229,961 hours (or 26 years!) asleep. In the 1800, little over a thousand years ago, the average human lifespan was about 30 years. So, here we were in the modern age, the technological, pharmaceutical, economical, and general health peak of human existence, committing entire lifetimes to the void -to nothingness.

Perversity, she reasoned, in the most extreme sense of the word.

This morning, a Monday, the smiling, well dressed, male anchor on her television was talking about a local kidnapping. Apparently, an Arcadia woman was last seen jogging the Friday prior, and was found Sunday morning dead in a ditch.

"When we return,' he segued, chiseled jaw, perfect teeth, 'find out the latest in local cuisines. Boudin melt subs, Turkey Cranberry, and new ways to make French Dip Deluxe!"

Cynthia took her two daily sumatriptan migraine pills, then she splashed water on her face in the bathroom while the news and commercials droned on in the background, regarding the contradictions of skin the color of roasted chestnuts under sandy brown hair, sapphire eyes from her French North African father against high cheekbones and full lips characteristic of her Afro-Guyanese mother.

"You are the miraculous product of multiculturalism,' Brisa, her middle-school teacher mother used to tell her when she was a girl, "a living expression of worlds consolidating, the beauty of different cultures, different nationalities, coming together as one human family."

There was this habit she had of reintroducing herself to her surroundings every morning, of perusing the décor of her small two bedroom house while thawing herself out of sleep and engaging the day. While others in her age and economical bracket, 32 with a budding professorial career, would be saying their good mornings to housemates and/or family members, she was affectionately scanning the collection of magnet sculptures she'd procured over the years, the shelves of books covering the entire wall separating the kitchen and the living room that served as a backdrop to a modest office space, the tribal wooden busts and figurine statues of African women in headdress, Zulu warriors carrying colorful shields and spears, and hand carved Maasai Laibon leaders with their chins held up with nobility, pride, wisdom.

The first thing she'd do is go out to the garage for a thirty minute session of kickboxing on the heavy-bag. High intensity. Then, a twelve ounce coffee while listening to an audio book. This particular morning, it was Invincible Summer by Albert Camus:

"*...In the midst of chaos, I found there was, within me, an invincible calm.*

I realized, through it all, that... In the midst of winter, I found there was, within me, an invincible summer. And that makes me happy. For it saysthat no matter how hard the world pushes against me, within me, there's something stronger -something better, pushing right back."

She then gets dressed for work, grabs her satchel and helmet, proceeds from there to wheel the white Kawasaki ZX6R out the street.

Every morning as she did this, she'd hear her father's voice.

"There's over eighty-nine thousand motorcycle accidents a year, honey. I worry about you riding them things."

"That's still barely 1%, dad," she replied, before kissing his forehead. "Way more car accidents than that."

She took the 1-10E from Lafayette to Baton Rouge. Her father would wince if he were around to see how fast she rode, but she was a card carrying member of the AMA and had competed in amateur racing her first couple years as an undergraduate in college. By now, finishing up her Doctorate in Literature, moving fast on two wheels came naturally to her. Anyway, dad was no longer around to complain.

There wasn't much traffic at that hour, especially on the specific route that she'd carved, so what should have taken fifty-five minutes just over forty. She'd pull into the parking garage at LSU campus just before 6am every day, with an hour to spare before her first class.

Rather than mingle or linger in the book store, library, or the food court, and suffer student, sometimes other teachers, hitting on her, Cynthia preferred going straight to her classroom to enjoy its emptiness, the quiet, and meditate at the podium before greeting her first wave of freshmen students.

This was part of her Doctorate program, teaching an undergraduate class of the literature track while working on her dissertation.

Some days, she regretted the subject she chose to teach. Especially because of the hate mail she'd get from disgruntled parents, usually Christians, wondering why she was teaching their kids that if Jesus lived, he spawned from some random person's imagination first.

Kids.

"Yesterday morning, they found the body of Jody Fischer, the jogger who went missing last week,' Cynthia began her lecture, at 7:15 after the last of 38 students had settled into their seats. She was bespectacled now, her hair tied in a bun, stoic rectitude saturating everything from her posture to her voice. "What kind of plans did she have for the weekend, before the thought ever entered her mind that she would never see it? The people who knew her, family, friends, coworkers, how much of themselves have died with her upon hearing the devastating news? These pieces of their identities dependent upon that stolen relationship that before they believed were static, inexorable, permanent aspects of who they were as people? The gulf between last Thursday and today, that draining void into which no shortage of broken promises, shattered dreams, and bespotten beliefs have been lost, is there any chance that even the apprehension of the murderer and justice being served might recoup any of that? If we're honest, the answer is no. If we're honest, in fact, we'll accept the perhaps debilitating and incurably demoralizing reality that murders can never be truly avenged, that justice which doesn't involve the prevention of lost life can never truly be served.

Maybe this is the underlying psychological reason that we humans, smart or dumb, young or old, educated or ignorant, are all so captivated by the idea of superheroes and mythological beings devoted to saving lives, pantheons of Gods all representative of some higher facet of equity."

Cynthia had left the podium by now and was pacing the aisles, a thing all her students were used to. She glanced down to her right and saw someone, a young man, writing in his notes. *"higher facets of equity"*.

"This brings us back to Theosophy," she continued. "I trust that everyone took time over the weekend to complete the reading on Alexandra David-Neel."

Cynthia was good at reading people, so when she turned to scan the room after saying that, she noticed that the body language of several students suggested that no, they didn't complete the reading. She had to hold back her knowing smirk.

One hand went up toward the back of the room, a twenty-one year old Native Choctaw woman.

"Yes, Talulah?"

"Well,... Ms. Degruy, I finished the reading. But I'm still a little confused."

"About?"

"About the credibility of the text. Or, maybe, how I should read it."

"Please, elaborate."

"Ok so..., David-Neel studied to Tibetan doctrines on tulpamancy. She concentrated on meditation and visualization to create her own tulpa, the Friar Tuck-like monk."

Talulah shifted in her seat, sitting forward and leaning her elbows on the desk.

"She created this guy who... started appearing to other people. I mean, in the story, she actually succeeds in manifesting a living thought form."

"But?" Cynthia challenged.

"But.... are we supposed to read this as a literal account? Do we believe that this really happened, or that the text is a metaphor of some kind?"

"Siddhartha Gautama," Cynthia countered. "Born to a wealthy family during 5th Century B.C., in present-day Nepal. He is considered the founder of Buddhism, and while the historicity of him as the Buddha himself is rarely questioned, but the story of his miraculous birth and life should bring pause."

She turned her attention then from Talulah to pace some more and address the entire class. The lights went dim in the room and a projector came down at the front wall, all by the remote prompt that Cynthia was carrying in her hand. With each click, the projector slides cycled pictures of the different people she was talking about in the lecture.

"He shares with Mihavira, the supposed founder of Jainism, a miraculous virgin birth. So does Jesus of Nazareth. The twin founders of Rome, Romulus and Remus, were born to the virgin Rhae Silvia. Horus was the son of the virgin Isis. Ancient Greece tells the story of Dionysus, son of the virgin Seleme. Were all these people and many other mere metaphors, or did they walk the earth? Perhaps, a combination of both? Could they have started as imaginary figures, oral stories passing from culture to culture, sharing some details and changing others, and people believing so strongly in them that these people came into actual sentient existence?"

Cynthia clicked again and the room brightened up slightly, the slide on the screen now back to a statue of Buddha.

"Circling back to Gautama," she also brought her attention back to Talulah, whose eyes were beaming with attention and fascination. "It is widely believed that immediately after he was born, he took seven steps north and then sang, *I alone am the honored one above earth and below heaven.*"

Then, she finally let a smile loose and again addressed the class, arms outstretched.

"What do you think? Fact, fiction, or intense thought and visualization brought to life?"

No one said anything at first, but several students were trading glances and contemplating the question.

Finally, a young Caucasian man seated next to a very pregnant young woman raised his hand. Cynthia nodded in his direction.

"Yeah, Ms. D., I was thinkin'. My Linda here is due in about two months. Maybe if we start thinking hard on it now, our kid will come out singin' *Faith* by George Michael."

Linda laughed embarrassingly, elbowing him.

There was a scatter of more laughter in the room. Even Cynthia was amused, appreciating the injection of levity.

"Well,' she reasoned, "It will sure beat the crying."

———

THE UHF BUG TRANSMITTER WAS HIDDEN inside of an antique Cloisonne vase in the trophy room with Coletrane and Poole. There, in fact, were several of them scattered around the house. Bugs, not Cloisonne vases. It was never something Poole, in charge of security, ever expected, so never something the team he hired for the task would think to do sweeps for. This is what Privett counted on. Time and Patience, the two most powerful warriors, were working to the hired spy and professional cat burglar's advantage.

"The story is still alive,' he listened to Coletrane say through the transponder connected to a laptop in the hotel room five miles away, that he was renting indefinitely. "Alive, but not well."

After seven weeks of service, he had finally come upon a conversation that fit the specific context of his assignment. It was enough to make him almost jump up off of the bed that he was lounging on, looking off into the space and watching the slow moving ceiling fan turn.

Jackson Privett wasn't a lazy man, but his surveillance job was sedentary enough that the effects of inertia would set in if he weren't careful. What Privett enjoyed was the thrill and challenge of infiltrating fortified mansions, and/or lifting jewelry and coveted arts from auctions and museums to be sold on the black market. He kept himself in shape by keeping a strict routine of early morning jogs followed by hundreds of sit-ups and pushups, practicing calisthenics to keep himself limber and yoga for flexibility. He in fact "conquered" yoga, having mastered the ability to perform all of the movements better than most teachers.

Privett was short at 5'7, did gymnastics ever since he was a child but got bored with competition. Fell entirely off the grid and was estranged from his family, so being alone for long periods of time was nothing to him. He relished the peace of not being bothered with people, a "hotbed of mediocrity", he often said to himself.

But after seven weeks of tedium, the sounds of a conversation at last relevant to the point of his employ excited him despite his otherwise stoic sensibilities.

Privett went over and sat at the chair in front of the laptop, turning up the volume on the transponder. He sipped from a bottle of coconut water as he listened.

"All these years,' Poole's voice said through the live recording, 'we've waited to learn if your father was right about the prophesy of your birth."

"We've always known he was right, Jonas. And everything has led us to this moment. As it is written, *On his 33rd he will seek it.*"

"Indeed, sir. But the second part is what concerns me. The part that reads, '*And they will seek him.*"

"I am less concerned than I am ready."

"Perhaps."

"Perhaps?"

"But who are the *they*, sir?"

"We'll find out soon enough. Call DeLoach and have him clear me a flight to Takayama."

Privett never spoke unless absolutely necessary, so he gladly removed the cellphone off the cordless charger that was on the desk next to the rest of his electronic equipment, punched in a number and began writing a text.

What Privett was writing, it reached all the way to a line in Venice, Italy. The top floor suite of a restored Paisiello apartment building, its balcony overlooking the San Polo canal. The Rialto Bridge could be seen from there, as well as the Rialto Market where street vendors sold fish and fruit to the locals. Landau Kier was on that balcony, reclined on a cushioned chair and holding a rock cut crystal tumbler half full of a pinkish ouzo -sweet with a touch pastis.

If he were standing, Kier was physically imposing at 6'9, but coasted on two hundred and fifty pounds of muscle with the grace of a feather in the wind. His long, dirty blonde hair was tied in a ponytail and his chiseled chin was clean shaven. He wore a white guanaco outfit that cost more than the average worker's entire month salary, the shirt open at the collar. And he spoke with the cadence of a man without a care in the world.

When his phone beeped, that carefree nature was evident in the nonchalance with which he regarded it. Frankly, he was more interested in when Qadr would return to the balcony to enjoy the view with him. He already missed her bergamot and vanilla scent. But even with all his imposing size and strength,

Kier knew that rushing the deadly Qadr Fakhoury was never a good idea.

Steam still rose from underneath the bathroom door from her shower, but she was in the mirror oiling her sandy umber brown skin. This was a ritual of hers, Qadr, she'd rub coconut oil on her tattoos and scars -of which there were many of both. The scars were memorabilia from her infantry service in the Israeli Army, and the tattoos were an ongoing mosaic telling the story of her life's traumas.

The uninitiated eye would see a beautiful tapestry of body art on an incredibly fit woman, but in reality she was a living scroll of misery and violence.

Watching her reflection looking back at her, Qadr considered the splinter in her mind; a recurring dream that she'd been having for weeks. She wasn't sure exactly how many times that she'd had it, actually. But she knew that it persisted enough to bother her in waking hours. There weren't many details that she retained, except for the lights. Twenty-seven of them, she was certain. Twenty-seven bright, iridescent lights reaching out an asphyxiating chasm of blackness so visceral that she could feel her breath being stifled just recalling the thought. So much so that she had to shake it away and then take deep breaths to keep herself from passing out...

When she finally came out to join Kier on the balcony, she was wearing that fragrance he loved so much, along with a white two piece bathing suit and a floor length crochet trim cover-up that dragged on the floor behind her. She looked at Kier through bug eye sunglasses but didn't smile. He loved that about her, the stoicism.

He'd finally read the message from Privett, which simply read:

Target planning trip, Tokyo.

"Bonjour, mon amour," she said, preferring French to English or even her native tongue. Kier loved the way it sounded spoken with her Moroccan elocution. But he could only nod in reply because he was already on the phone, checking in with his employer.

"Put him on, capo,' he said into the phone, 'Tell 'im it's Kier. He'll wan' the news promptly."

And on the other side of the world, that is exactly what the servant did. Recognizing the orders spoken directly from his boss. *"If Landau Kier calls and I find out you let me miss it, you're fired. At least."*

So, Bedros the short legged servant moved as fast as his legs would carry him out the veranda doors of the mountainside Redondo Beach Estate, across the grass and against a slight breeze to where his employer practiced his archery in the vast open field of his land.

A line of targets were set up at the place where grass became sand, just before the rock cut-off peak over sea water. But the obscenely rich student of archery was standing almost a hundred yards away, his sleeves rolled up to the biceps and eagerly practicing with his brand new compound bow -a carbon marvel of engineering. So far he loved the precise tuning of it, and the weather was perfect for testing its torque elimination on the draw cycle. But he stopped when he noticed Bedros moving hurriedly towards him with a cellphone in tow.

"Mr. Cross,' Bedros said, trying to not insult his boss' sensibilities by hyperventilating, 'a call for you. Landau Kier."

Jeremiah Cross looked like he barely aged in the last twenty-two years, he was more fit than he'd ever been in his life but his bald head now was a natural affectation of age, and his beard was now a dignified storm of gray and black. He took the phone from Bedros, noticeably disgusted by the small man's display of fatigue.

"You will join me for the morning jog starting tomorrow, Bedros. Your poor conditioning is repulsive."

"Of course, sir," Bedros said, nodding twice before moving away to give Cross his privacy.

"You know I have archery at this hour, Kier," Cross said into the phone. "I presume this is urgent."

"Maybe not as urgent as a bomb threat in a mall, capo. But.."

"The jokes will come out of your fee, Landau. And I am not your *capo*."

"Your man with the cadre of fetishes, he's taking an impromptu trip out to Japan. <u>That</u> sounded urgent. Should I put my people on it?"

"Yes. Of course. And Landau, while I have you on the line..."

"Shoot."

"Your associate, Fakhoury. I've another assignment for her."

"She'll love the news."

"The name Nicolaou Steinitz. Do you know it?"

On the balcony at the Paisiello, Qadr turned away from the sun and leaned back on the railing, watching Kier after realizing he was speaking of her. She lit a cigarette as he spoke in the phone.

"Yeah,' he said, nodding. His blue eyes were looking up at Qadr. "Chess prodigy from Prague.... Uh huh. Well ...sure. On it. Listen, Mr. Cross. You should try hatha. It's good for the Kundalini. Hello?"

Kier shook his head as he closed the phone, with a wink for Qadr.

"That guy does not have a sense of humor," he added, before putting down the phone and taking a sip of his ouzo.

"So... Un travail pour moi?"

"You guessed it, chérie. Beirut."

"What? Tu plaisante, n'Est-ce pas?"

Nope. Serious as a bomb threat in a mall," he winked again, then lifted his tumbler in a cheers gesture. "Pack up."

————

A TRADITIONAL STYLE DOJO WAS BUILT on the Marx property about twenty years ago. High ceilings with climbing ropes near the west wall, the *Shimoseki,* or Metal element corner, where there were also weapon racks and a wooden dummy, green slate stone flooring at the northern front and the southern back, *Kamiza* and *Shimoza* for Water and Fire respectively, separating these spaces from the wide open theatre of polished teakwood flooring. The place in the center, *the Embujo*, it represented the element of Earth -*honesty*.

And this is where Coletrane was, in the center of that floor. Shirtless, barefoot, blindfolded, and open-handed. There were nine other men circling him, none wearing blindfolds and all bearing a training weapon; jo, bokken, Kali sticks, or black rubber axes.

Poole was walking along the eastern corner, the *Joseki*, and the circling men were all waiting for his prompt before engaging Coletrane -who was still as a statue and maintaining steady, focused breaths.

He was outwardly calm, Coletrane was, but inside he was experiencing a fantasy of the night that his parents were murdered. Instead of entering that room as a precocious, frightened eleven year old, he walked in as a man wielding a sword of his own. Vincent and Adaeze were still alive, over by the corner of the room by the bed, wrapped in each other's arms. The demon Kojiro was about to attack them when instead he turned his attention to Coletrane upon hearing him enter the room.

Without hesitation, Coletrane lunged at the demon and clocked him across the jaw with a flying crescent kick. And then upon landing, fired a side kick into his stomach that sent the phantom samurai slamming against the wall. Coletrane readied himself in a low, wide standing Ko Gasami No Kamae combat stance, the blade held high and reaching out at eye level, its tsuka held close to his face. Black tar instead of blood shone on the lip, the demon Kojiro smiled, standing back upright off the wall and readying into a Shin No Kamae, his sword hand at his center torso with his other arm folded underneath, the blade jutting out and resting in the hinge of his left arm just under the bicep.

In reality, Coletrane had balled his fists. And on Poole's call, the men attacked him with their weapons. All at once!

In the fantasy, Kojiro, the pupils in his eyes doing the formidable figure-eight, attacked as well. But Coletrane was ready! He parried the demon's first two strikes, returning volley with a strike of his own under an attempt for his head, that cut under Kojiro's armpit with a spirt of tar but otherwise no effect!

In reality, he'd already moved under a jo strike attempt from one man, flipped him over his shoulder, sending him crashing into two of the others. He'd sidestepped two slanting slash attempts from one attacker's bokken, first left and then right, catching behind his arm after the second and popping his elbow. This caused the attacker to drop the bokken, which was hurled across the floor. Another tried to attack from behind, but Coletrane sensed it and swept his leg, rolling to his right in the direction of the fallen bokken and picking it up at the end of his roll. Still, the blindfold held. But now Coletrane had a weapon.

In the fantasy, Kojiro was back on him. Their swords created sparks on contact, every miss cutting furniture or a wall, bedsheets, pillows - sending up feathers, glass, debris!

Poole was impressed with Coletrane's technique and dexterity, his quickness and focus. But there was concern. Poole knew his ward well enough to know that his practice with those men was becoming more than that. Committed violence.

Coletrane was now going against the tall man with the Kali sticks, another with a jo, and a third with a bokken. He was careful to keep moving the fight to where only two or three men could engage him at once, sending the others either tumbling or stepping clumsily in each other's way long enough to move again and refigure the odds. Coletrane twirled his bokken and attacked the Kali stick wielder high, spinning around on that technique to attack the bokken wielder at midrange and then spinning once more, faster than the Kali fighter's reflex, to pop him behind the knee and knock him off his feet.

Kojiro, in the vision, blocked that same leg strike but Coletrane flipped off the momentum of the block to kick him twice with a backwards double cyclone kick. Only, Kojiro also countered off the momentum of the second strike that hit him, immediately turning into a horizontal slash that Coletrane was just barely quick enough to escape (evading certain death!) and open the distance between them with a lateral Esquiva side roll he learned from his observance of Brazilian Capoeira over the years.

He pulled a few similar Capoeira moves during his sparring match with the nine men, and Poole, a keen eye, noticed this. Cracking a brief, proud grin at the thought, "My boy, he never formally studied this discipline."

Now the men were up again, stalking Coletrane as he loitered slowly like a feline at the ready.

And in the fantasy, he and Kojiro were circling each other as well. This is when the demon finally spoke. With Vincent and Adaeze to Kojiro's back, he said,
"You think you are a man but you are not. You are still just the frightened little boy. Nothing you do will change that you are the cause of what has happened. Nothing you do,' *he paused to crack a smile,* **'will save them."** *And then he turned away from Coletrane and lifted the diabolic version of Hatsukoi overhead, in a move meant to cut down both Vincent and Adaeze at once!*

"NOO!" Coletrane screamed, throwing his sword at the demon like a spear. It flew across the room with so much force that it went all the way into the demon's back, chucking him forward and completing its trajectory by cutting right through Coletrane's parents as Kojiro crashed into them and then into the wall! The three of them skewered like a shish kabob!

Vincent, again, gets out just one word before his eyes go blank, "S-s-son..."

This set Coletrane off in reality, creating a snap in his mind. He rushed the men and leapt, doing a cross kick that hit one man in the chest with his left leg and another in the face with his right, twirled on his landing, flipped the bokken and ended on the turn with a yoko giri strike so strong that it broke the third attacker's jo in half in the block attempt and cracked two of his ribs on contact. A kesi giri strike to the left and then another to the right, busting, in that order, one ax bearing man's shoulder and breaking the other one's arm as he tried a futile parry with a Kali stick.

"THELONIOUS!" Poole yelled. But Coletrane didn't hear it.

In the commotion, the blindfold finally came off. What Poole saw then sent him running into the fray!

Two of the remaining men stepped away, frightened by Coletrane's sudden turn for the berserker! Of the two remaining, one hesitated -but Coletrane hurled his bokken at him, that spun like a boomerang until crashing longways into the man's stomach. The other still tried to fight with his two axes, but was quickly disarmed and mounted, Coletrane tearing into him with a fusillade of punches while screaming!

Luckily, Poole made it to them before Coletrane killed the man and tackled him to the floor. Holding him tight until he finally snapped out of it.

"Thelonious! Calm down! CALM DOWN!"

IT TOOK HOURS FOR COLETRANE TO fully regain his composure. When he finally did, evening was announcing itself in the dimming sky with a tint of sapphire. In the center of the hedge maze on the property, the twelve foot jadeite statue of the horse-bound feudal warrior with his unsheathed sword pointed upward, it looked like cobalt marble in the lighting. And Coletrane was there, his hands tucked in the pockets of his black knee length lapel coat, looking up at the statue as if silently asking it for answers, for wisdom. Maybe this, he wondered, is what drove his father; an unspoken desire in the man to translate the language of the surrounding area so that he may gain some sagaciousness from things that preceded, and would outlive him.

Poole would join him shortly, but was taking his time along the way between the many turns throughout the maze designed to throw off the path of the uninitiated. He was thinking about what he saw in Coletrane's face earlier at the crisis point of that martial arts practice session; *Coletrane's eyes did the bizarre figure-eight like Kojiro's and the moon, the skin around those eyes collecting with irritated veins coursing with vibrancy.*

So, as Poole walked the memorized path, carrying two iced goblets of Glenfiddich 50, he considered his regrets. One of which, not heeding the warning of those teachers who told him to not allow Coletrane to continue training in martial arts. He remembered a particular date not long after his parents' death, after the wound on Coletrane's chest healed and when it was deemed acceptable to release him from juvenile confinement after the trauma (suspicion) surrounding the murder of Vincent and Adaeze.

He remembered the therapy for Coletrane that followed, when the therapist told him,

"For the average rich kid,' the therapist warned Poole, as they watched the boy through a two-way mirror, sitting alone in a room with his eyes turned down, 'empathy is a little difficult to establish. Not to mention, the basic concept of need that facilitates the development of friendship and connection to other people. For Coletrane, especially after losing his parents the way that he did, it will be even more of a challenge for him to form lasting bonds and to interpret other people's emotional cues and expressions."

When Poole arrived at the center of the maze, seeing Coletrane looking up at the statue, he remembered the therapist's lasting admonition, **"Be careful with him."**

"Addison,' Coletrane said, of the man whose ribs were broken in the sparring match, 'how is he?"

"He'll live,' Poole replied, approaching. And as he handed Coletrane his drink, he added, 'So will Braga."

Coletrane shut his eyes a moment, in shame.

"I didn't mean to do that. Any of it."

"They know."

Then, changing the subject, Coletrane regarded his glass.

"This is three fingers, Poole."

"Yes. Figured you could use a little more. Because I saw it, you know?"

"Saw what?"

"The eyes... I saw your eyes."

Coletrane turned away, took a sip of his drink. He struggled to form emotional bonds, but Poole had become a surrogate father figure to him. As such, Poole knew all his tells and cues. So, when Coletrane began rubbing his index finger with the thumb of his free hand, he knew this meant that he was rattled inside despite his outward display of stoicism.

"Why didn't my father teach me about the prophesy before my mind created chaos?"

"He was only beginning to understand it himself."

"It's no excuse, considering the danger of it."

"Vincent thought he had more time, Thelonious."

There was a thing that Coletrane did with his shoulder, coupled with the twitch of an eye, Poole knew this meant he was experiencing guilt and anger.

"No matter,' he said, 'now I have to clean it up. There is a lot of blood on my hands now, Poole."

"Do not be so hard on yourself."

"Are you kidding?" Coletrane's voice went up a bit, a rare outward show of chagrin. "First my mother and father, and… **what happened to Marcus**.., but it's no telling how many more will have to die because of me before all this is done."

"That wasn't you. It was-"

"It <u>was</u> me! Kojiro is my creation. And I am going to find his sword in Takayama! Then I will the connection. I will have answers. But already, the implication of it all, physical evidence of a manomāyakāya, is enough to impact the very face of human history itself. And with it all our assumptions about the unknown, not to mention our place in the universe. Speaking of which, I have another idea that, well, you're not gonna like it."

Poole gave Coletrane a sideways look, but Coletrane disarmed him with a wry grin. A grin, Poole noted, that immediately vanished from Coletrane's face.

"Let's go back inside so you can make yourself another drink before I tell you."

He didn't wait for Poole's reply, before beginning his stride along the maze's exit path.

———

AND NEITHER OF THEM KNEW, THAT Coletrane's words were reverberating across the breadth of time and space, obeying no laws of either, and arriving in the ear of one of the Three Interstices.

Early morning, Cypress Swamp in the Everglades, the rhodium dust of Manthis's body solidifies into physical form, his bare feet now standing in the mud of the quiet forested wetlands. "*It was me! Kojiro is my creation,*' he hears Coletrane say as the ebony crystals of his eyes come into focus. '*And I am going to find his sword in Takayama! Then I will have the connection. I will have answers.*"

At the same time, Paul Whittaker was waking up on his overworn futon bed. He lived alone, "off the grid", in a one room shed house not far from where Manthis was standing. In fact, Manthis was close enough to the tumbledown home that

Whittaker's rottweiler, Barron, was pulling against his chain and barking up a storm. There was a yellow Gadsden flag bearing the picture of the timber rattlesnake flying on the slanting flag pole that Barron was chained to, and there was also a Confederate flag flying underneath it.

Paul was dreaming about what it would be like to command wealth when the barking woke him up. He was angry when the woman sucking his pecker disappeared upon opening his eyes.

"Gat-damnit, Barron!" he yelled. 'you shut it, mutt!"

Barron kept barking.

Paul worked himself off of the thin mattress and stumbled over to the small crate stack that doubled as a dresser. He reached behind it, in a reflex, for his shotgun. Instinct kicked in after the surge of annoyance, the realization that Barron doesn't usually bark like that early in the morning.

"Boy, I'm comin'."

He cocked the Winchester.

When he exited the front door, still in his boxers and a tank top stained with splotches of spaghetti and cheap rum, he saw right away what Barron was barking at; Manthis, standing not more than forty yards from his door to the left, at the tupelo trees along the bank of the bayou.

"Hey!' he yelled across the clearing, 'Hey you there!" Then he cocked the Winchester again, so the intruder could hear it. "You's on my proputy!"

Manthis didn't move, or in any way acknowledge the threat.

Paul, not one to put up with disrespect from anyone, especially not on *his* land, hot footed the rest of the distance. When he was close enough, Paul could see the dark skin of

Manthis' arms under the cloak, so his anger intensified as it registered in his mind that the intruder was a black man.

"Hey nigger,' he said with disgust, 'you turn around now! Imma shoot ya, ya don't!"

He lifted the gun, pointing at Manthis' head, "Turn around!!"

The immortal, unfeeling Interstice finally decided to acknowledge the human speaking to him, and turned to look at him over his shoulder. His turn was enough that Paul could see the crystal eyes.

That's when a pain shot through his body so great that he immediately dropped the gun to the muddy grass, and every one of his muscle joints were razed with a sudden quake of trauma. It was like a heart attack, except that his left arm wasn't the only part of him constricting. All the blood in his body began to flow in the opposite direction, wounds tore violently open at random points on his every extremity, his bowels evacuated burning excrement, and he swallowed his tongue so could not scream.

Paul tried to limp away, but this effort was futile. Also, it was cut short when his left leg gave out. All the bones in it became so brittle that they collapsed on themselves and dug into the flesh like a dropped bag of coins. Manthis watched, undisturbed. But he did not deliberately cause this to happen to Paul. It was Paul looking into Manthis' eyes that did it, the consequence of seeing one's own reflection in the Interstice.

It fascinated the immortal to watch the human man continue his painful journey towards death. But only momentarily distracted Manthis from his purpose for manifesting there in the Everglades...

———

THERE WERE HUNTERS IN THE SWAMP, a few miles removed from Whittaker's shack, foolishly hunting what they believed to be a rabid *felis concolor coryi*, or rare Florida panther, that a few locals thought was responsible for the mysterious disappearances of some people in the area. Including the leader of the hunt party, Felix Tradeau, who lost his twenty-five year old son seventy-two hours prior. Just vanished, no trace left.

Tradeau and his men were right about their quarry being responsible for those disappearance, but they'll prove dead wrong about the culprit.

"Walsch,' Tradeau whispered, looking to the man at his right, 'the time?"

"5:47," Walsch replied after checking his watch.

Them and five other men, all outfitted in camouflage hunting gear, were creeping through the dense thicket of deciduous conifer and fog. They could barely see more than twenty feet ahead in any distance, but their collective anger outweighed their natural, raw fears. Four of those men were friends of Tradeau's son, and two others recently lost people of their own within that same seventy-two hour timeframe. Most of them were carrying bolt-action rifles, but Tradeau had a 9mm semiautomatic carbine. He was the expert hunter of the group, and he owned, in fact, a shooting range that he operated with George, his missing son.

Manthis could see the men from his distance through telescopic vision, and could but wouldn't intervene. There was the sound of Coletrane's voice playing in his mind like an omen. *"How many more will have to die because of me,'* Manthis heard the words in the form of a question, *'before all this is done?"*

"Spread out some,' Tradeau whispered, 'but be quiet. Stay on alert."

The men complied, opening up the radius of their party like slow moving cats navigating the scattered about narrow spaces between puddles of water.

Walsch saw something move up ahead to his left, swiftly turning his gun towards it. There was nothing but bushes. Sudden movement up above between tree branches, this time Tradeau and two others turned their sights up. Still, nothing. A stillness took hold of the surroundings as the group advanced, each man sensitive to abrupt movements in their surrounding vista. Not only was the *rabid panther* they thought they were hunting a more dangerous creature, but there was other wildlife in those parts they'd be unwise to disturb. Gators, snakes, black bears, there were no shortage of perils that lie in wait to balance the scale between failure and consequence.

But as alert as these men were, none of them could see the invisible varnish coming over them, a living quintessence washing over the trees and grass and air.

By the time Walsch could smell its sulfuric scent, it was already too late.

"Hey,' he called to the man nearest him, in a hushed tone, 'do you sme-", that last word cut off by a falling leaf that he didn't notice, which went suddenly from fluttering downward to slanting like a thrown shuriken -going across Walsch's neck. His head was already rolling off of his shoulders before he realized that he was dead.

The man who saw this panicked and screamed! Fired a shot with his rifle on reflex before tripping over a vine and landing on his ass. In less than a second, a part of the invisible quintessence concentrated down from the trees in a shape like a giant piston and slammed into the man's middle torso so hard that all his ribs and internal organs were crushed. He was killed instantly, but the loud sound of his bones breaking along with the muffled murmur of his blood soaked death yell assaulted all the men's ears.

The man to Tradeau's right looked him square in the eye and dropped his rifle, turned tail to run. But then a long, thin tree branch shot downward in a slant, going right through the man's skull and into the ground. He was skewered standing up, his twitching legs dangling like the bottom half of a towel hung up on a clothesline. With his semiautomatic, Tradeau fired several shots in various direction, hoping futilely to hit something. A bullet grazed his ear from the rifle of another of the men who had the same earnest albeit inefficacious idea in a desperate scramble to preserve his life. Maybe he thought he would succeed, this man, perhaps he hoped to be that lone survivor to return home to his family and tell of the story of his brush with the supernatural and with death itself. But no. Within the space of moments that could only generously be described as seconds, Tradeau watched a translucent blade-like structure shoot through that man's back and come out his chest, sending his broken, dislodged heart flying across the clearing.

Then that structure solidified as a small hand and arm, that then yanked out of the man's chest after balling its invisible fist. As his body fell, Tradeau could now see what was standing behind it. A young naked woman in a feral ready stance, with a fiery mixture of brown, blonde, and black hair. Her body, vein riddled like a new born baby until smoothed out and silky in a matter of seconds. Her only clothing was the generous blood spatters of the men she'd just killed. This was **The Ghost Orchid**, Astrid's new form, in this new world setting, realizing, as she instinctively consumed the life-force of those she'd killed, that she lived before. *The first thought she had was of Ittei, the married samurai from another, mythic time. He wrote at one point in his life about a supernatural being much like what she had become in this life, and he used that term to describe her -Ghost Orchid.*

Tradeau fired a bullet at Astrid's head, and without even having to look in his direction, she reflexively (and quite casually) moved out of its path. The sound of the bullet as it passed by her ear however triggered a memory; *She remembered herself as Astrid, a world creator, a goddess..., she remembered falling to the earth and experiencing the mysterious reverie of her translucent self -pregnant with the suffocating cosmos and the miniature moons preserving her modesty.*

The stray bullet cut through the neck of another of the men, who tried to stop himself from dying by grasping the bleeding wound with both hands. Astrid reached back and grabbed him by his shirt, hurling him over her shoulder with incredible strength.

Tradeau had to dive out of the way to stop being hit by his friend-turned-projectile, and the body slammed into a tree with so much force that the spinal cord was jutting out the side of the hip as the body fell to the mud. The crash shook out a fall of leaves from the cypress tree. Those leaves fluttered down around Tradeau like slow-moving rain.

The other two remaining men were trying to flee. But then Astrid blinked, and then the falling leaves flew at them like heat seeking knives, cutting the men to pieces.

It was then that Tradeau would learn what happened to his son.

As Astrid, now the Ghost Orchid, closed her eyes and focused on the memory of the cosmos, she saw that version of her smiling in the reverie. And then it, she, whispered, "In the Tomorrow World, you will find Freedom."

Gripped still by the memory, as if it were providing her sustenance, Astrid arched her back and began to breathe deeply. She balled her fists and petrified her musculature, the many fallen body parts of what used to be men began to collapse into a pinkish volatile liquid -all of it collecting like ventricles towards Astrid as their source. She sucked up the entirely of their lifeforce until there was nothing left of them but tattered piles of bloody clothing.

While this was happening, she imagined the cosmos in her diaphanous and self-usurping like the vacuum of a black hole.

When she was finished, she walked over towards Tradeau. She didn't make eye contact with him. She didn't even seem to notice that he was there, pleading for his life.

"P-p-please. Please don't kill me," he said while slowly beginning to thaw out of catatonia and crab crawl backwards.

But to his surprise, she walked right past him and kept going.

Manthis, having watched these curious events unfold from a distance, narrowed his eyes and wondered,

Why is she here?

——

IN THE MARX MANSION, THERE IS A ROOM. It has black soft woven tatami flooring, and shōji doors that open onto a shaded, elevated Zen garden. At the back of the northern wall, in the center, there was a black and gold iron katchu armor set propped up on a wooden stand. The fabrics were gold with blood red trimmings here and there, and the Dou armored plates and Kabuto helmet were shiny, polished black. The leather watagami straps attaching the sode were red, and so was the silk brocade Kote sleeves bearing black armored plates connected with golden kusari. Those black plates bore samurai crests specific to Kojiro's lineage in the forgotten history, and the forehead of the kabuto was a gold double pointed maedate that looked like the horns of a bull. In its center was another Kojiro crest. The menpo mask was golden and looked like the face of an Oni. This is a face that haunts Coletrane's dreams.

He purchased this O-yoroi armor at an auction in Giza years ago, and the auctioneers believed it was the armor worn by the famous samurai Kojiro Sasaki, who lived during the Edo period and fought Miyamoto Musashi in 1612. This, they explained as a selling point, was why the armor was so elaborate and flashy in design; because Kojiro Sasaki was known for his vanity in life.

But Coletrane knew that this story was false. This particular armor was worn by Kojiro ko-Mitsu, the one no history books told stories about because it was Coletrane's own child mind that made him real. *Like a spirit, demon Pinocchio.*

He paid five million for the armor.

Next to the armor set was a vertical sword stand holding the onyx Lionbear sword of Kojiro's, **Jun**. Coletrane found this artifact at an auction house in London, sold at $2,700,532, and incorrectly credited to Toyotomi Hideyoshi, the "Great Unifier" of the late Sengoku period.

And on that evening, as he so often did, he was sitting on his knees before the O-yoroi in the seiza meditative position. Breathing deeply, and thinking about the conversation he had with Poole after exiting the hedge maze the day prior.

———

"SPOILED AND NUGATORY,' POOLE READ from a magazine, "a microcosmic image of the modern day Richie Rich."

"I like his use of that word, *nugatory*," Coletrane replied. He was pouring he and Poole a drink. They were in the wine cellar.

"What more has this Coletrane Thelonious Marx done with the vast resources left him by his parents,' Poole continued reading, 'than fund a profligate study of violence, and indulge his late father's fetish for collecting art from the around the world?"

Coletrane grinned, handing Poole his drink.

"I knew you wouldn't like the idea, Poole."

"Why would you want to bring a hack journalist with an irrational vendetta against you on this Japan trip?"

"Perhaps so he can see my *profligate study of violence* up close and report on it."

"This isn't a game, Thelonious."

"And I'm not playing one. This hack journalist was also a war photographer who, armed only with a camera, kept his cool in the middle of conflict scenarios just to get the great shots. He is a world renowned journalist with a voice and platform, telling entire stories through the brilliance of the perfect shot. Who better a vehicle to carry the story of Kojiro ko-Mitsu to the world, and make said world believe it?"

"Perhaps you're right, but I'm concerned about the potential dangers of this world being told that story at all."

"It wasn't my father's intent to keep all this buried. Archeology for him wasn't a vanity. It's like Krishnamurti said, Poole. The world needs to be freed from the known. But they can't be freed from the known if they do not know it."

"Again,' Poole tapped glasses with Coletrane and took a sip, 'perhaps."

———

BUT THEN THE AYAHUASCA STARTED kicking in, causing Coletrane's mind to wander away from thoughts of his own memories and into the realm of his higher spiritual vibration. The brief euphoria was never why Coletrane took ayahuasca, despite that -the psychedelic effects, the extrasensory and sexual stimulation- being chiefly the reason others, women exclusively, enjoyed it with him. For him it was all about the temporary reprieve from the traumas that defined him, and how his mind would drift and expand into augmented awareness.

This time, with his body down in the meditative posture and focused intensely on deep breathing, it brought him all the way back into the mythic time of Kojiro -into *his* memories, into *his* trauma. **The night he lost Taya**...

————

AND ON THE FATEFUL NIGHT, IN THE Zsu Ch'an Northern Province, it was quiet enough. There was a full moon out, and the whispery voice of eleven year old Coletrane was in the air, unknowingly creating the world.

"He will be unstoppable,' the boy's voice said, *'but troubled even beyond death. His weakness can be his emotions, and it will be his strength too. His passion. His love."*

One of the local sake dens was brimful of peaceable warriors, artisans, merchants, and farmers alike that would meet and drink together. They'd tell stories deep into the night and listen to beautiful songs sung by Taya Hideki while she danced and performed an ikebana display with the grace of a samurai master.

She was the enchanted daughter of the den owner, Basumanu Hideki, and sworn bride to be to the local living legend Kojiro ko-Mitsu. Again, there was young Coletrane's voice, *"He is strong in a way that frightens him, but his great sword feeds him courage with its every kill. Peace only comes from his love, but that is taken from him,"* Taya had a psychic power that allowed her to make the flower stalks grow out the fertilized bowls on command and contort in the ikebana designs she intuited with her kenjutsu dance. And indeed, she was beautiful, in some ways that no one other than Kojiro could ever have known or understood. The way, it seemed, that she turned the brute in a man back into an unvarnished beginning –restoring his humanity with how deeply and fully she could love.

But that night an unknown vagrant would wander into the place. Taya had just finished a song and was bowing to the cheering crowd. Kojiro was at a table having drinks and trading war stories and philosophical ideas with some of the local artisans and writers.

"At first glance,' Kojiro said, 'you'd wonder how it is certain that Buddhism gets rid of the discriminating mind. But it is true to the knowledge of warriors that the character for "cowardice" is made by adding the character for "meaning". Meaning, of course, is discrimination. When a man adds discrimination to his mind he becomes uncertain; he becomes a coward."

"Hmm.. I am not sure if that is a fair assessment,' one of the artisans retorted.

"Well,' Kojiro offered, shrugging his shoulders and taking a sip of his drink, 'then tell me this. In the way of the samurai, can I become more courageous when discrimination arises?"

The vagrant was horribly unkempt, and it appeared as though he was already drunk by the way he tottered on his feet like he could fall at any moment if it weren't for the people and objects he found to lean against or hold himself up.

"Yummy yummy,' he yelled, cutting in the way of Taya as she was trying to pass. "Lookie what we have here! Some honey for a starving man!" Then he tried to reach into her kimono and put a hand on her breast.

"Don't touch me!,' she commanded.

Hearing her distressed voice, Kojiro leaped from his chair. One man went to grab the vagrant when the vagrant got violent and shoved him so hard that he fell over a table that collapsed under his weight.

Kojiro strode across the room with so much rage in his face that every-one there moved out of his way like a parting sea. The vagrant smiled at him as if he just didn't give a shit about the big bad warrior!

Taya tried to stop him but Kojiro moved past her and punched the vagrant square in the jaw. Two of his teeth flew but not faster than his body did when he went tumbling out of the door and falling off the veranda, hard on his backside in the dirt.

Kojiro got down, hot with rage only amplified by the sake. The vagrant raised his arm, laughing the entire time, when Kojiro pulled Jun the onyx Lion-bear from her sheath! Slashing down faster than the eye could capture and lopping off the vagrant's right arm.

It spun and slid in the dirt, the upper part of the now useless space shooting blood from shocked arteries. The bastard wasn't laughing anymore! Kojiro stood over him, breathing hard and looking down with feral rage no less intense.

But then the vagrant's shoulder stopped shooting blood and he started laughing again. His arm miraculously appeared back in place; perfect and new. He stood to his feet and then changed form for everyone to see.

The vagrant transformed into the terrible trickster Oni, the immortal Inca Tan'mo. Yellow eyes with fiery red pupils; cracked, dry skin covered in desquamation that gave the look and texture of cracking porcelain; his kimono, dark, shadowy gray; his hair, silver with streaks of black dropping steamy coal dust as it moved. **On his hip materialized a blade like no other, gift of the sun goddess Amaterasu herself -the unbreakable Tsurugi. Kojiro would never forget it shape and regality.**

Taya ran outside and pulled at Kojiro's arm. But the warrior stood his ground and held the devil's gaze.

"Not wiiise to disrespect me,… so-called Deadly One,' the Oni said in a cold, lifeless voice with enunciations that conveyed the fear of God. 'Not looking soooo deadly now. With your pitiful sword… your pitiful pride… your pitiful woman."

"But who is the coward?!" Kojiro screamed. "Who is the fraud ..that would never fight a man's fight on mortal terms?! Such big words you can speak though!" Then, with his free arm, Kojiro pulled Hatsukoi and was now holding both his swords. Ready to fight a battle he knew he couldn't win.

But then the unspeakable and unexpected happened. It happened in front of her father's eyes. The Inca Tan'mo shot a bolt of energy from a palm-heel strike that splintered the air and went into Taya's chest!

She convulsed once as if struck by lightning, and screamed so loud and horribly that it would never stop ringing in Kojiro ko-Mitsu's ears. Then, she fell to her knees and blue veins spiderwebbed across the surface of her skin as her muscles spasmed and her body collapsed to the dirt.

Kojiro sheathed his swords and ran to Taya's side, took her in his arms.

He looked into her blank eyes in search of her, finding not death, but a far-away catatonia. She was there but not there, gone but not gone; lost in time.

"Taya! Tayaaaa!"

But she offered no response. She just looked off into the distance, her now lifeless eyes searching past Kojiro as if he weren't even there. At last, the throbbing blue veins calmed and went away.

Taya's father, Basumanu, he rushed over and took Kojiro's place at Taya's side as the warrior rested her gently in his arms and then stood.

"What have you done to her?!" Kojiro demanded of the Tan'mo, his voice trembling, and Hatsukoi redrawn.

"What have I done?", the Oni laughed, 'You mean, what have you done!?! Or better, what are the sins of your arbiter?"

"Arbiter?!" he lunged at the Tan'mo, twirled Hatsukoi and slashed twice, horizontal and then vertical -but the demon easily flitted out of the way of each strike as if he were a tendril of smoke.

"DON'T SPEAK TO ME IN RIDDLES!" Kojiro yelled as the Oni stood upright again, smiling from ear to ear.

"I tell no riddles, Deadly One. I am powered by the same source that gives you breath, and I am but your consequence. Your Taya is every bit an illusion as the strength you think you possess."

Enraged, Kojiro tried again to strike but this time the Inca Tan'Mo did not bother to move. Instead, he effortlessly grabbed Kojiro's striking hand at the right just before contact. And then open palm struck him in the chest with his free hand with so much force that Kojiro released Hatsukoi and flew backwards ten yards!

He held his chest and spit blood. The Tan'Mo, he tossed Hatsukoi over to him, in the sand like a worthless trinket.

"Arbiter,' the Tan'Mo said, and then whispered it again, 'Arbiter..

Remember the word. Responsible for your arrogance, for the foolish faith that you have in yourself, and for the suffering that comes with what you have done today. Enjoy it, Kojiro. Savor every drop."

And then, he vanished in less than a blink. The ragged clothes he was wearing dropped to the dirt, letting loose a scatter of insects from beneath the pile that went every which way until they vanished beneath the sand.

———

COLETRANE OPENED HIS EYES, BUT IT was the noise that made him do it. Suddenly rushing towards him was the demon Kojiro, fully dressed in the O-yoroi. And before Coletrane could stand, Kojiro lifted him up by the throat and took him over to the back wall, slamming his back against it with the force of hatred. The menpo mask, Coletrane noticed, resembled the cracked face of the Oni in the vision.

"Arbiter," the demon's voice was deep and bitter, inhuman unlike Kojiro's actual voice. He took off the entire kusari, menpo with it, and slung the thing at the floor. It shattered into bits. Kojiro's black hair fell loose, his skin was pale, and those eyes bore the figure-eights.

Coletrane struggled under Kojiro's grip, hitting him and trying to break loose from his hold. But Kojiro held him firm as if a small child. He clenched his jaw and the black tar emitted from his teeth.

"Arbiter," he repeated.

"Let...me...go," Coletrane gets the words out, barely finding enough breath for them under the tightening grip on his throat. Demon Kojiro held him so tight that his eyes were bulging, watery and red.

"YOU FIRST!", the demon screamed. But there was more agony in his voice now than anger. And that momentary slip was enough for his focus to career, causing both Kojiro and Coletrane to experience a shared flashback of Adaeze and Vincent's deaths.

They saw as, still in shadowy form, the seven foot wraith stood over Adaeze's crying, wounded body. They saw together as she pleaded with her last breath to be allowed to live, for her son. They saw Vincent's gallant attempt to fight the beast. But, like Kojiro himself against the Tan'Mo, his efforts were in vain.

This flashback hurt them both, Coletrane and Kojiro. But it effected Kojiro more, this sudden contrast between fighting an Oni and being one himself.

He released Coletrane and the both of them fell to their knees.

Coletrane gasped for air, Kojiro looked up at him. The frightening figure-eight pupils vanished from Kojiro's eyes, they became normal, and Coletrane could see that they were grey with splashes of hazel. In Kojiro's face and skin there remained the struggle between demon and legend; that is, an oscillation between deathly pale and vibrant tan. There were the start of tears welling in his eyes when he whispered,

"I am not... evil."

Poole rushed into the room at that moment. The door opening is what shook Coletrane from his trance. The samurai armor was back in its place on the stand, but Coletrane was still lying against the wall -the dark bruises still on his throat. He could feel the sting and the swelling.

This wasn't a dream.

AFTER KOJIRO AND JUBEI AGREED TO leave the horses behind for the journey to **acquire the power to take on gods in single, fair combat,** Jubei gathered the Live Crew. They were 32 warriors in all including himself, Kojiro, two women, and the artist Ittei. They were a small, rag tag arsenal of some of the world's greatest, most diverse and incredible warriors. Every man among them either owed Kojiro his life or Jubei some money. All were loyal to the fold, and many would lose their lives before this quest was over. But none cared, and all couldn't wait!

Among them were the five Kiyoshi Brothers from the feared Chinmoku Aki Clan, a family of deaf mercenaries who, if not born deaf, are made deaf through ritual in order to prepare each pupil for the study of the Sacred Arts. These Chinmoku, they can *hear* in a way that no other living creature can. What they hear is really feeling, a sense of the intentions of all things even before those intentions arrive in the mind of the thing. Also, while it is true that they are *deaf*, it is likewise true that by some strange dark Seishin-teki kyōkō magic, the Chinmoku can make it where no one within their surrounding area can hear anything that they do if they choose to not let them. No matter the noise, it will be absolutely soundless to the people under the Chinmoku spell. *Imagine then, the ease and danger of one sneaking up on you...*

They are the swordsmen Gorou, Hajime, Ichiro, Jirou, and Finn, five affable brothers who doubled as Kabuki performers when not fighting at Kojiro's side.

Otaku was there, the four-armed brute who was stolen as a child from an underground experiment in the Korean peninsula that remains entirely unknown to everyone. He was stolen by a mysterious cult called the Sekiharan Monks and raised to be an assassin. It wasn't until he was an adult that the Sekiharan were exterminated by Buddhists and he escaped to be his own man, a ronin, eventually finding his way to Kojiro. Otaku, named for his octopus' arms, was special for another reason. The rugged, stocky warrior was an infighting expert at disarming men no matter what his weapon, and he was top cut in more hand to hand combat styles than most could count. Each hand had a preference intuited from his mind, and each combination of two used a different mixed set of fighting styles. It was never quite sure who or what kind of fighter you were fighting at any given moment when facing **Otaku the Freak**. Lucky, Kojiro often thought, that the roughhewn guttural bastard was a friend!

There was Kana, aptly named for her unmatched finesse and skill, who was one of two women in the group and the lead tracker. She was small in frame, seemingly frail even, but these details as misleading as the allure of her exotic rainbow colored eyes.

Kana was master of the kusarigama, a deadly chain sickle with which she was so adept that she could surgically take out any enemy within a forty yard radius. She was also an expert knife wielder. It was never certain how many she carried on her person at any given time, but it was known (and feared) that she possessed a certain magnetic chi power that enabled her to draw those knives back to her after precision kills.

The other woman of the group was Tzukuba. She almost never spoke. No one knew her real name, so she is called Tzukuba after her weapon, the iron-piked sodogarami that split into two weapons; One a short tzukubō that doubled as a baton with spiked bards down its bludgeon base, and the other a narrow onyx sword. Like Kojiro's Lionbear, the Onyx Sword was an honorary weapon from Lord Tzu Ch'an's Collection, given Tzukuba for her allegiance to the Live Crew, and to honor her seven- year undercover service as a spy among the Ashigaru. The sodogarami was self-fashioned to fit as a combining weapon and sheath for the Onyx.

The rest of the Crew were mostly peasants, conscripts, farmers, teakiyari, but all great warriors of special talents. Talents that had to be special for them to be allowed into the fold. Any man who failed initiation, it meant death by disembowelment.

The Live Crew was that kind of strong.

The Crew traveled for hours following the paths that Kana tracked, through regions that were unwise to cross and nonetheless necessary. They all mostly walked in silence, moving mostly under the cover of night to avoid bounty hunters looking for opportunity since word would likely travel fast that the fugitive Kojiro had left the safety of the respected and feared daimyo Tzu Ch'an.

Ittei would later write in his journal:

Though none would speak it, we all knew that some of us would not survive the many dangers that lie ahead. But still we trekked on, as warriors do, against the perils of mind and body, and the anxieties that would cause others of lesser grit to dither and quake.

It is not that we were better than those who would turn from the call, or that we were bound, any of us, to Kojiro by duty or debt. It was rather that we were like fossil trees from which no flowers could be gathered, and that like our enemies we were but drops of dew that would dry and bolts of lightning that would vanish. We were joined in the embrace of life's delicate nature as well as in the rejection of the laughter of gods who would mock it.

At one point along the way, after many hours of walking and when passing through an edulis bamboo forest of giant timber reaching as high as 28 meters into the sky, Kojiro and Jubei had enough distance from the rest of the group to talk privately -in hushed tones.

"I shouldn't say..,' Jubei began.

"Then don't," Kojiro cut him off. His friend almost smiled.

"I wouldn't be Jubei if I didn't."

"Fair," Kojiro replied, sucking his lip, and knowing too well that Jubei was right. On the one hand, Kojiro was cursing himself for being friends with this asshole and on the other, he was grateful for Jubei's unfiltered love and persistence.

"I want to say first that I am sorry I wasn't with you. But even if I were, who among us could stop an Oni?"

"I did not know at first that he was an Oni. But that is the point of this trip, Jubei. We are men and women and children, of simple bone and flesh, living out finite lives while these so-called *gods* play games with us like we are pieces on a *Go* board.

None of us should tolerate it, and every living being should be freed from the consequences of their celestial boredom."

"Maybe," Jubei said, after a brief bit of thought and a shrug of his shoulders.

"Maybe?"

"Yeah, maybe... Maybe it is not so clear cut and dry. Maybe even if it is, there is no truly available recourse beyond the premises of myth -a thing a child might dream up. And maybe if there is that recourse, it is like the perfect blossom: a thing worth seeking for the betterment of self, but never meant to be attained."

Kojiro went silent to think about it, but Jubei knew that his friend was only humoring him. Or, at most, only considering the words intellectually. This journey would not have been embarked on if Kojiro was not already completely resolved to the idea that he could literally attain the power to take down the gods. It was more determination than fanaticism, Jubei also knew, because the sutras that speak of such a power do not lie.

Kojiro's mind, in the silence of walking, began to drift into the premises of memory -of regret. What he saw in his mind would have drawn tears to the eyes of a les focused man:

> Taya, Kojiro's beloved Taya... Her big family, not of the samurai caste, were farmers and merchants who lived in a well-kept minka at the threshold of a rice and buckwheat farm. The modest, elevated pit house, made of cypress, pine, and cryptomeria woods, had engawa verandas, tatami mat flooring, and sliding doors that bore painted images of the ikebana structures that Taya's mysterious though beautiful power enabled her to make. In fact, the house itself was decorated on

the outside and inside with illustrious growths of moss covered vines on which were intricate and impossibly twined sprouts of purple sumire, bright orange and sweet scented kinmokusei, and the pink cherry blossom Sakura from which Kojiro got his feared and fabled sobriquet. The Deadly Sakura.

The large family consisted of her father, Basumanu, an uncle and two aunts, Akio, Ema and Ichika, respectively, and her five siblings -three older brothers (Haruto, Touma, Yamato), one younger brother (Aoi), and one little sister (Miu).

All worked the farm, except, of course, for Taya, who was now bedridden and stuck in catatonia -suffering the curse put on her by the Tan'Mo.

Her brothers Touma and Yamato, they protested that Kojiro shouldn't be allowed to visit her. But the ever peaceful Basumanu kept them calm, sending them off to their harvesting work so that he and the heartbroken samurai could talk alone. They stood outside on the engawa for this.

"We can but get her to eat," Basumana said, the despondency just under the surface of his usually cheerful voice. "She just lies now in bed... Eyes always open, but no life in them."

Kojiro said nothing for a moment. It was taking all the effort and focus in him to keep his shoulders from slouching.

"The flowers,' he finally said, regarding the plant structures.

"Yes," Basumanu sighed, "We've noticed. Slowly... Almost imperceptibly..., they are dying."

"I would sit with her alone for a moment, if I may."

Entering Taya's room for Kojiro was like journeying willfully into the fiery domain of Jigoku, the Hell known to him by way his Buddhist scholarship. Her heavily padded shikibuton was flanked by warousoku candles and burning sage. Her head was rested on a bean filled pillow, and her eyes, now more inert than angelic, just stared off into the distance -forever locked in melancholic bewilderment.

Kojiro went over to his beloved and sat down on his knees before her, took her hand in his. Since he was alone, and, more, because he hadn't the wherewithal to resist, he let tears roll down from his eyes.

"I am sorry," he whispered, crushed inside by the futility of the words. "I am sorry, my love."

———

HE DIDN'T SPEAK AT ALL FOR A WHILE after experiencing this hard memory, every bit of him engaged in the struggle to not weep in front of those who counted on him for strength and leadership.

Jubei, knowing his body language, made no attempts to prompt him.

Kana sped up her gait after Kojiro and Jubei fell silent, to report a necessary shift in their path.

"Hold up,' she interjected. 'We can't keep going straight. If you could smell it, you'd know that up ahead is a storm that would set us back at least a day."

"If we could smell it?" Jubei quipped, always playful in his incurable misunderstanding of Kana's tracking skills.

She rolled her eyes at him, adding,

"Northwest from here, through the swamps. That's the best path."

"You are sure of it?" Kojiro asked.

"I'm always sure," she said, and then began walking in the northwestern direction without waiting for Kojiro's approval of her advice.

Jubei followed suit, not missing the opportunity to flash a rictus grin at his friend in passing. Kojiro sighed.

A little while later on Kana's new path, just upon dawn, the Crew made it to the Owari Crimson Swamps, where it was known that the family of bipedal water buffalo required offerings for mortals to pass. It was also known that if they were unsatisfied, the Buffalo Tribe would take a life of your party as an offering fit to let the rest of your team go on their way. And if they made this decision, it was known that successful defiance of the Buffalo Lord's edict was impossible.

"Ko-Mitsu, I recon,' The Buffalo Lord called, his voice reaching the Crew and Kojiro's ears on the wind a great distance before they were close enough to meet eyes with the *Crimson Family* and their patriarch.

Startled, the Crew drew weapons. All but Kojiro and Jubei.

"Settle everyone,' Kojiro said. "We are not in danger."

Then came the bellowing laugh of the Buffalo Lord.

"Ahh, but you <u>are</u>,' he said, his voice coming from a different place. Crew members spun left and right, trying to find the source. "You are always in danger."

Kojiro smiled.

"In a dream I saw you,' the Lord continued, his voice reaching them like music on the wind. "Each one ready and strong. But carried on wings for some reason. Dead, I thought, at first. My mind creating a metaphor for departure. But how, my son suggested, does a Buffalo Lord imagine something he can never experience? Death…, such a strange thing, that."

The flute player Ittei, he noted that the voice was like a suizen melody richer than any instrument could produce; scary at the same time, gruff and deep, and yet soothing – supernatural!- a sort of elixir for restoring strength in mortals.

Then without warning, the surrounding trees began to move. After a moment, it was clear the Buffalo, twelve of them, were emerging from the trees as if before they were camouflaged. They were a sight to behold, formidable in stature; an amazing twelve feet high stood the tallest of them, lean at the waist but carrying no less than seven hundred pounds of muscle capable of at least four times their weight in strength. An otherwise modest clan of aborigines, with their moss covered camouflaged and Cheetah-spotted skin, tree-length spears for weapons and nose rings the width of Jubei's neck, with their blood red eyes and 13-inch Smilodon teeth, their poison taloned fingers and coarse hair like African bushmen.

"Already,' the tallest of them said, their leader walking out to the front of the pack and towering over Kojiro. "Yet only at this moment face to face, and already my voice has bequeathed you."

"It is why your enemies will never hear it,' Kojiro intoned, looking up at the regal beast.

It was clear that the *small man* Kojiro's reputation preceded him, and that the Buffalo Lord was an admirer who held him and the Live Crew in reverence.

"Indeed,' the Lord said, 'why give an enemy the advantage of my voice when we can just take their meat and let one of them live to tell stories about us? You know, Ko-Mitsu, warriors taste better than any other sort of game."

"I often feel the same,' Kojiro responded, then was amused at himself, adding, 'not about the meat part, anyway, but, well, about letting at least one of an adversary's party leave with his life for the purpose of stories… Is it our similar minds, I wonder, that allows for us to stand here, the lives of my party and I still intact while in the presence of the great Crimsons?"

"Perhaps it's the salt in your flattery,' another of the Buffalo said. This one who spoke, he stood close to the Lord and looked the most like him. "We Buffalo are not big fans of salty foods."

The Lord looked at his son and stifled a laugh; such enormous, powerful, and war-built creatures, all the more fascinating for their silly nature.

"Don't mind my son, Ko-Mitsu,' the Lord offered. "But tell me this before you pass. In the interest of stories, of course, where are you going and why? It is the only offering I require, because it intrigues me so that you would risk so much to disturb the tranquility of our domain."

Otaku cut a glance at Kana, who shrugged in reply. She was completely unruffled by any suggested criticism of the path she chose. In fact, she was nonchalantly eating dried persimmon pieces from her hip pouch.

"Vengeance, Lord,' Kojiro admitted, his voice free of pride, bitterness, his voice free of everything but urgency and fortitude. "Vengeance against the worst enemy of Nature and of People."

"And by what means will you procure it?"

"We are heading northeast to find the Tabernacle of the Thalatha."

"Hmm. And what do you seek to acquire at the Tabernacle?

"A weapon, an answer, a secret."

"So, you don't know."

"We will find out when we get there," Kojiro said, narrowing his eyes. If he felt as though he were being put on the spot or being made a subject of ridicule in front of his crew, he did not show it.

"Ahhh,' the Lord mused, glancing up at the sky in thought and speaking as if delivering an impassioned, prophetic soliloquy. "The predicament of Man, *to most easily discern the shadows and the likenesses or reflections of themselves and other things in the water. To live shackled with their faces to the wall and their backs to the light. To imagine themselves free to shake off those tethers and venture into the Unknown.*"

The Buffalo Lord was standing far enough away from Kojiro that he didn't have to turn down his chin or kneel to make eye contact with him, so there was space enough between them for him to fold his arms behind his back and pace while considering Kojiro's premise.

"I will tell you a brief story, Ko-Mitsu. If you would honor me."

"If?" the Lord's hungry son was both surprised and a bit embarrassed for his father's reverence of this simple samurai of a lesser race.

"Quiet, Musuko!,' the Lord commanding him, whose shoulders slouched, only slightly, in submission. "You will enjoy this as well. It chronicles the tribulations of a warrior of virtue, an archetype for not just his people but his entire world...,' a pause, the Lord making piercing eye contact with Kojiro, '...as seen through the eyes of a child."

This line, it was curious to Kojiro's ear. He looked to Jubei, who also narrowed his eyes in suspicion.

"Soliciting your friend will not help you! He is as oblivious as my son on the matter. But *Iiii* know, and so do you."

"Pretend I am a drunk who has lost his memory,' Kojiro joked. "Tell me what it is that you know."

Then he looked at Musuko, and nodded -adding, 'If you would honor me."

"I know this, Ko-Mitsu,' the Buffalo Lord lowered his body some, despite not having to. He squinted in an odd, arch way that the samurai would query about for many sleepless nights. "I know that this vengeance your palate craves is far less than you will ingest. And I know that the child's mind is not restricted by such trivialities. I know that the Tabernacle you seek is not the stuff of fables, but the hearts and determination of those who would find it probably are."

Kojiro motioned to speak, but the Lord cut him off.

'Smile on your tracker,' he said with enthusiasm. It was Kana's turn to cut a glance at Otaku, and wink.

"Be assured,' the Buffalo Lord continued, "You are going the right way. One favor though."

"Of course."

"When your journey is won, pass back this same way. Tell me how it went."

ACHRAFIEH. BEIRUT, LEBANON. OUTSIDE a white, regal mansion on Rue Sursock street. It is late at night in the modern world, quiet. Not a single cloud in the dark blue sky. Along the strip are some of the historic mansions from the 18th and 19th centuries, but there was a scatter of modern apartment buildings now in the place of the mansions that were no longer there. You'd find no litter or vagrants on Rue Sursock, and nary a stone out of place. But anyone with a keen enough ear could hear the screaming otherwise muffled by soundproof walls.

Inside the mansion where the screaming originated, a suited guard was falling backwards down Tabriz carpeted stairs. His body was falling in pieces from cuts that came so fast that the severed limbs were playing catch up with time.

A shiny object flies across the high ceilinged room, cutting the cord on a chandelier. More shiny objects fly from several directions, taking out lights, and downing more chandeliers in loud glittery splashes of flying crystal. Two armed men run up the stairs where the body parts settle, their Uzis are trained above. But atop the stairs on the next level, a black, indecipherable figure blurs by in a roll across the floor. One of the men is suddenly hit in the neck with a shuriken, he falls awkward and, in a final reflex, unloads an entire clip on the other man.

Five guards burst into the front door, three others from the hallway behind the staircase where the body parts lay strewn. Everyone looks about with their weapons held up. They're using flashlights since the central lighting of the house has been disabled. Some are hardened men with no fear, but a few of them were young and secretly terrified -the scopes of their guns shaking despite themselves.

It wasn't the attack that frightened them, however. It was the imperceptibility of the assailant. No one there believed in ghosts, but it was as if they were fighting one. Those three men that came out from under the stairs, a shadow attacked the last of them in stealth -broke his neck, quietly. The second to the last heard something, and turned to it only to be stabbed in the forehead by a jambiya dagger that silenced him forever.

The two in front turned to the death rattle to see their colleague's Pietro Beretta taken from him and turned on them. One tried to fire on the shadowy figure but hit their man's body instead, being used as a shield. And then just as fast, they were dead too by shots fired from the Pietro.

The other five guards were greeted with a smoke grenade tossed out into the living area that quickly engulfed them all in a blinding purple haze. Two of them were each taken out with a kīla that flew across the room, hitting one of them in the throat and the other in the nape of the neck.

That's when she rolled out of the shadows to right in front of a third man, who saw her silhouette through the haze and was quick enough to turn his weapon towards her, but not quick enough to avoid her last second parry before firing a shot that mistakenly took out another of his final two colleagues. She engaged the man with two karambits drawn from hip pouches, cutting the joints in his arms and legs. He fell then to his knees and was incapable of moving. The last remaining man, as the smoke was clearing, turned his gun to the silhouette but she was too fast a moving target for him to take aim. She dashed left and then rolled right, sweeping him at the leg and then stabbing him in the chest with a Bowie knife as he slammed hard on his back. In the commotion, the doomed guard's hand happened to snatch off the black scarf that was covering her face.

He stared into Qadr Fakhoury's eyes as his life faded out, her countenance, the last thing he'd ever see, looking near angelic in the fusion of purple smoke and dwindling light.

The last of the smoke was clearing as she rose to her feet. All the dead men only saw black shadows when they engaged her because that is what she was wearing, black from head to toe; black long-sleeved, high neck cat suit with belt, light weight Kevlar vest, weapon pouches and arm/leg holsters all matching the camouflage. Her hair was braided and tied in a bun for maximum mobility.

"P-p-please,' the other man, who couldn't move but was still alive, said. She almost forgot about him. "Don't ki… Don't kill me."

Qadr regarded him, with pity -tilting her head to look down on him as an adult would look at a pitiful child that he or she doesn't like.

She shook her head, whispering, "Je suis désolé", before pulling a tactical Triton short sword off her back and slicing his throat.

———

UPSTAIRS IN THE MASTER BEDROOM, the chess genius Nicolaou Steinitz was discovering that his panic buttons and phone lines had been disabled. He fumbled about in a silk bathrobe and boxer shorts, covered in sweat and so terrified that he'd forgotten about the gun he kept in the end table drawer next to his bed. By the time he discovered it, Qadr was casually walking into the room.

"Stop there,' he said to her, the gun shaking in his hand. 'I'll.. I swear, I will kill you!"

Qadr offered no reaction, nor movement, nor emotion. She was an effigy to indifference.

For a moment, it was like the closest thing to a Mexican standoff or an old Western confrontation at high noon -Qadr, arms down, standing there on one side of the room, and Nicolaou, the gun aimed, standing at the other.

But that illusion was shattered when he fired, the bullet sailing less than an inch past Qadr's right cheek as she moved ever so slightly out of its path, throwing a shuriken in the space of the same moment.

As it sailed towards Nicolaou's head, time seemed to slow from his perspective as his life passed by his eyes. From childhood to this moment, he was at once confused by the flashes of a mythic version of Feudal Japan that invaded his memories. Even Qadr saw it, the millisecond when Nicolaou's eyes glazed over and an unexpected reflex from him triggered fast enough that he could shift his position and catch the shuriken that was intended for his forehead. **All the fear and cowardice before displayed was suddenly, magically, replaced by the confidence of training he only could have acquired in another lifetime.**

Both Nocolaou and Qadr were surprised.

But that moment passed.

Qadr dashed over to him, a karambit in her left hand. Nocolaou leaned backwards to avoid Qadr's first slash at him, and then elbow blocked the second. He hit her at the wrist with his free hand in follow to that move hard enough to disarm her. They traded a few blows until she could draw the Triton and cut Nocolaou twice with it -once across the stomach and then at his right forearm. He caught that move with his left hand and twisted to elbow strike Qadr to the chin with his bleeding right.

She dropped the Triton.

The two kept going after her deft recovery and trading empty hand to hand blows and parries and blocks at close quarters until Nocolaou managed to grab one last remaining shuriken from Qadr's hip and pivot off that move to underhand slash at her with it – cutting her at the outer right deltoid.

His follow up attempt was too zealous and Qadr took advantage, not only blocking but popping the elbow to loosen and retrieve the weapon, and then lodge it deep in his left armpit. Nocolaou grunted at the pain but had the unexpected warrior endurance to keep going, so Qadr slipped one of his advancing moves and flipped over him, twisting in the turn. She pulled a wrist-bound garrote cord in mid-flip, wrapping it around the chess man's throat. When she landed, she snapped forward in momentum with enough force to rip right through Nocolaou's throat -beheading him!

Hyperventilating, again, unexpectedly, Qadr felt... something, from this simple chess man who became a warrior in his moments of death.

——

Global Dollar Magazine's quote of the day: *"Your employees need to feel like you are working for them, as opposed to them working for you. Because community is strength, and strength is prosperity."*
-Tyler Lincoln, American Businessman

LOS ANGELES, CALIFORNIA. After closing a gargantuan 500 million dollar deal with Schröder & Vogt: Anlagekapital, a high profile investment firm based in Düsseldorf, Germany that specializes in communications, billionaire industrialist Jeremiah Cross set forth on a project that could be modestly described as "unprecedented". He bought out capital space for six different businesses to shut down four entire upper floors (41-44) in his Los Angeles headquarters for Rain Forest Inc. Why? For renovations that would turn the space into an Information Technology Research and Development facility known to the public only as TRIVIUM. When asked whether the name was an acronym and, if so, for what, when asked for clarity on what the project would entail, the cryptic businessman, in a reference that calls to mind the philosophies of Ayn Rand, offered only this: "Trivium will prove to be a technological advancement more momentous than any the world has ever seen. And it will shield us against the *fast approaching stage of ultimate inversion.*" That was thirteen months ago. What of Trivium now?...

THERE WERE TWO VERY LARGE AND armed security guards stationed at the Red Elevator on the ground floor of the Art Deco style office building in Los Angeles. It was a skyrise that reached as high as the highest buildings in LA. That special elevator with the mahogany doors took its passengers straight up to the top most floor, just above the top secret TRIVIUM, which in its entirety was the CEO's private office and conference room. No one got up there unless by appointment, confirmed at the guarded doors by retinal scan.

Qadr, dressed in a navy blue business skirt and carrying a black combination locked military-style Pelican case, approached the guards and had to look up at the towering men to make eye contact. The left side guard held out the retinal scanner that tracked a green light over her eyes and then beeped. The guard read the appointment confirmation and then pressed the button on the door placard for it to open.

The long ride up didn't present the sensation of movement, just floor numbers climbing by the second. Qadr was usually expert at clearing her mind when engaged in any professional endeavor, but despite herself the thought of Nocolaou Steinitz invaded her focus. *The glazing over of his eyes,* she thought, *it surprised both to him and her as his body took on a muscle memory that wasn't his own in that fateful moment of distress. Even his posture changed. What was it that happened to him?,* she wondered. *And why did it seem oddly familiar?*

When the elevator reached the top, floor number 45, the doors opened right into Jeremiah Cross' office. There was a high vaulted ceiling and gray smoke patterned marble floors. The entire level was one office but it was subdivided by clear glass walls that gave the room upon its entrance a holographic maze-like feel. You could see the giant conference table to the right, and a replica of Auguste Rodin's Thinker statue to the left that, like the conference table, matched the marble flooring as if an extension of it. To the back, on a raised level, was Cross' desk. There was a pool table and chess table across from it. The outer walls around the desk area were all windows. Not ordinary windows, but windows that doubled as virtual glass screens that, at that moment, cast imagery and nature sounds of a shadowed summer canopy.

Cross was seated behind the desk, his fingers laced and thumbs under his chin. He raised two fingers to beckon Qadr to approach. Her heels made a light clacking noise as she crossed the floor that led a b-line through the glass pillar walls cutting a path directly to the desk.

"Ms. Fakhoury,' he said when she got close, 'your renown is as august as your glamor."

She didn't smile at his compliment. Instead, she put the Pelican case on his desk and took a seat in the chair in front of it.

Cross, however, did smile. He stood and made to open the case but then saw the combination lock. He looked at Qadr.

"0,3,5,9," she said on cue.

"Ah. The Thue-Morse. A bit dramatic but, I suppose, droll enough. Did you choose it?"

"Landau."

Mildly amused, Cross shrugged.

The virtual screen changes at this point to reflect the Canadian Rockies, as an eddy and river flow behind wind-blown reeds and grasses. Cloud shadow-patterns from the skies overlay the landscape with a cape of shade, and the whine of mosquitoes chorus to the sounds of wind contrast against the muted rage ever present in the self-hallowed industrialist.

"Mr. Kier,' Cross scoffs, 'the man fancies himself a comedian."

He then opened the case and looked into the dead, open eyes of Nocolaou Steinitz. Cross took the head out of the case with his bare hands, examining the clean throat cut and the rogue dressing Qadr applied to make the head presentable.

"Very nice. And you even cleaned it."

"Une question de respect."

"Yes. Of course. Respect. We live in a world that has forgotten its worth, Ms. Fakhoury. Things like respect, honor, integrity."

Cross put the head back inside of the case and sat.

He picked up the cellphone that was on the desk and punched in some numbers before putting it back down.

"Confirm receipt of payment, Ms. Fakhoury."

Qadr took out her phone and checked her account. Her payment, $7,000,000, was there.

"I look forward to doing business with you again. Very soon, in fact."

Qadr nodded and stood to leave.

"Tell me one thing,' he said when she turned to leave, 'as a matter of professional curiosity."

Qadr turned to face Cross again, nodding for him to proceed.

"I am told that you know at least six languages, fluently. Why do you prefer to only speak French?"

Qadr lingered for a moment but didn't answer. She turned again and began her walk towards the exit.

Up on a ledge, several buildings away, and outside of the normal visual sphere of unassisted human eyes, there was someone watching this exchange.

It was Clymene, seeing everything through the andradite crystals of his eyes. The wind at that level barely rustled his robe, let alone disturbed his long beard or his perch at the narrow ledge. This was an interesting case for him. For the entirety of his consciousness, he had been aware, as well as his colleagues, that he should not intervene in the affairs of humans. But as his interest grew in the developing machinations of Jeremiah Cross, he began to wonder if maybe adhering to this edict might result in greater consequences for the world. It led him suddenly to experience something that he was not familiar with -anxiety.

———

THE BLACK AND SILVER LEARJET 60 WAS fueling up on runway II at the Orlando Executive Airport. The pilot, Matthew DeLoach, was standing at the open cabin door taking in the afternoon sun and blowing the steam off the rim of his coffee.

Poole was by the hangar waiting patiently as a yellow cab pulled up, his arms folded and trying his best to not look annoyed by this greeting of a man who was already almost twenty minutes late. Coletrane hadn't arrived yet either, but this was his party, Poole reasoned, so he could be as late as he wanted.

The cab passenger exited the backseat in a brisk, apologetic demeanor. He wore a white open collar dress shirt with the sleeves rolled up over khaki pants. A Labradorite pendant adorned his neck. He had hazel-green eyes and sandy brown hair, a little too spikey in fashion for Poole's taste, and he was carrying one leather satchel carry-on bag and a black camera case. When the war photography turned journalist extending his hand to shake Poole's, after first tipping the cab driver, Poole was reluctant to take it but did so in spite of himself.

"Hey hey, how's it going? Mr. Jonas Poole, right? A pleasure."

"You're late, Mr. Elliot."

"Yes, of course. I'm sorry about that. Traffic on the interstate, cab didn't pick me up until ten passed the scheduled time. Murphy's Law all around. But please, call me Patrick."

"What's the going rate for excuses in your field, Patrick."

"Yikes. Ouch. Ok, touché! But speaking of tardiness, where's Mr. Marx? Held up at an orgy?"

Poole didn't respond. And he wasn't amused.

Almost as if on cue, the melodic sound of a buzzing, powerful torque heralded a black Lamborghini Sian pulling onto the asphalt. It got the attention of Poole, Patrick, DeLoache, and airport workers too. DeLoach, in fact, lifted his coffee in greeting even before its driver turned off the humming engine.

An attendant hotfooted over to the car as the driver door lifted like a wing, and out stepped Coletrane to toss the attendant the keys.

Coletrane's outfit matched the black of the car, his favorite knee length lapel coat over tapered black pants and a black turtleneck sweater. He wore sunglasses as well, and his hair, as usual, in the topknot-like bun. The uninitiated would look at him, the way he strode, the confidence and agency of his every step, the way he accessorized himself with glamour, and think of him as "cool" and a subject of envy. But Coletrane Thelonious

Marx's inner reality told a different story, one of indissoluble turmoil ever

affixed to the replaying memory of Vincent and Adaeze's brutal murder.

He wore black, Coletrane did, but he always saw red.

The enigmatic rich man barely glanced over at Poole and Patrick as he made his way to the plane, but that subtle glance was enough to say that it was time to go.

"I'd recommend not trying to be too cute on this trip, Mr. Patrick Elliot," Poole said after checking the contents of his bag and handing it back to him. "Mr. Marx may be privy to indulging you, for whatever his reasons, but he is also not above leaving you in Japan to find your own way back."

———

THEY WERE WELL OVER THE ATLANTIC and nearing the land masses of Portugal and Morocco before either Coletrane or Patrick decided to break the ice. They were seated across from each other on beige leather chairs, a koa wood table between them that matched most of the cabin's palatial trimmings. Immediately upon boarding, it seemed that a power play had been ignited. Coletrane didn't care much for interaction, really, with anyone. If anything, he brought Patrick along so that the journalist could see first-hand how much reality contradicted his assumptions. And Patrick, well, he already felt himself an unwelcome guest. And as such, he was as much suspicious as intrigued to have been invited on this trip at all. There was opportunity in it, however, to see Japan and to gain up close exposure to an enigmatic, reclusive figure that could lead to a very much coveted Pulitzer. But at what cost?

The silence between them was both the coterie and disunion of men, that there could be a common interest between them and yet an unspoken need for prominence in agency, that on the ground zero of any post mortem of interaction there needed to be some rock on which one could stand that would represent or at least imply a hierarchy.

Coletrane was looking out the window, engaged in his thoughts. Patrick decided that he was the one with both the most to gain from breaking the ice and also the most to lose from not, so he said,

"I was surprised at first to get your invitation for the trip, Mr. Marx. When my publicist told me about it, I thought he was joking. In fact, he does that sort of thing often."

Coletrane looked away from the window, assuming a reluctant and disinterest eye contact with Patrick, then saying,

"I wonder if his history of glee in this regard is a testament to his subject's penurious self-esteem."

Patrick was set aback, but then he demurred.

"Is this why I'm a tag-along then, for amusement? Because it kinda proves that my assessment of you in the articles that you've surely read was fair, in retrospect."

This was the first time that Patrick would see Coletrane smile.

"Relax, Patrick,' Coletrane said, 'you're not a prop. We've got several hours before we land so I figured, why not make a joke? But I'd seriously consider firing that publicist of yours."

"He's my uncle."

"An even better reason."

Patrick laughed, "Touché. I am curious though, why <u>did</u> you invite me?"

Coletrane looked up in reflection, considering a memory before answering.

"'*Apathy is perhaps the nature of the bequest, a characteristic typical of the world's history of people who are born into money. Brats that never overcome the distinction, children who never grow up, and privileged nobodies touched by nepotism that are never inclined by the rigors of life to ascend above ground level.*'.. You wrote this in an article about me five years ago."

Patrick was nonplussed, "Wow. Good memory."

"To a fault," Coletrane said, the look in his eyes giving Patrick an impression that reminded him of the many soldiers he'd known who suffered PTSD.

"That still doesn't quite answer my question," Patrick added.

"No. But it answers one of mine."

"Which is?"

"Do Patrick Elliot's talents extend beyond making death and despair look picturesque with his camera? I was a fan of your war photography long before you took the pen to denigrating me. That Desolation expose you did on Desert Shield in Kuwait reminded me of Gordon Parks and the way his '41 series on black ghettos in the South Side of Chicago captured the haunting nature of racism. You're good at capturing haunting natures and, like Parks, using your camera as a weapon. It's probably why I've never taken offense to the things you've written."

"Thanks,' Patrick shifted in his seat, unsure where to put his mild sense of embarrassment, 'but really, is it denigration?"

"Sure, it is. The affluent are not all *brats* and, certainly, aren't as monolithic as you'd have your audience believe. And it's a bit presumptuous of you, a white man, to assume that you can speak from a place of knowing on the constitution of a black man, wealthy or otherwise."

"You brought me along to argue the integrity of race politics?"

"I brought you along to learn something, and to write from a place of knowing. Maybe that Pulitzer you've been coveting will come of it."

"How do you know that I'm gunning for a Pulitzer?"

"Isn't every writer?"

"Touché again, Mr. Marx."

"Train. Call me Train."

"If I remind you of Parks, Train, does that make you my Ella Watson?"

"Watson endured the insult of segregation and was a firebrand of dignity in the Jim Crow South. I wouldn't presume to command her level of strength."

Patrick gave Coletrane a quizzing look.

"What? Not the answer you expected from a brat?"

Despite himself, Patrick smiled and held back from saying touché again. In response, Coletrane merely smirked. But there was gravity to it.

"Sure,' Patrick said. "I'll admit it. That's not the kind of answer I expected."

"Yeah, I know. But now I'm gonna disappoint you, Patrick."

"Disappoint me?"

"That's right. Another reason I brought you along is that I'm intrigued. My butler, Poole, he thought it was a bad idea to bring you on this trip. But he doesn't get it like I do, that power struggle in you between the photographer and the writer. The duality of it. The writer, I admire. The photographer, I pity."

"Pity?' Patrick exclaimed, "The hell for?"

"Because his task is insurmountable. Pictures, they don't capture reality. They imitate it. And the imitation is poor. This is the challenge of the photographer, to bring wealth and vibrancy to this deficit. The writer, on the other hand, is only limited by his imagination. Or, in the case of the journalist, his mastery of the instrument of language."

"Wow.. Well, I'm not sure if I fully agree with your assessment, but either way, Train, you... you just keep getting curiouser and curiouser." Patrick, a little rattled, was not sure how else to respond to the impromptu deconstruction of his vocational identity. But then he added, "If we accept your hypothesis that pictures do not capture reality, then what about the thing you just said about Parks and haunting natures? The hypocrisy of flowery speech or just intellectual dishonesty?"

"Neither. Because there is a difference between haunting natures and reality. Haunting natures are impressions, but reality is a static thing. It's like memory versus fact. A picture can curate memories but the facts of the referenced moments remain elusive. It reminds me of the tug of war between the ego and the id, or man's obsession with the archetype of Jekyll/Hyde."

Coletrane looked outside his window, and just then the land mass of Namibia was visible through the clouds that the plane was passing over. He looked back at his guest, and decided.

"Speaking of which, I would like to show you something."

"Sure," Patrick said.

Coletrane then, he simply pulled down the collar of his turtleneck sweater to reveal the bruise on his throat left by the phantom of Kojiro. Even on his brown skin, the red, black, and purple marking was prominent enough to make Patrick lift his eyebrows.

"Ouch. Pretty nasty BJJ souvenir."

"This isn't from a sparring session,' Coletrane offered, far too casually. 'A demon did this to me, in a dream. A tulpa."

"What? Look, man. I'm.. I'm.. I can't really apologize for my articles, as I stand by what I write, but, you know, journalistic integrity dictates that-"

"This is not what you think. I am not playing with you, or wasting your time. Take a closer look at the bruise and you will see that it is a hand print. You've done your research. You know of my martial arts background."

"Prodigy of the fighting arts."

"Right. Is it likely, in your view, that I would allow an ordinary man to do this to me?"

In his research, Patrick had made himself familiar with the many martial art styles that Coletrane had mastered. He was aware of his skills and, in fact, had commented jokingly in one of his articles on Coletrane that it was a bit gratuitous how much time a rich brat put into martial arts when he could have otherwise been putting his time and resources towards helping the world. Never mind that Coletrane continued to run his mother's non-profit botanical foundation Anexity Works and related programs to address social problems and advance human potential as well as promote equality through science, medical research, and education. Never mind that he himself also founded an organization in honor of his father; The Vincent Marx Initiative, which was geared towards funding reparations for chattel slavery and providing free college tuition for budding architects and archeologists from low income families. These details didn't fit the narrative of the privileged, detached, and apathetic rich kid. And, anyway, Patrick knew that most charity and outreach programs funded by the wealthy were merely tax write offs and a complicated system of moving money from one pocket to the other designed only to make them appear philanthropic.

So, Coletrane's display of his mysterious bruise, this was just an extension of a culture of posturing that Patrick had attributed to him. But he was quickly becoming uncomfortable under Coletrane's gaze, uncomfortable, that is, because Patrick's time in the military had sharpened his instincts -and Coletrane did not appear to be lying.

Just then, back home in the trophy room at the Marx estate, the golden buckle latch on the ancient book unlocked itself. The onyx crystal on its cover lit up, the book shook on its shelf and popped open to somewhere in the middle, the last page that bore writing. New passages manifested in the blood ink, filling several pages of script in the unknown language.

Coletrane, somehow, could feel it. In his bones, in his nerves, it worked on him like a conscious influence prodding him to divulge more.

"My father was a scholar of Theosophy. Much of his archeology work was influenced by his study of concepts such as the Tibetan sprulsku. He was obsessed with the works of Judas Ulehla, to the point of theorizing that Ulehla was the key to answering a lot of questions posited by the world's great thinkers."

"Judas Ulehla?"

"Never heard of him? Many who have heard of him believe that he never actually existed, that he himself was just a legend like... Robinson Crusoe. But my father found three of his statues before he died. And those statues bore a puzzle to a prophesy concerning his son."

"You?"

"Yes. Me. How are you at math, Patrick?"

"I can count to ten," he replied, with a shrug but no wink.

Coletrane, amused by the sarcasm, followed up with, "Tell me, what are the odds of my father forming an obsession with a sculptor from ages ago, finding lost works by him, and translating a message in those works that would concern his own son?"

"Not great, I'd guess."

"You'd guess right. But the phenomenon of the tulpa, it presents answers."

"Well, was it..' Patrick stopped himself, embarrassed by what he was going to say. "No, never-"

"Finish the thought,' Coletrane insisted. "I'm a big boy."

The silence between them as Patrick considered his wording, it was wide as the sea the plane was crossing over.

"The case of your parents' murder, it was never solved. Do you belie-"

"No,' Coletrane interrupted again, 'I don't believe it. I know. And I saw him with my own eyes. He is the one who did this to my neck. He is also responsible for a scar on my chest from the night he killed my parents."

Patrick just examined Coletrane like a man unsure of what he was looking at or how to respond to it.

"You're still skeptical,' Coletrane added. 'Good. A regular idiot is fine, but I'd lament having invited a gullible idiot into my sphere."

Distracting Patrick from the not-so-subtle insult, Coletrane said this while unzipping a small, black travel bag and placing a tablet on the table between them. He turned it on and opened a photo file before turning the screen around for Patrick to see.

Patrick investigated it. When he clicked on the folder, a splay of photos of the Ulehla sculptures popped up. The emphasis was on the glyphs. Each image being a closer photo of it until, at very close, the one larger glyph was revealed to be a puzzle-like structure of several other glyphs.

"A cipher," Patrick said.

Coletrane nodded in confirmation.

"What does it mean?"

"That's the prophesy. **Upon his 33rd year, he will discover the means to redress a demon of his own creation.**"

"Demon? The tulpa, I presume."

"Correct."

"How do I know you didn't just make that up?"

"Could I have made this up?" Coletrane countered, as he rolled up his left sleeve. He showed Patrick the birthmark that matched the glyph.

Patrick tried hiding the surprise in him, but he was at war with his skepticism and could not, however, hide his interest.

Instinctively, he knew that he had to say something to get the ball back in his court. However ill advised, he remarked,

"All of this, is it why you abandoned your friend? Marcus Green?"

Coletrane let slip the anger that Patrick's words triggered, and it would be the first time Patrick would see that muted, everlasting rage that simmered just below the surface. He said very seriously, calm, firm,

"I did not abandon Marcus."

And then, not a moment later, Coletrane managed to put away the anger and replace it with a wry grin. He sat back in the cradle of his comfortable leather chair, never averting his hold on Patrick's quizzing gaze. He said,

"No worries, Patrick. Worst case scenario here, I am just some nut short of peeing in mason jars and yelling at the moon in his underwear. You gain the benefit of an all-expense paid trip, bed some exotic women, and then return to the states to pen an unflattering, reward worthy exposé on the enigmatic magnate."

Sometime later, about nine hours into the sixteen hour flight, Patrick was left alone while Coletrane napped in a bed cabin out of sight. There was one designated for the war photographer turned journalist as well but he couldn't sleep while in the air, and, anyway, preferred to burn the midnight oil while alert and restless.

He got a head start on his chronicle of the trip.

Our acquaintance would begin at about forty-thousand feet above ground, which was somehow appropriate; the illusion of safety provided by the ostentatious trappings of a rich man's luxury jet were the perfect juxtaposition against the familiar gambit of feigned niceties exchanged between two men who could never be friends.

In pure Brothers Grimm fashion, there on the one hand was a world weary scribe expected, by both himself and his betters, to spin gold from straw. And on the other hand was an enigma, a modern day Rumpelstiltskin wrapped up in the disguise of a 1%er given to philanthropy. What pretenses were hidden behind the cool packaging of Coletrane Marx? And would I prove worthy of discovering them? Only time will tell...

IT WAS THE HOUR OF THE BOAR, approaching midnight. Follow Kana's astute direction, the Crew made it into Mino shortly after passing the Weathering Bamboo Thicket, a bayou engulfed in thick, aromatic fogs produced by haplomitrium mnioides, a light green moss that was virtually everywhere, and tremella samoensis mushrooms emitting a false, toxic tranquility that could subdue you with the distractions of Nostalgia and Dream -leaving you trapped walking in an endless loop until you eventually died of exhaustion, dehydration, hunger, or all three. The group only survived this passage due to a jutsu spell that Tzukuba performed at Kana's behest, which cast a protective counter aura over each member.

"We all still have to remain focused," Kana warned, "lest the powers of this place breach our protection and consume us all."

"Remind us why we came this way," said Jubei. And again, Kana rolled her eyes at him instead of responding verbally.

They set up camp near a lake where the Kiyoshi brothers could fish and gain strategies from the spirits of the water. Most huddled in small groups of friends that talked and ate together. Some, Tzukuba for instance, chose to spend time alone practicing their weapons.

Otaku told stories of the fabled Dragon Kings. "They are more like angels than gods,' he said, 'envying humans for their emotional experience in the world. This is why I laugh at the Buddhist teachings about suppressing emotion. Nonsense! The Dragons would laugh too, if they could. They seek us out like men seek drug and drink. They seek only the strongest among us to touch with their power."

Ittei, the humble poet, he fed goji berries to wolves that he somehow could summon from the forest. Sometimes he'd summon only one or two, or usually just his favorite that he called Yuriko, but this time it was Yuriko and a few of her brothers and sisters. The men could only see their eyes looking on from deep within the shadows, not until they'd one by one reveal themselves to eat goji from Ittei's hand. "What do you think, Yuriko,' Ittei whispered, 'will there be a great story for us to tell of this adventure when done?"

———

It took a few more hours for everyone to find the solace of sleep. Tzukuba was high up in the trees, away from the men, only pretending to sleep. Otaku was sitting against the trunk of a great oak, eating twigs and flowers. But this was how he slept, his body active and feeding itself while his mind and consciousness floated adrift in an astral cataleptic state. Otaku's body could fight with up to 75% of skill while his mind was asleep, and sometimes could actually fight better *–drawing powers from his imagination and pulling them right out of the dream…*

Kojiro, finally alone, was off by himself where at last he could think -and weep. His armor removed and wearing nothing but his kimono, his long hair down and all over his face, the warrior wept for his beloved Taya. He was overwhelmed by guilt whenever he thought of her, and anger for the Tan'Mo that cursed her and laughed.

But Kojiro distracted his mind from the grief of this to muse about the cryptic words of the Buffalo Lord.

"*An archetype for not just his people but his entire world,*' the Lord had called him, '*...as seen through the eyes of a child.*"

What child, Kojiro wondered. And what did the great, wise Lord mean about this mysterious child's mind not being restricted by the trivialities of vengeance? These riddles, they bothered Kojiro more than riddles usually did. There was a gravity to them that he couldn't place, but felt an unshakable need to.

He washed his hands in a small pond where he could see his face. The crude, pitiless reflection was enough for him to find glimmers of guilt again in his eyes, shame over everything that he is and isn't, shame over Taya, shame over his preoccupation with mystifying questions...

> The callous memory of Taya lying stolid and helpless on her shikibuton, it paid Kojiro a haunting visit and mixed like oil and water with the contrasting image of her spirited and strong, her feet in the shallow waters of her favorite riverbank of Hokkaido -a private place the two of them often snuck away to, where Taya would use her magical command of plant life to will spruce, fig, and larch conifers to come together into humanoid-looking formations that appeared to be dancing.
>
> "Look, my love,' he could still her voice saying, 'I'll make the plants dance since you are always too shy to ever do it."
>
> "Sure,' he replied, in a rare elocution of cheerfulness, 'if shy is what we're calling uncoordinated and clumsy now."
>
> She laughed, his favorite sound...

Tears welled up in Kojiro's eyes, distorting his view of his reflection in the pond. That's when he saw that reflection morph into another face, the face of a young boy with brown skin and wild hair. It was gone in as fast as a blink, but startled Kojiro enough to make him stand and tense his body.

This was a lucky moment, because it was then that he sensed the presence of danger.

———

KOJIRO'S SWORD HATSUKOI WAS always nearby. He never truly parted with her. She was designed by the priest Nichi-O of the Nichiren Clan, chief holy man of Myokakuji in Kyoto and the advocate of Fuju Fuse. Many who knew him thought that Nichi-O was insane, not least of all for his stories about Hatsukoi's steel having an *outer worldly*, "alien" origin.

Yet Hatsukoi nonetheless, whatever her origin, was a mystical blade. And was the true expression of Kojiro's soul.

She was also always attached to Kojiro's wrist on an invisible string that stretched out for an unknown length. Some believe the string isn't there at all, and that rather Kojiro and Hatsukoi had some sort of mystic connection, and that when Kojiro yanked forward his wrist to spring Hatsukoi into his hands, it was always an incredible sight to see.

But no one was there to record how quickly Kojiro turned on the phantom standing behind him at his right. No one saw sheathed Hatsukoi zipping across the air from behind the phantom's back, slamming into him and knocking him forward and on his face before Kojiro caught and unsheathed her in a bolting coruscation of speed!

He fought with Hatsukoi in a Tomita-ryu style, a hybrid kenjutsu that he taught himself on the beach of Okjotsk, the place where the Sasaki Kojiro of legend fought and lost his final duel with the famed Miyamoto Musashi.

But the slash that came down on the phantom completely missed its target, who sprung back to his feet and twisted to and fro in a dance-like bob and weave, a Capoeira ginga going left and right and over and beyond Kojiro's sword no matter how many times he tried to cut him!

Kojiro spun away to pivot and get a look at the phantom to its face. To his surprise, though the man's naked skin was dark, his hair African and wool-like, Kojiro recognized the face as his own.

"What kind of madness?" Kojiro yelled at the blackened mirror image of himself, that held no weapons and wore no clothes.

It offered no answer. Instead, it laughed.

Another fell down from the sky like rain, flanking the one. And just as fast there were four other phantoms manifest in the space behind Kojiro, now six men surrounding him.

Six different, naked versions of Kojiro ko-Mitsu, all some crazy manifestation of himself with the features of men from other cultures.

One of them appeared Hindu while another had brown stringy hair, blue eyes, and a face and body decorated in war paints. One man had the beard of an Egyptian, while another was either some sort of pirate or gypsy for his scars, body piercing, and tattoos. And surprisingly, one was a voluptuous woman with the eyes of an Eskimo.

They all laughed, advancing on the warrior. Kojiro felt the setting taking a poisonous hold on his mind. He could feel the fear building up in Hatsukoi's spirit for it was known to the sword that her wielder was losing his balance on his feet and his hold on her tsuka.

Kojiro moved the moment he felt this, lunging forward to come down on the African one in front of him with a blinding kiriage slash. But on cue the phantoms each shattered like black eggs, exploding in tiny twittering spasms of energy, whisking spirit confetti and tendrils of swirling smoke!

The firecracker distraction was what the real threat used as his intro, jumping into the fray from an incredibly high and distant lunge in just the right moment of Kojiro's confusion. He'd have to turn over his left shoulder to see the villain coming down on him.

And all he saw was a head of long, woolen hair and the two Vajra short swords crisscrossed over the man's body coming down, double outward windmill slashes meant to sever Kojiro's head that wound up being nothing more than an illusion.

One blink and it was all gone. Over. Disappeared, a mirage.

Kojiro never even got a chance to see what his aggressor looked like when the voice invading his mind whispered,

"That was Jericho... I was being nice... The real Jericho would have killed you."

Kojiro heard the voice, but looked around and saw nothing.

"You are silly, ko-Mitsu,' the calm, woman's voice added, *"Do you look around in search of your stomach when it growls?"*

Still, he was not convinced that the sound was coming from within.

There was no longer any trace of the so-called Jericho. All that remained was the grassy dark earth, the surrounding vistas, and the many small ponds and flooded depressions in the ground that shown a trail behind the trees leading to a lake down the scarcely oblique clearing.

He followed his instincts down the path, Hatsukoi sheathed but her handle firm in his grip.

That's when he found the small, cute, and seemingly unassuming woman aloft over the water.

Her body was folded in an Indian seating posture but rotating in a hover as if on an invisible clock-like axis. She matched the water in her blue/green Shaolin uniform, her white socks and black leg wraps, her black headband bearing a family crest that Kojiro didn't recognize.

Her eyes were closed, but she seemed to sense Kojiro watching her. She unfolded from her meditative posture and transitioned right into a Taizu Chang set while still suspended in air, her every movement slow and with perfect grace, blurred slightly by afterimages that her movements left, and emitting an unusual energy that made Kojiro feel as if he were watching the display of an inner expression from his own mind.

Her movements were somewhat menacing in that they bore into him in the same way that her echoing words did. It became clear to Kojiro that this strange woman possessed some kind of power not meant to be understood, let alone trusted.

She segued into a Xiao Hung Quan kata and a flowing mien of the five shaolin animal katas to communicate with Kojiro intuitively, telling him without speaking how much she enjoyed the stories that she'd heard of him:

The story of Lord Tzu Ch'an pardoning your great crime -a crime punishable by death- of leaving Japan and returning after having been "tainted" with the influence of outside cultures is, in a word, fascinating. The pardon being largely unrecognized outside of Tzu Ch'an's Northern Province, it was known to you that you would have to remain there indefinitely or else be pursued by bounty hunters. Yet here you are, having left still -without fear.

I always relished of the story behind why you left in the first place, to avenge your mother's murder at the hands of the ecclesia militants. This illegal journey took you way past the Yellow Sea on pirate ships that crossed the unsafe waters known for swallowing vessels whole. It took you into the bowels of the Bangladesh underworld, where you heard tell of babies being born with two or more heads and people disappearing and then being thrown back into the world from out of nowhere with stories of curious technologies from distant times in the future.

"Enough," Kojiro said out loud, "How do you know the tales of my life? Speak."

She stopped at once and stood upright, allowing her body to surrender to gravity and drop down into the water. Was only knee deep where she landed, walking to the surface with her arms folded behind her back.

"Are you my enemy then?" Kojiro asked, impatient of her taking so long to answer. He narrowed his eyes and gripped Hatsukoi's tsuka tighter.

The woman and Kojiro met face to face on the shore, with some distance between them and Kojiro poised in a ready stance in case he needed to strike.

She bowed respectfully.

"So sorry,' she said, speaking out loud for the first time, 'but Xiao-xiao Chen is no enemy of the honored Deadly Sakura. Only, you must realize. None of us are truly enemies at all, not in this world."

"More riddles,' Kojiro was already annoyed. "I've been assailed by many riddles lately."

"Did you hear the one about the little boy who wondered if the chicken or the egg came first? It was a question that cost him his family, and gave vibrance to our world in the same gesture of fate."

"A little boy?" Kojiro was instantly suspicious again, thinking of the reflection in the water "Have you invaded my mind, to play tricks on me?"

"No,' she replied simply, simply enough that Kojiro detected no subterfuge. "I haven't invaded your mind at all.. But we are all connected."

"I am to believe it is a coincidence that you would prattle of a child's riddle? Shortly after.."

"Shortly after what?" Xiao-xiao Chen was genuinely curious. She truly hadn't invaded Kojiro's thoughts as he assumed. But she was aware, much like the Three Interstices in Coletrane's world, or a far reaching narrative that the consciousnesses of those participating could not fully grasp. This awareness, it was the source of her power.

But Kojiro's strength was rooted in his fastidiousness, in his mastery of the sword and the spirit itself of cutting through obstacles. This obstacle was a revelation codified in a viscosity of words; words of the Buffalo Lord, words of the Tan'Mo, and words now of Xiao-Chen.

As he was considering whether he would answer Xiao Chen's question, a familiar noise from a distance distracted him. It made him tense every muscle in his body. Then Xiao Xiao Chen sensed it too.

"Now is not the time for us to talk then, Sakura,' she bowed. "Go."

———

THE BATTLE-CRY WAS COMING FROM over three hundred yards away, the voice of Otaku alerting all members of the Crew to a threat that was upon them.

Kojiro broke into a sprint towards their camp, dashing past the trees and underbrush in his way.

He cursed himself for having wandered so far away. It burned, this anger, with a ferociousness so great that he felt like his energy was bursting out of his pores! His strength seemed to increase the further he ran.

Gripped now by rage, Kojiro screamed in spite of himself.

And that is when it happened. When myth became truth, when Otaku's drunken stories came to life at no man's call or beckon.

Three Dragon Kings that no present warrior could see appeared high up in the sky above Kojiro's outlined course. They were Noboru, the Virtuous One; Ringo, spirit of Eternal Peace; and Samuru, the essence of God's Wrath. Each one, together in agreement, wanted to taste the power of Kojiro's determination.

So, they came down on him. They shot into his body like crashing bolts of lightning. He was thrown three times by the force, burned terribly but healed at once. He felt a glow that no other would see emanating from his body. He knew, Kojiro did, that three Dragon Kings had now offered their assistance. And yes, he used it.!

It came on him upon recovery like a breath of new life. He ran faster, felt stronger, was ready to pounce in the air in one… two… three…. NOW!

Kojiro leapt an incredible distance, over three tall trees in a single bound, through hanging arms of fully leaved branches, disturbing nests, the slumber of raccoons, owls, critters in the night. He removed his kimono top in midair and tied it around his waist, freeing him from restricted mobility and exposing the muscle density of his upper torso and arms!

Coming down from the air, he could see more than fifty all in all of the Bafuku Ashigaru attacking his camp. Most of them were Green Knights while only twelve of them, Takauji's Twelve, were the Gray Ryu. He saw Jubei, first and urgent, with his broadswords split and taking on two highly skilled Grays when an arrow shot from the bow of a Green Knight was heading straight for his head.

Kojiro landed just in time to snatch the arrow out of the air not a moment before it would have made contact with Jubei, spin around and hurl it back in the direction of its initial path. It flew too quickly for the bowman to move, and went in his head and out the back. It then pinned one of the Grays through the throat to a tree. All other eleven Grays felt it as their one man died. But Takauji, yanking off his mask and revealing his leper-scarred face, felt it more than any other. He took in a deep breath of hot air and furious anger, then released it as a breath of life that revived his fallen clone.

Takauji maker made eye contact with Kojiro. The clone maker's scars and the texture of his skin made him look like a ghoul that used to be handsome. His shoulders bore the broadness of having been trained in chopping trees since childhood. He wore a gray headband that bore the crest of the Gray Ryu, and had the eyes of an eagle.

Holding his hurting throat, he said,

"Cursed if you survive this day, Sakura!"

"You are late, Takauji,' Kojiro taunted. "I am cursed already!"

That's when Takauji got to be the first to witness a display of the *Dragon Chi*. Kojiro's body rippled with new muscles right before Takauji's eyes. He seemed to even get taller, metamorphosing into an outer expression of his inner beast -a berserker.

The Dragons etched burning brand-like tattoos of themselves across Kojiro's back and chest, circling his arms. Unsheathing the hungry Hatsukoi, Kojiro sprinted towards Takauji.

Kojiro's eyes, Takauji would tell stories about it later, changed in a remarkable way; the three spirits, merging with his own, created a balance of four spirits within him. This made the pupils in his eyes double, like figure-eights. This Takauji saw as Kojiro lunged at him with his sword held high. Their blades sparked a glinting light when connected, setting off a dance of a fast moving bladed contest of Hate vs Vengeance.

Jubei had his hands full cutting down Green Knight after Green Knight with his incredible broadswords and brute strength. Otaku was dashing back and forth through the trees, overwhelming his opponents with his four arms, taking and killing them with their own weapons.

The Kiyoshi brothers spread out, each man with conscripts fighting by his side, and used their mastery of the Chinmoku *te* to anticipate the movements of the surrounding Ashigaru at least seven moves in advance. They dashed and crisscrossed through the forest in the thick of the fight like flashes of shooting light, but somehow even this could not diminish the numbers of Ashigaru fast enough for the Crew to gain the upper hand.

Many conscripts were falling left and right. The Ashigaru tried to subdue Otaku by attacking him four or five at a time, but Ichiro and Hajime joined in to even the scales.

Kana used her kusarigama like a whirlwind, keeping the multiplying Ashigaru at bay and taking them out one by one with precision strikes from a distance. She was so deft with the weapon that she would take the sickle handle in one hand on a flip and upon landing throw three or four knives at other Ashigaru closing in, then use her magnetic power to draw those knives back to her and then resume swinging the kusarigama with seamless transitioning.

Jubei rushed to fight at Kojiro's side when five and then six and then eight of Takauji's Twelve tried to overwhelm them.

"Not today, Takauji" Jubei yelled. "Not when any nose around can still smell a coward in his way!"

"We'll show you cowardice, pig!" Takauji shouted back.

Kojiro laughed.

"Hahaha. You hear that, Jubei?! I told ya' you were getting fat!"

"Better fat than anorexic and short like you, yuujin!"

Between shuriken and the use of her Lion Bear sword, Tzukuba was unstoppable. She was also angry and possessed by the knowledge that each kill against them or cut she sustained herself was personal since she lived among them for years as a spy. Tzukuba was never taught the multiplying technique, but she knew how to fight like the Ashigaru and was privy to their tricks. This is how she knew they would dash up into the trees in attempts to gain leverage and then come down with attacks from above while opponents were distracted by one or two of them on the ground. Tzukuba knew to be ready for a trick like that, and maneuver in ways that would work the trap against them, causing Ashigaru to crash into and kill a member of their own by mistake when she would tuck and roll out of the way.

Ittei fought hard with his naginata. He longed to put down the deadly weapon once and for all and commit to his arts, writing and music, but when he held it and fought, *that* was his art. And the battlefield his canvas. Like with Kana, the attackers struggled to get close against the twirling pointed spear. Ittei's techniques were like ferocious halos of wind, small hurricanes of death reaching out for souls to consume! Yuriko and several of her tribe joined the fight as well, leaping into the fray from out of the trees and surprising the Ashigaru. But even this effort, as great as it was, just wasn't enough. The Ashigaru soldiers just kept coming and coming.

Otaku and Kana, as well as heavy-set Gorou with his bludgeoning kanobo, joined to give Tzukuba cover while she did a series of *Kuji-In* hand sign jutsu techniques. Her eyes glowed a bright iridescence as she did a crescent-like motion with her arms, sending a wave of energy over the clearing which formed ghostly hands that grasped the throats of at least fifteen Ashigaru all at once, and then snapping their necks. Then she split her weapon and, mimicking one of the Ashigaru's own tricks, dashed up through the trees to come back down with an attack on two others from above.

Another two warriors engaged her, both of them much taller and noticeably stronger than the others. But she took them on without hesitation. Both of them armed with a katana, they tried to close in on her from front and back. But she did a windmill kick to knock down one of them while she sword fought the other. What Ztukuba lacked in size and strength, she made up for in speed. She broke through the man's defenses after three moves and landed a killing strike off a parry. Her blade however proved difficult to immediately pull out of his chest, and in this moment the other man was drawing near from behind. This distraction would have surely cost Tzukuba her life if it weren't for the sickle lodging into the back of the assailant's head. She turned around in time to see his body lurch backwards as Kana yanked the kusarigama back to her.

The two of them, Tzukuba and Kana, they held each other's gaze for just a few moments -but long enough for an unspoken bond to form between them.

"Jubei,' Kojiro yelled, 'the cave!"

A cave, it came out of nowhere! Before its sudden appearance, the Crew were being surrounded and strategically pushed into a dead end of mountains. But here now was this exit formed for them, beyond the trees to the left of the battlefield going East.

Jubei knew exactly what to do.

"Gorou!" he called. And then broke into an incredible sprint, lunged forward and with his broad sword cut clean through the base of an old cedar. On cue, Gorou leapt higher and hit the tree with his kanobo. Everyone reacted to its falling by scattering, except for the Crew members who all knew this was a diversion for them to escape into the cave.

Kana and Otaku threw a splay of explosive black eggs all designed on the four main points of the Ashigaru attack. The tree crashed down on several of them in the commotion.

"Quickly!" yelled Kojiro, and everyone headed for the cave.

As everyone was rushing towards the cave entrance, Kojiro experienced a vision of how it was formed.

It was Xiao-xiao Chen from way off, still on the shore of the sea. She did another Shaolin kata, and that was a "spell" that created the cave for them.

Kojiro didn't know why she was helping them, but didn't have time then to think on it. They had to get away before the Ashigaru regrouped!

"Hurry in!" Kojiro beckoned. And everyone did.

After everyone was inside, Kana called,

"Jubei, the entrance! Destroy it!"

He did so immediately by throwing an explosive shuriken at the crust of the rock ceiling after everyone was safely inside. Still multiplying in numbers, the Ashigaru were so aggressive and smooth that seventeen of them made it through before the way was blocked off. But in this small, darkened space now made by the sudden, mythic cave, Kana and Otaku, seemingly in competition with each other, shared in the responsibility of relieving each of the Ashigaru attackers of their heads.

From here, the Live Crew wasted no time getting deep into the cave and following the path before them.

As they went, Kojiro looked back at the smoking rubble of the makeshift barricade. He intuited Xiao-xiao Chen again, still at the beach doing calligraphy in the sand and intuiting words back to him.

"*Consider it, Sakura,*' she said to him in his mind, '*if a child could fashion the world, would his mind not be unhampered in imaginative expression? Would he not envision mythic power, creatures, people, and locales?*"

They kept walking in silence until coming upon an open space that looked like a buried, upside down cathedral. There were two paths now in front of them, one to the left and another to the right.

"We should split into two groups," Kana suggested, stopping to feel the walls and communicate psychically with the ground under her feet. "One to take the northern pass, and the rest to travel southeast following this here course. Both passages will lead eventually to the same exit, but down the northern path there is a detour that Otaku can set traps in, and the Kiyoshi can use their Chinmoku talents to chart a decoy for the Ashigaru to follow if and when they make it past our barricade."

Ittei kneeled to pet the one wolf that joined them on their journey, Yoriko.

"Good job back there,' he told her. 'We will pray together for those that fell."

Jubei addressed Kana.

"You are certain that both paths lead to the exit?"

"I am always certain."

All eyes turned on Kojiro, who didn't waste any time in his reply.

"Two groups then,' he said. "and no rest for either until we reach the other side."

THE GHOST ORCHID, NOW PEARL white with vein riddled, semi-translucent skin, is looking up through purple, double pupiled eyes. *A third pupil, this one gold, appeared in them both, syncing now with the enduring splinter in her mind of the vision; the cosmos, the silhouette, the twenty-seven lights -three of them mini moons. The freedom promised her in an echoing, haunting whisper. Maybe this is what was driving her, perhaps this is why she was here... But for now, the memory existed as but a question...*

She's looking up at the actual, present moon that, to her perspective, is also doubled in the figure-eight. She is standing naked in the middle of an interstate highway, I-95 in Miami, as incredulous and angry drivers zoom past and swerve to avoid hitting her. Astrid is aware of the presence of all this late night traffic and the noise of car horns, but she doesn't care about any of it. And, anyway, she couldn't be harmed by mere modern vehicles if hit. She couldn't be harmed, Astrid knew, by anything of this curious, primitive world.

The sound of sirens approach as Astrid examines her surroundings, the network of intersecting roadways that looked to her like arteries in a circulatory system. Somehow, this revelation reminded her of who she was and where she came from. That image of the brilliant inner workings of a living organism, it hastened the dawning of her senses, her mental understanding of emotions rushing in as dismay formed first as their herald. That flushing trepidation came with remembering that she is not supposed to be in the presence or visual sphere of humankind.

At this point those sirens were getting closer. She turned to the sound to find two police cars creating a barricade to block traffic in two of the four highway lanes. The cars parked but the sirens remained on. The red, blue, and yellow flashing lights, they made Astrid think of both the onset and denouement of consciousness; the first and last thing that a sentient being sees is a vibration of colors. She wasn't sure whether to frown or smile as the two officers approached her. One man, the other a woman.

"Ma'am,' the female officer, who led the approach, said to Astrid as she took careful, unthreatening steps towards her. She had one hand on her holstered sidearm and the other up in a gesture as if offering assurance to Astrid that she was safe. "Ma'am, are you ok? Do you know where you are?"

The male officer followed close but was angling his approach to the left, his hand also on his sidearm.

"What is your name, miss?' the female officer continues her attempt at consolation. "Are you ok? Do you know where you are?"

The cops close to her, Astrid's eyes are closed now. But the female officer makes the mistake of putting a hand on Astrid's shoulder, making her recoil from the touch and open her eyes. Both cops see the four glowing pupils.

Astrid's jaw makes motions as if to say "No", but no words emerge. She closing her eyes again. But it's already too late.

The female cop's arms go limp at her sides.

"Janet? Are you...?", the male cop begins to ask, before he experiences a painful sensation in his chest.

Janet turns to him, her face now festooned with throbbing veins. There are tears streaming from her suddenly bloodshot eyes. She looks ghostly, eerie. As she tries to speak, her head spontaneously explodes!

"Ja-', the male cop tries to scream but his voice is stifled by extreme shock, his hand fumbling with the now drawn gun that he immediately drops in response to the now more intense pain in his chest. His racing heart detonates like a grenade, his ribcage and entrails blasting out through his Kevlar vest and shirt. Both bodies fall as Astrid breaks into a sprint across the highway, through now swerving cars and blaring horns. When arriving at the road shoulder, Astrid looks over to see more ventricles of road beneath the high bridge of the street she is currently leaning over. There's a moment where she considers what it would look like for a cancerous cell to make its way through a human nervous system. But then she shuts her eyes again and leaps over the side.

Global Dollar Magazine's quote of the day: *"Is the world a better place because of the work we did today? If we can answer 'yes' to that question, then we have been successful in the workplace."*
                                   -Wilson Maddox, **Founder and CEO of Maddox Oil**.

LOS ANGELES, CALIFORNIA. Last year, a Zogby poll commissioned by 24/7 Wall St. found that 33% of respondents reported negative customer experience with Rain Forest Inc, including but not limited to their telecommunications products and PC equipment. Additionally, the company scored only a 64 out of 100 on the American

Customer Satisfaction Index. But in less than a year, since the still obscure development launch of the TRIVIUM project, as well as significantly decreased product inflation since Jeremiah Cross' deal with Schröder & Vogt: Anlagekapital, the company's ratings and public image has skyrocketed. The ACSI approval rating has gone from that unflattering 64 to an eyebrow raising 83, and Zogby reports 72% customer satisfaction.

Trivium, the company's spokesperson stressed in pointed out to the press, is not even publicly available yet. But look at how much it has already positively influenced research and development!

JEREMIAH CROSS SPENT SO MUCH time in his office at his company, Rain Forest Incorporated, that he practically lived in the enormous Art Deco style building. This was one such night, after 2am on a Saturday. The Silicon Valley magnate was seated in his plush cold-cured chair and watching a news broadcast on the plasma tv screen set up on the wall. He was enveloped in darkness, the only light was coming from that screen, and he would appear to anyone looking as if he were an animated gargoyle the subject of shadows.

"Just after midnight this evening,' a reported said on the television, 'two police officers were slain in an apparent shooting on I-95, just south of Miami metropolitan. Their names have not been released to the press. A disoriented woman was walking in the nude in the middle of the street and disrupting traffic when the officers responded to a call on the incident and.. the reports indicate that she opened fire on them with an apparent shotgun when they attempted to approach. Conflicting reports from witnesses say she had no weapon at all, which is clearly unlikely, or that she was hiding it on her side at an angle that the police couldn't see until it was too late.

No dash cam footage is available due to the way the two police vehicles on site were parked.."

Cross changed the channel, finding another report playing on the same I-95 incident. He changed the channel again, and the broadcast was on that station as well.

"Shotgun," Cross mockingly repeated under his breath.

The com on his desk beeped twice while a red light flashed. Cross turned off the television, and pressed a three button sequence on the remote next to the com. An overhead light came on, but it only provided dim lighting to replace the luminance that was coming before from the tv. He sat back in his chair, faced the front of the room and laced his fingers.

The elevator doors opened and in walked a middle aged Hindi woman in a lab coat, carrying a clipboard. She hurried over to Cross' desk.

"You called, Mr. Cross?" there was a mild film of disdain in her cadence.

"Yes, Dr. Upadhyay. How has the Steinitz head taken to the mainframe?"

She was reluctant to respond. Tentative.

"Doctor?" Cross repeated, a hint of menace to his inflection.

"Um.. Quite well, sir. The data pathways of its chemical synapses sync with all peripheral processor units, expanding the overall power availability of I/O channel networks. The steady flow of glutamate to the excitatory transmitter yields favorable support. Above average, in fact. There is.., at this point, no hitch in development, in other words. Only... Only six more to complete the needed halocarbon signature."

"So, the **Trivium** will go online as scheduled?"

"Yes, sir. Provided we …get the six."

"Oh you'll get the other six heads, Dr. Upadhyay. I've hired the best to make sure of it. The mind, as the axiom follows, is a terrible thing to waste."

Dr. Upadhyay wasn't amused by Cross' morbid joke. He noticed something in her face, an unspoken response she didn't intend for him to see.

"Is that fatigue, or apprehension?" he asked.

"Sir?"

"Your face. I'm aware that you have been uncomfortable over the ethical implications of your team's assignment, as well as the existential. But stay focused and think on the good your groundbreaking work will do for society once it's complete. The good it'll do for the world that your children will grow up in, and your children's children."

"Perhaps,' she countered, "but… some might consider murder a little higher up in the hierarchy of ethical gray areas."

"Nonsense,' Cross almost laughed. 'There's no blood on your hands save what small minds would splash on them in their campaigns to legislate sentimental gibberish. And as far as ethical gray areas are concerned, consider how fraught with controversy the derivation of pluripotent stem cell lines from oocytes and embryos is. While ignorant theologians quibble over speculations of *personhood*, stem cell research is steadily offering a great deal of promise in the real world of disease treatment, myocardial infarction, spinal cord injuries…"

The doctor glances down at her shoes, then looks back up at Cross.

"Of course, Mr. Cross," she replied, instead of giving voice to the many thoughts that flooded her mind.

There was an awkward moment of silence.

Going for reassurance in the only way he knew how or cared to learn, Cross offered,

"I am sure the money I am paying will cure any remaining ambivalence in you if the greater good isn't enough."

Neither Dr. Upadhyay nor Cross could see her, but Zhrontese was there in the room, watching them from the shadows. She knew that she could not intervene, and she also knew that Jeremiah Cross was lying.

She was distracted however by something else that she was intuiting from the other side of the continent.

———

CYNTHIA DIDN'T HAVE ANY FRIENDS, not really. She had lunch often with Paulina Mitchell, her mentor and a tenured history professor at LSU. There was a Mediterranean bistro about three miles from the campus. It was comely, quiet, and decorated like a museum slash eatery with Persian and Mesopotamian refinements. It was Cynthia's preference to meet there mostly on Wednesdays, away from students who might interrupt them with questions on lectures or requests for paper deadline extensions. They always sat at a booth by the windows.

Paulina was a white woman from Nevada who dressed like an entertainment agent from the City of Angels in her designer pantsuits and platform heels. She wore her curly red hair short and was never seen without impeccable makeup. For lunch, always with a steamy *ellinikos kafes* (a Greek coffee blend), she would usually have the Souvlaki platter, or sometimes, when in a particularly good mood, a Mousaka dish with eggplant, potatoes, and bechamel sauce, served with a Greek salad and pita. This was one of those days. Cynthia, she was so consistent that she could tell any waiter "the usual" and they'd bring her a Tabbouleh; parsley, bulgar, onions, tomatoes, cucumber, peppers, and olives all served on a bed of iceberg lettuce.

"So, he tries to argue with me on the conquest of Constantinople,' Paulina prattled on, a mile a minute, more confident than smug, "forgetting this is my field. No, he says, *the janissaries of Orhan weren't paid salaries as the books suggest*, as if this misreading of the histories will somehow support his idiotic theory that minimum wages aren't inhumane and unlivable, and that the Ottoman Empire wasn't directly instrumental to the watermark that ended the Middle Ages."

"Why you even bother having these conversations with Hisari is beyond me," Cynthia replied, referring to Nicholas Hisari, another tenured professor at the college whose subject was not history. "The guy deludes himself with the belief that the study of geology makes him a de facto authority on every subject above ground."

This made Paulina laugh, almost choking on the sip of kafes she was taking.

"Maybe I'm part masochist,' she offered, 'or maybe I think kinks in fragile masculinity are cute and endearing on some level."

Neither Paulina nor Cynthia noticed him, but outside the window and standing in the middle of the sidewalk, was a man watching them. Watching Cynthia, actually. Standing there casually with his hands in his pockets, staring directly at her. He was wearing a knee-length charcoal black coat over a camel brown turtleneck -overdressed for the weather, but unphased by it. His seventeen inch braided beard and andradite crystal eyes, along with the outfit, would make him stand out if anyone could see him, but Clymene was making himself invisible to humans. Even pedestrians walking by on the sidewalk, they'd pass right through him as if he wasn't there.

Cynthia grinned at Paulina's quip, shrugged. Then she winced, rubbed her temple.

"What's with you today?" Paulina asked. "That migraine acting up?"

"It's always acting up."

"Seems like something else is making it worse though."

"Maybe. I mean, you'd think a college professor wouldn't have to suffer an endless barrage of hate mail from clingy parents."

Paulina sighed, knowingly. Cynthia, in her peripheral, could (somehow) see Clymene standing outside the window and staring at her. She could sense and was made uncomfortable by the presence, but didn't respond to her instincts just yet.

"Welcome to the fold, grasshopper," Paulina joked. "None of us ever really grows up. Not really. We're all children in the sense that we always have a blind spot, a point of ignorance that keeps us hopeful enough to keep on existing. I think most parents, especially religious ones, are at least subconsciously privy to the existential dance and want to keep their kids off the floor, no matter how old they get. And look at your subject! You're challenging their most fundamental beliefs."

"Isn't that what higher education is supposed to be about? Challenging the beliefs and ideas that we take for granted?"

"Not as far as the people paying the bills are concerned."

It was Cynthia's turn to chuckle at Paulina's witticism, but then another biting pain in her head prompted her to glance to the right, seeing Clymene, and then back at Paulina. She did a double take and, in that instant, Clymene was gone.

"Wait, what?" Cynthia said, fully looking now out at the street.

Paulina turned around to see what was the matter.

"What are.. You ok?" she asked.

"I coulda sworn..." Cynthia shook her head but kept searching. There was nothing but pedestrians, shoppers walking the strip, cars passing by, the sun beating down on the asphalt. "I saw somebody. A man... standing right there. Staring at me."

What she didn't know was that Clymene was still there, wondering to himself how she had seen him. Or, rather, confirming the suspicions he had which drew him to her in the first place. He removed his hands from his pockets and opened his palms at his sides -ascending to a hover as his clothing morphed back into robes. He became more translucent as he floated up higher, the clouds in his andradite eyes began to swirl, and then he vanished entirely. What he took with him was the lingering question, the image of Cynthia looking aghast outside that window -only subconsciously aware of what she'd seen.

———

THE IMAGE FOR CYNTHIA, THE subconscious memory of Clymene watching her, it lingered in her mind as well. But in a way that kept her restless and disturbed.

That Wednesday night was a cool one. It had rained a little just before evening, so the light wind that followed at dusk was crisp and serene. Usually on nights like these, Cynthia would grade papers over lavender tea, and/or prepare new lectures for the coming days, but the splinter in her mind had cracked open the levees to a flood of thoughts not easily ignored. The subconscious image grew conscious, and imagination began to fill in the blanks of the unknown.

She saw those eyes while replaying her conversation with Paulina in her mind, the andradite crystals swirling with clouds that intensified the revelations as she spoke.

Isn't that what higher education is supposed to be about? Challenging the beliefs and ideas that we take for granted?

She could even see him vanishing as she did her double takes, looking back to find him and feeling those eyes still staring at her from the void.

This enduring restlessness prompted Cynthia to change into leggings and a t-shirt and then go out to the garage to spend her energy on the heavy bag. She put on an audio book to detox her mind while at it, *The Devil Finds Work* by James Baldwin:

"Identity would seem to be the garment with which one covers nakedness of the self. In which case, it is best that the garment be loose, a little like the robes of the desert, through which one's nakedness can always be felt, and, sometimes, discerned. This trust in one's nakedness is all that gives one the power to change one's robes..."

The punching and kicking, the reader's voice, and adrenaline, sweat, noise of Cynthia's gloves crashing over and over into the bag, none of this was drowning out the image of Clymene staring. None of it buried or quieted the question of it. What concerned her most was the phenomenon of Tulpamancy. Had she in her loneliness unconsciously created one, like David-Neel's monk? Was it the long dead explorer's monk himself, now haunting her instead?

"An identity is questioned only when it is menaced, as when the mighty begin to fall, or when the wretched begin to rise, or when the stranger enters the gates, never, thereafter, to be a stranger..."

Fatigue finally set in after forty minutes of nonstop bag work, leaving her body drenched in sweat and her muscles on fire. The image of Clymene endured. In fact, she saw what she didn't see; his modern clothing becoming his ancient robes, and him ascending until vanishing into molecules. Cynthia gritted her teeth and punched the bag once more in anger.

The dream that night, after the tug of war between sleep and consciousness, was just as tempestuous. Her surroundings were the bright blinding whites and constant symphony of beeping machines of an intensive care unit, in Harlem, NY five years prior. Her face was wet with tears and gaunt with sleeplessness, and she was sitting at a bed containing the unmoving body of Yves DeGruy -her father.

The heart rate monitor machine indicated by its jumping blue, green, and purple line sequences that he wasn't dead. Yet. But there was no movement from him, and Cynthia was ensnared by the desperateness of a tight focus on the faint rise and fall of his chest. At least, she reasoned, he is breathing.

It seemed like hours she was sitting there, and maybe it was. Time loses all meaning and substance not only in dreams, but in the awful perpetuity of waiting for loved ones to depart this mortal coil. The sounds in that room never leave you, the smell, the cold, though the people will. They'll be retreating in your memory forevermore until, finally, you yourself leaves. And so there Cynthia sat for minutes, hours, days -the sun and moon shuffling back and forth in the dream, callously mocking her senses in the way that only Time could.

Eventually, she got tired of it and stood. She took one final look at her father, then turned to walk toward the door.

"You'll leave me?" his deep, quavering voice called her back. Again, she turned to him, to face his accusing, bloodshot eyes. "You would leave me now?.... Like this?"

"Breaking news!" exclaimed the different, though just as familiar voice from Cynthia's television, clicking on at 3:45AM.

Her eyes adjusted to the brightness of morning, finding the smiling anchor on the screen wearing a green tie and gray suit today. "Twelve people were killed last night in a drive by shooting at a Valero gas station just south of Guilbeau. Four of the victims were teenagers between the ages of 13 and 15. Though no suspects have been identified, witnesses say the car was a beige Acura Legend Coupe with a broken left tail light last seen heading west on New Iberia…"

———

TAKAYAMA WAS RENOWNED FOR A number of things, from its sansai mountain vegetables to its lacquerware and pottery, the narrow streets of the Sanmachi Suji historic district and the biannual Takayama Festival. Like the festival, its rich culture and wooden merchant houses dated all the way back to the 1600s. But Coletrane and Patrick's trip would bring them into Tokyo first, where they'd explore a far different bequest of the feudal era: Nihonbashi, the red-light district formerly known as Yoshiwara.

"In one of your articles,' Coletrane said to Patrick upon the plane's landing, 'you referred to me as a modern day Richie Rich… but tell me, is it a cautionary tale about child prodigies, or is it secretly a Jekyll/Hyde story wherein Casper the friendly ghost is cast as the former? Maybe the publisher of Harvey Comics knew something of tulpas. Maybe you do as well, Patrick,.. subconsciously."

"I'm still not convinced of your tulpa story, Train. Intrigued, though."

"We'll mull over it later. After a respite from our objective here."

"Respite?"

That first night, Patrick would learn of Coletrane's meaning. The night life of the small, moat-surrounded city was neon lit with a spectrum of vibrant color, the many nightclubs, restaurants, and love hotels all moving with the crowded tension that earned the place its sobriquet as the "Sleepless Town".

Coletrane insisted that they walk through the streets and soak up the surroundings, breathe in the life of Nihonbashi. This was fine for Patrick's sensibilities as a sight seer. But unbeknownst to him, they were being followed by three covert operatives hired for the task of reconnaissance by Landau Kier. Two men, one woman: Elrone, Spoone, and Lyza. They were all deftly spread out like spies behind enemy lines, each of them carefully blending in with the other people out enjoying the vibrant night life. Patrick didn't notice them, but Coletrane had spotted each one of them without cluing to the fact. He simply made a mental note of their presence as he and Patrick passed them in the street. This was a product of his lifelong paranoia, weaponized to his benefit.

"Do you believe in determinism, Patrick?" Coletrane asked as they were passing under a red neon gate that served as an entrance way between two tall buildings onto a street lined with shops, restaurants, and bars. He asked this on the one hand to make conversation, and on the other to appear distracted enough to not tip off those watching of his knowledge of them.

"Determinism?' Patrick replied, surprised by the question. "Well, it's certainly an intriguing school of thought. But I'm more a free will kind of guy. What brought that up?"

"Just thinking. I'm looking around at all these people and wondering, what if their every movement is already predetermined? How crippled would they be to discover this as fact, not belief or *school of thought*?"

"They'll probably rush to a scientific conclusion to justify rejecting this knowledge, citing the fundamental randomness of quantum mechanics."

"Even the religious? Even those who don't know what quantum mechanics are?"

"Is this an addendum to the _Why_ in you bringing me here?"

"Fly you seven thousand miles to talk philosophy?' Coletrane laughed. 'Not quite, Copernicus. Just wondering if there could be a reconciliation between the two, between Determinism and Free Will. We're here running down the flotsam of a prophesy, after all."

"_You're_ here running down the flotsam of a prophesy,' Patrick corrected. "I'm here to write an exposé on a notoriously prodigal rich man." He winked when Coletrane glanced at him.

"Ah. The Pulitzer?" Coletrane replied, amused.

"Yep." Patrick grinned.

Back in Florida at the Marx estate, in the trophy room with Poole there watching as it happens, the open book was filling more blood red script on the empty pages. Poole had an unsettled look on his face as he watched this, sensing, though he couldn't read it, that the words being written were not a report of good tidings...

On the downtown streets of Nijonbashi, Patrick took so many pictures of the brilliant architecture, the Kabuki street performers, the aggressive memorabilia vendors conducting their business with the charm of thieves; he moved about deceived by the illusion of safety presented by the gaudy veneer of the surroundings. His commitment to work, however, calmed down when they entered an establishment with half naked *yujo* girls moving about seductively on latticed verandas.

"Maybe put your camera away for a while," Coletrane warned, 'lest you attract some unwanted attention that I'd be too amused to protect you from."

"Yeah, sure. But.. Protect me? I can take care of my-"

"No, you can't,' Coletrane laughed. 'Not here. You're a long way from Kuwait, soldier."

The establishment's hostess, a tall woman at 5'11 in a form fitting Gemini gold kimono, approached them as if she'd anticipated the visit from the high born rich man from America. While she glanced at Patrick with a note of indifference, she regarded Coletrane with enthusiasm,

"Welcome to the Lotus Oiran, Mr. Marx. Your patronage brings us great honor."

"I trust you've prepared us a booth," he replied.

"The finest. Come."

She led them up to the second floor level. Used to the finer things, Coletrane's demeanor was blasé towards the manicured resplendence of the place's make out. Everything was polished, fine lit, and adorned in regal artistry. But everywhere left and right was also bedecked with people interacting with each other as if within the walls of a brothel. Indeed, behind the curtain of refinery, that is exactly what the Lotus Oiran was. Patrick had never been in a place like this and it showed. Anyone seeing the way he looked around would spot him as a tourist. But, at least, he wasn't taking pictures. No patrons paid him attention, however. Both the men and women were too busy being entertained by the staff. Even at the booths they were passing were people engaged in various degrees of affection. Some, making out. Others, enjoying the gyrations of toned hips. And others still, dry humping in darkened corners while feeding each other their tongues.

The hostess brought Coletrane and Patrick to a red Shoji door enclosed VIP platform with multiple couches surrounding an ice chamber for bottles of champaign.

"Do you know what an oiran is, Patrick?" Coletrane asked him when the hostess left them.

"No. Can't say that I do."

"Well,' Coletrane chuckled, pouring champaign into two glasses, 'you're about to find out. *Oira no tokoro no nee-san,* Patrick." He handed the war photographer his glass, continuing, "The *nonpariel* courtesans of this place."

His wink was as if a cue, heralding the five disarmingly beautiful women that entered moments later. Skilled seductresses, snakelike in movement, their bodies oiled and adorned in edible paint designs, revealing lingerie, and open, low cut *uchikake* brocades that defied any notion of modesty.

Two of the women sat on opposite sides of Coletrane, together caressing and flirting with him, sipping champaign as well. A third stood in front of him, between his legs, swaying her hips to the music. The other two women, sensing Patrick's discomfort, went over and beckoned him to stand and dance with them. It wasn't a request. They simply each grabbed a hand and lifted him off of the couch, laughing coquettishly as they did it. Patrick would learn right then and there how to loosen up, despite himself.

It went on like this for a bit, everyone getting more and more inebriated. The women, more undressed a little at a time until down only to underwear. Patrick, enjoying every aspect of his current station and growing *looser* with every drink -nearly to the point of hilarity. But Coletrane, he was cut from a different cloth. Outwardly, he pretended to be having fun and getting tipsy. But liquor tended to have little effect on him. And his anxiety level was secretly much too piqued for him to enjoy it anyway.

Like earlier when he spotted the three operatives following them, Coletrane sensed another presence amid them in the belly of the clublike love hotel. This time, a threat.

Bodies moving to music could be seen in silhouette through the red paper Shoji walls, but there was one shadow not moving at all. Though difficult to make out, Coletrane could see it; through the wall directly across from him, past the woman grinding in his lap, past Patrick on the other couch with now three of the oiran, he could see someone just standing there in the middle of the crowd. And he had an eerie feeling that this mysterious someone was watching him through the Shoji. This feeling was so strong that he no longer felt the woman grinding on him, so strong that he wanted to hop up and jump through the Shoji and attack whoever it was! He was almost overcome by this desire when, suddenly, he noticed more non-moving silhouettes through the thin paper walls. First one, then two others, then at least seven before all of them began to blur and blend in with the dancing shadows that served as their camouflage.

Coletrane could no longer make them out, and soon his vistas were covered by the topless women that moved into his line of vision.

He would not forget those menacing shadows in the darkness though. Ever.

Drops of dew, bolts of lighting, these images again weighing heavily on the mind as a spear would weigh if embedded in a man's chest and left there by its owner. The fate of victor and vanquished both held in this crude asymmetrical equality. The sharp-edged sword, springing to life, cutting through the void. A band of individuals joined in the darkness' seductive pull drawing them deeper and deeper into the squalid abyss.

What lie in wait for them is anyone's guess. What lie in wait for them, in fact, may silence their questions before they've a chance to give voice to them…

-Ittei's Journal, on passing through the mysterious cave.

MIRACULOUSLY RESCUED BY THE sudden manifestation of a cave, the Live Crew pressed on while in silent agreement to not think too much on the luck of it. For Kojiro however, there came upon him an unusual sense of repulsion toward death, assault, blood. It was the bodies of his crew members left dead on the field at their confrontation with the Ashigaru, it was those who remained ready still to die as well, it was Jubei standing next to him, relatively cordial under the circumstances, his regard for Kojiro not marred in any way by their losses that ironically filled him with an abiding sense of trepidation that he could hide but not ignore.

Takauji and his multiplying Ashigaru managed to take out twelve of their dedicated members, leaving them only twenty warriors strong. The fallen were conscripts, but each of them had family, friends, lives… Each of them represented a world now gone from existence. Gone, Kojiro thought to himself, as a direct result of his arrogance in offending a demon God like the Inca Tan'Mo.

One of those fallen conscripts was named Aito, who tended a rice farm on which his family lived. A pregnant wife, and two strong boys aged 13 and 9. The one on the way, if it turns out to also be a boy, Aito had told Kojiro in confidence, he will be named Kojiro after him. When the Deadly Sakura asked him why, Aito told him simply, "Because you honor me, and I will honor you."

Kojiro thought of this and winced. If he survived this journey, he promised himself right then that he would be the one to personally deliver the news of Aito's death to his family.

"I am weary of this path," Jubei said, snapping Kojiro out of the reverie.

The remaining warriors had split into two groups, on Kana's council. The one traveling southeast were Kana, Otaku, three of the deaf Kiyoshi brothers, Jirou, Finn, and Hajime, and six other conscripts. Kojiro's group included Jubei, Tzukuba, Ittei and his wolf, the other two Chinmoku Aki, Ichiro and Gorou, and the last three conscripts among them. They were taking a path going southwest. The wolf Yoriko was sniffing out the darkened passageway ahead and, by Jubei's estimation, moving forward with hesitation.

"You are always weary of something, yuunin,' Kojiro joked.

"Well, it pays that one of us be."

"But always with a smile. One can never place whether you are apprehensive, jovial, or some combination of the two."

"Add in dubious and you'll have a formula."

"Do you not trust Yoriko?" Tzukuba asked, interjecting, her voice having gravity for the rarity of her using it.

"He trusts nothing but the sinew of his own muscles," Ittei offered, defending his quadrupedal friend.

"More than any animal that cannot speak, Ittei,' Jubei snapped back.

"You shouldn't trust yourself then,' Ittei quipped. Jubei grunted.

Walking ahead to kneel down and rub Yoriko's fur, feeding her a few berries from his hip pouch, Ittei added, 'She hesitates because this is unfamiliar terrain. Not for fear of there being no exit. If this were the case, she would not have come down this way with us at all."

"Maybe she intuits a metaphysical origin of these surroundings,' Tzukuba offered, 'and like Jubei, is weary."

"That settles it then,' Ittei said, smiling, 'the two of them are sisters."

Ittei stood tall when Jubei made a motion to approach him aggressively, but Kojiro stood between them.

"Stop it,' he commanded. 'We are all tense and grieving. Lost too. We will not add infighting to our conflicts. And... Tzukuba is right. This cave was not there before we needed it. It opened like a mouth to save us."

"Or consume us," Jubei said, "like the Weathering Thicket. The presence of safety, perhaps an illusion by which we are meant to be subdued."

"There are no tremella samoensis here,' Ittei reasoned. "Yoriko would have smelled them."

"And I would have sensed them," Tzukuba added.

"Anyway,' Kojiro said, settling things. "This is the path we have chosen. We will see it to the end."

He walked ahead, not waiting for anyone to agree.

———

THE PATH OF THE OTHER GROUP WAS dripping with water from the limestone pikes hanging down from the ceiling, and they were unlucky enough to have to pass through narrow, swampy terrain on their way. The otherwise darkened path was lit by surface crawling crustaceans that moved on dozens of tentacled legs like nautilus. There were thousands of such creatures on the walls, responding to movement and forming together into living hieroglyphic patterns that would change as you pass them.

"I grew up hearing stories about these creatures as a girl,' Kana whispered. 'But I've never seen them with my own eyes, or renderings of them, until today. The anphitites, storytellers of the parasite family."

"Parasites?" Otaku asked.

"Yes. They will tell stories that reflect the relevant histories of those who see them, but if you die among them, the sutras say, they will eat your corpse and leave no trace of you behind."

Otaku scratched an itch on the back of his head with his top left arm, had the two bottom arms both carrying a knife at his sides, and the fourth, top right arm reaching into his belt for his sake gourd.

"I reckon them allies then, that they would clean up your messes." Otaku took a swig. "But my interest is in the stories they are telling us now. Look there, Kana."

Otaku pointed at patterns the anphitites were making on the upper left side wall.

"I see it," Kana said.

"Are you sure?" Otaku challenged, the jocularity and inebriation already in his voice. "My deaf brothers, Hajime? Jirou? Finn? Surely your eyes are keener than those of our illustrious tracker."

Jirou, who was slightly ahead, turned and gave Otaku a contemptuous look over his shoulder.

"They can't hear you, fool,' Kana reminded him. 'But they can sense your boorishness."

"Boorishness?" Otaku repeated, laughing.

"Get on with whatever you are trying to say," Kana shot, "before the sake takes hold and you begin slurring your words."

Otaku swallowed his laughter, replacing it with a grunt.

"Dragons, sister. Look closely. As those bugs change their arrangement, they form as dragons in the transition."

"Do you read the language?"

"No. But I know a dragon when I see one! Whatever story they are imparting to us, it has to do with our commander."

Playfully and without warning, Otaku slapped Kana's chest with the back of a free hand in an endearing gesture of enthusiasm. He was too used to doing this with the men, realizing too late that it was breasts and not chest that he slapped. Kana shoved him hard, and the drunken four armed brute stumbled and, almost falling, bumped his head on the cave wall.

"Asshole!"

"Ow!"

"Hurt? Good!"

"I'm sorry. I'm sorry. Please forgive. Excitement gets the better of me."

"It's sake that gets the better of you, Otaku!" she lectured, snatching the gourd from off his belt.

"Hey!"

"You'll get it back later."

There was anger on his face, but when Kana didn't budge - he smiled. Then laughed.

The group continued walking.

"What's funny?" Kana wanted to know.

"Nothing really," Otaku assured with a wave of his hand, then his excitement, in an instant, returned. "I'm just saying that I told you, the Bodhisattvas were true in their tellings of the Dragon Kings. Ahh! Imagine! **Imagine seeing them all at once, twenty-seven dragons alighting the sky with mystical colors and unspeakable magic!**"

"Twenty-seven?" Kana inquired, a note of prepackaged disbelief just under the question.

"That's right!" Otaku said proudly. "**Twenty-seven great Lords. All of them, each, representing a different source of power. It is even said that they are elements that together make up the physicality of the universe, the bridge between the real and the imagined, the toucha-uh.. the tangible and the non-physical.**"

"It is said?" Kana repeated, dismissively. "You speak of oral traditions, not of anything written in the Bodhisattvas, my soaken friend."

"Soaken?! Look, I am not drunk! And whatever, Bodhisattvas, campfire stories, what matters is they are true. We saw with our own eyes as they descended upon Kojiro. At least three of them!"

"I saw nothing, Otaku. And neither did anyone else here among us."

Otaku looked to the faces of the conscripts, to Jirou and Finn, to Hajime's back... There was no register of confirmation from any of them. Still, Otaku shrugged.

"I know what I saw."

"I do not deny what you saw,' Kana assured. "But aren't those kings the consistency of spirits? Your ever inebriated vantage point perhaps gives you a second sight. That is, when you're not being inappropriate."

"I told you. I am not drunk!"

"I do not accuse you of being drunk. Well... yeah, I kinda do. But my point is that sake is always flowing through your veins, Otaku. The loosened inhibitions this inspires, it perhaps offers you greater sensitivity to nuances that the tightness of sobriety disallows in the rest of us."

Otaku considers this for a moment, realizing that Kana was not insulting him.

"Fine,' he demurred. 'But you see it now, right? These bugs that you yourself named?"

"Sure. I see it."

"They are talking about him. I do not know their language, but I know symbols and glyphs. They are telling a story about Kojiro, and by extension, us."

"Perhaps."

"Haha! I'll drink to that!"

THERE WERE ONLY TWO WOMEN sharing the Caesar size bed with Coletrane in his top floor hotel suite. A menage a trois, intensity bordering on violence, his hungers were rapacious to the point of near irreconcilable malaise. Indulgences of the flesh for Coletrane were tempered by harrowing betrayals of the mind; *his thoughts journeying back to the waking chimera of Kojiro, the demonic version, a hand tightly gripped around his throat and squeezing the life out of him as the two pleaded with each other.*

"Let... me.... go!" *Coletrane said.*

"YOU FIRST!" *demon Kojiro replied.*

This memory played over and over again in Coletrane's mind as his sweaty body thrusted, making it impossible for him to be mentally present and enjoy the incredible sex that an ordinary man would kill to have. **The other presence of distraction in his mind were lights, the twenty-seven lights from his childhood dream, the humid, life sucking darkness out of which they irradiated; this uncanny herald to the waking nightmare of his parents' brutal murder. Those lights that stifled his breath in the memory, they were now seemingly charging him with more energy, greater blood flow through his veins, more sweat on his brow, greater fervency of thrusts, and something, finally, akin to orgasmic pleasure.**

Deeper into the night, the two naked women fast asleep in each other's embrace, Coletrane also naked and next to them on the overlarge mattress, the clock on the end table struck 3:26am when the restless billionaire looked over at it. He was awakened by some movement at the foot of the bed. Discovering it not the women, he looked into the eyes of his unwelcome visitor - whose own eyes were like scintillating rhinestones burrowing into his soul from out the envelop of darkness and modest light bleeding into the room through the borders of closed curtains.

The spirit was seated in the lotus position, leaned forward on its elbows with his chin rested on interlaced fists. Coletrane wasn't sure if this was a dream or not, but he was in fact certain that Kojiro was there in the room, on the corner of the bed, and staring at him for real.

"You remember the lights then," Kojiro nodded slightly, sighing his approval. And then without waiting for a response, he added,

"But do you know why you must succeed?" the spirit asked Coletrane, whispering. "Why you must win?"

Coletrane just stared back, his silence due more to incredulity than defiance.

"I will show you then," the melancholic phantom decided, "Lest you lose all perspective to womanizing."

This utterance, and not so subtle rebuke, transported Coletrane's mind into a memory not his own but no less intimate:

Late November, in the year of the Tiger, just at the yawning precipice of what would be a cold winter. It was still warm however on the day of this memory, but a brisk wind was flowing in from the east that was strong enough to lift hair and cloth, but not strong enough to corrupt the graceful acoustics of

Ittei's shakuhachi flute. He and Yoriko had come along at the behest of Kojiro, with a little prodding from Taya, to the young couple's secret place in Hokkaido to enrich their afternoon with music. He was rested up against a cedar tree and enjoying its leafy shade while playing a lulling honkyoku that he wrote specifically to represent the miraculous love shared between two people.

Taya and Kojiro stood together barefoot in the cool, shallow water at the river bank not twenty yards from Ittei's perch. The pant legs of Kojiro's lapis hakama were rolled up and ribbon-tied at the calves to keep from getting wet, and the hem of Taya's arctic blue kimono was tucked into the sash around her hips. She had a white cherry blossom pinned up in her hair over her left ear that matched the Sakura patterns on her attire, this giving her an ethereal aura under the balmy rays of sun. Kojiro, his hair down and flowing in the wind, the navy blue sleeves of the haori coat he wore over his tie-dyed obi rolled up like his pant legs, splashed water on Taya, making her squeal and protest. She would have skipped away but he grabbed her wrist and pulled her to him. They kissed and laughed.

"Tell me," Taya whispered in Kojiro's ear, "Tell me when."

"Eh,' he grunted in mock annoyance, "I told you already."

"You told me several times,' she corrected. 'Tell me again."

They stared into each other's eyes for several beats, Kojiro tried to hold a serious face until, despite himself, Taya's made him smile.

Ittei watching as he played, Yoriko still at his side and lying on her stomach. It was equal parts surprising and elating for the dexterous warrior, and perhaps for Yoriko as well, to see Kojiro this way; happy, playful -smiling.

Kojiro looked in fact several years younger when he was with Taya, so much so that one would be forgiven for assuming it was an effect of her ikebana magic -but it was not.

"I will gather oak, birch, and loquat,' Kojiro finally answered Taya, so close that his breath tickled her neck, "and with these, me alone, I will build our minka, right up at the top of this hill so that you will always have a view of the river. There will be engawa verandas, just like those built by your father Basumaru, and the sliding doors at the front entrance will open onto a bronze Buddha statue set against the opposing wall. We'll have beautiful tatami mat flooring, high vaulted ceilings, and a room just for Vipassana meditation."

Taya interrupted him with soft laughter,

"But will you meditate?"

"I will."

"Do you promise?"

"I do."

She smiled again, hugging him tightly and resting her cheek against his beating heart.

"I will fish every morning," he continued. "And in this fertile soil we'll grow all your favorite plants. Clematis, senna, honeydew and barley, all the herbs we can make space for so that you may develop your kampo medicines. It will be our own private Takamagahara... Our Peaceful Place."

"I love the way you tell it," she said, looking up into his eyes again. "I love you."

"This is my promise to you, Taya. It is not just talk."

"Soon?"

"Yes. Very soon."

Coletrane opened his eyes again. He was lying down now, and it was not yet morning so the room was still dark. Kojiro's spirit projection was gone, but the two women were still there breathing next to him.

The now troubled bachelor just lied there with his eyes open for the next few hours, waiting for the sunrise and thinking about how he'd never felt so alone.

———

THE NEXT MORNING, IN THE adjoined suite, Patrick's vision was blurred upon waking. His head ached, his body - flushed with fatigue. He immediately regretted how much he drank the night before. But what surprised him was seeing Coletrane sitting in a chair next to the bed that he did not remember going to sleep in.

"*I stand amid the roar of a self-tormented shore,*' Coletrane quoted, '*And I hold within my hand grains of the golden sand.*"

"What?" Patrick said, groggily.

"Poe said that of sleep. He also drank himself to death. You probably should have stopped at that fourth cocktail, Patrick."

Patrick sat up and put his bare feet to the floor.

He regarded Coletrane, who was dressed down in jeans and a dark brown tapered fit sweater with the sleeves rolled up. He regarded the plain though top-end surroundings, recognizing less as he saw more. The floor to ceiling windows that made up the entire front wall, the villa-like architecture, the bedsheets and carpeting distinguished by custom embroidery.

"Where am I?"

"A hotel. Maybe you've heard of them."

"I mean, how did I get here? Shit, I had that much to drink?"

"You had more than that much to drink, Patrick. But good news. The women enjoyed your company."

"I wish I remembered theirs."

On the other side of the bed, Coletrane saw the demon version of Kojiro, dressed in the black, tar drenched O-yoroi armor, standing by the wall and staring directly at him through the double pupiled eyes. He knew that Patrick couldn't see the lingering phantom, so he knew also not to react to the menacing presence despite the anxiety that was triggered in him.

"Well, " Coletrane said, standing and tossing Patrick a bathrobe that he picked up from the floor, "life gives a little and takes more as payment. Shower. Get dressed. We have an appointment in Takayama."

———

THE PURPLE HERON, THE DARK AND light morphs, the great egrets becoming physical and given life by a child's imagination stretched out across worlds. They come to life and coast on the winds, swooping here and there, as craters spanning miles and miles fill with sea water, as the mountains erect and reach into the sky, an august archipelago of deciduous broad-leaved forests, aerial grasslands of high ranging flora, Yabutsubaki and Shii trees further than the eye could see. Entire ecosystems of marine and land-bound wildlife fill the forests and rivers; a rich biodiversity of species coming to life in open and isolated habitats; terrestrial mammals, vascular plants, there were giant flying squirrels, macaque, red-backed vole, other heron of all types and colors, serow running in the fields, black woodpeckers excavating the bases of trees for dinner; each animal, while not sentient, were all intuitively aware of the cave growing in the mountains above them like a caterpillar in its cocoon transforming into a butterfly. Magic...

———

IN THE PRESENT, JUST OUTSIDE THE city of Takayama where relics of the feudal era remain, a Ryukyu flies amid blue skies and then swoops down, diving low along the slopes of mountain, through fissures in rock and aerial pathways that would kill her instantly if she were to crash or make one mistake at her current speed. She glides above the water, her reflection below, pure poetry in motion. Orders of nen-gyo fish swim to the surface, hopping up and snapping at the Ryukyu, but she gracefully avoids becoming their lunch. Some trout and silver carp join in sport, but are all equally unsuccessful. Bored, the Ryukyu goes back up in the sky, abreast the clouds. The city lies not far from her line of vision.

The covert operatives hired by Kier: Spoon, Lyza, and Elrone, they are there again spread out and blended in with the packed-in crowds of pedestrians at Kami-Sannomachi, historic, Edo-period streets lined with traditional style breweries, merchant houses, shops, and eateries. Coletrane was aware of them again, but, again, not showing it. Even Patrick could not sense his apprehension.

The two entered a tachi-nomi establishment where Coletrane asked a random woman, in her native tongue, a question. She pointed across the street where stood a modest kaiten-zushi restaurant.

"What did you ask her?" Patrick wanted to know.

"We're looking for a man," Coletrane replied, as they passed under the sign of the place called Tomoe House Sushi.

It was a busy restaurant, renowned for its hida beef and gyoza, and impressive even for a district known for always being busy with tourism. The strong, rich aromas coming from the work of chefs at the open kitchen filled the atmosphere, along with the wait staff and cleaners moving through the congested tables filled to capacity like the gears of an unflagging machine.

Coletrane and Patrick worked their way to the chef's table, a rounded marble fixture, with four cooks inside, that served as the place's steamy center and raison d'être. But before they got there, their path was intersected by a waitress. She was petite and had a welcoming smile.

"Kon'nichiwa,' she said to Patrick, 'Welcome to Tomoe! I help you find seat?"

"No, thank you. I'm with him."

"He's with me," Coletrane repeated.

"Yes. Yes. Yōkoso!"

"Arigatōgozaimashita," Patrick said, adding a bow.

The waitress smiled and moved away. Coletrane was looking at Patrick with a quizzing look, a hint of pride and surprise.

"Don't get excited,' Patrick volunteered, 'How to say *thank you* is pretty much the only Japanese I know."

Coletrane's smile in response to that was sportive if not genuine. He turned then to face one of the chefs, who was so busy at work that he barely registered them.

"Excuse me," Coletrane said, leaning towards.

"Self-serve," the chef spat. He was lean with a chiseled jaw, muscular forearms and hands bearing the scars of a lifetime working in kitchens. There was also a scar under the left side of his cheek that added mystery to his otherwise plain and gaunt physiognomy.

"Try chu-toro,' he added. 'Tourist favorite."

"I'm looking for a man."

"No serve man meat. Try the Yakiniku a block over."

"He works here,' Coletrane ignored the joke but, behind him, Patrick smirked. "Tennen Ameeru."

"Ahh,' the chef didn't bother hiding his disgust. 'Ameeru, the entotsu! Out back. Again."

"Katajikenai,' Coletrane said. When the two of them moved away from the chefs' table, Patrick asked,

"Entotsu?"

"Chimney."

———

THERE WAS A COBBLESTONE AND GRAVEL road out back between buildings. A dumpster was by the back door of the restaurant, and about ten yards beyond that where the cobblestone patches ended and mostly gravel remained was a game board set up on crates with three men sitting around it. A fourth man was leaned against the wall watching the game of *Go* being played on the board. Two of the men were wearing aprons, the others just t-shirts and jeans, but all of them were smoking.

One of the seated men had a bald head and a barrel chest, gray patches of facial hair and a beer gut. He looked like he'd either been a marine or a convict in the past, and squinted as if he needed glasses but refused to wear them.

"You play sloppily, Shiro,' he said to the man seated across from him, a fella with a glass eye and a wispy thin goatee, 'Your mother ate sake engawa with you in the oven."

"Shut up and play, Ameeru,' Shiro replied with an impatient voice, 'your rhetoric smells of shit."

The man leaning against the wall, coughed, almost swallowing his cigarette, when he jovially said, "One of these days, you two are gonna fight."

"You mean one day Shiro will lose the other eye taking a beating on his feet as bad as he does at this table."

Everyone laughed. Even Shiro.

This is when Coletrane and Patrick walked up.

"Hey,' the fourth man said, nodding up at the two men approaching. "Look at these gaikoku hito."

"Ahh, I knew I smelled something,' Ameeru hissed.

"Sorry to interrupt,' Coletrane began, 'just wondering which of you is Tennen Ameeru."

"Hey Takibi,' Ameeru said to the man leaning on the wall, 'have you heard the one about the American who fled the kaiten-zushi that served pork, horrified that civilized people would eat his brothers?"

"That's funny,' Coletrane quipped. "Friend of mine likes jokes too. Chinese fella named Guang rui-Bai. Maybe you know him. Last I heard he was a fugitive wanted for Falun Gong crimes."

That got Ameeru's attention. He nodded for his friends to leave. When they did, Ameeru stood and lit another cigarette.

"What do you want, American?"

"I need a guide to the hanging coffins of Shikakami."

"Hanging coffins?" Ameeru was as surprised as he was amused. He regarded Patrick. "Your man here is a fan of Saturday morning cartoons."

"Is rui-Bai a fan as well?" Coletrane interjected.

"Your threats will only go so far, American. I cannot take you to a place that only exists in myth."

"You'd be surprised."

Ameeru was impatient, and, anyway, already didn't like this presumptuous American.

"Go back home to your country, gaijin. Or turn me in. I've got a shift to get back to."

He moved past them, bumping Coletrane's shoulder aggressively and giving Patrick a threatening glare.

"Two million for your guidance and a team," Coletrane offered to his back. This got Ameeru's attention again.

"What?"

"You can quit this dive and open your own kaiten-zushi."

"If you know Guang rui-Bai,' Ameeru threw open his arms, shrugged, 'then you know he isn't a cook by choice."

"Do whatever you want with the money then. Three million. For you alone. Tell your team I'm paying sixty grand a head."

Ameeru squinted while considering it, but this was a front. No way he would turn down that kind of money. He was, after all, a fugitive hiding in Japan under a pseudonym.

———

SPOONE FISHED A BOX OF NEWPORT cigarettes out of his suitcase, but before he could shake one loose, Elrone, who was looking over photos of Coletrane and Patrick that he had spread out on one of the beds, said, "Uh uh, broham. Not inside."

"What? Come on,' Spoone protested. "There's barely a balcony at this joint. I'll have to go down to the lobby, and all the way the fuck outside."

"First of all, there's plenty of space on the so-called *barely balcony* for your skinny ass to smoke. Second, Lyza's not having it."

Spoone looked to Lyza, who was seated at the chair in front of the only table inside their modest hotel room. She was reading a book that she doesn't look up from.

"Lyza's not having it, Spoone," she confirms.

"Yeah, well. Who made you the boss?"

"The contract," she replied matter-of-factly, repressing the urge to smile.

It was getting dark out, cold, and the three operatives, working in the employ of Landau Kier to spy on Coletrane Marx, were already annoyed with each other. They were in a two bed room despite there being three of them and one a woman, Spoone was always anxious for not being allowed to smoke inside, and Elrone was sour due to having lost the coin toss for the other bed.

Spoone, restless and undecided about that cigarette, was pacing. This annoyed Elrone.

"Look, either go have your smoke or make yourself useful."

"What's your problem?" Spoone spat.

"Your pacing, the whining. Take a number. How about, do the write up on Marx and his tag-along."

"Pfft. Write up. You make it sound like this job is anything but a gyp."

"The frequent flyer miles are worth it,' Lyza said, still not looking up from her book. 'Not to mention the paycheck."

"Well, that's about it. We're following around one rich dick for another rich dick. To what end?"

"Rich?.. Jeremiah Cross isn't the client, Spoone,' Elrone reminded. "Kier is. And who gives a shit about the whys? Let's just do the thing. Imagine it's like an FBI surveillance gig. Hours and hours of following and recording boring conversations, taking pictures and following some more."

"FBI?' Spoone screwed up his face, took his laptop out of the suitcase and sat on a chair. He propped the computer on the edge of the same bed Elrone had the picture display on, opened it. "Now it sounds like science fiction. Why would the FBI waste man hours on an unremarkable trust fund baby? Dude's no Fred Hampton."

"Hey, well, this guy Marx is a playboy, sure. But he's also got that reparations project. And the campaign to dismantle highways that were originally designed to displace families that couldn't suburbanize, nothing to sneeze at. He wants to do in Florida what they did in Boston and move the central arteries of I-95 underground. Any idea to bring rich and poor or black and white communities together is enough to disturb the American infrastructure. Who's to say Kier isn't looking for dirt on this guy to sell to the feds so they can shut him down?"

"What would Cross have to do with it then?" Spoone was now twirling one of the cigarettes between his fingers. "Sure, he's a capitalist but-"

"Again, Spoone,' Lyza finally put down her book, 'the client is Kier. I don't give a shit about some Silicon Valley industrialist and neither should you."

"Right right. Focus on the job. But so far this Marx guy is just fucking exotic women and, what, spelunking? He came all the way out here just to go climb some mountain?" He shook his head, dangling the unlit cigarette from his lips.

"Just do the write up, broham," Elrone put his attention back on the splay of photos. "Something is up with the dude. The devil is in the details. And by the way, speaking of which, didn't he kill his parents?"

Spoone lit up with memory.

"Shit, right! I read about that!"

"Doubtful,' Lyza added. 'A little boy kills his parents with a sword that was never found and then slices open his own chest to cover it up?"

"Stranger things have happened," Elrone argued.

"No,' Lyza persisted, in the tone of an irritated, sarcastic parent. "Stranger things have not happened, Elrone. And even if they did, that would be pretty fucking out there even for the world's standard of strange."

Something about the way Lyza cursed, it made Spoone laugh, loosen up, and sit back in his chair.

"Either way you slice it,' he said, 'there's some screws missing with our enigma of a subject. I mean, there's gotta be to wanna waste millions to tear down highways and call it altruism."

"Wait a minute,' Elrone says, noticing something in one of the pictures. "Look at this." He picks up the photo and brings it to Lyza. Curious, Spoone walks over to them.

"What's special about it?" Lyza asks.

"You don't see it? Marx is looking directly into the camera. You think he's aware of us following him?"

"Let me see?" Spoone takes the picture from him. "I shot this one. No way he spotted me."

"Yeah sure, but look at his expression. It's like he's almost smirking. Like he's subtly saying that he knows you are there."

"You calling me bad at my job?" Spoone hands the photo back to Elrone. "Because that's some bullshit, ya know? Neither one of you play the stealth game better than me. Hell, I could teach a class on it."

"Sure, make it about your ego."

"Fuck you, man!"

"Both of you relax,' Lyza mediates. 'Elrone, you're being paranoid. Spoone, you're full of shit. Only kind of class you're fit to teach is one on the art of consternation."

———

A GROUSE, THE PTARMIGAN, WORE plumage of white against the snowfields of Takayama. Aloft a rock ledge some two thousand meters above ground level, the young bird would be surprised, if sentient, to witness the group of seven humans hiking along the mountain range that would be the death of any non-flying creature that slipped. The path was narrow, the winds heavy, and the bamboo bridge they sought to reach still more than four hundred meters north of their position.

Tennen Ameeru and his team of four cragsmen were all armed, and outfitted in hiking gear and heavy coats for the cold. Patrick and Coletrane were likewise dressed for the affair, but unarmed (besides each having a knife, which was a standard hiking tool). Patrick, however, <u>did</u> have his camera, and he snapped shots to document the views whenever he safely could.

Before the journey, back at the hotel, he wrote:

> What the Epicurean Orphan, I'd decided to call him, had in common with despots, fuhrers, and pharaohs was the kind of charisma often associated with narcissists and sociopaths. While they used their talents to convince their subjects to perpetrate crimes against humanity, Marx used his to steer desperate men down paths of self-destruction. Here they were ready to stake their lives against risks unknown and for monies unseen, all predicated on the ever elusive promise of prosperity. The word *exploitation* comes to mind at once as the synecdoche of man's industrial history, the immortal sin of the Haves standing on the broken backs of the Have-nots to get a peek beyond the veil...

The group stopped to rest on stable terrain. Coltrane and Patrick were at the tail end.

"As far as I know," Ameeru said to Coletrane, "the cave entrance on this mountain is not far from here. But as for your quarry.."

"Find the cave, we find the quarry."

"You really believe it exists? The hanging coffins of Shikakami?"

Coletrane smiled at Ameeru, then said,

"Ernest Hemingway said that the best people possess the courage to take risks, and the capacity for sacrifice."

"You Americans,' Ameeru scoffed. "Your Hemingway also said that those same people wind up wounded and destroyed. I don't care to be the best anything. Paid will do."

"Then temper your concerns. You'll be that whether my query is real or not."

Coletrane then went over to where Patrick was fiddling with his camera, and looking quite troubled while at it.

"You look disquieted, Patrick," Coletrane said.

"Not so much disquieted but.., well, the last thing I expected was to be hiking in the mountains on this trip."

"Would you feel better if you had a gun?"

"Maybe. But really, I wonder why any of us need them."

One of Ameeru's team, a tall, stocky man of ambiguous heritage but with jet black hair and features that suggested an Ecuadorian descent, overheard them and approached. His name was Hugo, and on his hip was a wooden-cased Talibung sword with Mindanao carvings on the sheath sides. This made his background even more equivocal to the eye.

"Do not be misled by the tranquility of this mountain,' Hugo warned. 'The higher up we go, the further from civilization, the more dangerous the potential surprises."

"Can it, Hugo,' another of the men, Yuri, quipped, 'we were not hired to scare the Americans. Just preparation is all. Wise." He was trying to quit smoking so he hoarded nicotine gum, which was probably worse -spit out a worn piece and then popped another after his joke. There was a fighter's twitch to the way he moved, and burn scars on his ugly, grinning face from a long ago accident.

"I am not scared,' Patrick was annoyed. 'I've been in war zones with nothing but this camera."

"Right! Of course,' Yuri, unimpressed, was rather confident and jocular with the 3-9x40 scope Ruger carbine rifle hung over his shoulder, 'the war photographer John Rambo himself."

Hugo and the other men laughed. Patrick gave Yuri the finger. Coletrane shook his head. But Ameeru, he was unamused and impatient.

"All of you shut up,' he said. 'prepared or not, we can still freeze and become dinner for the Ussuri!"

"The Ussuri are vegetarian," Hugo said with a questioning inflection.

"Not all of the time," Ameeru snapped back.

"I've got dinner for the Ussuri right here,' Yuri replied, referencing his gun. Ameeru glared at him. This deflated the smug grin.

The men got moving again.

"Ussuri?" Patrick asked Coletrane, discreetly.

"I pegged you an outdoorsman, Patrick."

This drew a look of querulous fervency from Patrick, but no reply.

"Nothing to worry about," Coletrane shrugged. "Just a genus of bear the size and aggression of the Kodiak."

He walks ahead of Patrick, moving along with the group. Then Patrick sighed and said under his breath,

"Sure. Nothing to worry about."

———

THE PATH UP THE FINAL FOUR HUNDRED meters leading to the bridge was the most dangerous part of the ascent. Up until that point, most of the climb offered pastoral trails winding upward around rocky ridges that served as earthborn staircases. There were patches of inexplicable meadow lands, and stable exposures of bedrock on which maintaining an integrity of balance was relatively simple. But the closer they got to the summit, the greater the frosty winds and the more tapered the vertical cliffs. They had to use trekking poles and flip lines with swivel snap carabiners for safety when the walkway became too steep. At one point, with a bit of irony not lost on anyone, it was Yuri who tripped on a loose rock - dropping his Ruger carbine down the cliff.

"Fuck!" he yelled, watching helplessly as it tumbled over the peak, breaking on rock and getting smaller on its way down to oblivion. Patrick had to stifle a laugh.

When the team made it to the bridge, the winds had reached an intensity that required them to raise their voices to a decibel of screaming in order to communicate. The fog was so many layers thick that the bridge vanished beyond twenty feet, making it impossible to measure its distance or even gauge the dangers of crossing it.

"Would our chaperone like to take point?" one of the other men, Daichi, asked.

"I'm flattered,' Coletrane yelled. "But I'd have to deduct that from your fee."

"That is not our deal,' Ameeru stepped to Coletrane, 'The fee is final."

"The fee is what I say it is. Your men are being paid to guide, not play cute."

Daichi was the tallest among them, towering over Coletrane at 6'5. In his lifetime he had been a competing powerlifter and a bodyguard. Now, he was an out of work lumberman that needed this payday. But he had a chip on his shoulder and enough class hatred that Coletrane's haughtiness was enough to trigger him.

"We are far from the watchful eye of civilization, rich man," Daichi threatened. "Maybe it is you who should caution playing cute."

Coletrane smiled.

"Daichi, is it? Try me."

Daichi was motioning to do just that when Ameeru blocked his path, backhand slapping his chest while saying, "What Daichi means is that of course we will go first! He wouldn't journey this far just to compromise his pay." Then he gave Daichi a warning look, "Or any of ours."

The truth is that, underneath all of the bluster and posturing, all these clashes of testosterone, each of the men were yet subject to human nature and thus afraid of the unknown that lie beyond the steps of that rope rail bridge that disappeared into the mouth of a yawning fog. The wind made the path sway on its suspension ropes, the groaning sound of it suggesting instability and a precursor to peril. Only Coletrane's heartbeat wasn't excitedly beating in his chest, betraying his conviction the way the other men's all privately were. Ever since that night when he watched the demon kill his parents, ever since the memory of his mother's destroyed body branded itself in his mind, fear eluded him to the point where he envied those who could experience it fully. Normally. He envied those men on that precipice, even Patrick; Coletrane wanted to fight Daichi out of this unique sense of jealousy alone.

But nothing would come of it. The moment passed and the men, their silently agreed upon totem being a commitment to bravery, pushed on and engaged the bridge. Each of them moved along while firmly gripping the rope rails, careful to not lean their weight too much to either side so as not to capsize the platform. After about fifty yards and still no sign of the end, Ameeru began to worry about just how long this bridge was. But he didn't voice his concerns. Just after these thoughts arose however, the team was surprised by a large white-tailed eagle that swooped up out of the fog from below, sailing so close that its talon knocked off the hat that one of the men, JoJo, was wearing. He yelled and buckled in surprise. Luckily, Daichi, who was walking in front of him, did not panic and was able to reach back and grab hold the strap of his backpack to stabilize both him and the shaking bridge.

"JoJo, I got you!" he exclaimed.

But JoJo wasn't the only one that flinched. Even Hugo did, who was walking seven paces behind Jojo, drawing up his bolt action rifle and firing on reflex as he slipped and bumped into Coletrane behind him. The bullet grazed the seventh man, Hinata's, ear. He ducked and grabbed it.

"Goddamnit, Hugo!" he cried.

"Shit!" Hugo wailed.

"Everybody calm down!" Coletrane called.

"Hinata, are you-" Ameeru began, but his voice was swallowed by Patrick's, saying,

"Son of a bitch! Son of a- LOOK OUT!" Patrick warned, seeing peripherally before anyone else, as a family of twelve other white-tailed eagles came flying upward from random zigzagging directions from below and above, left and right, all swooping out the dense cloak of flog after themselves having been panicked by the echoing gunshot. Not only were the birds wild and menacing while unnerved, but they, all of them, were distinctively overlarge. So big that they could have been feather covered pterodactyls! Hugo threw his rifle strap over his shoulder and drew his Talibung instead, started swinging it to keep the frantically swooping birds at bay.

"THOSE THINGS ARE WAY TOO FUCKING BIG!" Yuri yelled, regretting even more now that he dropped his Ruger.

"Keep moving!" Ameeru commanded. "Quickly! Come on!"

The urgency presented by the giant nerve-rattled birds washed away any remaining apprehension the men had for the unclear vistas ahead. Everyone rushed forward on Ameeru's call, eager to get across to the other side of the bridge -wherever it was, wherever it led. One by one, a man was swallowed by the fog as the one following several yards behind fled into that same anonymous void. Until it was Patrick's turn, and one of the largest of the birds swept over and low -hovering in his path with its wide wings spread, its large talons taut, its beak ajar and squawking loudly. The great bird looked from Patrick's vantage point to be like a rising phoenix, grave in its intent and stupefied, magnetized, by an insurmountable need to attack him! Patrick took out his hiking knife, was ready to fight with whatever reflexes of his old, unused military training he'd retained over the otherwise dull years of the life that was at that moment flashing before his eyes. But just as the bird was about to jet towards him, BOOM! -went the firecracker sound of another gunshot! The bullet destroyed the bird's throat, and the velocity of it sent the body falling down into the abyss.

It was Hinata, blood on his face from the accidental shot to his ear, that took the bird out with a silver revolver.

"Come on, you idiot!," he said, snapping Patrick out of his moment of catatonic shock. "Come on!"

On the other side of the bridge was a grass-barren clearing of sandstone riddled with fissures the result of denudation. This spread for a radius of thirty yards, beyond which was the opening of a cave in the shoulder of the mountain. It was colder here, and all the hyperventilating men could see their breath as it added to the concretion of fog.

"I took you for an outdoorsman,' Coletrane said to Patrick, 'but not a birdman."

"I'm glad you're amused,' he replied, leaning his hands on his knees while catching his breath.

"I'm not amused. Just trying to lighten you up. You ok?"

"I'm fine."

Ameeru's voice turned them around.

"This is your fabled cave then, Mr. Marx?" he said, in a questioning tone that yet seemed a declaration.

Coletrane stepped closer to examine it.

There seemed to be nothing out of the ordinary about the cave, at first glance. But then upon closer inspection, Coletrane saw three identical and evenly situated petroglyphs carved into the crust of the entranceway -one on either side, the third at the very top and center. He recognized them at once. It was the same design on his arm.

"Indeed, it is," Coletrane confirmed. The relief in him was matched only by his foreboding. This conflict of emotions, it was the closest he'd ever been to experiencing fear since the night his parents died.

"Strange," the big man Daichi observed. "This opening is like... like a talus. But look above. The surface shows no clue of crags. Neither does the history of this mountain."

Patrick recognized the glyph too but it registered in his mind as an experience of déjà vu. Suddenly he was assailed by a jarring vision; *at first, a voice, Ittei's, saying, "What is it, Yoriko?" And then the loud echoing crash of blades colliding! A red eyed, growling tribal child wraith, lean but supernaturally muscular, quill and tattoo riddled, soaked in tar and brandishing a broad sword made of bone, holding that bone sword against the sharp nihonto blade of Ittei's naginata. Yoriko leapt out of the darkness, biting down on the wraith's arm! But this monster in a child's body, so powerful and violent, slings her off. She slams against the cave wall, and Ittei uses this moment to shift the angle of his nihonto, slipping the wraith's broad sword and then cutting a gash in its neck. Then a yell is heard. It is Kojiro, now him dashing out of the darkness, Hatsukoi in hand, rushing in with an overhead strike but-*

The image vanishes and Patrick is brought back into reality, dropping to one knee and shaking off the wooziness of the head trip.

"No time for rest, Rambo," Yuri said. Smiling. Patrick ignored him. Coletrane helped him back to his feet. There was a knowing look between them, but nothing said.

The group entered the cave with caution. Coletrane insisted this time that he led the way, breaching the darkness with a flashlight with Ameeru and Daichi at his left and right flank. They had rifles trained on the blackened unknown. Jojo had two Smith and Wesson handguns both outfitted with an LED strobe; he loaned one to Yuri. Patrick was between Jojo and Yuri, effectively in the center of the group as he was walking directly behind Coletrane. Patrick still didn't have a gun, but he was brandishing a trekking pole. Hugo was at the rear, his hand firmly grasping the 9mm CZ 75 that was still in its chest bound case.

The passageway was dry and humid, at certain points along the way getting so narrow that only one man could pass at a time. Those tight spaces became worrisome after a while, getting tighter and tighter, until the path opened up again to allow them space to spread out and breathe. There was movement on the walls from critters going in and out of fissures and glimmering mineral deposits peppered along the jagged surface, and sharp stalactites reaching down from the cave ceiling casting shadows that looked like the mouths of beasts or the reaching arms of phantoms. Eventually they passed through an area where there was a descend in the ground. They had to pass under calcite flowstones and angular patches of speleothem around a U-like curving path.

"You hear that?" Daichi asked no one in particular, referring to the sound of flowing water. "There's a grotto up ahead."

And surely there was, not two hundred yards at the tail of the curving path. There was moisture underfoot as gravel became mud, and then swampy water for them to pass through after coming out of the path.

The foyer to this opening was like a lava tube, and out into the swamp there was an uneven walkway littered with high reaching stalagmites. The ever flowing waters fell into a sinkhole leading into what appeared to be a bottomless chasm, and the velocity of the incredibly cold water was such that the men had to be careful when passing through it so as not to be pulled into the flushing doline.

"Karsts in this region," Daichi was becoming more and more incredulous, "it makes as little sense as the talus opening outside."

"Where the hell does it lead?" Yuri asked, frustrated by the effort it was taking to pass through the swamp.

"Better not find out," Hugo warned.

"This place does not appear to have occurred naturally," Daichi concluded.

"It didn't," Coletrane knew.

"How do you know that?" JoJo asked.

"Good question," said Ameeru.

"Just keep moving," Coletrane said, unwilling to answer these questions. He moved ahead to make this clear.

At this point they passed under a formation of hollow cylindrical tubes of mineral rock just before the opening of three tunnels, where the water stopped and cold air from inside was pushing against them -as if to say, *Do not pass this point.*

Patrick sighed, "Which way?"

"If only we had a map," Hugo lamented.

"Isn't that Daichi's role," Yuri offered, "the cave expert?"

"Shut your trap, Yuri," Daichi warned.

"We don't need a map," Coletrane declared. He stepped closer to the tunnels and looked at them, left to right and back again. A memory of his childhood came over him, of that night when he and Marcus were unknowingly fashioning the mythology of Kojiro, the foundation that would become this curious reality. It was by osmosis that he said,

"We'll take the far right path. Southwest."

"How are you so sure?" Ameeru wanted to know. He was beyond the incredulousness of Daichi. Ameeru had reached the degree of suspicious, bordering on violence. "If you have been here before,' he continued, 'why did you need a guide?"

"I have not been here before," Coletrane announced. "I just... know."

"Too esoteric for my tastes, Marx," Ameeru replied.

"How about for your wallet? Let's go."

Coletrane's instincts proved correct. The tunnel, which was not far, took them to a deep, calcareous catacomb with sepulchers dug high in the surface of the walls. In those sepulchers, which were evenly spaced out in a row that went all the way around, were stone sarcophaguses each bearing hieroglyphic markings; These were the hanging coffins of Shikakami.

There was a four foot ledge that everyone had to jump down from to reach the floor of the domain, and all across the surface of that floor were maze-like arrangements of patterns that bore resemblance to a network of crop circles. Three points of this elaborate work converged on a circle in the center of the floor, inside of which stood three stone statues -of powerfully muscle bound humanoid gargoyles, each wearing loincloth. They were seven feet tall in stature, had the bodies of men, and heads of bison with curved horns and looped nose rings. The two on the left and right were standing tall, them both holding a golden sheathed ōdachi sword turned downward like a guard at post. The one in the center was kneeling, holding a rectangular case in his outstretched arms as if humbly presenting it to a lord.

Coletrane's eyes zeroed in on that case. A hunger and excitement grew in him, but he held it at bay.

"I stand corrected, Mr. Marx," Ameeru said, taking in the surroundings through eyes aglow with awe. Sulfate spikes of gypsum were jutting out of random places on the cave walls and ceiling, presenting the appearance of an array of crystals casting reflective lights in the dark, yawning chasm of rock.

Patrick, of course, took pictures. But not before taking it all in with his own eyes. What stood out to him were those reflective gypsum, as well as the statues, which were mysterious, in his mind, to the point of inexplicability. So much power suggested in the vascular arms holding those ōdachi, he thought, and he noticed also, suddenly, that the statues were wearing bracelets and tribal gemstone chokers with a dragon image emblazoned on the center stone.

"Strange," Patrick said.

"What?" Coletrane wanted to know.

"Look at the jewelry on those statues. How old did you say this tomb was?"

"I didn't."

"But you know. Right?"

"Of course. Everything you see here was manifest sometime between 1300 and 1600 CE."

"Manifest," Daichi repeated, suspicion in his tone, "don't you mean built, constructed? You say *manifest* as if it were not crafted by human hands."

"Astute of you," Coletrane replied, with no irony. This made Yuri shrug and grunt with amusement.

Patrick continued, "1600 CE..., well, why do the trimmings on these statues, the jewelry, why does it all appear so ..modern?"

"You already know the answer, Patrick. We talked about it on the plane."

That clue triggered a thought, but Patrick didn't believe it even when releasing it on the air,

"Judas Ulehla?"

"Judas Ulehla," Coletrane confirmed.

"Who?" that was Ameeru.

Yuri, impatient, chimed in, "Hey, Marx. Why don't we get whatever it is we came here for, eh?"

"Good idea," said Hugo, his attention split between the eerie limestone speleothems above, the patterns under his feet, and the hanging coffins themselves. "This place is giving me the creeps."

Jojo was using the LED strobe of his handgun to examine the cave walls, anxious and doing something to occupy himself and distract from this feeling. Then it was curiosity that gripped him as the strobe came to more series of patterns, hieroglyphic markings that piqued his interest for their familiarity. When he was younger, he studied the artform of hieroglyphic storytelling -particularly the Egyptian legends passed down through generations. As he walked along examining more of the developing markings, he noticed some similarity to the story of Sinuhe, a nobleman who fled Egypt upon learning of the death of Pharaoh Amenemhat I.

Only, the story that Jojo followed along with his light, was not of Sinuhe. Rather, it was of a figure he had not heard of, and whose name he could not translate; **Kojiro**. Some of the glyphic imagery chronicled the journey of Kojiro and the Live Crew thus far, the encounter with Takauji and the Ashigaru, with the Buffalo Lords, Xiao Xiao Chen, the feral tribal child covered in tar... There were images of the Inca Tan'Mo, characterized as a Trickster-like archetype. There was a contrasting depiction of Kojiro's rival, who Jubei referred to as his "friend", **Katsurou the Prometheus**. And after to Katsurou were **The Hamarufa**; Centaur-like creatures who were horses below the torso, with humanoid upper bodies and the head of deer. They had long, intimidating antlers, and carried spears, swords, daggers.

Like Sinuhe, Kojiro was depicted as passing from a place of familiarity through the realms of these many dangers and wonders.

Coletrane looked over at what Jojo was doing. He raised his flashlight to see what Jojo was seeing. And unlike Jojo, he could fully read the language.

"What have you found there, Jojo?" Ameeru asked, whose attention followed Coletrane's.

Jojo, so engrossed in trying to decipher what he was reading, did not immediately answer.

"Hey,' Hugo called, "Jojo!"

"I can't read it all,' he finally replied, eyes still on the wall, squinting in the LED light, "but it reminds me of the ostracon I studied in school. Mr. Marx, what do you know of this? This warrior who fled... something. Who.... Wait..."

"It doesn't say *fled*," Coletrane corrected, walking closer to the wall, reading further.

"Yeah, I noticed. I-"

"Let's cut to the chase, Marx," Ameeru said, a reluctant alliance in sentiment with the impatient Yuri, "You hired me to gather this team, bring you out into the mountains and find this cave. We're here now. But what for? A paleontology lesson?"

Coletrane turned to him. He didn't say so, but he liked Ameeru's use of the word, *paleontology*.

"You are standing right by it," Coletrane said, nodding in gesture at the statues to Ameeru's left. He walked over while continuing, "A man once lived whose exploits however prodigious came to pass just under the surface of our comparatively prosaic history. Another timeline if you will, the stuff of myth as we know them, bleeding into our timeline and retroactively writing himself and his world into our recorded history. Like looking at yourself in an imperfect mirror."

"What?" Ameeru replied in a way that would have been comical if not for the seriousness in Coletrane's continued delivery.

"His name was, is, Kojiro ko-Mitsu," He glanced at Patrick when saying the name. "A samurai, from a magical world that was washed away when it collided with ours, not unlike the catastrophic event of sixty-six million years ago when an asteroid brought the 180 million year reign of the dinosaurs to an end. What's left of Kojiro's world are fossils, phantoms, objects mixed in with things relevant to our history and incorrectly associated with it. I found his O-yoroi armor at an auction in Giza, attributed to Sasaki Kojiro, the great warrior from our time who dueled Miyamoto Musashi. I found his onyx short sword *Jun* in London, attributed to the Sengoku period and said to have been owned by The Great Unifier himself, Toyotomi Hideyoshi. But these… very expensive *facts* were both wrong. And here…,"

Coletrane said with a note of vivacity, having walked past Ameeru, now standing in front of the kneeling gargoyle. "…here is *Hatsukoi*, his most beloved katana, his closest confidant."

The rest of the men, even Patrick, they all looked at the stone statue, the stone case that it was holding, all a unified piece of masonry expertly crafted -but stone, nonetheless.

The men regarded each other uncomfortably, Hugo squinted, Daichi grunted, Jojo sighed.

"I see a lump of stone, Marx," Ameeru as much annoyed as he was amused. "Not a katana. Fine craftsmanship but… still."

Coletrane didn't take his eyes off of the gargoyle's presented case, he didn't look at Ameeru when saying, intensely, "You would think so."

He then reached out for the case...

Back in Florida, on the grounds of the Marx Estate, Poole was out doing tai chi forms under light of a gray blue bourgeoning morning. In this midst of the form called Grasping the Peacock's Tail is when he saw it, a throbbing light coming from the window of the trophy room.

He immediately ran inside, up the stairs, down the hall, and then into the door of the room. The ancient book was open and shaking on its perch.

"Thelonious," he said to himself but out loud -worried.

... In the cave, as Coletrane was reaching for the case, Patrick's photographer eye was noticing unexamined aspects of the cave and its many inscrutable affectations: the hieroglyphic renderings amid the walls' glimmering dolostones, the hanging coffins tucked between speleothem cages, the crop circle patterns on the floor with three points intersecting at where the statues were. He noticed a fourth point at the end of the maze that the other three points branched from. Daichi was standing there. And Patrick noticed in the darkness above that there was a monolith of sedimentary rock not connected to the walls or ceiling, but suspended in midair as if magically paused in time.

At this moment, Coletrane's hand now touched the stone case. And in response to his touch, the case turned from stone to polished cherrywood before all the men's unbelieving eyes. And now Coletrane was able to open it and find a sheathed katana adorned in purple silk, resting in the center of the red felt interior. **The manuki grip decorated with golden ito hilt wrap with laces of red, her tsuba also golden with dragon designs etched in it, red and golden sageo cord near the mouth of an onyx black scabbard, and inside of that scabbard was a solid gold blade, impossibly strong, impossibly sharp, Hatsukoi was beautiful**. But now with the sword and its case animated, so too became the suspended monolith. Patrick saw it shift a bit, before he called,

"Daichi, move!" but it was already too late. The deadly bedrock fell from its impossible perch right onto Daichi as he looked up at it, crushing him like a bug! All the men reacted, Coletrane spun around. No one knew what else to do but to draw their weapons and look around for other sudden threats to besiege them. In the commotion, everyone was too gripped by shock and adrenaline to notice that Daichi's blood was now filling the depressed spaces of the crop circle maze in the floor, rushing like river water in a dam towards the end points that went under the feet of the stone statues. When blood connected to all three, the eyes of all three gargoyles came open, filled with lambent red.

From out of the dark crevices of the cave came the echoing sound of millions of flapping wings, herald to the swarms of bats that followed -quickly filling the room.

"Fuck!" Yuri screamed.

"What the hell is happening?!" Hugo yelled, swinging his talibung at the bats as they circled him. It didn't take long for the men to realize that those bats were flesh eaters, as Jojo and Hinata found out in the worst way. Jojo was engulfed too fast to retaliate, his gun proving useless as they ate through his clothes and all the flesh off his bones in less time than it took to pull a trigger twice. Hinata tried to help him, but the wound already on his face attracted the blood thirsty chirotera; they took off his head before he could even scream.

Hugo's talibung proved a better weapon in the lethal storm, spinning, slashing, and twirling the blade like a cyclone in a busy theater of death. Coletrane dropped to a knee, the energy emanating from Hatsukoi was keeping the bats at bay. But there were so many of them that he could barely see the men or even Patrick in the commotion. He did however see those red eyes of the now animated gargoyles, who thawed from their prison of rock, the stone however remaining on their flesh like armor. All the rock that broke off of them were at the joints, throat, and torse for bending, exposing pink and fleshy sinews of muscle. The two odachi bearers stood and were immediately attracted to the gunfire. Ameeru got one last look at Coletrane, regret for taking this trip registering in eyes. His final words were "Damn you, Marx!", before he was beheaded by one of the giants' ancient sword.

The other one attacked Yuri, who was lucky enough for a time to have some distance on him. He unloaded an entire clip on the beast, each bullet ricocheting off the impenetrable stone armor, before the fabled inhuman warrior charged at him, slashing the giant sword down at the man, who dove and rolled out of the way -surviving by a hair.

When Yuri stood, one of the bats flew into his face and plucked out an eye. He yelled and grasped at the gushing wound. The odachi bearer turned to him and lifted the blade, angling to slice him in half in this moment of excruciation. But then Patrick came rushing in, gripped by an unknown, phantom sense of courage, not to mention inexplicable skill with the trekking pole! He tapped into an unconscious knowledge that told him to aim his strikes at the exposed sinews at the joints, and so he did; he wielded the pole like an improvised jo staff, using the pointed end to slash at the beast's knee and the elbow hinge joints. It didn't down the beast, but it did make for a painful distraction.

The third of the Buffalo Lords came to life, it was looking directly at Coletrane, who returned his stare while drawing the golden sword Hatsukoi from her sheath. Suddenly, a great deal of energy and confidence surged through Coletrane as he stood to his feet. He felt within him, or at least nearby, the presence of Kojiro. And so too did the Buffalo, who Coletrane now recognized as the volatile Musuko.

"Ahh,' he spoke, "the Sakura reborn, to fail once again."

This made Coletrane angry, he swung Hatsukoi at Musuko's face. Musuko stood and chucked backwards two steps. He reached for his face to find a gash in the stone along his cheek, Hatsukoi proving the only weapon so far strong enough to cut through the armor.

Musuko turned his face back to Coletrane, a mixture of rage, surprise, and elation besieging him.

"Today you experience death again, Kojiro!"

"Not by your hand," a voice from behind him called, cutting through all the noise of countless flapping wings. Musuko turned in the opposite direction, seeing a blackened silhouette come strutting out of the shadows, panther-like in movement.

Barely perceptible in the heavily compromised lighting, but also very obviously the spirit of Kojiro -brandishing the ghost of Hatsukoi and dragging her blade tip in the dust.

In Musuko's distraction, Coletrane ran towards him, a battle cry erupting from his throat, and leapt into a flying side kick that connected to the goliath's chest and sent him falling backwards. Coletrane stood then in a low *Seigan No Kamae* stance, the handle held firmly by both hands and Hatsukoi's blade tip pointing at the savage opponent.

Patrick had his hands full with the Buffalo that turned its attention on him after the attack with the trekking pole. He was still brandishing it like a jo staff, edging backwards to maintain a relatively safe distance from the long reaching odachi.

In an effort of bravado, Yuri, though blinded in an eye, attempted to attack the Buffalo with a hunting knife while it was distracted by Patrick. But reflexively, it's upper torso turned all the way around and sliced Yuri's body in half at an angle with the odachi without even losing momentum on the turn, grabbed Yuri by the head with his free hand, and completed the 360 turn to where he was now facing Patrick again. The Buffalo held up Yuri's upper body, held from the back of the head like a basketball player palming the ball, taunting Patrick with a look at his own fate. Yuri, still alive, his guts and blood dripping on the floor, looked at Patrick through dying eyes subdued entirely by shock. Those eyes then began to fill with blood as the Buffalo tightened his grip, until he crushed Yuri's head like a melon and then dropped the body like a bag of useless weight. Piranha bats attacked the carcass at his feet. The Buffalo smiled at Patrick's fear and hopelessness.

In Orlando, Poole felt an invisible force of wind pushing him back as he moved towards the shaking book. When he touched it, a painful jolt of static electricity made him pull back the hand. He could but watch blood fill the pages with passage after passage, until on one page a drawing was being formed. On it, there were two mirror images of a samurai warrior cast adjacent and facing one another. Just then, the energy filling the room made the bulbs in the room's ceiling lights burst.

In the cave, Hugo was still holding his own against the bats, who were now clearing to make way for the third Buffalo to engage him. Though frightened by the sight of it, Hugo still bravely lifted the talibung. He also noticed the exposed muscle joints, figuring correctly to focus on them. The Buffalo was big and menacing, but Hugo was fast and determined. He sidestepped two attempts on his life, rushing inside and managing to stab the Buffalo just under the right bicep. He lost hold of the weapon as the monster recoiled however, and was grabbed at the shoulder by its other hand. The Buffalo was so strong that it crushed Hugo's rotator cuff as it tightened its hand and lifted him up. The man's scream filled the entire arena, echoing throughout the cave and down its halls!

With his wounded hand, the beast was still strong enough to grasp Hugo's leg and hold him upright. He then pulled and broke Hugo in two like a wished upon T-bone, tossing his parts aside as if they were nothing. He then turned his attention to Patrick and joined the other Buffalo in approaching him.

Patrick, alone with the trekking pole, just watched a superior fighter in Hugo get broken apart by only one of the Buffalo.

Now there were two drawing near him. He was certain that he was about to die. While edging backwards, he tripped and fell on his backside -dropping the pole.

Musuko drew two masakari axes from his belt and engaged Coletrane, but the rich man was deft with the sword and held his own, trading blow for blow with the loud clashing blades. Still, Musuko's strength proved overwhelming, and after a few moves was able to knock Coletrane off his feet at the result of a parry.

The two odachi wielding Buffalo stalked the crawling Patrick, taking their time as their query had nowhere to run. But to their surprise, Patrick climbed to his feet and lifted the trekking pole. Though his hands were shaking, it was a show of true courage that he would stand tall and proceed against the two faces of death. But this offended them, so they charged.

They were intercepted however by white streaks dashing out of the surrounding darkness from several random points. It was unclear what the fast moving creatures were until one of them latched onto one of the Buffalo's arm, and he tried futilely to shake free of the powerful ghost wolf's jaws. Another grabbed onto his throat and another his leg. Four attacked the other one, taking turns leaping on and biting through the stone of his back, torso, snout. A fifth lunged at him and tore one of its horns clean off! Soon both of them were overwhelmed by too many wolves flitting in and out of time and space to count. The leader of the pack tore out the throat of the Buffalo closest to Patrick, and when its body fell with a loud thud, the wolf turned her attention to the man that she saved.

Patrick, looking upon her, experienced a memory that was not his own; *Ittei feeding berries to his wolf friends in the forest, and then him sitting in the moonlight amid them, and then them helping him and the Live Crew as they were set upon by the tar bodied aborigines.*

"Yor... Yoriko?" he whispered, unsure of how he even knew the name. But it instantly sounded familiar to him after saying it.

The Buffalo Lord still standing, wounded but now livid and piqued, he shakes off the wolves, snatches one still gripped to his back and throws it. That wolf explodes in a burst of smoke against the wall. And the re-animated stone armored Buffalo Lord stepped over his fallen comrade (right on top of Yoriko, who also diffuses like a disturbed smoke cloud) and comes down with a heavy overhead strike at Patrick with his odachi. But Patrick dives out of the way of the strike, that connects with the floor so hard that everything rumbles and a spiderweb of cracks open up on the floor. Patrick runs behind the Buffalo, who turns to follow.

Musuko stalks on the downed Coletrane with a smirk in his gait and his two masakari held open in a gesture of taunting disdain.

"At last, the Sakura returns to self-spite,' he sang, 'having failed yet another team of squishy mortals foolish enough to believe the lore of his might."

Coletrane was winded, those few blows against the incredibly strong cave guardian having left him near completely spent. But the taunting gave him a second wind. Still, he couldn't yet climb to his feet.

But behind Musuko came the vitalized shadow of the Deadly Sakura himself, not amused at all by the insult.

He dashed forward and sliced through the stone armor of Musuko's back with a yoko giri side cut, then in front of him turns to follow up with an upward slash across the chest plate. The force sent Musuko backwards six tumbling steps.

While the jeering behemoth was regaining his footing, the ghost of Kojiro looked down into Coletrane's eyes. Now up close, Coletrane could see the figure eight pupil split and became hypnotized by them. This image that he feared since childhood, this phantom inexorable from the memory of his parents' brutal death, this manifestation of his guilt, was now standing there with a hand outstretched to him.

Without having to think, Coletrane grasped it and Kojiro hoisted him up. In the momentum of the pull, the two merged into each other. Kojiro's tenebrous body absorbed into Coletrane's, and the shadowy sword the spirit held coalesced with the shiny golden blade of Hatsukoi.

Coletrane could feel all their memories coming together, he could feel an explosion of power within his chest, he could feel two hearts becoming one. And then, in the moment between moments, a suspended millisecond –

> **-He saw before him a crackling fire, through eyes that belonged to Kojiro as a ten year old child. Beneath the violet dim of night, the young boy was sitting on side of the small fire and looking at the looming figure on the other side of it. This figure smiled at him, a jovial though serious and worldly presence much larger than any the boy would know for the duration of his life; his father, Akimitsu.**

The man wore a purple kimono and hoari coat over shoulders built for woodsmanship, a black obi belt and hakama pants. His jet black hair was fixed in a chonmage top knot, and the smile on his face was warmer than the fire.

"You could almost taste the sweet smell of igusa upon approach,' Akimitsu said, closing his eyes to the nostalgia. "And from a distance, that is all you think you are seeing; a bustling field of tall grass. But then as you get closer you see them."

"The swords, father?" the precocious young boy asked, excitedly trying to capture in his mind the image of what his father was describing.

"Yes. The Valley of Swords. And then beyond it, the Tabernacle."

"And you have been there? For real?"

Akimitsu hesitated to answer, but the smile never left his face.

"Father?", little Kojiro impatiently insisted.

"Yes,' Akimitsu finally said. "I have. But you must never go there yourself."

"Why?"

Leaning in towards his son, Akimitsu whispered,

"Because, little dragon, there are consequences."

Coletrane, now with Kojiro within him, returned to the present on a blink.

This was just as Musuko was coming down on him with a double axe strike that seemed, to Coletrane, to be moving in slow motion. He grinned, curving his brow. Then he sidestepped, parried, and countered with a move so deft that both Musuko's wrists gave in to the business end of Hatsukoi's power. Musuko screamed as he watched his severed hands fall to the ground.

Coletrane could see the other Buffalo out of his periphery just as it was about to corner Patrick. In a quick move, he threw Hatsukoi like a shuriken. She flew across the clearing like a spear, and lodged into the Buffalo's throat -going all the way through to the hull. Both its arms went limp, it fell to its knees and the odachi clacked down on the ground next to where Patrick stood.

Then Coletrane drew Hatsukoi back to him as if the sword were an extension of his arm held to an invisible magnetic energy, going back along the same path and shattering the Buffalo's head, then stopping right into the grip of Coletrane's hands in time for him to leap and spin, now taking off Musuko's head with a cyclone strike.

By the time Coletrane landed on his feet, Patrick realized that he wasn't dead, the remaining bats all turned to airborne dust, and all three of the Buffalo Lords turned back into statues now broken and scattered on the floor.

Coletrane took one look at Patrick, grinned slightly, and then passed out.

BOOK II:
ETERNAL RETURN OF THE SAME

克

" didn't want those men to die, Patrick.
I... I didn't count on, or expect it. You know that... Right?"
"I don't know what I know anymore. About anything."

克

AT THE LAC LA BICHE FOREST AREA, in Albert, Canada, the wildfire front pressed on over several miles wide with no indication of relent, a sea of black smoke uplifting from the trees and reaching for the clouds. It was a Saturday morning that found the air and trees seared in waves of thermal radiation, all small animals and vegetation succumbing to the fire whose origin would always be a mystery, it was through this that Clymene walked barefoot over scorched earth and sizzling grass. The blistering humidity cast the untouchable robes on his body to wave backwards as if he were passing through a windy, side-sweeping rain -yet, his skin and body temperature remained unaffected. He held in mind the real-time unravelment of a series of events that he needed to share with the other Interstices, a series, in fact, that was represented in the seemingly random, inexplainable pyrolysis of wood. Clymene's seventeen inch long beard was unbraided and adrift, red and black flames danced madly on the surface of his bald head, as his andradite eyes were looking many miles beyond the trees that were burning and coming down around him and over to what was happening at the place where Zhrontese also walked.

A tropical cyclone had erupted without warning in the Atlantic seas within seven miles of the Cape Verde islands, it became a hurricane in a matter of hours and peaked as a category five while coming into Lake Okeechobee, Florida. 146 miles per hour winds were devastating the empty streets, knocking down power lines, ravaging homes and any other real-estate unlucky to be in its path. Cars were being shaken, dragged and, some, flipped. Yards, gardens, and shrubbery patterns were coming undone as gulfs of debris swept over the land.

Zhrontese was walking through a concrete jungle of parking lots in a nine thousand square foot strip mall, that jungle's *wildlife* being pieces of neighboring buildings, hordes of broken glass, large rocks lifted and thrown, and mini jagged whirlwinds of objects collected in the commanding succession of squalls. She didn't have to step aside left or right to avoid any of the large objects tumbling towards her since anything that came into contact with Zhrontese as she walked towards the eye of the hurricane would break off of her like rain drops splashing against a solid surface.

Her hair was a three foot ripple of kaleidoscopic colors flowing against the push of ferocious winds. The swirling storms of gold and red dust that made up her eyes beamed like floodlights cutting a path in disarray, but what she saw was much more than a natural disaster happening all around her. She saw intuitively through Manthis' ebony eyes, hundreds of miles away, she saw what he was seeing.

In Bozeman, Montana, the acoustic effects of the vehement thunder were being suppressed by the many-mile scope of a spontaneous extratropical typhoon. Graupel and hail deposits scattered the land like gunfire, and the unwieldy rain quickly morphed into a killer snowstorm. Cold air masses moving through it picked up water vapor from the lakes, producing devastating waves of bellicose snow over the city facing the Rocky Mountains. Manthis was walking down one of that mountain's highest peaks, watching the storm attack on the city from an eagle nest's vantage point. Behind him was a curtain of royalty, the swathes of his robe like a billowing cape. He had a story on his mind that he needed to share with his equals, and he intuited as much back to Zhrontese in Okeechobee, who in turn intuited the same to Clymene in Alberta.

Three natural disasters, three freak occurrences happening simultaneously, as the Three Interstices each standing amid one of these events were having a meeting telepathically. The purpose of which being to combine as one mind and share separate but connected chains of events that were all relevant towards a single question: **Should they risk complete chaos and intervene in the affairs of people**?

Zhrontese stopped walking in the middle of an eight lane highway, her chin tilted to the sky as the hurricane rippled through, stripping buildings, powerlines, and tree groupings. She watched the roof of a small office collapse in on itself, a great oak fall on top of another office just across the street, cars sliding to the railings of a three level parking platform nearby and an uprooted public mailbox flying around -crashing out windows. The winds were so strong that entire palm trees were yanked out of the ground and thrown about as spinning projectiles, street lights bent and contorted, a broken-out fire hydrant zipping around on the air in a consistency of circular patterns. There was so much chaos that there was nearly no visibility of it to the naked eye, just a dusty, rain filled, smog of extreme opacity. But Zhrontese could see and think clearly as she intuited her message to the others.

"Four point five billion years," she began, her voice echoing across the wavelength of the three's combined intuitive frequency, "before the dawn of sentience on this planet, six million before the opening of the first human eyes, two hundred thousand of consciousness at this stage of the evolutionary trajectory, and just over six thousand years of modern, industrial civilizations, the bridging of intuition between the practical and the creative arrives in cataclysmic form prophesied in some way or the other in every human text that has ventured a guess at the future, every spiritual doctrine laying claim to the unknown, and every work of philosophy that has spoken metaphorically of towers of Babel and the consequences of constructing them."

"How many will die?" Clymene asked, already knowing the answer.

"Does it matter?" Manthis offered, "any number of people who perish will be meaningless in the grand scheme of the cosmos. People, in fact, are only as *meaningful* as their sentient minds suppose them to be."

"And yet," Zhrontese countered, "it is that same sentience that casts their very existence, history and ecology into a circumstance of extinctual risk. Don't speak or think of it as a trivial thing."

Manthis, thinking of it, could not help but agree. He didn't nod or confirm his agreement with the words. Instead, after a single beat, he said,

"Well. Indeed then, I have a story."

"So do I," Clymene added.

Zhrontese looked over her right shoulder, seeing a van tumbling down the street. Soon it was airborne, and after a few flips, it crashed through a row of parking meters and into the side of a corporate office -an explosion of glass and mortar. The slanting sea of rain sent large and small chunks of hail into everything in its path like a wall of arrows' end points. Zhrontese breathed a sigh,

"We all have a regrettable story to share."

"Should I then begin," Manthis said, "bearing the tale of the Sakura himself having finally merged with the spirit of his proprietor?"

"This Marx fellow is no proprietor," spat Clymene, his sensibilities disturbed by the notion, "just another expression of Kojiro, called "the Deadly Sakura" by the people who knew him."

"Perhaps,' Manthis argued. "But he or they, the illusion between them is that they are separate entities, separate consciousnesses, now coalesced as one -on a heroic journey, each his own, to achieve something specific that would perhaps answer the question of their life's meaning. Even Patrick's awakening to being the reflection of the philosopher Ittei, a revelation charged with as much ambiguity as intrigue, it is all relevant to the same enduring illusion that has brought the entirety of humankind to its current state of disrepair. And this herald of catastrophic conditions, it is represented in the carnage of the Marx/Kojiro awakening event, and will lead to more of it. As surely as I am now standing in the belly of a snowstorm."

"Defenders of subjective justice are every bit as responsible for their enemies as their enemies them," Clymene said, now looking at a handful of fire that he scooped up off of the ground. "Defenders and their adversaries, humans with their games of tug of war. All futile palliatives to ease the pains of the unknown. Like a girl named Qadr Fakhoury. She is on the path to an awakening of her own, as her ancillary involvement with the forming cataclysm becomes apparent to her *by accident*. She will inherit a dangerous enemy in the unveiling, and make herself an enemy to him. Both will fancy themselves being the ones making the heroic choices, because this will be the downfall of humankind whether we at last intervene in the forthcoming event, or not."

Then, Clymene took one last look at the small fire in his palm and then balled the fist, putting out the flame as a dispersed breath of smoke escaped between his fingers. "Consider,' he reasoned. 'Intervention corresponds to prevention, and what consequences would we put in the place of the circumstances that we impede? Who is to say, that it would not lead to something much worse? That we would not doom humankind to a more harrowing fate?"

Zhrontese outstretched her arms and tilted her chin to the sky, her hair wrestling the wind as her body lifted to a hundred feet up -a vantage point on the ferocious hurricane from over the peaks of the highest nearby buildings. From there she envisioned a devastating event of human history as a cryptic herald of things to come. She saw the city of Pompeii on August 24, in the late summer autumn of 79 CE. Fragments of volcanic debris rained down on the city as people ran for their lives, in vain against the dense carpet of lava and ash coming in from Mount Vesuvius. 1.5 million tons per second of molten rock, pulverized pumice, rolling ash and profuse thermal energy, it was much too much for the Bay of Naples to sustain.

She saw the stone statues that became of fleeing people when she said, "We do not know what *might* happen, Clymene. We know what *will* happen. As we now speak, a rival of Kojiro, and by extension Coletrane, comes into play. And the effects of his actions will assure that the cataclysm comes to pass. Something must be done."

"Something must be done by them," Manthis added, standing untouched in the midst of avalanching snow. "by them, and for them. It must be allowed to happen. Humankind seeks absolution for the damage they've done to the planet, so they keep creating crusades to fight, disasters to thwart, injustices to avenge. This is but another expression of it. It is for us to keep in mind that if the cataclysm does happen, the one object that will survive it will be the book containing the story of it."

Zhrontese looked beyond Pompeii, all the way to January 15, 1919, when 2.3 million gallons of molasses ravaged the commercial district of Boston at 35 miles per hour. She watched as the terrifying substance swallowed everything and everyone in its path, when she said, ominously,

"What good is a book, with no one left to read it?"

"PTOLEMY VIII IN ALEXANDRIA WAS THE first to appoint a voyage through the monsoon wind system of the Indian Ocean," Cynthia said, well into an intense lecture on a Friday afternoon. Her migraine was acting up worse than usual that day, but she was mostly able to ignore it while lecturing. The lights in the room were dim, and the projector screen had a map of the Silk Road extending from southern Europe through Arabia, Somalia, Egypt, Persia, India and Java until finally China. There was another image on the screen of the Greek historian Poseidonius, the lifeless eyes of his stone bust looking out across the length of the darkened classroom. The students were looking back as if Poseidonius himself were judging their engagement; fully engrossed, many taking notes, listening intently with a hand rubbing chin. An exam was coming up, Cynthia thought to herself, so of course everyone was paying attention.

"He sent Eudoxus of Cyzicus to sail Egypt to India twice, and it was a big break of sorts for the industrious explorer. By 118 BC terms, of course."

Pacing as usual, Cynthia hit the button on her remote and the image onscreen dissolved to a picture of Eodoxus. Another click, and next to Eudoxus came a male silhouette with a large question mark in the center of the outlining. A third click and between the two images was a picture of an old wool-jacket journal.

"Eodoxus' voyage is well documented, but what isn't talked about in most instructional texts is the journal he kept which talked about an unnamed shipwrecked sailor from India who he rescued in the Red Sea some time before the famous journey. This man was brought to Ptolemy, and he offered his knowledge of those waters as gratitude for rescue. He was made Eodoxus' guide, and was directly responsible for him getting the opportunity to sail the Indian Ocean. Why this is important should be obvious to anyone who is up to date on their reading."

Saying that, she put her eyes on one male student who was slouching in his chair, on the verge of sleep. She looked at him from over the rim of her glasses and added, "Right, Jacob?"

Jacob immediately perked up and fixed his posture.

"Of -yeah, of.. of course, Ms. D."

She smiled, continuing,

"In his journal, several months before the voyage, Euxodus wrote of dreams. Constant visions of meeting a man under the same circumstances. For at least three months he mulled over these visions to the point of recognizing the man's face when he found him near death on a rudimentary barge. Was this man a living tulpa? Or did historians, including Poseidonius and even Euxodus himself, simply forget to record any details about his life or even his name?"

Everyone in the room knew that the question was rhetorical, so no one attempted to answer it when Cynthia went quiet to let it hang in the air for a moment.

"That's something to think on over the weekend," she continued, "as you prepare for Monday's exam."

The lights coming on and the projector going blank was the cue that class was over. Students began packing their things and filing out. Cynthia took a moment then to massage her temples in a futile attempt to assuage some of the intensifying pain. Just then, one student approached her as she was putting folders into her satchel – Talulah.

"Hey, Ms. DeGruy. Can I.. Can we talk for a minute?"

"I'm actually in a bit of a hurry, Talulah. I have a meeting across campus."

"I gotta go by administration anyway. I can walk with you a bit."

Cynthia was going to decline again, wanting to take that walk alone as a buffer before having to endure the suffocating meeting with the dean. And, also, in hopes that the tranquility of it would calm the pain in her head. But she had a soft spot for Talulah, and could tell by the tension of her body language that the matter held a degree of importance.

"Ok. Sure."

It was a typical day on the Baton Rouge LSU campus, bustling with students and staff moving about the ventricles of the Italian-Renaissance inspired architecture. The Memorial Clock Tower, which could be seen from pretty much anywhere on site, had just struck noon as Cynthia and Talulah were passing through the area of the Huey P. Long Field House in the historic district. The sun was hot, but to their left was a row of tall oak trees in the well-groomed grass that provided some shade.

"I don't have a great relationship with my parents,' Talulah said, "never have."

"I'm sorry to hear that," Cynthia replied. She could relate, but wasn't expecting the conversation to go there.

"Oh it's... nothing really. Kind of a generational thing. Me being at this school alone, it represents, I guess, a kind of betrayal or an acquiescence to America's vacant culture."

"That's an interesting way to put it."

"Vacant culture?"

"Well, that, but really I was thinking of *acquiescence*. That specific word. Reminds me of the revolutionary thinkers of the 60s and the 70s. Civil Rights activism. Feminists navigating, and writing in, a systemically patriarchal society."

"See?!" Talulah was excited. "That's why I wanted to talk to you! You get it! You.. Hey, you ok, Ms. DeGruy?" This was in response to seeing Cynthia wince again, and rub at her temple with two fingers.

But she waved Talulah off with a hand gesture and smiled. There was a small group of students talking loudly and walking by in the opposite direction. When they were out of direct earshot, she said,

"I do get it, Talulah. Your family is from Alabama, right?"

"Yes. Choctaw, on my mother's side. My father was Cherokee and their families actually met during the Trail of Tears."

"A lot of rich history there."

"Yeah. A lot of animosity too. See, my father died when I was little so I was raised by my mother's family, which, well, let's just say they're a little antiquated in their beliefs."

"Antiquated?"

"Yeah, like *proud that their tribe fought with the Confederacy* antiquated."

"Ah. I see."

The two at this point had stopped walking, continuing their conversation near the entrance to Prescott Hall.

"I'm rambling, I think," Talulah demurred.

"No no, you're not. Please, go on."

"Well, ok.. The thing I wanted to talk about is, the more I learn here, the more I study, the greater the intellective gulf gets between me and my mother. She thinks school is swallowing my mind, she thinks my scholarship, and my acceptance of it, represents me falling for some kind of vast conspiracy to whitewash her family's heritage. It just… It's so exhausting, all of it. It doesn't make any…"

"Talulah?"

"Ms. DeGruy.. Your… Your nose."

Cynthia's nose had begun to bleed, and she didn't even notice it until Talulah mentioned it. Somehow a sense of lightheadedness accompanied the bleeding. The befuddled Native student momentarily forgot her family issues, and reached out to grasp the shoulders of her teacher who appeared to be on the verge of stumbling.

"I'm ok. I'm ok. I…," Cynthia began, but the words got trapped in her throat when she looked around and saw that other students walking around in the area had all stopped to stare at her, all of their faces suddenly replaced by Clymene's. She was surrounded now by those menacing andradite eyes.

That's when the vertigo kicked in, she began seeing afterimages of everything, and Talulah's now panicked, echoing visage was yelling something in a muted voice.

Then, nothingness.

———

LATER THAT NIGHT, SHE'D RECALL how she didn't quite remember passing out. She didn't remember the ride to the hospital either. But Cynthia will always remember her time in the doctor's office. This was her most hated place in the world, her most powerful trauma trigger. She sat there on the exam table, keenly aware of all the items in the cold, sterile white room; the hand sanitizers on the desk by the sink, hygiene wipes, hypodermic needles, blood pressure cuffs by the heart rate machine, the ophthalmoscopes on the wall.

The overhead LED lights were unforgivingly bright, but for Cynthia they were but a dark reminder of her father's final hours.

She barely noticed the doctor when he entered with his clipboard. When she did notice, Cynthia realized he'd already been talking to her for at least a minute.

"…and the X-ray's show-"

"Just be straight with me, doctor. I switched from rizatriptan to sumatriptan recently for the migraines. I was warned about side effects, sure. But blackouts and nose bleeds?"

"An anomaly, I'm sure but-"

"Anomaly? I'm not an inanimate substance on a petri dish. At least talk to me like I'm a human."

The doctor was just over 6 feet tall with dark brown skin, the sprinkles of salt in his full pepper beard putting him somewhere between his mid to late forties. His head was bald and he wore no tie under his lab coat. He had the demeanor of a man who either was never good with people or had over time developed a distinct arrogance that some doctors have which corresponds to a stony bedside manner.

"Of course, Ms. DeGruy. I was simply going to say that we don't think your symptoms are related to the medicine."

"What then? What's going on? The headaches have gotten worse."

"Have you ever had epilepsy, or a palliative procedure called a corpus callosotomy?"

"No. Neither."

"Let me show you something," he said with no warmth, moving to the radiographic table to set up two X-ray images of her brain.

"Let's take a look at your brain," he used a pen to point out the areas he was referring to on the scan, specifically the highway-looking space between the two hemispheres. "This white matter tract is called the corpus callosum. This bundle of axons is the anterior commissure, and this one the posterior. In an epilepsy patient, the callosotomy is done to limit the spread of epileptic activity between them."

"Why does any of this matter? I just told you I've never had epilepsy or a collo-"

"Corpus callosotomy."

"Right. So?"

"So, you CT scan suggests that you *have* had this procedure, despite the lack of cranial evidence of surgery. There is also brain activity which reflects a conflict of two distinct personality types, a Type A and a type D."

"What? It sounds like you're telling me that my headaches are being caused by a phantom brain in my head or something."

The doctor's phlegmatic features momentarily broke a smile, amused by her confusion or perhaps made uncomfortable by his own.

"Of course not, Ms. DeGruy. But we'll have to do some more test to arrive at a more medically sound explanation. For now, I'm going to up the dosage of your prescription."

A phantom brain…

克

JEREMIAH CROSS LANGUISHED UNDER THE cover of darkness in his cold though spacious office. The virtual windows cast the images of hastily moving swaths of thick, gray fog over black forests and amid glimmers of rain. It was a setting as unnatural as Cross' penchant for calling 2am meetings with his staff of scientists, engineers, and his board of directors. The meetings were never in person. Rather, they were virtual just like the windows that surrounded him with interchangeable locales.

An oculus stereopticon with a three headed sphere was set in the ceiling above his desk, and it shown twelve chairs projected around him with a billowing digital landscape between them that served as their roundtable.

All each person in attendance could see were the others in their chairs, so no one saw the ominous figure standing in the shadows behind Cross.

Dr. Upadhyay was there with her colleagues, Dr. Wendell McDowell, Dr. Tejeda Lopez, and Dr. Walter Huynh. They were, save for Dr. McDowell, who was on a research assignment in Quebec, reporting from their office downtown. But despite not being physically present, they could all feel the stoic coldness of the other nine people in attendance. None of those suited business men or numbers experts were operating in defiance of a Hippocratic Oath for being in the employ of Jeremiah Cross. None of them held any moral misgivings over the Trivium project's morbid foundation of beheading innocents in service to a vague plan to "advance humanity" and make a lot of money while doing it.

The only person at the table that no one but Cross knew was Qadr Fakhoury, who Cross invited with no preamble, and was present upon his own insistence that she see behind the true value of the work she was doing for him. She was casually dressed in a smocked waist jumpsuit made of black silk, a golden Cleopatra necklace and etched metal arm band bracelets. She was twirling two Tiger Eye Boading balls like a scholar doing some casual midnight reading.

Cross, in contrast, was never seen dressed in anything but the gift-wrappings of the highest finery, for his vanity would never allow it. He was no Bill Gates type in this way. He did however favor the color black for these affairs, and was near camouflaged in the darkness of the room by his tapered satin peak lapels.

"If collectivism means the subjugation of the individual to a group,' Cross began, 'and I think it does, could it then be considered the bedrock of a global indoctrination that keeps humanity from achieving a *True* common good, with a capital T, rather than a series of idealized fantasies of such only mimicked, mocked, and meandered?"

He paused a moment so everyone could consider the words, a pause met with a deafening silence colored by the collective knowing that his question was rhetorical. "What then is Trivium, and what of our unique duty to the world as its stewards?"

Right then, as if on command by his voice, the sprawling elliptic table between the group roused to life and formed, one by one, a 3D animated image of the unnatural disasters witnessed by the Interstices; the snow storm, the hurricane, and the wild fire, all transmogrified as Cross spoke of them.

"In this past week the world witnessed, all at once, an unprecedented network of earthborn calamities. While Lake Okeechobee was being ravished by 182 mile per hour winds, the forests of Lac la Biche saw fires just as devastating. And during this still, Bozeman, Montana was subject to an unrelenting air strike of graupel the size and weight of full grown bison. Many hundreds of thousands, millions even -dead; billions in property damage all told."

Another pause, as he scanned the faces of the people. He noted, with a bit of admiration, that Qadr had no emotional regard for the words or imagery -at all. "But what if,' Cross continued, '...what if such a thing could have been prevented, or even reversed? Suppose humankind wielded this power but it was yet blocked by the bad economics that govern the modern world."

Cross, ever perceptive, noticed a subtle glance shared between Doctors Upadhyay and Lopez. And from this pebble cast in the waters of existential discomfort was a ripple effect that touched on the temperaments of both Doctors Huynh and McDowell.

Cross smiled.

"The number of people murdered by the earth in this recent series of events itself measures up to the honor of a Stalin or a Hitler, but ironically not to a Genghis Khan. Indeed, Khan even outdid the Black Death in its sweeping gesture of clandestine philanthropy!"

Cross could see that he got the desired effect from the use of that word, *philanthropy*, and it tickled his intellect. "Many of you, I'm sure, would balk at the word under the circumstances but, in the case of Khan, it is not so ironic when you consider that that the 40 million dead at the behest of his reign resulted in cooling the earth, an environmental benefit that brought the carbon in the air down by 700 million tons. So, armed with this knowledge, and with the dreamed upon power to decide what to do with it, do we move according to our indoctrination? Do we succumb to the urge of collectivism and damn the earth, and with it the future of humankind, to further ruin? Or do we take a page out of the great Khan's book, making the individualistic choice of doing as we please for our sake alone?"

"Mr. Cross?' Dr. Lopez spoke up, in a small voice that was full of conviction.

"Yes, Dr. Lopez, please contribute," Cross invited, the otherwise tepid delivery apostrophized by an affirmative hand gesture.

She was hesitant for a moment, perhaps sensing Cross' muted though dangerous disappointment with being interrupted.

"Why would we let all of this happen if we had the power to stop it? Isn't the power to stop disasters such as these the point of Trivium, the... justification for-"

"For a few rolling heads?," Cross quipped, Qadr grinned, and Dr. Upadhyay was getting visibly annoyed by the grating noise of Qadr twirling the Boading balls with defiant indifference.

"On the contrary,' Cross continued, "the point of Trivium is not the premises of Sophie's choices, but rather the doing away of that limitation entirely."

Even though no one but himself at this meeting was physically present in the room, Cross could feel their collective energy trending towards a keen interest, if not the intrigue of shared confusion, in the mystery of this Trivium project to which they were all contractually enjoined. He also felt the burning lust of the shadowy presence behind him; he felt its energy drawing near, the touch of its menacing, osseous fingers alight on his shoulders and squeeze. He felt the translucent beard scraping the back of his neck... This devil was pleased with him, he knew, and that was as much a palliative for his anxieties as it were a trigger to them.

"The Trivium,' he continued, 'a system that by design will expire all meanings of the word impossible. Science has shown us that thoughts are not ethereal, that they are instead representations of matter that as such have shape and weight. This is true even for imagination and dream, and for every possibility that exists within these perimeters. If minds proven to have coded data bearing memory of multi-life experience from planes of existence wherein mystical powers of myth and magic were commonplace, and if these forms of matter can be manipulated like any other, then we can put pressure on them like stones and create diamonds in our world. Put another way, Trivium can and will become a computer with the power to commodify Infinity itself."

"Commodify Infinity?" repeated Corbon Lars, one of the businessmen on Cross' board, in a tone more fitting epiphany than question.

Instead of responding to either possibility, Cross addressed Qadr.

"Ms. Fakhoury, have any good men so far been killed in the recruitment of the unique minds integral to the completion of our project?"

The attention of the group shifted towards her, who did not take her eyes off Cross in replying,

"*Rien,*" she said, meaning *none* in French.

"And what of the remaining list?"

"*Tous les méchants.*"

"All bad men," Cross repeated in English. "And that is the good news, Mr. Lars. We will commodify Infinity while in the process ridding the world of a few more bad men, missed by none but remembered by all for their contributions to the betterment of humankind."

克

THE DREAM COULDN'T HAVE BEEN WORSE, this enduring feeling of powerlessness that Kojiro felt while lying in a suspended state for more time than he could know. Dreaming of his beloved Taya, dreaming of his fault in her mental corruption, the curse that consumed her. Dreaming, lamenting, the consequences suffered by those who would link themselves to his cause and make the error of being his friends.

His memories assault him like a pack of starving dogs tearing at a half stripped bone, eating into him at every direction; an echo in his ear, pain in his loins, throbbing in his head, tears from clenched eyes and sweat from desperate pores.

Kojiro wanted to wake up, to gain control, but was absent the strength to will either result. He knew that he was in a dream because he could not account for his body. And if he were awake, Kojiro knew, his foolhardy sense of valor would lead him to some form of rash, ill-conceived violence, the sort of which that is always the undoing of impetuous men.

Why, he wondered, did men follow him at all? Why did women, for that matter? Was it a curse of his own that he'd be stricken with charisma only so that it may be used to lure others into the trap of devotion to him? Had Destiny chosen Guilt as his downfall, an enemy he could not fight with either of his swords?

"Wake up, Sakura... Wake up," a young female voice intoned, reaching out of a far distance in his mind's ear and cutting the black of guilt like a tanto knife.

"Your body is healed enough," the voice continued, "It is only your mind that has kept you down for so long... Now wake up, Sakura ko-Mitsu!"

Kojiro began to open his eyes, and he'll never forget how it felt like he hadn't done this in many months; he could actually feel the weight and muscle of his eyelids held down and atrophied from disuse.

But at last, they worked! Light hit his pupils harshly, a blaze of images and colors. Finally, as things became clear, he saw the woman sitting in front of him. This is how he remembered seeing her for the first time, as a wave of glorious color. A tender, caring smile, bright eyes full of hope, a thunder show of jet black and golden hair. This was important because her kimono matched it in color, marked with designs of dragons and sea monsters; depictions, Kojiro thought, of his many battles, and all quite reminiscent of his sword Hatsukoi... This observation made him very curious, and at once suspicious. He became quickly aware of the smells in the room, an elemental mixture of flavored incense -chamomile, bitter orange, patchouli. Beyond these wafted a thick undercurrent of rosemary.

Light shown from a hibiscus lantern held up above gave her young though mature face a welcoming glow as she continued to push two fingers at Kojiro's shoulder, nudging him awake.

"Don't be afraid," she said. 'I am Dr. Reiki Chiyu. But please, just call me Chiyu.

Instead of responding, Kojiro took in more of his surroundings. .

He noticed a gold tipped battle arrow lying on a pillowed shrine next to his resting place. This, he knew, was a Shinto practice of *norito* prayer. The arrow had likely been purchased from a nearby Shinto temple, and right now was supposedly being *charged* by the absorption of Kojiro's many impurities...

Kojiro didn't buy into these superstitions. Anyway, he hated the gods and what he called "tricks they play on the minds of innocent and earnest people."

He noticed then, his body. Like his heavy eyelids, his muscles had atrophied. And he'd accumulated an uncomfortable amount of fat in his midsection. He felt like a drunken peasant, a washed up wrestler....

The room he was in was much like a tent, curtained all around and "doored" with a drawstring closure -primitive, minimalistic. Glass casings of medicine were stacked all around the peaceful setting, and a black cat slept in the corner before a small bowl of fresh, untouched water.

"You've been asleep for some time. Do not try to get up just yet," Dr. Chiyu warned tenderly, placing hands on his chest as he attempted to sit up. There was pain in his back as he moved, but Chiyu's touch was like a witch doctor's ointment on an open wound.

"Make up your mind," Kojiro groaned, "get up or stay down?"

Chiyu laughed at the apparent joke.

From the lying position, Kojiro stretched his back and then touched his face.

Surprised, he said out loud,

"I've grown a beard."

———

IT WASN'T BUT A FEW MOMENTS LATER when, without warning, a surge of recollections flushed in on Kojiro's mind. All on its own, and despite the pain in his every rusted out muscle, Kojiro's body jolted to an upright seating position.

"Where is Jubei? Where are the others?"

"You need to relax, Kojiro," Chiyu said, trying to lightly restrain him, "Calm yourself! You are safe!"

"Where are they?! Where am I?! Ittei!!"

The tinge of rosemary in the air became more pronounced to his olfactory nerve when he said this, Ittei's name. That's when the flitting memories stabilized, zapping him like a bolt of lightning!

Kojiro, Tzukuba, Jubei, Ittei, Yoriko, the two Chinmoku Aki brothers Gorou and Ichiro, and the three remaining conscripts, were suddenly set upon along the southwest passageway by **Pau'gukdoza Wraiths***; agile, child-bodied creatures that looked like tribal warriors in both woolen loin cloth dress and bone-made weaponry, with gray/red skin and living tattoos all over their emaciated though muscular bodies that changed and moved constantly. They sweat and bled tar in excess, could travel in the shadows, and had red, demonic eyes.*

It was impossible to deduce how many of them there were, as they kept coming in and out of the shadows in a blink, to attack with makeshift daggers made of dragon bone! Two of the three conscripts were murdered almost immediately, Gorou was badly wounded after taking a slash across the left side of his neck and another deep gash to the right quadricep. Tzukuba saved him from certain death by intercepting a killing strike with her onyx blade and cutting through the Pau'gukdoza's body in a splash of tar that dispersed left and right to become two blobs that quickly grew into humanoid form. Jubei was immediately at her side to take on the newly born monstrosities, only to then get his hands full with three others that dashed out of the dark. But Ichiro joined the fight after briefly checking on his brother.

Kojiro jumped into the fray to fight alongside Ittei and Yoriko.

"What are they, Ittei?!"

"They are called The Pau'gukdoza in the sutras, my liege! They multiply with greater aggression than the Ashigaru! And they attack only warriors!"

"We'll make them regret that!" Kojiro yelled, cutting down two or three at the same time with Hatsukoi, the seven body blade. They would split and begin regeneration, but he would stomp them out and shred them with his sword before they complete or even begin their process. The berserker rage, the Dragon Kings still within, they gave him power and energy, making it such that he moved so fast and dexterous as if a living bladed tornado! The vexing dust of Hatsukoi's blade creating a haze that affects the seemingly immortal tribal demons, obstructing their sight and making them cough.

Then, abruptly, there was a pause in the assault. The Pau'gukdoza all squared up and edged back, moving into the shadows where their silhouettes barely shown and their eyes glowed.

"What are they doing?" Jubei called.

"Hold your ground," Kojiro replied.

That's when the laughter could be heard, up ahead, where the crew members could see a small light emerging from around the corner. After a moment, they could see that it was a man carrying a lamp. Even though it was over forty yards away, Kojiro could already smell the sardine oil from the lamp. And though none of the crew could make out yet the identity of the man, what with the distance, the shadows and glimmer of the lamp light, all camouflaging his facial features, Kojiro still recognized the voice and the self-righteous, swaggering gait, the bare feet and tattered, woolen shawl and cloak.

That familiar laugh, it was followed by familiar, irony-laced words,

"Hold your ground? Haha. Ironic advice from a runt always bad at holding his own."

"Who are you?!" Jubei demanded.

"KoKo knows," was the reply.

Kojiro hadn't been called Koko in years. Just hearing it set him off, activating his rashness, drawing out his less than leader-like instincts.

"BASTARD!" He called, as he ran past his men towards the light. The Pau'gukdoza pounced, attempting to attack and slow him down.

"Kojiro, no!" That was Ittei, but Kojiro did not hear him.

"Sakura!!" Tzukuba called, at once trying to grab his arm as he passed her but, in his rage, he pushed her off with such force that her back slammed against the cave surface.

He cut down Pau'gukdoza after Pau'gukdoza. Some he sidestepped or dashed past like a running-back avoiding being tackled, while others he drove through with Hatsukoi like a frenzied weed shredder.

The man did not move, but before Kojiro could get close enough, the man pulled out a bamboo straw and shot him with a powerful sedative arrow.

That is all he remembered.

"Did you see it?" Chiyu asked, when his shoulders loosened and he looked at her, the guilt and embarrassment impossible to hide despite the thickness of his beard.

"The rashness… of your decisions.. which led you here?"

"Where are they?… Are they all dead because of me?"

"You should be so lucky, yuujin,' came the surprising though welcome voice of Jubei as he entered the tent, 'to be rid of us that easily."

Chiyu frowned.

"Good morning, Jubei,' she greeted, 'but I do not think Kojiro is ready just yet for visitors."

"I'm as ready as I will ever be," Kojiro interjected.

"See?' Jubei added, with a wide grin. "He's ready."

Kojiro put a reassuring hand on Chiyu's.

"Can we have a moment, doctor?"

"Just Chiyu."

"Can we have a moment, Chiyu?'

She smiled and, though reluctant, she exited the tent-like room.

When she was gone, Jubei approached the bed.

"We were worried about you, yuujin. Three weeks you've been down, comatose."

"Three weeks?' Kojiro couldn't even believe it after saying the words himself. But then he regarded his body fat, his beard…

"I'm afraid so, but we needn't dwell. Everyone is well rested, well fed. We can get back on track. After another few weeks, devoted to getting you strong again, we can-"

"I can get strong again along the way. We have to move."

Jubei sat down on the edge of the bed, speaking now to his friend in softer tones.

"We should trust and follow the doctor's recommendation. The mystical woman you met at the lake, she made it so we could not be found in this place, and so that time would be suspended for us. Outside the three mile radius of these healing grounds, this hidden forest, the three weeks we have been here have only been about three hours out there."

"Impossible."

"It is so, yuujin... So let us focus on your healing, and the regaining of strength. Besides,' he smiled, quipped, 'you cannot lead with that belly."

"Now is not the time for jokes, Jubei."

"It is always the time for jokes! As laughter accelerates healing, and the weight on our shoulders as mortal men is ever heavy."

Kojiro sat back and took a deep breath.

"What of the others, Jubei? What were our losses in the cave?"

Unable to help it, the joviality drained from Jubei's eyes and expression.

"Jubei?" Kojiro prodded, after a few uncomfortable moments of silence.

"We lost the last of the conscripts to the Pau'gukdoza. Three men. And... Three Chinmoku as well. Jirou, Finn, and Hajime."

Kojiro began shaking with rage. He suddenly realized why Chiyu was weary of him having a visit in his current, vulnerable condition.

"Six men..."

"The Bastard is no doubt after the bounty on your head."

"As we knew he would be. You tried to warn me. Back at Tzu Chen's domain."

"The past is done, yuujin. We all knew the risks."

There was about a minute of silence then, Kojiro letting his friend's attempt to comfort him hang in the air.

"And the other team?" he asked.

"They got to us in time to shake things up. That's when the three brothers fell. They gave their lives so that we could live. We retreated out an alternate exit that Kana found."

An image passed in Kojiro's mind, of the mysterious lantern holding villain who shot him with the sedative arrow and spoke to him with such bitter familiarity. Just the thought of this man filled Kojiro with energy, with agency.

"If time indeed goes slow in this place, we must take advantage of it. I must get stronger than ever before. A brief detour from our quarry…. to get revenge on Katsurou!"

THERE WAS A MYSTERIOUS CHOLERA outbreak in Dhaka, capital city of Bangladesh, in southeast Asia. 1983. Something of unknown origin had gotten into the Buriganga River, infecting and killing thousands before doctors could even figure out that it was an unknown strand of Cholera. Adaeze, on the very first and only expedition trip that Vincent agreed to her attending, wound up being one of the infected. And it was this way, in the hospital bed, that it was discovered she was pregnant with Coletrane.

Vincent was at Adaeze's bedside in the ICU unit of the local Cholera hospital. It took every bit of his strength not to run from the room screaming, as hospitals had become a phobia over the years after seeing most of his family members and close friends die in them. The beeping from the heart monitor hit like bee stings, its display of blue, green, and purple lines racing from left to right taunted him, seeming to threaten each moment to just... stop. Or was that his paranoia, a trait his son would eventually inherit?

His son.... Even though he just found out that Adaeze was pregnant, he knew that she would birth him a son if she lived to do so. It was unlikely, however, the attending doctor told him, and very possible that both would die.

There's no sugarcoating in Dhaka.

Vincent held Adaeze's hand tightly. Even though she was unconscious and deathly sick, she still looking to him like a sleeping angel.

"Adaeze,' he said softly, his voice trembling and punctuated by remorse, 'I'm sorry. I... I should not have brought you here... I ...I won't let you die. I won't let our baby die."

He was only supposed to be allowed a ten minute visit, but he was able to talk (and pay) the staff to allow him forty-five minutes instead, which he pushed to an hour. After this, he slouched in a lobby chair downstairs to wait indefinitely. He refused to leave the hospital while his wife lie dying inside. Vincent even abandoned the expedition party that he was in Dhaka for; a journal of Judas Ulehla supposedly buried somewhere at 3000 feet of the Sippi Arguang, a peak located deep in Rowangchhari Upazila of the Bandarban district in the Chittagong Hill Tracts. He'd already secured a dig site, learned the tribal language of the local Bom nation, and hired a team for the job. But all of it, he called off at the last minute.

No archeological find was more important to him than Adaeze.

Many hours passed before anyone acknowledged his presence. He felt like a statue himself propped up in the room to lend it some color, watching for what seemed like forever for the black sky outside the tall windows to begin swelling with the blue of morning.

Vincent must have dozed off for a moment because he didn't hear the man walk up on him.

"Mr. Vincent Marx?" the deep African elocution startled him awake. He woke to find not a hospital employee standing before him, but a tall casually dressed man with dark, heavily melanated skin. He wore simply jeans and a black short sleeved polyester kenta shirt, a brown leather satchel over his right shoulder. His head was bald, and his chiseled face held at least fifty years of hard experience on this earth -if not more. When Vincent looked up at him, the man's broad, welcoming smile seemed to erase not only his years but also the hardness of his resting physiognomy.

———

ADEBOWALE NWOSU WAS A MEDICINE man from Johannesburg, South Africa. Like Vincent, Adebowale came from a wealthy family that owned most of the Soweto museums in the city. What he had in common with Adaeze was a passion for holistic medicine, and what he had in common with Vincent was a keen interest in the unknown.

There was orange tinted lighting in the small café, paintings and an assortment of artistic décor on shelved displays, comfortable prism chairs decked with ornately adorned throw pillows, all giving the place's ambiance a cozy, crafty aesthetic. Adebowale offered Vincent coffee at the shop across the street from the hospital. The medicine man had a small slice of chocolate mousse cake with an expresso. Vincent, just a black coffee with no sugar.

"You are a man of archeology,' Adebowale began, after two sips of his espresso and a small bite of his cake, 'that I have followed for some time, with a degree of earnest. I very much enjoyed the chronicle of your pilgrimage in Puttaparthi. Tell me, did you ever find it?! The hidden tomb of Sarah, *princess of the multitudes?"*

Vincent blinked, the incredulity stifling his voice.

"You,' he began, but Adebowale's faint smile took the question out of his mouth. Instead, Vincent sighed, holding back the tears and apprehension over his wife, made vulnerable, it would seem, by desperation, he began again, "this... expedition was... supposed to be, sponsored as anyway, a possible location of it."

"Ahh,' the inscrutable medicine man realized, 'was... It is how you secured the permits to dig then! But you are not here in search of a tomb."

Vincent just stared at him. The tension between the two men was interrupted by the waitress coming by to refill Vincent's half-drank coffee. When she left, Adebowale said,

"I can tell that you believe the stories, the memetic theories of William Price, on thinking being a source of spontaneous creation, on thought-forms, the Dzgochen and primordial state of Great Perfection..., on Judas Ulehla."

It was as if Vincent's emotional and intellectual exhaustion betrayed his suspicion of this man who knew so much of him, leaving only curiosity and intrigue.

Vincent was, of course, a rich man, but he was looking haggard in his sleeplessness and grief.

"I can't... I... don't care to think of Ulehla right now. It in fact is an obsession that has very negatively impacted my family."

"Indeed, it appears so on the surface, Mr. Marx,' the compassion in Adebowale's voice somehow complimented the grin on his face, 'but there are no coincidences in this life."

Before Vincent even has the opportunity to incorrectly connect Adebowale's words with a sentiment of dismissal for his wife's sickness, the medicine man pulled two things from his satchel; a rustic, buffalo leather journal with an antique handmade closing strap, and a small vial of amber liquid.

Vincent looked at both objects with a note of suspicion, especially the journal, which he regarded incredulously.

"Is that?...' he began, 'That's not what I think it is."

"A keen eye fit for the rigors of explorations!' Adebowale said, excitedly. 'Your plan was to go all the way into the Rowangchhari Upazila in hopes of finding the journal of Ulehla, but I have saved you the trip."

"How did....? This expedition was private." Vincent's dubiousness did not prevent him from reaching for and examining the artifact.

He opened it very carefully, and could recognize the handwriting of Judas Ulehla.

Full seriousness now, Adebowale leaned forward and spoke in hushed tones,

"The details of the prophesy are expressed at length within those pages. Ulehla knew that you and I would meet. And he knew that you would need what is in that vial. It took me fourteen years to perfect that serum."

"What is this serum for, Adebowale?"

"Your wife,' he said simply. 'Do not let the doctors see. Give it to her. Every drop. Both she and your son will be saved. And Vincent?"

He grasped Vincent's arm, squeezing tight to herald the gravity of the words that would follow.

"It will change your son in ways unimaginable. It will cast upon him the weight of all Ulehla's secrets, the truth behind tulpas, and the answers to your life's work."

"How do I simply trust a self-professed medicine man with the lives of my family, offering some… unknown questionable serum?"

Then Adebowale smiled again.

"Because you saw this already in a dream, Mr. Marx. The same kind of dream that guided Ulehla in his travels, his works, and all the days of his life."

Vincent could not readily respond. He knew the mysterious medicine man's words to be true, as their meeting felt to him like déjà vu.

———

HIS NEXT VISIT WITH ADAEZE, A FEW hours later, she appeared even worse than the night before. Her skin was much paler, and her hair looked like it was thinning. The heartrate monitor shown a BPM of 42, a dangerous indication of bradycardia. And she was on a high dose IV drip of doxycycline that alas did not seem to be having much of a positive affect if any at all. Indeed, this strand of cholera was something the doctors could not yet identify and thus could not yet adequately treat.

Seeing her this way, his beloved wife, it made Vincent's eyes fill with tears. He was very careful to avoid the gaze of the nurses moving about in the ICU, when he leaned forward at Adaeze's side, opened her mouth, and carefully poured every drop of the serum down her throat.

Vincent dosed off in the chair again after that, just for about a half hour, apparently, upon checking his watch. But while he was asleep, his mind was assailed by a strange dream that he wouldn't forget; *a grown suited black man with a wild lion's mane of coarse hair, in a darkened cave armed only with a golden Japanese sword. He fights a giant stone humanoid buffalo wielding an impossibly long-reaching odachi sword. In the man's face is the determination and focus to topple empires, and in his eyes are double-pupiled figure eights.*

To Vincent's surprise, Adaeze was awake when he shook out of the dream. She still looked weak but noticeably better. Her heartrate had risen to 94 BPM, she was a little elevated now in the bed and her face had a slightly exfoliated glow.

"Ho…ney,' the word weakly slipped from her lips. "Honey,' she repeated, cracking a smile. Vincent sat up and leaned towards her, his eyes now filling with a very different kind of tears.

He grasped her hand with both of his and that is when he noticed, to his surprise, that her eyes now were green instead of hazel.

What, he wondered to himself, and despite the rush of joy to see Adaeze awake and lively, *have I done to my wife? What, in fact, have I done to my unborn son?*

———

COLETRANE USED THE VHF RADIO HE'D been hiding on his person to contact DeLoache, giving him the coordinates to pick up he and Patrick at the precipice of the cave by chopper. From there, they were taken directly to the airstrip where they hastily boarded the Lear Jet for a rushed trip back to the states.

The two barely spoke or ever made eye contact for much of the chopper ride and half of the plane trip to Florida. Patrick, he was in shock and still adjusting to the memories of Ittei that were flowing into his mind and changing his perspective on the entirety of his life. He in fact was experiencing tremors similar to liquor withdrawal, blurred vision, and lightheadedness. It was only sitting by a window and looking out at the clouds that helped him to maintain his equilibrium.

Coletrane, on the other hand, had dismissed himself from the main cabin entirely. He departed to a private room, the sheathed and mahogany packaged sword at his side, to watch an interview of his father's on a tablet, a video recorded back when he was an infant.

"I am excited to be a new father,' Vincent told the bespectacled, conservatively dressed journalist -a white man with skin the color of bleached bone and thinning gray hair that still bore streaks of black. They were on a dimly lit stage on plush leather chairs with a coffee table between them, both he and the interviewer nursing a steaming mug of coffee. "But I also feel pregnant with suppositions and theories begat by recent discoveries. As you know, I've followed the works of Judas Ulehla for the better part of my adult life. I even hold a private journal of his that led me to the unearthing of the catacombs of Kom el Shogafa. The question that comes of it is this. How does a tomb featuring influences of Greek, Roman, and Egyptian cultures, a burial chamber from the 2nd to 4th century, somehow bear evidence of being the final resting place of an 18th century samurai forgotten entirely from recorded history?"

"An intriguing question indeed, Mr. Marx." The journalist, he sat back in his chair and folded his right leg over the left, lightly stirring his coffee with a spoon. "But how much of it is relegated to the strict confines of heresy? For instance, what evidence have you of this samurai being associated with the Kom el Shogafa?"

"Beyond the careful details embedded in Ulehla's journal? None.. Yet. But he wrote this of tulpas and the catacomb: *Many a necropolis, from hidden sepulcher to the myths of hanging coffins, will bear evidence in detail, if one knows what to look for, of a jumbled historical context, a context laying waste to the flotsam and jetsam of a disturbed human subconscious. What then,* he continued, *if the mysteries and seemingly unanswerable questions of historical findings are evidence of tulpas? How many people in the future, indeed, will come to believe that I myself was a tulpa, a myth dreamed up by some bored, drunken author?"*

Coletrane's jaw tightened more with his father's every word, an anxiety growing in him that he recognized consciously as anger, as rage. He had to stop the tape upon realizing that he was holding his breath while listening.

"**You have to go speak with him,**" Coletrane heard, rather clearly but somehow not surprisingly, Kojiro's voice in his mind's ear, "**You have to set him at ease before a blood vessel pops in his head.**"

———

PATRICK WAS STILL SEATED IN THE FRONT cabin, watching the clouds outside his window. The shakes were beginning to subside, but the flashes of memories of him almost losing his life to giant sentient statues, the memories of the gruesome deaths of those who weren't so lucky, it all persisted and set his teeth on edge, teasing out beads of sweat on his forehead and in the palms of his hands.

He continued taking deep breathes, which was helping -a little.

He didn't hear Coletrane walk up on him.

The enigmatic rich man, without speaking, lowered himself into the seat across from Patrick. He was carrying two ceramic mugs with steam rising from their brims. Handing one of them to Patrick, he said,

"It's chamomile and lavender, and… a little something else for potency. Should help with the nerves."

"What's the something else?" Patrick whispered; his cadence laced with wariness.

"Adaptogens. Polygala from my mother's garden, eleuthero, astragalus…"

"Eleuthero?' Patrick recognized the word, from the brief time that he studied herbal medicines long ago. "Devil's shrub?"

"Yes."

"Appropriate,' he spat, colored by a note of deprecation. "Is that you then, the devil?"

Coletrane stared at Patrick for a long time, seeming to not even blink while holding eye contact with the war photographer turned journalist. Then he did blink and drew in a deep breath that ended in a sigh.

"I didn't want those men to die, Patrick. I... I didn't count on, or expect it. You know that... right?"

"I don't know what I know anymore. About anything."

Coletrane shut his eyes, shaking his head.

"It all was a blind spot in my mind... I should have.."

"*It was no blind spot, yuujin,*" Kojiro, in his head, interrupted.

"I should have seen it. But everything was clouded by.."

"*Ambition.*"

"Hatsukoi."

"*It was your destiny to find her, no matter the consequences. All men die. Do not succumb to guilt.*"

"Why do I know that name," Patrick questioned, after blowing the steam from his tea and taking a few sips of it. Then he began to feel the effects of the tea as those few sips settled in his stomach. "Wow this... this tea *is* good."

"My mother dedicated her life and garden to making sure that it would be."

"But to my question," Patrick said, recovering from the brief euphoria and returning to the subject.

"To your question," Coletrane repeated, not sure yet how best to answer.

"Whose memories are these? Of white wolves.. Of a naginata.. Or another life? I even remember some goddess that I was friendly with in another skin. I remember things that are impossible."

"Not impossible,' Coletrane warned, 'just unknown. I spoke to you of the prophesy. You didn't believe me... But it's true and all apparently affects more lives than my own. The mark now is gone,' he added, pulling down his color to reveal that the deep bruise that was on his throat has vanished without a trace, "the demon, now within me."

"You traveled over seven thousand miles to absorb a demon?"

"For an inexorable purpose."

"One recklessly vague and undisclosed to all who would follow."

"I'm sorry, Patrick."

"You are not sorry. And I am no demon," Kojiro told him, his contempt building in Coletrane's chest like the sensation of acid reflux. ***"It is you who are the demon. You, the harbinger of chaos. The child in the reflection."***

Just then, Coletrane experiences a memory spasm, of Kojiro, from his time, looking at the reflection of young Coletrane in the pond.

He quickly shakes off the vision, returning to reality, as Patrick says,

"You alright?"

"Yes. I'm fine. But there is much for us to do now. Much to face. Much to accept. But first, finish your tea."

———

ST. CLOUD, FLORIDA. AT THE BLACKWOOD Center, an 84 bed psychiatric hospital billed as a tranquil, comprehensive healing suite for those afflicted by mental illness, substance abuse disorder, Anxiety, Depression, and PTSD/Trauma. The facility addresses a broad spectrum of patient needs, proudly offering Detoxification, Inpatient Rehabilitation, and Partial Hospitalization programs.

The building, from the outside, its architecture looks like a private school in an upscale district, its grounds enveloped in colorful, resplendent shrubbery, hedges and gardening reflective its promise of tranquility, a permaculture of low-maintenance evergreens, purple beautyberry, pyracantha, and a vibrancy of white, coral, pink, yellow, and red camellia. There were rock trails bordered by winding rows of blue liriope, there were vine arbor tunnels and weeping atlas cedars complimenting an all-encompassing sun shield thicket of live oak.

Inside the facility however, to indefinite inpatients such as **Marcus Green**, the place felt more like a prison. The obsessive over-sanitation of all his surroundings gave the rooms, halls, common areas a cold, unlived-in aesthetic. Like a doll house put on display in a museum. The staff always displayed creepy, inauthentic *smiles* easily detectable by the naked eye as being quite off, and they were trained to lie about everything in order to keep patients placated.

Marcus had followed his father's footsteps into the fighting arts. Starting at 16, he was an undisputed champ for twelve years with a 33-0 record, but he fought for the last four of those years with an untreated epidural hematoma. No one's fault, really, unless you blame his father for paying his doctors to go soft on reporting any injuries that weren't absolutely urgent and/or life threatening. This was never proven, mind you. Maybe the doctors just didn't catch it. Marcus, after all, was the pinnacle of health. He was an adored champion, a charismatic leader, and more positive and inspiring than a pixie in stardust.

Privately, however, after the artery tear caused by the epidural hematoma, he started thinking a lot about that night from his childhood, the night he and Coletrane created a samurai called Kojiro.

He started hallucinating, to the point where he had convinced himself that, somehow, the character they created for a mere school project was real, had come to life and, in fact, was the answer to the riddle of Coletrane's parents' brutal murder.

He even tried talking to his friend at times, though they'd drifted apart after high school, and would always get the same dismissive stonewalling.

"We were just kids, Marcus,' Coletrane would say, eye contact subtly averted which every time clued Marcus to the lie, 'our creation was fiction, and nothing more. Besides, we're adults now and you have an upcoming fight to be focused on."

Marcus, each time, would smile and assure that he could beat the upcoming opponent in his sleep. They'd laugh and laugh, change the subject, and move on... But what Coletrane didn't know was that there was some truth to the *sleep* part, as in the ring, ever since the start of his brain damage, Marcus would slip into a fugue state; he would be assailed by a burning apprehension in his chest that would manifest in him a berserker rage, and to his perspective, his opponent would morph into a yellow-eyed demon wearing a flesh-like yōkai mask with long horns and sharp fangs. Its color was always different, red, blue, black, green, silver..., but what remained consistent were the distracting memories it would trigger in Marcus, from a different time, a magical world, danger. The opponent would draw close to Marcus, moving in slow motion but leaving blurry footprints with his every move, lingering afterimages that eventually would make it look to Marcus as if he were in a kumite against several men at once.

Each time, the rage in him would lead him to find the real one and beat him by knockout in the first, second, or third round. Until finally, the in-ring hallucinations becoming too much, he squared off against an opponent who held his ground, was much tougher than the rest, and tore into Marcus enough that a new brain injury occurred, an intracerebral hemorrhage, that put him on the mat and resulted in him being rushed to the hospital.

There, he talked openly about living demons and fantasy worlds written onto the history of man, he talked about wanting to hurt himself and others... This got him onto the Baker Act. He's been a resident at the Blackwood Center since. Five years now...

———

FOR THE LAST TWO WEEKS, MARCUS HAD been feeling stranger than usual. The small, single bed room he resided in seemed smaller. The common area, where patients were allowed to watch television for two hour intervals, took on a phantom smell that made it insufferable for Marcus to be in there for more than a few minutes at a time. He became restless and just paced the halls all day, barely ate, and restarted an old nervous tick of scratching his right thumb with the index finger of the same hand.

His thoughts of Kojiro, they were several miles past obsession by now. Marcus was never an artist, but suddenly he could render professional-level pencil drawings of the mythic warrior who wielded a *seven body blade*.

That single bed room, all the walls by now were nearly covered entirely by those pencil drawings plastered on them by scotch tape. An eagle-eyed viewer would notice that those pictures, they were telling an ancient story of Kojiro every bit as cryptic as the blood-borne passages being self-written in the book back at the Marx Estate.

Marcus, he didn't look much like the boxer that he once was. He'd lost a great deal of weight and grew in exchange for his muscles a generous swath of facial hair to match the wild fire of brown wool on top his head. If Moses were black and insane, he'd be Marcus Green at the rock bottom of his life; locked up in a mental hospital and drawing pictures of a man he deeply hated but didn't know (or remember) why.

He was working on a new drawing, of Kojiro going through a dark cave, when, unbeknownst to him, there were two trench coated men wearing identical Hannya Kabuki Demon masks, one black and silver/the other black and green, walking into the front entrance to Blackwood. They were behemoths at 6'4 and 6'2.

The receptionist, a friendly looking café-au-lait brown skinned woman in her mid-40s, immediately lost her affable glow upon seeing them. But before she could get a word out, there was a silver Desert Eagle mark XIX .50 pointed at her forehead.

The portly, armed security man, toffee colored and too old for this, rose from his perch at the corner of the small lobby, but the second of the two bald assassins had already drew a burnt bronze semi-automatic FN F2000 from his coat, pumping 17 rounds into the guard that didn't have a lick of a chance.

Those shots rang throughout the building. Marcus, who was on the second floor, heard them as loudly as if the assault was happening in the next room. But it just sounded like music to his troubled mind, a cause more for curiosity than panic.

So, he listened for more *music* as the otherwise uneventful minutes dragged on, the pencil in his hand continuing to render more details on his 8.5 x 11 inch canvas. Interrupting both the music and his drawing were a sudden potpourri of memories from another, distant time.

Another gun blast was heard outside somewhere, and then three more, triggering the image in Marcus' mind of *a man (himself?) wearing a rough, woolen cloak, walking barefoot in the muddy water of a darkened cave, and holding up a lantern to light a path through the darkness ahead.*

He shook the memory off, briefly, continuing his drawing. But even as his hand carefully traced in lines of detail, his mind's eye still played memories:

of Kojiro rushing up on him, the mysterious figure in a woolen shawl, in the cave. Marcus felt the glee in the man, as he pulled out the bamboo straw and shot Kojiro with the sedative…

There was another shot outside, the booms getting closer, that again briefly jolted Marcus out of the confusing reveries.

Kojiro, in the memory, spoke to him. He was on the ground now after getting shot, holding his neck and slowly losing consciousness.
"I will…. I will find you again, bastard! Coward! Villain!"
"I am worthy many names then,' Marcus, as this man in the memory, felt himself saying in reply, "Flattering, that. You honor me, old friend!"

Another shot, BOOM! Another and another… There was screaming in the halls, the sounds of glass shattering, the commotion of chaos ringing not far from Marcus' room door. Between this and the invasion of memories, he was distracted enough that he put down his pencil and stood. The noise of gunshots and screaming and running, it was no longer musical to Marcus' ear. It was like rationality was dawning on him as a defense against the influx of suffocating thoughts. Suddenly, he began to sweat. His throat tightened as another foreign memory invaded his mind.

Deep within the oasis of an unnamed forest, the sun's light invading from just overhead, its rays shooting down between the patchy bright red shade of palmate maple, Hogyoku, and weeping Green Cascades. Three men could be found laughing. One of them, the shapeshifting Jericho, whom Kojiro once encountered in a test-like reverie cast upon him by the mystical Xiao Xiao Chen. There was another, much taller brutish man with a barrel chest, broad shoulders and brick-layer hands. He had a scar over his dead right eye. This was Omphalos. And the third man, their leader, the barefooted mystery man with a woolen cloak and a bokken in his belt. He was sometimes referred to as the Prometheus.

A now healthy and strong Kojiro, still bearded, accompanied by Jubei, Kana, Tzukuba, Ittei and Yoriko's pack, Otaku, Girou and Ichiro, they were walking up on these three confident men who stood around laughing, it seemed, at them.

The Prometheus, Marcus' remembered perspective, he took one look at Kojiro, smirked, and said, "It seems you've found me after all, old friend! Persistent!"

Another loud BOOM, this time right outside Marcus' door, it shook him out of the memory, shifting his mind further along in the timeframe of that same event.

A fight had broken out in those woods between Kojiro's crew and those three men. The Prometheus called more of the Pau-gukdoza, that assisted him in the cave, to join in the battle.

There was a moment when Kojiro's man Ichiro fell to his knees and tore open his shinu shirt, his eyes aglow a bright amber and a tattoo on his chest of a Ningen sea monster began to burn, bleed, and move involuntarily. Marcus remembers Kojiro yelling to the man, "NO, ICHIRO!! CONTROL IT!!!" But it was too late. The ground beneath everyone's feet transformed into a cross between muddy flooded swamp and shallow river water. The Prometheus, to maintain footing, leapt up onto a large boulder, that was now floating in a magical current of water. He looked hatefully across the clearing at Kojiro, who himself was now riding the trunk of a fallen tree as the water level grew. A giant blue-gray arm burst forth from the swamp and then-

-the memory was shattered by an explosion at Marcus' door, the door handle blowing off from a shotgun blast and then the taller man kicking the now broken door inward.

Marcus, in a panic, backpedaled all the way to the dead-end that was the back wall, his arm held up in surrender and his mind expecting that these were his final moments.

The two assassins calmly entered the room, lowering their weapons after confirming their quarry. Both lifted their masks, revealing bone white skin, clean shaven faces with chiseled jaws that could slice bread, and bald heads. They would look like brothers if it weren't for one of them, the taller man with the black and silver Oni, having a long, deep distinguishing scar over his dead left eye.

The Cyclops smiled upon making eye contact with Marcus. "Time to go, my liege," he said. "Now."

"W-w-what?"

"We haven't any time to waste, Katsurou," said the other man.

"Kat-who?" was Marcus' reply.

———

"IF COLLECTIVISM MEANS THE SUBJUGATION of the individual to a group,' Qadr Fakhoury remembered Cross smugly saying in that virtual meeting, '...could it then be considered the bedrock of a global indoctrination that keeps humanity from achieving a True common good, with a capital T, rather than a series of idealized fantasies of such only mimicked, mocked, and meandered?"

She'd known men like him her entire life, suave megalomaniacs who piggybacked the philosophies of Ayn Rand to justify opportunistic schemes running the full spectrum of perversity. These men made up her entire network of employers, and their monies furnished her lavish lifestyle, they kept her and Landau Kier residing under the roofs of the world's most ostentatiously rich and luxurious condos and hotels, no Saturday morning under the same sun twice. Jeremiah Cross, she was learning more and more, was the worst among them. And it was this revelation that was beginning to maraud the fulcrum of her cold-blooded resolve.

Another thing that bugged her was the memory, the mystery, of that night in Buirut, when she collected Nicolaou Steinitz's head on assignment. As with every target, she vetted him thoroughly before engaging. So, she knew that the prodigious chess player had no training in the fighting arts.

How then, at the end of his life, was he able to spontaneously manifest the skills to go toe to toe with her -if but briefly? How did the fear and cowardice in his eyes switch from that to a warrior's twitch? And why, again, did this transformation seem oddly familiar?

Between jobs, her globe-trotting travels to collect the other six heads needed for Cross' Trivium project, she found herself staring in the mirror for long sessions at a time, sometimes as long as an hour, trying to see past her eyes and into her own soul. Trying, to no avail, to decipher a lingering existential riddle.

She'd never met Steinitz before the night that she killed him, but in the moments of his turn from coward to fighter, she …recognized him.

She recognized Ingvar Oliyath too, her next quarry, an architect from Copenhagen, Denmark, whom she found in a high rise building of his own design that overlooked the Baltic Sea.

The Aerospace Engineer Javi Castillo, found vacationing in Jounieh, Lebanon, eerily took on a distinct body odor that evoked dubious recollections of a previous life in Qadr, at the moment when she pierced his heart with a pearl handled stiletto knife while he was sleeping.

Her encounter with Lev Illsley Knopfler, M.D. was much different, more complicated. Maybe she was made slightly, subtly slower by the revelations of each hit, maybe the creeping existential questions began to weigh so heavily on her shoulders that it was making her sloppy at her job. Surely, it wasn't because she was growing a conscience.

Knopfler, a world renowned cardiologist by trade, teamed up about twenty years prior with a pharmaceutical company to develop a groundbreaking anticoagulant medication that, unlike others on the market, could not only cure heart disease, unstable angina, and reverse the effects of ischemic strokes, but could also clear atherosclerosis and the linked diseases that account for the leading cause of death in the United States. Only, the pharmaceutical company was corrupt, and the medicine's claims were short-term and exaggerated, leading to debilitating opioid addictions. The company, in fact, Lehdnonovan, was a money laundering front for Knopfler's business partner, Carlos Wagner, secret head of a German-Columbian drug cartel.

"Ms. Fakhoury,' went the memory of Cross' smug voice playing in her mind, *'have any good men so far been killed in the recruitment of the unique minds integral to the completion of our project?"*
"Rien,"….

So no, it wasn't a matter of conscience that slowed Qadr down when set to dispatch the sketchy doctor. She crept into his home like any other, a decedent mega-mansion in Los Angeles, California. Before slipping in through a window, it took her about twenty minutes to disable the security systems and send all the doctor's fifteen guards into the big sleep.

"And what,' Cross continued in her memory, *'of the remaining list?"*

"Tous les méchants."

"All bad men," Cross happily translated, the words bleeding through the fissures of his perfect teeth.

Knopfler had no family. Beige furniture accenting the silica and quartz tile floors and high ceilings, the huge home was a narcissist's affectations of prestige. So Qadr knew that he was alone somewhere in the big ostentatious, four-story gold-laced home. Like a wraith, she stuck to the shadows in her black cat suit, a 27 inch straight blade scimitar sheathed in black leather on her back, an M-9 Bayonet knife holstered on the front strap across her breasts, a Glock 43 strapped to either thigh accompanied each by two extra magazines, and both her hands holding a Karambit knife. Her stealth skills were to the point of perfection, edging forward with deliberate steps that made no sound at all.

But something was off.

The main lighting in the living room was blue, coming from an internally-lit wall length aquarium that took a curve by the staircase and stretched all the way down a hall that led to a veranda to the backyard.

The glass held snapper, mulloway, and King George whiting marine life. But it was the slightest of reflections cast against the blue-lit surface that saved Qadr from certain death.

She dove backwards in a flip and rolled behind a couch just as three shots rang out that would have taken off her head hadn't she moved in time. Two of the three shots that missed Qadr, they hit the aquarium and shattered it, all the water, the snappers, mulloway, and King George fish spilling out onto the floor as the entire surface of glass collapsed under the pressure. Shards going everywhere in an exploding salvo.

Those shots came from a long barrel 357 Magnum, wielded competently by Knopfler, in a bathrobe and high socks, standing himself in shadows over by the darkened entrance to the kitchen -which was exactly thirty yards across from the staircase/assassin trap.

"Look at you!," Knopfler yelled, before firing another shot that put a large hole in his sofa, and then another, "deceiver!! Traducer!!"

One more shot, "Benedict-Arnold!," and then he dropped the shells from the chamber and pulled a speed loader from his robe pocket, while saying, "playing the long game! Thinking you can ever escape your responsibilities to the people who trust you!"

The words confused Qadr. She'd never met nor held any form of allegiances to Lev Illsley Knopfler, but now wasn't the time to make sense of that. She drew one of her Glocks and reached over the top of the sofa, firing shots in the robed doctor's direction. But like a trained operative himself (which, Qadr knew, he wasn't!), Knopfler moved out of the path of the bullets and sheltered himself behind a wall.

"I invented the techniques you are using,' he yelled beyond the wall, closing his gun's chamber, 'I am the precursor! And I remember you!"

She couldn't see it, but Knopfler was using a palm sized mirror to look beyond the wall, seeing that Qadr was rising from behind the couch with her gun training in his direction.

He waited until she was fully standing, then he turned and fired-

-at nothing! She was gone, vanished. The entire movement, being caught in the mirror and all, was a set up. Before Knopfler could look to his right, Qadr was already there, slashing his bicep with the Karambit and relieving him of the gun.

He wouldn't go down easily, however. The gun fell to the floor, clattering and sliding just within ten yards of their stand-off. Knopfler was good, he held his own with parries and counters against two very sharp Karambit knives, only getting cut here and there as they scuffled.

Knopfler managed to get an elbow strike in to Qadr's face, making her stagger backwards. He took this opportunity to dive and roll for the gun. But she was on him. He was quick enough however to turn and fire, but only once before she impaled the forearm of his gun hand, making him drop the weapon again, and then, in barely a second's time, disabling his arms and legs with several slashes in just the right places. She grabbed him by the throat before his body could slump backwards. That's when she noticed she was bleeding from her left side rib. Knopfler smiled,

"I got you,' he said, "...Tzukuba."

His utterance of that name, it at the same time frightened and surprised Qadr.

She screamed while drawing the sword from her back, twirling it once, and then with it separating Knopfler's head from his neck.

——

QADR, AS A RULE, USES LOW INCOME HOTELS when on jobs in the states and always checks in under a pseudonym. The architectural criteria was that any place she stayed at had to be set up in a way that provided room access without having to pass through a lobby. This time, at a Villa hotel not far from the Culver City district, she was Carla Jaziri.

She staggered into her room at about 2am, having already lost a lot of blood from the gunshot wound just below her left rib. It was a through and through shot, luckily, so she wouldn't have to dig for a bullet to remove. And that she made it this far was enough to assure that no vital organs had been hit. But the pain and blood loss were real threats. If she passed out from shock before treating the wound, Qadr knew, she would never wake up.

So, she immediately stripped and washed the entry and exit wounds. She then cauterized them with the heated blade of the M-9 Bayonet, stifling the scream that an ordinary person would have let ring.

This focus on subduing the pain, it's why Qadr didn't feel the presence in the room. The cloaked, translucent figure drawing near her, step by deliberate step, a cloak flowing behind against the push of nonexistent wind. She didn't see the changing flow of hair, the gold-red dust that made up the skin of the invisible cloak wearer, or the crystal, memory-stealing eyes watching her that swirled with monsoons in the place of pupils.

Those eyes, they could see right through Qadr. And they could see that she was fatally wrong in medical assessment of her injuries. What Qadr didn't catch was that, yes, her spleen had been ruptured by the bullet. And she would surely die despite having stopped the bleeding and dressed the wounds.

"This is unacceptable," Zhrontese said to herself, watching Qadr lie down on the bed and stare up at the ceiling fan that was slowly making its revelations.

Tzukuba, Qadr repeated in her mind, that name that Knopfler used for her. It made her think of another vague, repressed memory from over ten years prior. The first time that she heard that name, when she absconded from the Israeli army.

Qadr was an IDF soldier stationed at a remote camp in Deir ez-Zor, a scorched earth patch of Syrian desert land not far from where the infamous Armenian genocide that took place in the early 1900s. She was the unprecedented (and unwelcome) leader of a unit of twelve men positioned in the middle of nowhere to await, indefinitely, instructions from Northern Command. Those instructions never came, and after more than four months of target practice, drill cycles, and endless waiting, the men grew more restless, bitter, and tired of taking orders from a woman. One night, a mistake, they tried to rape her. Qadr blacked out in the height of the assault, and then woke up some time later in a pool of all twelve men's blood. She had vague musings of a ninja woman named Tzukuba during the blackout, but remembered only the name upon waking up.

She was never heard from again by anyone who knew her.

Both Zhrontese and Qadr recounted this distant memory as the stoic assassin lie there on the bed, unknowingly, dying. But then Zhrontese said again, "No. This is unacceptable," before deciding to break her coven's rule against intervention.

Still invisible, the powerful Interstice drew close to Qadr's bedside. She reached for the wound and rested her hand upon it. Qadr could not see the hand, but she could feel the sudden rush of burning pain that its touch caused.

This time, she couldn't stifle the scream.

———

"DO NOT LET THE HERO IN YOU BE SUFFOCATED by the hand of lonely, impatient frustration," the grievous, echoing voice spoke to the Objectivist business man's back. "Your own life is your own ethical purpose. Every thought that you have toward achievement, it must war constantly against the myth of selflessness and the suppositions of any and all who would oppose your ultimate wisdom. Every spark of your fire is irreplaceable."

"Yes,' Jeremiah Cross agreed, his eyes intense and drunk with conflagrant zeal, his body and mind inebriated by the scotch from the half empty snifter held in his right hand, dangling at his side as he stared over the horizon of the city through his office window, the morning sun somewhere beyond the building tops and beginning to invade the purple/blue sky. "Every spark of my fire…"

"Is irreplaceable,' finished the voice coming from behind him. A voice that grew louder, drawing close, casting a shadow over Cross' back that suggested a figure walking up on him of no less than seven feet in height. He made a movement to turn and look when the presence snapped,

"DO NOT LOOK AT ME!"

Cross immediately obeyed, that commanding voice filling him with an arresting fear.

"Never attempt to look at me. Not unless I tell you to," the presence warned, the voice again calm.

Moments passed, time enough for Cross to resume breathing, and then,

"The small minds that would oppose you,' the wraith argued, 'that would oppose a man of virtue, greatness…, they are not unique. Across the trajectory of human existence, the meek have always held the few who realize that their own happiness is their moral purpose, and productive achievement their noblest activity, as evil, despotic, autocratic. The short memories of the many, who look at death and destruction only in a negative light, fail to see the value in every event that they label in their books as an atrocity, a human rights violation, a black mark on human history, they fail to see the influence of these events, how they inspire lateral intellectual mobility, how they cast man several steps ahead on his evolutionary path, how they clear the grounds for so much more, so much better."

"Like the great Khan. Like the Black Death!"

"Clandestine philanthropy!" the phantom added with aplomb, "Like you so eloquently said to your workers, many of whom remain fearful of the great work that they are doing."

"But they will come around."

"You will make them!" the voice, drawing even closer, the shadow over Cross getting larger, the footsteps louder and heavier on the tile floor. Despite the urge, Cross didn't dare again to turn. Instead, he said,

"I will make them."

"Or else," the voice, now speaking directly into his ear. Hands now reached out of the living wraith-like shadow, the pale skin covered in desquamation and bearing the texture of cracking porcelain. Then a face just over Cross' right shoulder, looking down on him from the vantage point of seven feet in height, dark shadowy gray hair, and yellow eyes with fiery red pupils, the only thing that changed about the Inca Tan'mo's appearance was that now he sported a wild, chaotic beard that added to his menacing mien. "Or else they will die for the greater good, as many others already will."

克

COLETRANE'S HANDLING OF THE black Lamborghini Sian rivaled that of a professional racecar driver, but it didn't make Patrick feel any better over sitting in the passenger seat of a car going over 110mph on the I-4, pushing the singing v12 engine to the max. They were heading to the mansion from the airport, zipping past other cars so fast that it felt, and looked, as though the two were traveling in an earthbound jet.

Their bags were in the back, but Hatsukoi was tucked between the right side of Coletrane's seat and the vehicle's center console, her gold-wrapped tsuka pointing upward at a 95 degree angle.

They didn't talk much on the plane, not after that one conversation precipitated by Coletrane bringing the spiked tea to calm Patrick's nerves. And not a word passed between them since unboarding the plane, loading the car, and fishtailing out of the lot.

After a while, it began to rain. And Coletrane was still speeding, pushing the car to its 117mph max. That's when Patrick broke the silence,

"Don't you ever worry about getting... a ticket?"

At first, Coletrane was too focused on the road and his thoughts to answer. He was focused in fact on a conversation he was having in his mind with Kojiro, that accounted much for his urgency and recklessness behind the wheel:

The two of them, Kojiro and Coletrane, were standing together at the edge of a high, narrow ridge in the vision, an escarpment among many surrounding others in an unknown place beset by garish corrugations of fog so thick and expansive that every earthen surface looked like rock-borne lily pads adrift on a gray, black sea. The sand under their feet was copper pearl in color, but felt and smelled like the detritus from a long ago cataclysm. The sky was bereft of color and vibrancy, but every few moments there shown a spider-web of lightning in the far reaching distance of despair. The wind would have pushed both men over if they weren't firmly planted in the desolate earth.

Kojiro's kimono was entirely black, and so was Coletrane's suit and double-breasted knee length coat. In the former was an eminence of melancholy, and in the latter was a strong sense of curiosity that made him want to speak, to inquire. But Kojiro, looking out at the fog instead of turning to face Coletrane, spoke first.

"Men are ...arrogant by nature. And mistaken,' he began, 'across every age, race, region, culture, or creed. Their lives in fact depend upon the error in thinking that their failures accompany their bodies to the dust in the end. But in reality, it is never over. Your failures, and the memory of them, are eternal. They echo out into the beyond like a stone skipping across water."

That's when he finally turned to Coletrane, stepping close and staring him dead in the eye.

"Can you see her?" he asked. "Can you see Taya's fate in my eyes, that came to find her in my failure to acquit her of it?"

Coletrane couldn't speak. It was like the words he wanted to say were caught in his throat, or like the feral version of Kojiro's hand was still squeezing his windpipe. He wanted to turn from the twilight samurai's eyes, but couldn't. So, in them he could see Taya; still in her room in Basumaru's house, many years after Kojiro's apparent failure to reverse the Tan'Mo's curse. It is late at night. She is all alone, her only company the still burning warousoku candles and sage that she couldn't smell.

Her skin had become grayish, still technically living but sucked dry of life-force, transparent enough that the blue of veins could be seen, as well as the many bed sores underneath from being immobile for so long. Her black hair had thinned and developed streaks of white. There were webs of frown lines about the corners of her mouth, a superhighway of stress lines across her brow, and her face was so emaciated and devoid of effervescence that only the rise and fall of her chest from breathing could convince anyone that she was alive at all. Those eyes though, they continued to stare up at the ceiling; looking, waiting, hoping (in vain) that her love would one day save her.

"Don't you worry about getting a ticket?" Patrick repeated. "Hey. Train?"

Coletrane gripped the steering wheel tighter, narrowed his eyes and steeled his jaw. After a few long moments he finally said, simply,

"I own the police in this city. And they know my car."

———

THAT LONG HALLWAY IN THE MARX Estate, the one leading to the trophy room, wherein lied the ancient buckle-latched book propped up on an etagere pillar, it was a narrow passageway with a vaulted ceiling lined with acrylic prism lights. The hand woven runner underfoot was a woolen Maasai imported patchwork of beige, rust red, olive, burgundy, several browns, green, and light salmon. The African Blackwood walls held rows on either side of hand painted portraits of great Black inventors from history; Henry Blair, Thomas L. Jennings, Sarah

Boone, Otis Boykin, Madam C. J. Walker, George Washington Carver, Garret Morgan, Elijah McCoy, Mary Kenner, Alexander Miles, Sarah E. Goode, Marie Van Brittan Brown, Norbert Rillieux, and others.

Patrick took notice of this while walking with Coletrane through this seemingly endless, curving tunnel, recognizing many of the faces but not all of them, and marveling most specifically at the hall being so long that it could hold so many portraits of so many people.

Poole met them just before the entrance to the trophy room, the weariness in his face making it look as though he'd aged a few years while they were abroad. But Coletrane made no acknowledgement of it besides a subtle look of the eye that only Poole himself would recognize as an unspoken apology. He, Coletrane, held out Hatsukoi for Poole to examine. The old man took the sheathed weapon into his hands, somewhat reluctantly.

"At last then, the sword,' he said, 'the totem of your every misfortune."

"The blade that killed my parents…"

Poole sighed, pulling Hatsukoi just halfway out of her saya to examine the dragon designs etched into the golden blade, and then closing it back.

"That book,' he said to break the awkward silence, 'it wrote over a hundred new pages in your absence."

"Perhaps now, having found Hatsukoi and merged at last with my quarry, I can read the language."

"*I would not recommend it*," came Kojiro's voice in Coletrane's mind, "*and yet… You must.*"

"Are you ready, Thelonious?" Poole asked, and then looking over Coletrane's shoulder at Patrick, "and you, Patrick-"

"Ittei,' Patrick corrected.

"What?"

"That, apparently, was my name long ago. In this other life. And I am as ready as I will ever be to understand."

"He is not," Kojiro confided. Coletrane tightened his jaw, narrowed his eyes, but did not turn away from Poole to regard Patrick behind him. Did not want to make any movement that might shake the war photographer's resolve.

"Very well," Poole offered, standing aside for the men to pass into the room.

———

AT THE ETAGERE, COLETRANE FELT AN eerily prohibitive force pushing against him as he went to engage the mysterious book.

"Focus," Kojiro told him. *"That is just your own energy trying to protect you from the known."*

"Fear," Coletrane whispered.

Poole and Patrick, they stood back a few yards, one man to Coletrane's right and the other to his left. Up above at the ceiling, whom no one could see, was the hovering spirit of the Interstice Clymene -watching. He had just now seeped in through the walls.

After hearing Coletrane say fear, Poole replied,

"Thelonious?"

"Fear, Poole,' he spoke up. "Fear is why I couldn't read it before. Fear is why I lacked control."

"What does it say?" Patrick asked, as Coletrane read the blood passages, carefully going from page to page.

"It is the story of Kojiro ko-Mitsu. Of he and his gang. The story of a curse put upon him by a devil, and his vainglorious efforts to seek revenge."

"Shi-ne,' Kojiro said, basically meaning *fuck you, 'little modern man of privilege. No action of mine was done in vain. We are still here, now, together, and the Tan'Mo still seeks to bring the world crashing down."*

"Vainglorious was a poor word choice,' Coletrane. Corrected. "Kojiro could not succeed in his time because... I stopped consciously creating the story. My subconscious took over after the shock of my parents' deaths. My trauma."

Then, Coletrane turns from the book to look directly at Poole.

"My father was the vainglorious one, Poole. Had he taught me more, had he prepared me-"

"Your father had not fully grasped the phenomena of the tulpa, or the mysteries of Ulehla's work. He wanted but to protect you, for you to have a normal life."

"But instead, he cursed me,' Coletrane offered, walking over to Poole, "Doomed me every bit as much as Kojiro's demon doomed him."

"Listen to yourself,' Poole, now raising his voice, offended by the unfair accusations being leveled at his dead employer, "Kojiro is a manifestation of your mind! This is your doing, all of this! Your imagination run amok! Vincent and Adaeze-"

"Don't you say it!" Coletrane warned, fearing, knowing, that Poole was ready to vocalize, in front of Patrick, the crushing indictment that he himself had murdered his own parents. "Don't you dare!"

"Is it possible," Patrick interjected, to dissipate this tension that was rapidly spiraling out of control. Both Coletrane and Poole regarded him. "Is it possible that Vincent... never fully believed? Not in the prophesy, not in the theories of Ulehla that would undo everything that humankind had come to take for granted about the surrounding world... Maybe this was his way of trying to protect you, Train. If only he could find some scientific explanation that would tie everything up. Often the greatest skeptics become the greatest holy men."

"This man,' Clymene said telepathically, while watching this drama unfold before him, 'as truths dawn upon him, comes to the realization that he must do something to bring balance to the universe."

"Before two worlds collide,' rhodium particles drifting upward from the floor not ten yards from Poole, Patrick and Coletrane, imperceptible however to the human eye, solidifying into the translucent countenance of Manthis as he continued speaking telepathically to Clymene, "before Fact and Fiction, Fantasy and Reality, eat each other like the ouroboros. But is he ready?"

"A test then?" Clymene suggested.

"Yes," Manthis immediately liked the idea, almost smiling, "a test."

———

LATER THAT NIGHT, MUCH LATER, JUST after 2AM, Poole in his room beneath the stairs and Patrick in one of the guest suites, Coletrane lie in his enormous bed with the company of three women. Those women as well as the ayahuasca, they were supposed to be enough to distract Coletrane, at least for a while, from the troubles and the questions that were set before him. But it was getting harder and harder for hedonism to quell the troubled beast.

Coletrane began to sweat. He was shifting in the bed as if in the grips of a nightmare. None of the women however were disturbed by his movements, the nighttime darkness remaining a salve for the unburdened minds of sirens.

There was silence. Stillness. Life suspended in a panoply of dreams, or, in Coletrane's case, nightmares. But then, shaken by instinct, he opened his eyes just in time.

Coletrane shifted awake and dove from the bed at the moment a beamlike blast of flaming andradite shot from out a darkened corner of the room and hit the bed at its center, burning all three women to a crisp before they even had a chance to scream out in pain. The bed itself collapsed in dust as Coletrane rolled across the floor to a stand on which Hatsukoi was placed. He drew the golden blade and narrowed his eyes, which were now transformed into the double pupil figure-eights. He was naked save for a pair of boxer shorts, his unbound hair was an untamed forest on top of his head, and every muscle in his body was taut and ready.

That's when Clymene stepped out of the corner from which the fiery blast had come, a portal behind him closing on the Taklimakan Desert. Instead of a cloak, the bearded Interstice was wrapped in gaudy 8th century cord and plaque armor from the High Tang Dynasty, aglow in a pulsing silhouette of red light. He looked directly at Coletrane, whose body and life were protected from the instant implosion of an Interstice's gaze by the figure-eights.

That's when Manthis emerged from another portal on the other side of the room, a portal closing behind him on the Dome Argus, his body adorned in wintry iron plated nomadic armor of gambesons and chain mail. On his pronounced chest plate was a familiar crest -the Ulehla glyph.

Both of them were larger than life, standing near eight feet tall and looking down on Coletrane with subdued contempt colored by intrigue.

"It is time then for us to see," Manthis said.

"See what, demon?!"

"You would call us by your own epithet?" Clymene asked, more amused than genuinely surprised.

"Can you identify the face of your enemy?" Manthis wondered, "Or will you strike out recklessly at any perceived threat, real or imagined, thus dooming yourself and the world too?"

Coletrane offered no response. Instead, he just stared, standing high and readying the sword in a Te Ura Gasami stance.

"Very well," Clymene said.

And then on cue, Manthis leapt towards Coletrane and attacked with two short double-edged kindjal swords drawn from air, both of them engulfed in flames. They made sparks when colliding with Hatsukoi, and Coletrane's skills proved deft enough to avoid their fiery tips. The Interstice did get a cut in across Coletrane's arm, but was countered by a horizontal slash from Hatsukoi along the torso. That would have killed a mortal man, but the Interstices could not be killed. Coletrane spun around off of that last move and transitioned into an overhead strike that would have gone through Manthis' shoulder, but right in the moment before impact, Manthis changed his form to appear as Adaeze -smiling at her son.

Coletrane, seeing this, reflexively pulled back on the strike just in time -and barely!- to but make a small cut across his mother's cheek. He staggered.

"It's ok, bien-aimé," she said, immediately filling Coletrane with rage for how perfectly gratuitous the imitation was. He spun Hatsukoi and then rushed forward, only to pass right through an explosion of reflective dark amber beads, and then find himself now fighting Clymene on the other end of it, who would have taken off his head with an unexpected swing of a Dao! The second strike however cut along his chest, the third one too! But Coletrane parried the third and spun behind his supernatural opponent, slashing diagonally across the surface of the cord and plaque! The force of the strike pushed Clymene forward, but he immediately regained his footing, pivoted off his left foot, and spun back around from the right side -serving Coletrane a fusillade of deadly slashes.

Coletrane was able to block most of them with Hatsukoi, and then he became suddenly aware that he wouldn't be this fast if it weren't for Kojiro within him. This realization, it made him faster! It saved him from Manthis, who resolidified from the bead scatter and joined in on the fray from Coletrane's right. He had to duck under one of the kindjals, which passed through

Clymene's body instead but had no effect, and then sidestep the second kindjal and turn into a counter with Hatsukoi.

The slash cut Clymene's head in half at a slanting angle, but it came immediately back together just as Clymene smiled and then kicked Coletrane in the chest, throwing him backward seven yards -crashing into a curio and then slamming against the wall!

Though hurt and wounded from several cuts to his unarmored body, arms, legs, Coletrane quickly climbs to his feet, spits blood out on the floor, and pivots himself to re-engage the two warriors before him.

He lunges left to attack Manthis first from the right, parries and rolls under the counter to attack Clymene next -playing both of them against each other by maintaining tight proximity and moving in crescent-angled steps off each blow, requiring his opponents to constantly turn and shift and move out of each other's way.

At one point Manthis becomes Poole, and Coletrane, instinctively, avoids striking him in that form. Then Clymene, just as Coletrane is bringing Hatsukoi down into a body cut, would become the youthful image of Marcus, cause Coletrane to quickly pivot again and draw away the strike, shifting his momentum into a swirl that would bring Hatsukoi's blade clattering fiercely against one of Manthis' fiery kindjal!

This goes on for several more minutes, with Coletrane getting futile blows in on the Interstices that would all immediately heal, and them sustaining cuts on himself that wouldn't. He continued to hold his own, working against the pain and fatigue.

"You are wiser than I would have pegged you," Kojiro said in his mind, *"knowing to avoid them when they transform into someone who isn't a foe."*

"They gave away the answer to the riddle," Coletrane responds, also in mind, "when they mentioned the reckless potential of not being able to identify the face of my enemy."

Briefly, and in more of a feeling than an image, Coletrane saw himself and Kojiro together in his mind, as separate entities, sitting across from one another in a dinghy cast somewhere out in the middle of an unnamed sea.

But it was a gash across the surface of his right quadricep made by Clymene's Dao that snapped him fully out of the reverie.

That is when Clymene stood before him, and transformed into Jeremiah Cross.

Coletrane, at first, was unsure how to respond. He didn't know his father's friend to had been an enemy. So, he stood there, frozen for a moment long enough for Manthis to attack him from behind, slashing across his back and creating a wound with the kindjal that immediately cauterized by the fire.

Coletrane screamed and staggered forward. Clymene, still in the form of Cross, sidestepped so that Coletrane would crash through a slender glass wall that divided his bed quarters and the shower room. There was now glass and destruction everywhere, Coletrane bleeding from more cuts than could be counted. But still, he got back up. The Interstices waited patiently for him to do so.

Clymene as Cross, he still stood before him with his hands in the pockets of his beige long lapel coat.

"That,' Kojiro began, he and Coletrane again at sea in the mental image. He stood up in the boat and looking off at a developing storm in the horizon, ***"That is not your father's friend. He was never your father's friend."***

"Who is he then?"

Instead of an answer, Coletrane narrowed his eyes as he looked upon Manthis/Cross standing before him in the room. He watched as the skin of his face began to go pale and crackle. He watched at the eyes became yellow, with bleeding red pupils. He watched in disbelief as the now smiling image of Jeremiah Cross became the menacing countenance of the Inca Tan'Mo!

No longer hesitant, Coletrane sprang towards the Tan'Mo with every intention to cut him to shreds! But then-

Poole quickly gathered up his robe upon hearing the screams in the house, exited the room and rushed up the stairs. By the time he reached the second floor and the hall to the east wing, Patrick was already standing at the door to his own room, looking out as three distraught women came running down the hall in Poole's direction and away from Coletrane's room. They each had a blanket or large towel covering their naked bodies, and none of them were wounded in any way -certainly not burnt to a crisp as before seen.

The women ran past Patrick and past Poole too, and then on their way towards the stairway at the end of the curving hallway. When Patrick made a gesture to exit his room and join Poole, the distressed steward made a hand gesture indicating that Patrick should hang back and wait.

Watching Poole continue his trek up the long hallway however, Patrick watched and in a blink, the semi-translucent image of Yoriko appeared standing in the center of the carpet. Watching him with her bright, hypnotic eyes.

"Thelonious?" Poole called after knocking once on Coletrane's door. "Thelonious?" he said again before opening it.

The entire room was trashed, the bed sheets were soaked in splatters of blood. There was damage all over the walls that appeared to have been made by blades, two shattered curios, glass all over the floor. Hatsukoi was still sheathed and on her stand. But Coletrane was on the floor on the other side of the bed. Poole had to rush all the way into the room to get to him, and when he did he found his surrogate son covered in bleeding knife wounds and convulsing, still unconscious and lost in a nightmare.

"THELONIOUS!" he yelled, running to him and propping him up on his knees, cradling Coletrane like a child as he shook and slapped him a few times to wake him up. One more cut was slowly forming on Coletrane's face, going down the side of his cheek and opening up. Until, suddenly, and in a moment that seemed to last forever, he finally opened his eyes and then the cut stop. His connection was broken from the dream.

Patrick stepped into the room then, but he remained in the doorway. He watched Poole helping Coletrane to his feet. That's when his and the rich man's eyes locked, the unspoken gravity of the moment becoming ever clear.

ABOUT TWO HOURS LATER, POOLE HAD finished patching up Coletrane's wounds (since he had foregone going to a hospital), a hired limo service had gotten the girls home safely, and the sun had reached its peak in the morning sky. Patrick stood out on the balcony to his room, looking out on the resplendent, tranquil view that it provided, of the vast botanical gardens, lakes, the hedge maze, statues. He thought while taking in deep breaths of clean air about how the equanimity inspired by these quiet, serene vistas were but an illusion draped over the violent chaos of life. Of his life, currently, and all life in general. Humans enjoy beauty, luxury, the many coruscations offered by temporal comforts, because they know that just underneath and beyond them lie misery, uncertainty, sickness, disappointment, death...

Patrick turned these thoughts in his mind as, below, Coletrane and Poole were sitting on a bench in front of the lake.

Poole, by now, was fully dressed in an off-white sweater and black pants. Coletrane, his many wounds all fully dressed in bandages and gauze, was still in but a bathrobe and cradling a steaming ceramic mug in his hands. It was filled with a holistic tea mixture from Adaeze's garden; kava, rooibos, lapacho bark, calendula, and a touch of chrysanthemum. It had a strong taste matched only by its potency.

"They were.... not phantoms or demons," Coletrane explained, recalling the events of the previous night. "They were some form of messengers... Their assault on me was some kind of test."

"Does the condition I found you in suggest that you failed this test?" Poole asked, subdued sarcasm coming naturally to him in order that he might ease the tension of otherwise pressing moments.

"Very droll, Poole. But no. I think I passed it."

Then after a few moments, a few more sips of the piquant tea,

"What do you remember about my father's old friend, Jeremiah Cross?"

Surprised by the question, Poole thought a moment,

"I remember never liking or trusting him."

"You never quite like or trust anyone, Poole. What was different about this guy?"

"Don't you remember?" Poole asked, then after a thought, "Perhaps you were too young... There was always something suspicious and ulterior about his interactions with Vincent. Most men from old money, they cannot help but to be clinically unscrupulous in some way or the other. But this man Cross, this... Silicon Valley magnate, there was always something particularly cold and snakelike about him. Vincent, he regarded him like the brother of sorts. The poor fool never noticed the man's air of duplicity. But I always did."

On that note, Coletrane sat back on the bench. Contemplated Poole's revelation for a series of beats.

A black-crowned anhinga came flying into view beyond an imperceptible sheen of sunlight cast across the blue, cloudless sky. The darter bird with its long fanlike tail swooped down to the water of the lake, splashing in and then coming out with a pickerel impaled by its beak. It returned skyward then, disappearing behind a bright, leafy thicket of bald cypress.

"Set me an appointment with Mr. Cross," Coletrane finally said. "It's time I had an audience of this ersatz uncle."

———

THE STEADY DRIP FROM THE CONDENSATE drain line in back of the three story office building seemed louder in the stillness of night. Each drop of water in the little puddle it made on the asphalt below rang out like the resonate, echoing sound of a mallet hitting a gong. There were two dumpsters out back, a stone veneered building to the left and an abandoned restaurant to the right, together forming a small oasis on a 16 x 20 foot patch of concrete that gave way to a rocky border just before a wide open grassy field that undulated across its surface enough to account for hummocks and ditches when it rained. There was a small pond beyond that field, and on the other side of it, about a quarter of a mile out, was a backroad that used to merge into an onramp to a now closed interstate highway.

Spots like this were scattered all around the city of Orlando, which boasted upward of 2,000 homeless people in Orange, Osceola, and Seminole counties at any time of the year. When the shelters were full, which they often were, destitute people had to get creative to find places to lay their heads at night.

Being a stranded goddess with only a fraction of her power, who couldn't fly or conjure or teleport or do much of anything else except unwillingly cause destruction to those with whom she made eye contact or violently take human life force to sustain her physicality, made the *Ghost Orchid* Astrid count very much as destitute. She'd found an old, threadbare vellux fleece blanket at some point that she used to cover her naked body. Astrid didn't remember how she got it, as her memory since coming back into the world was spotty at best, but she didn't remember a human dying in the exchange.

She was curled up in the blanket and huddled on the floor near the drain line, that dripping water somehow giving her comfort. The consistency of it, a form of stability for a mind still adrift in confusion. Cold, this was a new sensation for her. So was pain, which she discovered she could experience after getting cut on the leg by a nail when she passed too close to a ramshackle wall.

The dripping helped Astrid concentrate on her thoughts, vague memories of her previous *life* in the mythological mock history created by young Coletrane. She remember Ittei and Kojiro and the Live Crew. She remembered having a psychic, spiritual connection to the earth that, now, was either severed or nullified. Maybe she was never a goddess at all, she considered. Maybe, she was but a primordial personification of Gaia, the spirit of the earth. Maybe this possibility made sense of why looking into her eyes would instantly kill any human, maybe the emptiness she now felt accounted for why she had to keep absorbing the life force of those who would return to the dust in order to sustain the tangibility of her physical body.

One glance at the moon above reminded her of the enduring, haunting vision of her translucent self. Her eyes lingered on that moon, being somewhat hypnotized by its quiet radiance, and then,

"Will you accept it?" her own voice said to her, and she looked down from the moon and saw the vision before her - sitting in the lotus fashion. The three miniature moons that covered the vision's privates now glimmered, and seven of the smaller ones had emerged from the cosmos within her and were now circling her head like a rotating crown of coruscating luminescence.

The vision, in this way, appeared to Astrid as a sage of sorts, and now, in this moment, she was feeling a shortness of breath as the vision/sage then said,

"Will you even recognize your own intuition, and go towards the Freedom being offered you?"

It had quickly become too hard for Astrid to breath to concentrate on forming a response. She blinked and turned away, shaking her head. When she looked back up, the vision of the cosmic sage was gone.

So, then she wondered again about the thought of being a personification of Gaia, and how this possibility related to the admonitions of the haunting, conscious memory. She considering the possibility of it being more a point of epiphany than inquisition. And without thinking at all, perhaps unconsciously reluctant, she reached out a slightly quivering hand to place it down open palmed on the ground. Concentrating...

It took a while for her to intuit beyond the layers of man-made concrete, but eventually she could feel the rigidity, the brittleness of the lithosphere, that relatively thin layer of rock that made up the earth's crust. And though there was a breeze in the air, her body started to feel the warmth of viscous silicate as if it were blood flowing through her veins; olivine, garnet, pyroxene, and a couple thousand degrees Celsius beneath sheets of calcium, sodium, aluminum, and potassium. But then...

These musings, this psychic existential journey toward the center of the earth, were interrupted by the sound of approaching footsteps. The nearing gait was tentative and light footed, but getting closer quickly enough that its sounds, having disturbed the rhythm of the water drip, had set every muscle in Astrid's body to tension. She remembered then that the body she inhabited could be hurt, she remembered also that humankind was as violent purposefully as she was subconsciously. So, she arched her shoulders forward, tightened the cover of the battered blanket, and readied her eyes to show whoever was coming their end.

A shadow reached out from around the corner, stretching out long enough to suggest the coming figure's height of at least 6' ft or more. But then,

"Hello?" she heard, a child's voice. "Lady, you still back here?"

Astrid then loosened her shoulders, the illusion of the shadow breaking upon the small boy stepping out beyond the wall. He was underdressed for the cool, in only an old, dirty t-shirt, jean shorts, no shoes. His skin was biscotti brown and his coarse, bristly hair was hued somewhere between umber and cedar. Standing just over 4'3 in height, holding something yet unidentified in his hand, and so skinny it was a wonder that he wasn't lifted by the wind, the boy turned to look over where Astrid was sitting against the wall.

She remembered herself in time to shut her eyes and turn away to avoid making eye-contact with him. The boy perceived this as fear, perhaps over some form of trauma -maybe the trauma of homelessness.

"Oh, I sorry!," he plead, 'I see you earlier and wanted to bring something. If maybe you hungry."

He approached her, slowly as to not cause alarm, and knelt down in front of her at a distance of about three yards. Then he reached out and lightly tossed what he was carrying towards her; a small, wrapped single serving piece of vanilla pound cake.

"It's all I could get. Tried for trail mix too, with raisins and nuts and granola.. But the store guy almost catch me. Had to run very fast!"

Astrid lifted her eyes, careful to only open them enough to see the pound cake and the boy's knees, not up at his face.

"But very good though," he assured. "They very good."

After a few beats, and no response from Astrid, the boy added,

"I Joaquín!" he offered with a bit of excitement.

Astrid, instead of responding, curled up more in the blanket. Joaquín noticed that she was slightly shivering.

"Is ok,' he assured, standing, "probably, I see you tomorrow."

And then he left. Astrid opened her eyes then, watching as the small, malnourished boy turned the corner -his hands in his pockets.

When she was sure that Joaquín was gone, she finally reached for the pound cake.

———

CYNTHIA HAD NEVER BEEN A BIG FAN of the occult, despite, or perhaps because of, the Obeah traditions passed down through the matriarchal bloodline of her mother's family, through Ghana, the Ivory Coast, and the African diaspora in the Caribbean and South America. Her mother told stories about them all the time when Cynthia was a girl, the esoteric healing and justice-making practices of the *obayifo*, or Akan witches, and obeah priestesses referred to as *bonsam komfo*. These were slaves from Africa brought over to the West Indies, so Cynthia became more confused, resistant, and embittered by these stories as she got older. Because what kind of "justice-making" rituals would allow innumerable scores of people to live in chains, what sort of healing was this that would prove ineffective at convalescing the bone-deep lividity of generational trauma?

> *"We are all Abosam," Brisa once told little Cynthia in her thick Guyana accent, while tending to a cut she got on her knee at the playground, "children of Nyame. And the one who would send us suffering, cause us pain, enslave our people, this is Abonsam. Do you understand?"*
>
> *"No, mama," Cynthia replied, her face still wet with tears, "Because why does Nyame not protect us from Abonsam?"*
>
> *"Little picknie,' Brisa reasoned, "learning to protect ourselves is how we arrive at strength."*

She never bought that argument, no matter how many times it assaulted her ears, and had by this point spent the entirety of her educational life in defiance of it. So, Cynthia wasn't much enthused by Paulina's idea to visit an herbalist and self-described *holistic doctor*. But the migraines continued despite several prescription changes and inconclusive hospital visits, so desperation was beginning to set in and Paulina was nothing if not persistent and persuasive.

"Is that really his name," Cynthia asked from the passenger seat of Paulina's Cadillac CTS, on the ride to the healer's office.

"Yep. He even showed me his driver's license."

"Come on, Paulina. Black Christopher?"

"Maybe he got a legal name change."

"Or maybe it's a fake ID."

"Always the cynic."

Cynthia's cynical attitude wasn't improved upon arriving at Black Christopher's office, especially considering that it was in a rural neighborhood several miles removed from the business district, and because the location itself looked like a small home converted to a tattoo parlor or daiquiri shop.

The place had the appearance of a rustic bayou shack elevated at its base on brick piers. There was a four-step gabled front porch to the narrow *caille* with a thatched roof, shuttered windows, and hickory-brown stucco walls. "Caille" is what these cramped, rectangular West African to Taino style homes were called in Haiti, shotgun cottages made popular in southern states, especially Louisiana, when Haitians migrated to the US after Haiti's rebellion and independence in 1804.

As nuclear families grew larger in the closing decades of the 20th century, these style homes became less accommodating for even the poor as homes proper, so many were refitted as small businesses; hair salons, BBQ shacks, bail bondsman offices, etc.

There was a sign out front in the grass next to the steps, reading "Dr. Black Christopher's Healing Den" in bold Teutonic font.

Doctor.

They'd passed three churches in the area before arrival, one right there on that same block at the end of the corner of Cathedral Street. Those, a gas station, a couple thrift marts and a neighborhood grocery, were the only businesses in a fifteen mile radius. There was a dog barking somewhere in the vicinity when they exited the car, somewhere close but unseen -like the muted screams of Cynthia's protest.

It was just over 85 degrees out that Saturday afternoon, but didn't feel it. The low humidity made the temperature balance out at somewhere in the mid-70s against the ataraxia beauty of a high sun. One could almost pretend this wasn't a low income bethel in Arcadia.

It didn't take long for him to answer the door after Paulina rang the bell. He was dressed in a red long sleeve dashiki embroidered with golden metallic floral prints along the center. There was a bloodstone wolf-head pendant around his neck, and thick bead bracelets on both wrists made of zoisite crystals that changed colors depending on the angle that light hit them. His long brown hair was done in beeswaxed dreadlocks that reached all the way down to his bellybutton, several random locs adorned with silver hair pearls bearing pharaoh and Anubis etchings.

His big smile was decorated by a patchy beard.

"Greetings! Greetings! Please come in," the white man said, moving out of the way for Paulina and Cynthia to pass into the oasis of burning sage. "I've been expecting you."

He gave both of them the double-hander handshake, which is a favorite of politicians attempting to express warmth and trustworthiness, but for Cynthia it just felt weird and overly-familiar.

"Please follow me. Let me offer you some tea or coffee," he said while walking passed the foyer threshold and into the first room. When his back was to them, Cynthia cut her eyes at Paulina and mouthed the words, "*Black* Christopher?"

The house had no hallways. Within the wooden frame were three rooms lined up one after the other; the living room followed by the bedroom followed by the kitchen and restroom. The doorway dividing the first two rooms was just a frame with no door, making it all just one long tunnel room divided only by a bamboo beaded curtain bearing the image of the sun and moon. The uncarpeted floors sported round polypropylene area rugs with multicolored Mandala patterns that synced with the surrounding New Age Feng Shui aesthetic. Tree of life chakra wall ornaments, a coffee table bearing a bronze Himalayan Singing bowl, and maroque crescent moon shelves holding assortments of herbal healing tonics and CBD items.

Black Christopher led them into the second room which was set up like a consultation office. There was a love seat and a two sitter couch with a small two-level emerald agate geode table between. On the teal top surface of the table was a silver pot that had been broken but welded back together with gold lacquer. In front of the pot, facing the two-seater couch, was a placard that read, "*Kintsukuroi, evidence of beauty after having been broken and repaired.*"

This one detail in the entire house is what made Cynthia intrigued by the white man with Black in his name.

He served Paulina a coffee upon request and, for Cynthia, chamomile tea meant to relax her for the session. Then he introduced her to what was called a Mindplace Procyon, a hypnosis tool that looked like an 80s Walkman. It had a neurotransmitter device and a tricked-out electrocardiogram unit that used magnetic resonance imaging through sensors that attached to the patient's index and middle fingers. He also gave Cynthia a pair of large, Oculus-like goggles and an earbud.

"It's all completely safe,' Black Christopher reasoned, perched at the edge of the love-seat while setting up the device, "The sensors record physiological indicators like blood pressure, pulse, respiration, and skin conductivity. The information feed provides unique light show imagery through the goggles to induce hypnosis while the earbud plays you effervescent music."

"What?" Cynthia asked.

"It's a lot less complicated than it sounds," the cyber-eccentric herbalist assured. "Paulina has done this procedure before. We had fruitful results."

"Did you?" Cynthia gave Paulina another cross, sarcastic look.

"Remember the chronic pain in my legs I complained a lot about last fall, that limp I sometimes had?" Paulina asked, prompting Black Christopher to sit back in his chair and beam with pride.

"Yeah," Cynthia replied. "That vascular issue. I remember."

Paulina was referring to a blood flow obstruction caused by the abnormal positioning of one of her left ribs. Doctors recommended surgery to correct the issue, which she planned to get that following summer. She talked often about it during their lunches, which the two started routinely having when Cynthia was taking one of Paulina's history courses.

"Didn't you have the surgery last summer?"

Paulina grinned,

"Nope. Hypnotherapy right here in this chair cleared it up."

Black Christopher sat forward again, reaching out to grasp Paulina's hand in joviality.

"Hypnosis is the epitome of mind-body healing," Christopher added. "Of course, it is not meant to replace modern medicine. But there's no harm in exploring or acknowledging its limitations. Maybe there is something embedded in the subconscious that a neurologist's CT scans cannot detect."

Like her mother's arguments, Cynthia wasn't entirely convinced by Christopher's pitch. But the same desperation that brought her to his door made her rationalize at least humoring him.

So, he finished setting up the Procyon, had Cynthia put on the goggles and sit back comfortably on the reclining couch, and then started the light show and music.

At first, the lights and the music were nothing more than a minor annoyance to Cynthia. Nothing seemed to be happening besides the sensory bombardment of a rhythmic series of flashing colors; a spectrum of blues, purples, greens, reds, all swishing together like a meandering stream of psychedelic incandescence.

This went on for several minutes, until time began to fade - blending in the stew of consciousness, memory, space, and the differences between past, present, and future. She didn't realize at all that she'd been sitting on that couch for over forty minutes that felt like no more than three, when new unfamiliar sensations assuaged her senses. There was the smell of Igusa grass in her nose, of sandalwood, mimosa, jasmine. There was the cantaloupe-like flavor of persimmons on her tongue and the moisture of tropical vegetation. She could see the blue-green waters of an archipelago that she somehow knew was in the Western Pacific somewhere between Hokkaido and Sakhalin. That's when she heard the clashing of blades and commotion of battle. She could see a chain-sickle swinging about in the imperceptible chaos of sensations, but then the sensation of fear returned to pull her out of the hypnotic state.

Cynthia started awake and took off the Oculus goggles in a panic. Paulina was still sitting next to her and now rubbing her arm, while Black Christopher leapt from the love seat to get down on his knees in front of Cynthia -his palms up in a gesture as if to say *it's okay, everything is okay.*

"Cynthia?", that was Paulina. "What happened? Are you ok?"

"It's alright," Christopher assured. "you're still right here in the office. Nothing in the vision can hurt you."

She looked around, left and right. She noticed suddenly that she was sweating.

"What did you see?" Christopher asked, in a tone that barely masked his intense curiosity. "What revelations found you?"

———

THE THREE LEVEL DUPLEX WAS IN THE downtown area of Orlando. There was a twelve step cobblestone stairway from the street leading up to the dais that opened into the first floor. Like the one above it, the wide open, rambling space was baronial in structure and instead of walls had partitions and pillars separating the different spaces on the floorplan. Each floor had an elevated space with a built in bar, and the top level, which was actually an open party space on the roof, was shaded only by tentlike tarp that was retractable by remote. The entire place used to be a triple-level nightclub owned by a developer named Thibaut Maxwell from Louisiana, but after a mass shooting that claimed more than fifty lives at another club directly across the street, Maxwell shut it down and sold it to an unscrupulous contractor by the name of Noa Kovács. This was five years ago, and Mr. Kovács was the scarred man who, with the company of his partner Gordan Juric, broke Marcus Green out of the Blackwood psychiatric hospital not three days prior.

Kovács and Juric helped Marcus acclimate to the fact that they were friends of his from another life, Omphalos and Jericho, and that he was the formidable and feared ronin called Katsurou the Prometheus. Though Marcus had been experiencing clues to his past life for as long as he could remember, and especially after the brain damage and during his stay at Blackwood, it was still difficult to swallow being told to him, confirmed, and said out loud by others. The steady flow of whiskey they fed him however helped these facts go down easier.

Kovács and Juric discovered themselves not long after meeting each other in college, almost twenty years prior. Both immigrants, Kovács from Budapest and Juric from Zagreb, the cultural hub and capital city of Croatia, they became fast friends as freshman business students at Columbia University in New York. They also partied too hard, and both OD'd on barbiturates one night while hanging out together on the Saturday of a long weekend. Both of them would have died that night, but the Universe and the freshly awakened spirits of their previous selves had different plans for them...

Marcus, for each of the first three nights of liberation from captivity, experienced a recurring dream of Katsurou, a memory/nightmare, really, of another form of captivity *-the bitter ronin's incurable hatred for Kojiro ko-Mitsu*:

> As vividly as if it were happening currently, right there and then, and in reality instead of in a dream, Marcus remembered a time when the warrior known as the Prometheus had earned the mysterious moniker. It was when he became aware of the goddess Astrid, and, in his hubris, offender her and was sentenced, much like Sisyphus from Greek myth, to roam for four hundred years in a desert-like limbo world called the **Barren Bastille of Oblivion**.

There were salvos of living wind pushing against his body without relent, seeking to dissuade and discourage him against advancing further into the mouth of stupefaction. He could seldom see beyond the storm of sand, this granular assault that were cutting not only his inflamed pupils but also the surface of his skin, but he kept on walking, grabbing hold of bamboo sticking out of the ground or tree limbs, high grass, anything he could get his hands on to steal a few moments of rest and propel himself forward.

He was determined not only to survive but to best the formidable tricks set upon him by the rancorous deity.

"You hear me!,' he yelled against the wind, 'huh??!! I am Katsurou! You cannot captivate me!! You cannot hold me hostage in my own mind!! You phantom! You BITCH!!"

He taunted and cursed and yelled, but Astrid wasn't even aware of Katsurou's voice. She was elsewise occupied…

At random, wraiths of dead men from the brutal ronin's dueling past materialized in front of him –challenging him with their weapons, against his loquat wood Suburito Bokken (the only weapon he ever used). He fought them off with his bokken, cutting through their bodies and defenses and watching them vanish into smoke and then reappear to engage him again and again.

"TEMPEST!" he yelled. "DEMON! I killed these men! I WILL KILL THEM AGAIN AND AGAIN!!'

But that's when he saw him, the first phantom to strike him with fear and speechlessness -the image of his father Murasamu Tadao.

"Still a coward,' Murasamu Tadao spat, displeased as ever for the weaknesses of his son, 'still reveling in weakness, still its greatest disciple."

"Shut up, old man,' Katsurou cried, even though he knew that his father wasn't really there.

Tadao had only one arm, just as Katsurou remembered him. His right. An adept of the two sword style, he lost his left in a duel. And was remembered in life mostly for how much his kenjutsu had actually improved since the maiming. *The true warrior*, Tadao's philosophy, *always grows much more in despair – benefiting exponentially from failure*. But in his eyes, and he never shied from mentioning it, his only son was doomed to become the exact opposite sort of man. And it was all because of Katsurou's response to **a defining event of his childhood that would mar him forever** in the eyes of his father...

Curse her, Katurou thought to himself of Astrid, reminding him of this!

"Look at yourself, son,' the deceased warrior yelled in disgust, as for just that moment Katsurou's gaze became clear enough to see Tadao step into the light and morph, just momentarily, into a mirror image of himself just while saying, 'I am near ashamed to even call you that, boy! To call you son."

Then the sand assailed Katsurou again, so harshly that he could not help the fall of bloody tears from his eyes as the winds picked up and the entirety of the storm began to hone in directly on his body from all angles and sides and directions.

Enormous black and red birds, bat-like in their make and mythic in every way, appeared out of nowhere in droves. Assaulting Katsurou more and multiplying by the dozens. He'd tell a friend at a later date, Omphalos in fact, that *"the memory was about as beautiful and deadly as chaos could ever be!"*

Katsurou shut his eyes much more in grief than in the pain of the hot blood coming from them. He looked up again, determined this time to not turn away. That's when he noticed that his father had already drawn his nodachi blade from its bronze scorpion-plated sheath, the long black blade a ruthlessly intimidating though beguiling sight! Tadao slashed at Katsurou's body before the subdued ronin could react or move.

"Noooo!" Katsurou screamed, only to realize as the blade swung past and dug into the ground that the dead man's sword could not physically touch or harm him!!

The look in Tadao's eyes, the disbelief that his great sword could not kill or even touch the unwanted prodigal son, it was most frightening and awe inspiring and existential proof available to Katsurou's senses that, yes, not only was there life beyond death, but consciousness was itself eternal!

Katsurou, in misguided hubris, smiled and lunged forward in an overhead attack with the bokken.

But in that moment, tendrils of plant-life and vine sprouted from Tadao's empty left arm socket, catching Katsurou at the throat in mid-lunge.

It was the phantom's turn to smile.

"You are a fool, son... A FOOL!... that you would let pettiness damage your bond with the man destined to be your greatest friend!"

Katsurou could barely breathe with the grip on his throat. He dropped the bokken and searched his father's eyes for sympathy -finding none.

"Father," he could barely get the word out.

"Do not call me that, boy! You are weak! And your misplaced rage will be the end of you!"

Katsurou knew that Tadao was speaking of Kojiro, his childhood friend turned enemy.

"Why?' he fought against the tendril's grip to say, "why should I... think of him... as friend?... After what... he let happen to me?"

"Because, you coward!" Tadao yelled, bringing Katsurou close to his face. "He is the only real friend you will ever know, in this life or the next!"

EACH MORNING, FOR THOSE THREE DAYS, Marcus would awaken from the dream in a cold sweat, his hands shaking, his heart racing in a panic. His throat would hurt, but still he would run down the anxiety with three fingers of bourbon whiskey. He'd grab a swivel barstool and sit at the outdoor bar table, resting his elbows on the black graphite countertop.

"Same dream again?" Juric asked him on the third morning, as he did the two before it.

Kovács would sleep late on a futon on the second level, and so it would be Juric that greeted Marcus every morning, before dawn, up on the ceiling-less upper floor.

"It's why I prefer to sleep up here," he said. "beneath the sky, cradled in natural air. I'd suffocate otherwise, Juric. You know?"

Juric did know, remembering the hard transition to life after returning from near death all those years ago and becoming aware of this spirit of Jericho which resided within.

He pulled a green pack of Newport menthols from his back pocket, shook one loose and then pulled it out with his lips. He offered Marcus one before lighting it, but the marooned, brain damaged boxer declined.

"These rank number three on the list of best cigarettes. Fucking three, man. A couple years back, four. But I spent enough time in New York to know that dat's sum bullshit. The euphoric, light-headedness they provide, unmatched -all the way. Reminds me of the lie, the illusions wrapped all around the dermis of the world."

"Dermis?" Marcus asked, his form of higher education having been the flotsam and jetsam of innumerable punches to the body and head.

"The skin, buraz!" Juric added gleefully, and then took a long drag. "Ahh… And then the taste, closest analog to kiseru pipes from the homeland. You remember?"

Marcus tightened his eyes, thinking back as the secondhand smoke filled his nostrils. He could just barely make out a glimpse in memory of Jericho, leaning against the heavily shaded trunk of a camphor and enjoying his kiseru pipe.

"If he remembered,' Kovács, having entered the upper platform at the surprise of both men, 'he'd slap that cancer stick right out of your mouth."

"Ehhh, come off it!" Juric waved his hand in mock exasperation, walking a few steps away to blow his smoke up into the air in case Kovács' words gave Marcus an idea.

"Would I?" Marcus asked.

"You would indeed. Katsurou hated Jericho's damned kiseru. You… hated Jericho's damned kiseru, my liege."

"You can stop calling me that, man," Marcus shook his head, "Call me Marcus Green. It'll help me get my bearings."

"I will call you Katsurou when you are ready to be addressed appropriately."

Marcus stood up from the swivel high-backed barstool and reached for the bottle just waiting for him on the graphite, poured himself another three fingers of bourbon. He walked, staggering a little from the empty stomach inebriation, over to the balcony edge and leaned on the 42 inch rustic brass railing.

The view of the city and the tall buildings in the distance helped steady his racing mind and balance his focus against the liquor.

"I used to watch your fights,' Juric said, joining him at the balcony but at a distance of about eight yards, so as not to disturb him with the smoke. "I didn't believe it at first, buraz.. That you were Katsurou reborn. Not until that Diezel fight."

Marcus looked over at Juric, instantly getting the reference.

Timothy "Stone Hands" Diezel was Marcus' 24th fight, and his seventeenth win by knockout. It was also the fight that triggered the epidural hematoma. Diezel had a solid twenty pounds of muscle over Marcus, longer reach, more power and more speed too. That carried him for seven rounds, five of which he won in points and shots landed -a lot to the body, most to the head. By the end of the 7th, Marcus' left eye looked like he was hiding a baseball under the lid, his jaw was worn, vision rattled. The announcers didn't expect him to make it to twelve. The champ, they said, was done. He'd finally lose the title.

But they were wrong.

When that next bell rang, a switch went off in Marcus. The next brutal headshot he took from the warrior aptly dubbed Stone Hands, it set off not only the epidural hematoma but the rage of the long dead ronin.

"I won six hundred dollars that night,' Juric proclaimed. Marcus gave him a quizzical look. "Yeah, man!' he continued, 'whoo, and I thought I was gonna lose my shirt! But then you came out in the seventh, different style, different posture. You fought all seven rounds before it orthodox, then came out suddenly a southpaw! You were playing the swarmer against the slugger with superior reach. And playin' it badly, for seven whole rounds! Then boom, out comes the boxer-puncher! Precision defense, lightning speed, jab combos to humble giants! You're switching styles on him too, suddenly you're the slugger, the swarmer again, the out-fighter! All within the span of..' Juric snaps his fingers to remember, then, "What was it, Noa?"

"Not even two minutes," Noa Kovács obliged. Marcus now, he's looking between the two men as they tell his story, replaying the choppy visual reel of it in his mind.

"That boy,' Kovács continued, "the block of stone from Joplin, Missouri, he was down in about a minute twelve."

"Done!" Juric intoned, enthusiastically waving his hands like a referee declaring the fight over.

Marcus saw a flash of it, a suddenly vivid memory of the referee's gaunt, sable black face. He saw his tired left arm being lifted in victory by his trainer, Gus De Luca, the blinding assault of lights from cameras everywhere snapping shots of him -still light heavy champion of the world.

That's when Kovács walked up to Marcus, a whiskey filled snifter in hand. He cozies up next to the boxer in forced retirement, touches glasses with him in cheers.

"That's when we knew,' he said, holding Marcus' gaze for fifteen seconds that seemed longer, enough time for the gravity of the words to sink in. After a sip of his drink, he added "we were certain we'd found you. The walk..., the confidence of a man who, in a past life, dueled with a bokken against live blades and won -every time."

"Every time?" Marcus echoed in question, growing more and more intrigued, more impressed… with himself.

"Every time," Kovács touched glasses with him again, still intensely holding eye contact.

"Then why,' Marcus' cadence was tinged now with an allusion to anger, "did it take you five years to liberate me from that... Hell?"

Kovács' grin was matched with a grunt,

"Asked a man who walked for four hundred years in a psychic desert. The true you, Katsurou awakened, he would have had it no other way. Because suffering, as you used to always say, is –"

Marcus, not even thinking it, cut him off with the unexpected flash of memory,

"Is the manna of kings."

Kovács couldn't help but smile at the incredulity in Marcus' face as memory grew greater in him. Even Juric, tossing the butt of his smoke over the brass balcony railing, could barely contain his excitement.

BOOK III:
THE QUINTESSENCE OF DUST

怫

"I would hurl words into this darkness and wait for an echo,
And if an echo sounded, no matter how faintly,
I would send other words to tell, to march, to fight,
to create a sense of hunger for life that gnaws in us all."

-Richard Wright

佛

IN THE NEAR FUTURE...

DELOACH WAS GRATEFUL FOR THE aerodynamic improvements made to the Learjet 60, especially the reduced interference drag between the wing chord and the fuselage, the ogive winglet trailing edge and the addition of two ventral fins instead of one for augmented stability. These came in handy for navigating the cataclysmic horror show at forty thousand feet. At Mach .76 and on a fuel burn of 1,300 pounds, the 60 was being pushed to and beyond its limits against hot, dust rich tertiary trade winds at south east over Kalkata and the Andaman Sea, lightning strikes that seemed sentient and gunning to bring the plane down, large committees of oversized and impossibly aggressive gallinazo vultures attacking the plane in kamikaze strikes and, a great many of them, flying ahead of the plane and collecting together to form giant piranha-like mouths in the sky that tried biting at the jet's wings as it went by.

DeLoach couldn't believe his eyes, his heart beating so fast that it was a wonder he didn't go into cardiac arrest, but he was able to flip and dive the plane just out of reach of these *bites* that would chomp down hard enough to produce dangerously powerful pressure spikes against the wings. The turbulence all this created inside the cabin was unreal, but it didn't stop the sword fight that was happening inside; Coletrane brandishing

Hatsukoi with the deferred indignation of Kojiro against a duel African Konda blade wielding Marcus enlivened by Katsurou's rage!

The executive cabin was now a twisting and diving theater of war with a cubic volume of four hundred and fifty three; the fighters' blood stage just over five meters, the tunnel space for the savage testing of their swordsmanship a tight 5.9 by 5.7 feet, their blade clashes were a cacophonous symphony of light, spark, and steel.

Both men were dressed to the nines, but bore blade cuts and blood that brought them back down to savagery. There was no illusion of innocence here, a memory ringing out in Coletrane's head as he tried with earnest to end the life of his best friend before the man succeeded in doing the same to him.

Men are arrogant by nature.

Marcus' aggressive windmill style with the Konda short swords kept Coletrane often on the defensive, parrying and ducking under slashes meant for his head or limbs that would instead cut through the dark wood veneers in the galley, a cabinet or a coffee table, or burst open the plush leather of a cabin swivel seat. A counter strike from Coletrane would destroy an upholstery-mounted telephone, slice a mahogany work desk clean in half, or break apart one of the overhead baggage compartments. Emergency LED lights were flashing on and off, oxygen masks dangled from the ceiling like animated moss, a broken defibrillator unit and two loose fire extinguishers were now deadly projectiles crashing all over the place that the men had to avoid while they fought. Deloach would make a sharp turn or dip to avoid the elements or the ferocious birds, and the jet's 46,000 pounds of thrust would send the two fighters tumbling from one end of the cabin to the other.

They both landed hard against the wall of the galley tower. Marcus, in the tumble, let loose one of the Kondas and its blade tip lodged into the door to the flight deck, which was just over Coletrane's left shoulder. It hit close enough that it cut into his trapezoid.

He screamed! Marcus tried to come down on him with an overhead strike with the other Konda, but Coletrane dropped Hatsukoi and caught Marcus' hand, turning him around and flipping him over the hip. Marcus landed down hard on the floor!

In that second, one of the fire extinguishers was flipping towards them from the other side of the plane. Coletrane picked up Hatsukoi again and cut the extinguisher in half when it reached them. A high pressure burst of monoammonium phosphate created a dense, blinding fog.

By the time it cleared, the plane had somewhat stabilized though was still rocking back and forth. There was a space now between Marcus and Coletrane; the former now with one Konda held underhand in his left, the latter tightly gripping Hatsukoi with both.

Marcus looked at Coletrane with the intensity and hatred of at least ten men, and Coletrane, the hair atop his head a wild untamed fire, looked at him with something akin to commiseration.

"I am sorry, Marcus!" he said.

"Not yet you aren't!" Marcus called back through a mouth of bloodied teeth.

DeLoache, drenched in sweat, was working the controls in the flight deck like a bedeviled composer whose life depended on the perfection of every chord. Those impossible vultures were overlarge, flying higher than their species is known for, and continuing to collect together into mouth-like formations set upon biting the plane. He did his best to keep the plane stable while navigating around them.

"Fuck! Fuck!' he said to himself. 'This can't be... Mayday! Mayday! Mayday!"

"This is Air Traffic Control,' the male voice out of the radio, "What is your emergency?"

"Giant birds, Control!"

'What?"

"Giant fucking birds!"

One of the vultures chose that moment to crash into the windshield, setting off a spiderweb of cracks that made sight even more challenging for DeLoache in the commotion of elemental and wildlife bombardments. Then something even more unbelievable appeared; the vultures were accompanied by a swarm of the same white-tailed eagles that attacked Ameeru's search party on the bridge in Japan. They again were the size of pterodactyls, and every bit as aggressive as the vulture committee. DeLoache's eyes widened upon seeing one of them swoop past and under.

In the cabin, Coletrane and Marcus had reengaged, Tachi versus Konda.

Coletrane sidestepped a stabbing attempt from Marcus and, hitting the blade near the hilt, managed to relieve Marcus of his weapon. The shellshocked boxer ducked under three of Coletrane's attempts to cut him with Hatsukoi. On the third he found an opening, catching him behind the wrist and hitting him in just the right place behind the elbow to make him drop the sword.

The two were now both unarmed, giving Marcus a slight advantage for his professional boxing skills -especially in the tight space. His second consciousness, Katsurou, smiled within.

Marcus threw a series of combinations at Coletrane that resulted in him getting the upper hand. A right hook sent Coletrane over a seat and crashing against a window. Wasting no time, Marcus was on him. Using leverage with his knee against the seat, he pushed his weight on Coletrane and locked his forearm under the rich man's chin. The position put their faces close together, but the angle gave Coletrane a clear view of the chaos just outside of the plane. He recognized those pterodactyl-like eagles that were mixing with the vulture swarm.

"I...,' Coletrane struggled to get the words out, Marcus' elbow pressed against his windpipe doing him no favors in this regard, "I…. am not …your enemy."

Again, Marcus bore his bloodied teeth. But when he spoke, it was Katsurou's voice that came out.

"Too late for that."

In Coletrane's peripheral, in this exact moment, one of the white-tailed eagles came torpedoing toward the plane, slamming against the window that Coletrane was looking out of -causing a blazing eruption of wind and glass!

HATSUKOI'S SHARP EDGE SLICED THROUGH the bamboo tameshigiri like a knife through butter, flipping then in Kojiro's hands and cutting through another. There were at least thirty more of these set up in the high grass field wherein the troubled warrior toiled to regain his strength. The night before he had a strange dream about some distant future, imperceptible in waking and yet enough to get him up before the sun.

Two months had passed by the *slow time,* so Kojiro's body had grown strong again by din of pushing himself daily to the brink of exhaustion and beyond. Muscle replaced fat, but the beard he grew while sleeping remained -only much longer now, like a holy man of violence.

And even though time moved slowly in Chiyu's secluded, magical homeland, Kojiro was still moved by an unshakable sense of urgency for rebuilding his muscles and skills to much greater than before, much greater than they'd ever been. He was possessed by this exigency ever since he was able to stand without help after awakening fully from the long sleep, he practiced in a place already prepared for him not far from the small hut in which he slept, an area that could only be described as an orphic everglade surrounded by mountains and rivers. Chiyu described the place as a village, but she was the only human who inhabited it. The trees and mountains and rivers were her family, she said, and they kept her safe. They would keep the ten remaining members of the Live Crew safe as well, from the Ashigaru who were surely still hunting them, Katsurou and his band of tar-borne aborigines, or any other threat that awaited them, for the duration of their visit, each of them residing in their own private hut that, as Jubei told it, "grew right out of the ground for us, one by one; woods, lanterns, candles, and all. This place, yuujin, is alive!"

And this fact was made apparent to Kojiro in the field in which he practiced, as each of the tameshigiri he cut down with his sword would grow back after a few minutes and form more targets for him to work against. In a burst of energy, and to test his endurance by pushing beyond his limits and beyond the lactic acid burn, Kojiro lunged left and then right, dashed forward, back, and diagonally, cutting down tameshigiris with each move and every pivot, so fast that it was like one single ongoing breath, one symphonic typhoon of bamboo cutting wind! Until he pivoted and heel-turned, sweat drenching his face, pulsating arms, and the white shitagi that was now open and dripping at the breast.

He looked on the results of his work, but while he hyperventilated to regain his breath, and before he even had five full seconds to marvel his fluency, all the bamboo cutting pillars grew back taller, stronger, thicker.

Kojiro sighed, almost laughed even at the thought of how closely this regenerating practice area reflected the futility of man's efforts in life.

"You are the one they call the Deadly Sakura," a deep, husky voice from behind him interrupted his philosophical moment. When Kojiro turned to face his visitor, he was surprised to find not a tall powerful Lord to match the voice, but instead something that he remembered only from a cave drawing.

The centaur-like creature had the lower half of a horse, a lean humanoid upper torso and arms, but the head of a deer bearing a crown of honed, spindly antlers. He wore a beaded wolf tooth choker around his neck, and stacked leather bracelets on either wrist bearing hematite and obsidian stones. The creature held up his chin with the pride of nobility, and looked at Kojiro through purple eyes.

"You do not look so deadly," he added. Kojiro immediately did not like him.

"I can give you a demonstration," came Kojiro's reply, the threat in his voice not subtle. He fixed the neatness of his shitagi and slightly put his right shoulder forward.

The deer headed centaur chuckled.

"If only it didn't belie the occasion."

"Which is?" Kojiro narrowed his eyes.

Taking a few unthreatening steps forward, the creature of myth offered,

"I am Bwana of the Hamarufa race. And I come at the behest of a friend you will remember. Xiao Xiao Chen."

Kojiro remembered her, the woman who floated on water and created a cave with her mind for him and the crew to escape the overwhelming numbers of Ashigaru. But he was more interested in his visitor's name.

"Bwana,' Kojiro repeated. "I do not recognize the genealogy of this name. From where do you come?"

Bwana laughed, "A place you will never see."

———

KOJIRO FOLLOWED BWANA THROUGH a dense meadow vegetated with tall hakone grass and lush peonies filling the air with a sweet and citrusy aroma. They didn't talk along the way, as Kojiro's voice was caught up in his fascination for the way the living vistas changed as they went. Soon the meadow led into a path through a thicket of maple and wisteria trees, their sloping blooms looking like a magical fall of purple to pinkish rain forever suspended in mid-air.

It was subtle, but those trees moved for the two travelers, making the winding path before them more apparent and easier to pass through. When they reached the other side of the thicket, what Kojiro saw defied the scope of his imagination.

The ground beneath their feet went from earthen dirt to an ethereal swirling platform of flattened, diaphanous clouds that could have been still-damp acrylic blues, grays, and whites on a fresh, breathing canvas. There were little ponds everywhere full of tropical water and jumping multicolored koi fish. Instead of mountains for as far as the naked eye could see, there were giant water sculptures suspended over lakes and some on elevated patches of land. The shape of a woman splashing water on her face; another of a man drawing his hand from the pond, the sparkling aqua falling from his palm and through his fingers back into the source; on two sides of land with the lake flowing between them, a structure on one side was the upper torso and head of what appeared to be an extraterrestrial with a key sticking out of its forehead, on the other side was another upper torso but of a monkey instead, the alien's key pointed at its forehead; there was a full body depiction of a curvaceous woman rising out the center of a lake as if a sea-borne phoenix with her head held back and her hair flowing back into the water; one even looked like the translucent face of a spirit rising from out the prison of a human bust.

This last one interested Kojiro the most. He stared at it in fact, to the point of near hypnosis. So much that he didn't hear her walk up on him, and was startled by her voice.

"To ask the question is a waste," Xiao Xiao Chen said, her arms folded behind her back. She was smiling. "A waste, evermore, when you yourself are its answer."

She was dressed much differently than last he saw her, this time in a long baby blue gown, her hair in pigtails tied with cords that matched her dress. Even her lips were polished in blue, only a bit darker and cerulean.

"We have to let go of the life we planned," she continued, her peaceable voice denoting an unassailable air of wisdom, "in order to arrive at the life that is waiting for us…. A writer from an adjacent future will say something like this in his letters."

"An adjacent future?"

"Yes, Sakura. Like the reflection of the boy you saw in the water. I know it still haunts you."

Kojiro didn't deny it. He sighed instead, and tightened his jaw.

Bwana was standing some distance away, bathing under the waterfall created by the sculpture of the giant man drawing his hand from the lake. He had his arms outstretched and chin turned up, just letting the water wash over his body. His obsidian and hematite jewelry glimmered in the reflective sunlight. After a moment, another of the Hamarufa leapt off one of the nearer earthen cliffs and galloped over to Bwana, joining him in the water. It was lighter brown in color, and appeared female. They joined hands and touched snouts affectionately.

"You had a dream last night," Xiao Chen said, less a question than a statement.

"How did you-" Kojiro began to asked, then realized the relative silliness of it upon looking at her. "Of course."

"Tell me about it."

"There isn't much to tell. I barely remember it."

"What *do* you remember?"

Kojiro took some time to reflect. Looking up at the sky, he found that the equanimity it offered back in return made it easier to think. It in fact whispered reminders of the dubious dream.

The color pattern of the heavenly azure were swaths of blue, purple, and violet, mottled here and there by densities of air just faintly recognizable as clouds. No sun or moon in view, the bright flickers of ivory lights that illuminated the sky bore the appearance of taraxacum blooms, white dandelions that every moment seemed just upon the verge of breaking apart.

"Lights," Kojiro finally said, his eyes still turned up to the sky. "Twenty seven of them, arranged in a specific pattern. They were drawing close and coming out of an imperceptible though suffocating darkness."

"Suffocating?"

"Yes. I remember not being able to breath or turn away. I felt like a voyeur witnessing life itself being.... destroyed.. It was like-"

"It came to me in a dream…", Kojiro heard, faintly, a child's voice. A familiar child's voice.

"Did you hear that?" he asked Xiao Xiao Chen. Instead of answering, she smiled and stepped out of the way. Beyond her he saw a pulsating, champagne-colored light in the ephemeral, cloud-like floor about twenty yards away. This is where the voice was coming from, and curiosity drew Kojiro towards it. It was instinct however that brought his left hand up to Hatsukoi's hilt.

"It came to me in a dream," the voice said again. Kojiro stopped walking a few paces away from the light, was just close enough to look into it; the appearance of it was like illuminated water beneath a thin layer of ice, water that vaguely gave way to a window into a dream of the future. Through this window was the barely perceptible and near vertiginous image of young Coletrane talking to his friend Marcus.

Instinct again gripped Kojiro. With a quivering lip, he would have turned and run away if it weren't for Xiao Xiao Chen coming up behind him and resting a hand on his shoulder.

"It came to me in a dream,' the voice repeated once more, *"…lights coming out of darkness… pitch black, except for the lights… Twenty-seven of them, I think… Telling me a story… a warming… I woke up real fast because I couldn't breathe."*

"The boy," Kojiro realized, his eyes suddenly rheumy. And then he said again, realizing that he was slightly shivering when he did it, "The boy…"

The wind picked up then, it was cold and damp, and the white taraxacum blossoms in the sky scattered as if actual dandelions blown apart and then reformed. A comet passed in the deep space just beyond the humid empyrean of violet and blue.

It began to rain or more like drizzle, but this was enough to hide the tears that would have otherwise betrayed the Deadly Sakura's stoic resolve.

"What does it mean?" he asked Xiao Chen.

"It means that you are afraid."

Kojiro glared at her.

"I fear nothing of this world or beyond it."

Xiao Xiao Chen grinned, warmly and in no way mockingly, and lifted Kojiro's right hand for him to see it.

"Your shivering hand would disagree," she murmured.

Kojiro jerked away, saying nothing.

"Do not be angry, Kojiro. Your fear but means that you are on the right path."

"And what of the hauntings of the boy?"

Instead of answering, Xiao Xiao Chen just stared. And then, Kojiro, impatient, yelled,

"TELL ME!"

Suddenly out of nowhere, on cue of his burst of aggression, he was surrounded by Bwana and dozens of his kin. Not all of them brandished weapons but those who did held spears or long single-edged scimitars at the ready. Each of them, male and female, were clearly strong and muscularly toned; they all had crowns of powerful antlers, threat and poise in their exotic eyes, and tribal earth-stone jewelry shimmering on wrists and neck.

Kojiro pivoted and turned his right shoulder slightly forward, resting his hand on Hatsukoi's tsuka. He half-expected to be pounced on by the mob and torn to shreds. Welcomed it, even!

But instead, they opened a path for him behind Xiao Xiao Chen that led back to where he came from.

She said simply, stepping aside herself,

"That is for you and you alone to decipher."

"If I may," Bwana said to Xiao Xiao Chen, lowering his proud chin in a slight bow. She nodded back as if to say proceed, so he took a step forward to address Kojiro directly.

"Earlier, Sakura, when you queried as to the origin of my name."

"Yes."

"It tells me something of great importance about you. And my people would agree."

"What does it tell you?"

"That your curiosity is both genuine and stalwart, and that it will take you far. Perhaps beyond boundaries unknowable, and past the ambits of consciousness itself. If any mortal man were to prove strong enough to make sense of his place in the universe, his connection to voices reaching out to him from beyond the pale, it would be this breed of unflappable grit that would prove requisite. One warning though."

"Speak it," the inquisitive samurai said without hesitation.

"When one goes looking for answers, they are more often cursed than blessed by what they find."

Kojiro scoffed, more so to break the tension of the moment than anything else.

"You are definitely one of Chen's subjects, Bwana. You both talk almost entirely in riddles."

———

THE DRIZZLE BECAME RAIN BY THE TIME Kojiro made it back through the path. When the trees opened up for him to exit back onto the clearing, he saw Jubei and Tzukuba sparring, he a jo and her a bokken, in the field that Kojiro inhabited before -its space now clear of the tameshigiri and full instead of swaying igusa grass.

They stopped upon seeing him approach.

"Seems I saved you from her besting you again, Jubei," Kojiro quipped.

"Don't think this new beard you've painted on would acquit you the same fate," Jubei countered.

Ztukuba, very much used to their banter, just smiled and shook her head.

Suddenly, the moment for playfulness passed.

"Where are the others?" Kojiro asked.

"The Chinmoku brothers are enjoying tutelage in Chiyu's homely remedies," Jubei reported. "Ittei is probably writing, and Otaku I'm sure has convinced Kana to drink with him by now."

"Well,' Kojiro shrugged, 'they'll have to sober up. It's time for us to go."

Global Dollar Magazine's quote of the day: *"When I ask other successful CEOs how they did it, mediocre ones all point to some self-congratulatory explanation or the other. But great CEOs, they all cite their unyielding determination."*

-Reid Carnegie, **CEO of Lonsanto Agrochemicals**.

LOS ANGELES, CALIFORNIA. Rain Forest Inc. founder and CEO Jeremiah Cross under fire for having flown to Wichita, Kansas to meet with notoriously hand-over-fist business brothers Samson and Daniel Oderbrecht, who are known for shockingly cruel business practices such as exploiting small counties by pennies on the dollar to run mineral mines abroad, and whose privately owned power conglomerate Oderbrecht Energy Solutions, has been linked to everything from segregation and voter suppression to gutting the US Social Security System, and from manipulating college university hiring practices to causing cancer clusters due to pollution outside of their plant headquarters. The purpose of said meeting was to negotiate a seven billion dollar deal to expand Trivium pending a successful public implementation of the technological systems at 100%. This calls into question the true purpose behind the Trivium project, and lends credence to rumors that the project is less about improving quality of life, as it has been ostensibly marketed as, than about securing more power for the upper 1%. When the subject came up in a recent interview, the ever-vague Mr. Cross simply smiled, saying, "The public tends to not know what it wants or needs until it receives it. And as always, the unknown is a hollow, frightening space that the uninitiated will use their cynical imaginations to fill with the worst of possibilities."

IT TOOK 300 BILLION CELLS, AND OVER a hundred watts of electrical power, to facilitate the neurotransmissions at the hub of the Trivium motherboard. That meant a superhighway of cell membranes and complex voltage stabilizing circuitry configurations between three amalgamated brains was a constant necessity. That combined with a support system of mutated microbial rhadopsins patented by Cross' neurological research team (simply dubbed the NRT Division of Rain Forest INC.), and erosion proof bus interface cables linking the motherboard to a network of twenty four other data units (brains) for the system, a form of scientific magic, to theoretically work at full capacity.

"Imagine a search engine that worked like a 3D printer," the white lab coated Dr. Upadhyay said to Cross and Landau Kier through the virtual screen that hovered between the two seated men. The international intelligence contractor, dapper in a brown tweed blazer over a beige, white, and gray floral embroidered Cuban collar shirt, flew out to the states to personally apologize to his employer for the failure of the team put on the task of surveilling Coletrane and Patrick in Japan. He came for that, and to report that the team had all been fired. To Landau's surprise, however, Cross set up a meeting with him and his one operative that hadn't been let go; Qadr Fakhoury.

Cross was professionally outfitted as usual; in a dark blue double breasted suit, brown snake skin shoes and watch, no tie, and the white collar of his baby blue shirt open two buttons down from the top. There was a small patch of gauze on the left side of Cross' temple, just over the ear. He made no mention of it and neither did Kier.

"With the inclusion of the six remaining, um.." Dr. Upadhyay stumbled, still on the fence about the ethical implications of her work. Not to mention the unquestionable illegality of it!

"Don't be shy, Dr. Upadhyay," Cross assured. "Our guest is under contract and a… gravely binding NDA."

The threat to Kier in that, barely veiled by Cross' smile and natural charisma, didn't faze the man, and wouldn't anyone more governed by money and the sanctity of contracts than any form of ethics or what he called *"man's finite illusions of decency."*

Dr. Upadhyay could tell as much from the moral vacancy of Kier's eyes and demeanor that were viewable from her end of the video feed.

Not much could be seen by Kier or Cross on the doctor's end, but it was clear enough that she was reporting to them live from the Trivium lab and that behind her was a wall of flickering blue, red, and white lights, computer systems and SATA cables connected to brains preserved in suspended spheres of preservatory formalin fluid.

The doctor sighed,

"Um.. With the inclusion of the remaining six interdimensional brains, the Trivium can go online at vertex."

"Vertex?" Kier asked. Cross smiled. Then he nodded affirmatively when Dr. Upadhyay glanced at him, seemingly, for approval to speak freely.

"Full potential, Mr. Kier."

"Ahh,' he replied. "Of course."

"What about its current potential, doctor?" Cross interjected, lightly tapping the gauze patch on his head. "Fit enough to activate my chip for a small demonstration?"

———

MEANWHILE, QADR DIDN'T NEED ANY kind of dressing on her gunshot wound. She was miraculously alive after the night that she should have died, looking at herself in the mirror as she dressed, and marveling at how the wound had disappeared.

Not magically either, because she fully remembered what had happened. The near unbearably hot sensation of having Zhrontese's hand pressed down against her abdomen, the smell even of her flesh burning as it healed! She remembered the semi-translucent hand, and the spectral face peeking out of an astral plane of existence that should not have been perceptible to the human eye. She could not make out the features of that face, or see the eyes, beyond the blur of her own tears, but that voice continued to echo in her mind while rubbing the surface of the now vanished mortal wound.

"No. This is unacceptable."

———

"FIT ENOUGH TO ACTIVATE MY CHIP FOR a small demonstration?" went the echo of Cross' question in Dr. Upadhyay's ear, it registering twice for the sheer aberrancy and prematureness of it. She was immediately torn, as on the one hand she could decline on the premise that it would be dangerous since the system wasn't at full capacity, in the event risking Cross' embarrassment in front of an audience of Kier. And on the other hand, she could respond affirmatively, thus possibly pulling the switch on her boss' lobotomy in the presence of that same audience.

"Well?" Cross prodded when she took too long to answer.

"Of course, Mr. Cross."

"Very good then! Proceed."

Dr. Upandhyay kept the apprehension that she felt inside from appearing on her face as she typed in a command sequence on her handheld touch-screen control board.

Silently, a prayer before hitting ENTER.

————

QADR'S LIFELONG TRAINING IN STOICISM proved sufficient enough a firewall behind which her many anxieties struggled for reconciliation despite the abiding placidity of her surface demeanor. That struggle persisted as she prepared for her scheduled meeting with Cross. She had "delicate items of merchandise" to deliver, two each held in suitcase-sized cryopreservation units provided her by Rain Forest INC.'s NRT Division. These items were the heads of Nicolaou Steinitz, Ingvar Oliyath, Javi Castillo, and Lev Illsley Knopfler; all murders she committed for hire that, before Knopfler, didn't linger in her mind as stains on her immortal soul. But now? Qadr couldn't help or deny the existential implications of those sudden bursts of muscle memory experienced by the people she's slaughtered in their moments of death, and neither could she extenuate the relationship those instances of anamnesis had with her own responses to extreme trauma. That time her trusted colleagues attempted violation of her dignity, her blackout and their subsequent deaths as a result, in what way were these removed from the calling out of those souls whose eyes forever blotted out in death now looked up at her from the open cryopreservation cases? She closed those cases quickly, less to prevent damage to the integrity of the units' vitrification than to acquit herself the leering condemnation of dead men.

Still, outward stoicism kept as she checked herself out of the hotel, stored the two NRT cases in the trunk of her nondescript rental Toyota, and took to the street to arrive fashionably late to her morbid appointment.

———

LUCKILY FOR DR. UPANDHYAY, NOTHING bad happened to her employer when she hit ENTER on the touch screen. He flinched a little from a mild electrical shock, but then Cross smiled and said,

"Thank you, doctor. That will be all."

Cross pressed a button on his desk and the video projection screen went off.

Kier at this point thought the two of them were alone. He couldn't see or detect in any way that there was another presence in the room, certainly not one that commanded more authority than his host. But he was there, and Cross could see him. Several feet behind where Kier was seated, over by the Auguste Rodin's Thinker replica and hovering about three over the marble floor, was the Tan'Mo; his arms smugly folded behind his back, his pale face still the texture dry, crackling porcelain, his eyes still yellow with red threatening pupils, his silver and coal black hair tied up in a bun, and dressed in a gray modern-day business suit instead of the kimono of the same color.

It amused him that Cross was making sure to not look at him, as before commanded, amused enough to smile.

"Happiness,' Cross began, his attention on his guest, "is not merely the pursuit of knowledge and sublimity, Mr. Kier."

"No?"

"No. It is the pursuit of these heights unfettered by the depressingly quotidian limitations of the body. This is what Trivium will bring at last to the world, a Revolution of the Mind."

"Ah,' Kier shifted in his seat, switching from his left leg crossed over the right to the right crossed over the left, "I was going to ask about that thing your scientist mentioned. *Interdimensional* brains?"

"Yes,' Cross beamed with enthusiasm, "the only specific kind of brain that could power the system, else an ordinary brain such as your own would do."

Kier imagined it for a moment, Qadr's blade severing his head.

"Guess I should be relieved."

"Indeed."

"So, my operative's shopping list, all people in possession of ...interdimensional brains?"

"Correct."

"And you just need six more?"

"Two," Cross glanced at his watch, "after Ms. Fakhoury arrives."

———

THE HIGHWAYS IN LOS ANGELES WERE always packed, especially in the afternoon. Qadr was grateful for the delay. She was in no hurry to see Kier, who could sniff out her apprehension where others couldn't, and she didn't care much to be in the presence of Jeremiah Cross either -whom she never liked to begin with, and despised even more now due to her awakened consciousness or, rather, conscience. As she pressed along, inch by inch in one of the worst traffic buildups in the US, northward bound on the I-710, the rogue military veteran turn hired assassin realized for the first time since childhood that her palms were sweating under the firmly gripped steering wheel. In her mind played the memory of a man she once secretly loved in a previous life, one characterized by the contradiction of being rough and violent by nature and yet nicknamed after the delicate, lilac scented cherry blossom. This inkling of thought was significant since she'd never experienced this emotion for any man in her current life (despite her relationship with Landau Kier, who no doubt deluded himself with the precarious notion that their professional liaison was exactly that; love, or at least a form of it). Maybe he was right, she considered. Maybe love in the modern would had quietly rooted itself in the argil loam of survival instinct, in the sense that it was a story people told themselves daily to stave off the turmoil of life's inescapable brevity.

———

"HOW ABOUT THAT DEMONSTRATION NOW, Mr. Kier?" Cross offered.

"Sure. I must admit I am a bit intrigued, in fact. So, what of this Revolution of the Mind that will take the pursuit of knowledge and sublimity past the limitations of the body?"

Cross smiled. He liked Kier more in person than over the phone. He liked how well that he listened and paid attention to detail.

"I am told that you are a collector of antique guns, flintlock pistols and revolvers and such."

"A man like you doesn't become a captain of industry without doing his homework."

"Indeed."

"I inherited the obsession from my father. He himself was a sergeant in the RAF, and an engineer. Fought in the Cold War and was one of the minds behind the first twin-engine Typhoons. I saw more of his antique munitions collection than I did of him as a boy."

"Off the top of your head, name one gun not currently in the collection, one gun your father could never get his hands on."

Kier chucked.

"There aren't many, I'm afraid."

"Humor me."

"Well,' Kier sat back, thought about it for a few breathes, "alright. I've been trying to get my hands on a variant of the 1849 Paterson Colt, a pocket revolver with a streamlined gold inlay."

"But?"

Kier grunted a grin, admiring Cross' attention to nuance every bit as much as the industrialist admired his.

"But… that wouldn't have made my father blush. A true gem that I or he could never acquire at any price is the 6 inch Derringer that killed Lincoln."

"No?"

"Nope. Forever locked away at Ford's Theatre in D.C."

"Really? Well…' Cross closed his eyes and lifted his right hand, his fingers fixed as if holding an invisible gun.

Kier watched for a few moments as nothing happened besides Cross tightening his eyes in concentration. And then, both to Kier's fascination and dismay, many thousands of micron particles in the air collected in the palm of Cross' raised hand. There were a few pulsating flashes of electrical charges, and then those microns solidified into John Wilkes Booth's infamous derringer. Cross opened his eyes and then pointed the gun at Kier, who leapt from his chair, astounded!

"Impossible," he declared.

"Isn't it?" Cross turned the gun around and offered its handle to Kier, who reluctantly sat back down and reached for the pistol. Even taking it into his hand, he couldn't believe it. He held it as if expecting it to vanish at any moment. It didn't.

"Welcome to Trivium, Mr. Kier."

"This… it can't be <u>the</u> actual gun."

"Keep your eyes on the news. You'll hear its disappearance from the vault at Ford before long."

The DING of the elevator interrupted this moment and the implications of it that were escaping into Kier's mind past the colander net of fascination and greed. The rhythmic clacking sound of her heels on the marble flooring announced her identity before she stepped out beyond the subdividing walls.

Both Cross and Kier stood, the former happy to see the cases she was carrying and the latter just happy to see her.

"Ah,' Cross began, 'Ms. Fakhoury. Welcome."

怫

DUSTING HAD BEEN POOLE'S FRIDAY evening ritual since before Vincent and Adaeze died. He'd quietly coast throughout the halls of the entire estate tending to every corner, every vas, every statue or bust, every inch of mahogany on every floor. He'd think of the things that troubled him while at it. And this time, there was enough to cover three whole revelations of dusting -if he were so inclined. He thought of the impending meeting that Thelonious wanted to have with Jeremiah Cross, a man he never trusted. He worried about what would come of the progression of the relationship between Thelonious and Patrick now that their shared connection to the mythic, alternate, menacing past was revealed. Patrick, as a journalist with credibility and access to the world's ear, would he use that platform to tell confirming stories about the phenomena of Tulpas? And would this decision have the same sort of effect on the world that definitive knowledge of aliens or the afterlife would? A destructive effect that would result in the undoing of all our presumptions, all the institutions that we took for granted, the very cohesive glues that kept society functioning? *Chaos*, he thought, *an inevitability of enlightenment, of change, of progress.*

By the time Poole made it to the trophy room, his worries doubled. The first thing he noticed before even crossing the threshold of the entrance was that the ancient book was missing from its shrine.

———

THE NIGHT SKY WAS PEACEFUL, QUIET. Stars peppered the swim of blue tinted black like chia seeds on pudding, the sky's buoyant texture suggesting pudding as well. Patrick, restless, had decided to take a walk on the vast, sprawling property. His mind however lingered on the last thing he wrote before leaving the guest room:

> Here I'd found myself sheathed between the tight confines of mystery and revelation. Every bit as nescient as I was at the outset, and Coletrane Marx even more an enigma now than he was then, I found myself on a path of what I'd hoped would be a filament of instinct that proved instead an indictment of awakened memory. My past as a war photographer was not a choice of my own, but rather a reflex learned in a previous life wherein putting myself in danger was a matter of course. Coletrane, he was not some hedonistic playboy burning his inheritance on frivolous joys of the flesh. He was a tortured voyager braving the seas between splintered consciousnesses. Not a man fully formed by anything resembling a normal upbringing, but rather the many contradictory pieces of Frankenstein's monster laboring perilously to cohere -to unlock Truth, to unearth Purpose, to quiet the cry of the soul.

Patrick wasn't sure if he'd use that, or if perhaps he would edit it later. The question of it escaped him however when he made it to the dojo on the property. The light was on, so he went inside. That's where he found Coletrane, his back to him, over by the *Shimoseki* corner where the weapon racks were. He was going through the motions of sharpening Hatsukoi on a whetstone, but more-so was simply admiring her beauty. Behind Coletrane to the left was the ancient book open on the floor.

Patrick doesn't have to announce himself upon entering. Coletrane already knew it was him by the tentative pattern of his steps.

"The sharp-edged sword,' Coletrane began, quoting from memory as he held up Hatsukoi's blade, running two fingers slowly across its body on the side with two dueling dragons etched on the surface, "springing to life, cutting through the void. A band of individuals joined in the darkness' seductive pull drawing them deeper and deeper into the squalid abyss. What lie in wait for them is anyone's guess. What lie in wait for them, in fact, may silence their questions before they've a chance to give voice to them."

Coletrane stood after finishing the quote, faced Patrick.

"Platonian,' Patrick recognized, "allegory of the cave. Man's reality versus his interpretation of it."

"More than that." He nodded towards the open book on the floor. "In fact, not *that* at all when you first wrote it… Ittei."

"My… My memory remains unclear. I-"

"But surely you're not still in disbelief."

He didn't answer, but there were words still trapped in his throat. Coletrane put Hatsukoi back in her sheath and crossed the floor to Patrick. Then, sensing something and turning his head slightly to the right, he stopped walking. Just for a moment. He experienced a memory of their time in Japan; *flashing lights, the company of beautiful women, dancing, and unmoving shadows -watching them.*

He blinked away the memory and resumed,

"Do you remember when were at the Lotus Oiran, in the VIP?"

"Yeah,' Patrick was a little surprised by the shift, "Uh.. Yeah, I remember."

"You were probably distracted by the lights and by the women. But there were eyes watching us. There were spies, of course. Amateurs, I spotted them right away. But I'm not talking about them. I'm talking about something else. In the shadows. Something supernatural."

"That's quite an abrupt subject change. Why are you bringing this up?"

"Because they're here with us now."

Before Patrick could even question it, Coletrane shoved him to the right and dove to the left, rolling to a crouch and redrawing Hatsukoi. Soon as Patrick stumbled out of the way from the shove and fell on his butt, Poole entered the dojo with a double barrel shotgun. Just in time too, because out of the shadowed corner on the other side of the room leapt an **Akumeza**; the skeletal demon of an Ashigaru, clad in a black ninja-yoroi and hooded cowl. He (it?) threw three shuriken in Poole's direction before landing light on its tabi boots. Only one of those shuriken made contact with Poole's shoulder, but the wraith caught a shotgun blast to the chest in reply -this sending it flying backwards and slamming against the wall, then disintegrating into steamy microns before vanishing all together.

Three other Akumeza emerged from the same corner of shadows, while two more came dashing in from the other opposing corners of the room. Each of them was armed with obsidian Shinobigatana swords. And though they were undead ninja, their skeletal bodies evoked an air of immortal pain and trauma all evinced by the anger in their faces under the hoods, the gold of their eyes sunken deep in the black space of their cranial sockets, their bloody though fleshless jaws and teeth.

Coletrane, channeling Kojiro within him, engaged two of them at once. They were indeed undead, but not lacking in skill.

Poole tossed Patrick a semi-automatic Ruger. This was not unfamiliar to the photographer that had seen combat, so he was right at home serving headshot after headshot. The wraiths however were multiplying as quickly as they fell. That's when Coletrane, or, rather, Kojiro, recognized them as *echoes of the Bafuku Ashigaru*!

One of them in the chaos tried to collect the ancient book up of the floor, but Coletrane noticed in time and cut him down. Then another engaged him, lifting his obsidian blade and pointing its tip at him tauntingly.

"You thought you could escape us in death, Sakura?" the Akumeza asked, his chilling voice not one easily forgotten. "You thought you could hide from us behind the face of a doro skinned man?"

Doro skinned.

Mud.

The absurdity of the fiendish creature slipping in a racialized comment like that, it only charged Coletrane with an implacable anger. It was his own rage, not Kojiro's, that cut the specter down. And then quickly three others who tried to subdue him by all engaging at once.

A fourth however was about to get the drop on him, when instead it took a blast to the back from Poole's shotgun.

Patrick was being closed in on by two, who moved so quickly that they were slapping away or slicing through the last of the bullets in Patrick's clip. When the closest one drew dangerously near, the ghost of Yoriko dashed out of nowhere to save him once again at the last minute. She tackled and chomped down on its throat just before it got a chance to bring its sword down on Patrick's. And then the other one, in this moment of distraction, took Patrick's last bullet right between the eyes.

Another full wave of Akumeza attacked; some emerging from the shadows, others coming in through the door from out of the darkness of the night, some even dropping down from a portal in the ceiling. The three, with the help of Yoriko, held their own against the assault. And though the undead ninja each disintegrated and vanished when dispatched, the black/red blood exsanguinated from them by bullet and blade remained -painting the men, the dojo floor and its walls, like a Jackson Pollock rendering of gore.

The band holding Coletrane's hair together snapped in the commotion, making it all fan out like a marigold in bloom! He wielded Hatsukoi with effortless ingenuity, fluent as if the blade were an extension of his own body, and nimble like the flitting wings of a dragonfly.

Poole gave Patrick another clip while Yoriko, about as swift as Hatsukoi zipping through air, covered them with deft lunges and savage teeth!

Then, all at once, the demon ninja stopped coming and the room fell quiet. Yoriko was growling, and her eyes were glowing blue. Patrick wondered if this were some unspoken power of hers, a canine séance of sorts that ridded them of their attackers. He glanced over at Poole, who had torn off a piece of his shirt to use as a cloth for putting pressure on the shuriken wound. But Patrick's attention was mostly on Yoriko, who rather than disappear as she did before had walked over near the center of the room with an air of regal ascendancy -cast in a yellowish empyrean aura.

"Is everyone alright?" Poole asked. "Patrick? Coletrane?"

Patrick nodded, but Coletrane offered no response.

He was still fighting to calm the berserker rage within himself, Hatsukoi still unsheathed, his face and body drenched in the blood of demons. Coletrane looked even like a demon himself in this way, bringing to mind for Patrick an idea of how he would later edit his unfinished passage from before.

> Coletrane Thelonious Marx, a man named after musicians but otherwise not fully or even partly formed by anything resembling a normal upbringing. He was a cypher, a paradox, the many contradictory pieces of Frankenstein's monster laboring perilously to cohere while navigating the peristaltic waves of fortune and loss. But if he was Frankenstein's monster, by what instrument of this world was he created?

HOW SHE MANAGED TO SAVE JOAQUÍN from the consequence of looking into her eyes brought the Ghost Orchid to the threshold of myriad revelations; among them, the control she could wield over her powers, her psychic relationship with the earth, and, most curious, an awareness of the Interstices and the entire unfolding story of Kojiro. At the same time these revelations were dawning in her mind, the ancient book at the Marx Estate was filling with more blood-written chronicles on its pages.

For several nights, Joaquín brought Astrid items of food he'd managed to steal. She'd avoid making eye contact with him to protect the boy from the violent death it would cause, while he'd sit and eat with her and tell her story of his life.

He and his father were illegal migrants from Mexico who had been in Florida for four years, flying under the radar by working menial low paying jobs and constantly moving like nomads on the run. **His mother died having him, and his four brothers had been kidnapped not long before he and his father made the trek to the border -without a trace or explanation, and little effort from the police to find them**.

Joaquín was twelve years old when he met Astrid, and just three months prior had been made an orphan after watching his father get shot by a man who was attempting to rob a 7-11 when the man heroically tried to stop him. And he would have been successful, Joaquín told Astrid, if it wasn't for the man's driver entering the store while the wrestled and shooting his father in the back of the head.

Joaquín didn't cry when telling this story, he'd already been hardened by the cruel hand dealt his family.

"America was 'spose to be different," he said, "but I guess it's just the same everywhere. Everybody smile. But nobody cares."

It was a Sunday night when Astrid's wariness slipped. Joaquín had left around the corner. She thought he was gone. But every night, the malnourished homeless boy made sure to say "See you later" to her. This was an important ritual of his, *See you later*, an affirmation of good tidings to come -an intimate promise of community. For some reason, this reminded Astrid of tribal societies that practiced ritualistic greetings which highlighted a communal cultural archetype. For some reason, this awakened a strong sense of humanity in her.

But that night, he forgot to say it. So, when Astrid removed the blanket from over her head, when she let her guard down from her spot behind the dumpster, he abruptly came back from around the corner in that sprite, urgent way that children do when possessed by an idea.

"Hey, I forgot to say..," he began, but, startled, Astrid turned to him and their eyes locked. The boy's voice was then trapped in his throat, inflamed veins spiderwebbed across his face. His cheeks began to swell, he staggered on his feet. And Astrid knew that he was about to die by combustion.

"No!" she yelled, speaking her first word. She rushed to her feet and took Joaquín into a strong, anguished embrace. His body was shaking, and through his pores Astrid could feel his fear and confusion.

Empathy is what saved his life.

It's what made Astrid's consciousness expand across the entire spectrum of human emotion, potential, and experience. She saw hundreds of kidnapped children working under deadly heat on cacao plantations, medieval Roman knights fighting Visigoths in ancient Italy; she saw agriculture developing in the Fertile Crescent and the many atrocities humans justified on its behalf; she saw countless millions of Africans being transported across the Atlantic to endure slavery in the Americas. Her mind tossing around history like a ping pong ball being slapped back and forth across a table, Astrid witnessed the *Hora de Sangre*, or Hour of Blood, when in the early 1900s white Rangers and law enforcement officials massacred Mexicans in Texas on the justification of racism; she saw the brutal reign of the Mongols, the bloody sectarian conflicts in Israel between Jews and Arabs, and the innumerable deaths on the hands of Christian Missionaries under the premise of "God's Will".

Her mind moving at the speed of Joaquín's adrenaline-fueled heart, Astrid experienced so much human violence that it all began to blur together until finally she saw Taya lying motionless on the padded shikibuton mat and Kojiro kneeling over her, silently weeping; she saw at the same time little Coletrane bleeding at the chest next to the destroyed bodies of his parents, at the time unaware of his own complicity in their deaths. She could see the cold opportunism of Jeremiah Cross, and how his greed, egged on by the Inca Tan'Mo, will mean the destruction of the modern world if not halted. She saw the urgency of it all compounded by the three Interstices beginning to break their own rules of intervention in the affairs of men. And she saw, finally, her connection to Gaia -.the reason humans died as a result of looking into her eyes being the subconscious, bone-deep guilt over the destructive violence that people have done (and continue to do) to the earth, that to save anyone from this fate would require a conscious forgiveness on her part.

So, to stop Joaquín from dying, to reverse the effects of her power, she forgave him. She forgave people their trespasses, their arrogance, their evil.

"America was 'spose to be different," the boy's voice rang in her head, *"but I guess it's just the same everywhere. Everybody smile. But nobody cares."*

"No," Astrid whispered in his ear, "I am different. I care."

———

KIER WAS SO TAKEN UP IN EXAMINING the Lincoln Derringer that he didn't actually hear the elevator ding. It wasn't until Cross said, "Ahh! Ms. Fakhoury," that he was shaken from his trance.

You'd have no idea that Qadr was a killer upon seeing her in public. She looked more like a fashion model, and had the typical effect on men that this would imply. She wore a red long sleeve, form fitting skirt that went just to halfway down her thighs, showing off her muscular legs and athletic figure.

Around her neck was a golden necklace with an oceanic labradorite pendant, and Maghreb calligraphy cuff bracelets on both wrists. Her eyes were hidden behind prism black sunglasses.

Kier grinned.

Cross, his attention on the cryopreservation cases she carried, grinned as well.

The pleasantries were short, formal. Cold. Kier and Qadr never showed affection for one another in public, seldom, in fact, in private either. A demonstration of Trivium was offered to the secretly conflicted assassin, since Cross was in rare form and a particularly good mood -but she declined. Kier insisted, showing off the new gun for his collection. She declined a second time.

The four heads were to the Silicon Valley magnate's satisfaction. He opened the cases right there and then, smiling down at each lifeless countenance. Kier didn't care, but it gave Qadr a chill.

"I took the liberty of transferring renumerations before the both of you arrived," Cross said, before sitting back down in his chair. "Please confirm receipt."

Kier checked his bank account on his phone while Qadr, stone faced, just held Cross' gaze until Kier flashed an affirmative thumb. Then, Cross handed Qadr a small white envelope with a red bow tied on it.

"Gifts?" Kier joked. "Where's mine?"

Qadr flashed an annoyed glare at him, saying "assignment" in French before standing to leave.

"The lady is astute," Cross replied, standing as well.

" *Je vérifirais ça plus tard*," was Qadr's reply, her back already turned to the men, the clack of her heels on the tile floor sounding off as she walked toward the elevator.

———

"YOU'RE MORE PHLEGMATIC THAN usual," Kier said to Qadr when they were alone in the elevator, going down. Through the glass wall, the many corporate office skyscrapers of Los Angeles that stretched across Figueroa to Flower, and from Olive to Grand could be seen. Law offices, banks, real estate companies, hotels, even the regional Metro rail system and the 230,000 square foot Bullocks Wilshire was visible from that high perch, its copper, tarnished green 73 meter tower tip a bold beacon in the sky like a secular, Art Deco tower of Babel.

"Did you miss me?" Kier wanted to know.

She didn't. But Qadr spared him this knowledge by sporting a marginally coquettish grin.

"This Trivium project of Cross'," Kier reflected, punctuating with a whistle. "Pretty intriguing, to say the least. I'm convinced it's gonna change the world. How does it feel to be part of that?"

Qadr shrugged, and then, in French as usual, she tells him, "*Every avaricious industrialist thinks they will change the world. We're in another Gilded Age that will be romanticized by the people who make all the money, vilified by the crushed.*"

Landau Kier chuckled,

"The Vanderbilts and Rockefellers of yesteryears never saw a gun pulled out of thin air."

She made a gesture as if to say, *Touché.*

Then she pulled the envelope out the one hip pocket on her dress, opening it.

"So,' Kier shifted the subject, 'who's the winner behind curtain number three?"

Qadr read the name on the card, then showed Kier before returning it to the envelope.

"A woman this time?! Well, I'll be sure to pour one out for her. To equal opportunity, ma chérie!"

Qadr rolled her eyes again, but did enjoy Kier's wry and persistent sense of humor. Appreciating it especially as a buffer for her conflicted mood.

She committed the name on the card to memory:
Cynthia Mélisœur DeGruy.

———

THE PORTE COCHERE FRONT ENTRANCE to Rain Forest INC. was as fancy as its owner. Just as Landau and Qadr were exiting the automatic front door, a black Bentley Continental GT coupe pulled into the porte cochere. The man who stepped out of it was a portrait of iron sanguinity. He wore black pants and a tapered green polyester/spandex shirt with a zip up turtleneck collar. Over that was a camel colored, light weight cashmere overcoat. His hair was done in boxer braids that ended in a viper's tail.

After handing the valet his keys, Coletrane encountered Landau and Qadr. He glanced at Qadr in passing, sensing something.

She felt it too, a subtle jolt of static electricity. A subconscious spiritual recognition between Kojiro and Tzukuba.

———

"YOUR GREAT GRANDFATHER OBASI was ahead of his time," Cross said when Coletrane entered. He was standing over by his window, nursing a snifter half full of scotch. "One of the first big winners of the petroleum boom, he got around. Knew a lot of important people. It's not written in any book you're likely to find, but he met Herman Sachs one time in Chicago."

Coletrane went over to the open flooring, but he didn't approach Cross just yet. Instead, he put his hands in his pockets and waited. Then Cross pointed out the window and said,

"You see the tip of the Wilshire just across the way? That's part of Sachs' legacy. Vincent never tired of telling me the story of how one night, over drinks, it was Obasi that inspired it. Paint it green, the old man said…"

Then he finally turned to greet his visitor, a huge though oddly sinister grin on his face, "…the color of money."

Coletrane smiled back, gestured to the snifter.

"Let me guess. Glenmorangie Grand Vintage?"

"Vincent's son indeed," Cross said, genuinely nostalgic. He gave Coletrane a firm handshake.

"Can I offer you a glass?"

"Too early for me."

"Another thing you've inherited from your father. Austerity," Cross quipped.

"Only when the sun's up," Coletrane quipped back.

Cross laughed.

"Please. Come sit with me."

A wall to the left opened up when he said that, revealing a lounge area that was off limits to most guests.

Cross spoke as he walked, a decidedly ceremonious habit.

"It's all very funny,' he said, 'I never was a fan of tall buildings when I was younger. They always called to mind the image of Picart's 1731 painting of giants attempting to scale heaven by piling mountains on top of each other."

"What changed?" Coletrane asked to Cross' back.

"My father died. And I grew up."

In the center of the space was a celestial crown of crystal overhead light, and a bookcase on the back wall flanked on either side by dark walnut paneling. Keeping with the symmetry, there were duel marble planter pillars in the foreground of the walnut -both of them showcasing a well-groomed bonsai. Dali artwork was gently backlit and stretched out on the adjacent wall, complimentary in mood to a set of dark brown chesterfield sofas. The third wall held a chocolatey walnut armory, geometrically sectionized and displaying several different combat swords against a dark gray backdrop. The gray and black scatter cushions on the sofas complimented the steel blades and leather scabbards. They also complimented the scotch display on the circular black table set between the sofas.

Cross took a seat on one of the sofas and gestured for Coletrane to take the one across from him. He did.

"I love this parlor. Very modern chic."

"Yeah? I was going for reticent and aloof."

"I'd have left out the bonsais then."

"Touché," Cross lifted his glass. "You sure I can't offer you a drink?"

"I'm sure."

"Hmm," Cross sat back. There was a subtle note of offense in the way that he stared at Coletrane, despite his display of affability. Twice now, his visitor had rejected his hospitality.

"Anexity Works. I've been checking up on it. Can't say I was surprised to learn that it's now the top ranked dispensary of herbal medicinals worldwide. Your mother would be proud of its success."

"Big pharma wouldn't. To them, I might as well be Mussolini. *Oppressing* their shareholders by offering poor people actual cures to their ailments rather than stringing them along with addictive half-measures."

Cross laughed heartily.

"May we both be remembered as such nefarious villains!"

"Right. I've heard on the vine a bit about a public secret you've been keeping. About something called Trivium?"

"Yes," Cross stood. He placed his now empty snifter on the scotch table, and proceeded to power pace -hovering toward the armory wall. "I intend to shepherd in the next big Renaissance in Human Evolution. Call it the Fertile Crescent of the Mind."

"That's… an interesting reference," Coletrane noted, slowly trusting Cross less and less the more the man talked. How, he wondered, was this man and his father so close?

"Forensic meteorologists attribute the disappearance of Mayan civilizations between 1517 and 1546AD to Spanish colonization, drought, and agricultural failures. But when the Spanish actually arrived with their Roman Catholic faith, many of the cities across the Yucatan peninsula were already abandoned. So, what happened to these people, who invented the number zero thousands of years before their concept ever entered the minds of European mathematicians?"

"I'm sure you'll tell me."

"Math happened, Thelonious. The only tenable form of transcendence. The Mayans discovered the equation for overcoming this world. And so, they did just that."

"The Mayans," Coletrane countered, objectionably, and probably because he instinctively didn't like Cross' presumptuous use of his middle name, "were also notorious for practicing human sacrifice as so-called nourishment to the gods. They tumbled the heads of men, women, and children down the steps of their lofty pyramid structures in service to one of the most brutal traditions the world has ever seen."

Cross was good at hiding his anger, but Coletrane was equally good at reading anger and frustration in the body language of bad actors.

"You've read the *Título de Totonicapán* then. Impressive. But isn't that a text written in Guatemala by the colonialists themselves?"

"The Madrid Codex, actually. Written by the Mayans themselves."

This chipped even further at Jeremiah Cross' armor, inspiring in him one of his least fond memories of Coletrane's father -a penchant for challenging, and embarrassing, his intellect. So his stare that lasted for just a few moments carried the weight and tension of several awkward, friction-charged minutes.

Sensing something, or, rather, responding subconsciously to a prompt given him by a secret presence in the room, Cross nodded toward the armory.

"You see this sword here?" he walked over to it, taking the center-most blade from off the wall. A double-edged Tsurugi. "It's long name is Kusanagi-no-Tsurugi. In Japan it is considered –"

"Imperial regalia. One of the three sacred treasures. I know the story."

And Coletrane knew that story not because of he was well cultured and read, but because of the sudden apprehension that gripped him -because of Kojiro's memory of it. For starters, it wasn't the regalia that it looked like. It was another blade of the same original design, a blade known only as the weapon which adorned the hip of the Inca Tan'Mo.

Coletrane could even see Kojiro's memory of it tucked in the Tan'Mo's belt that day when his true form was revealed outside the tavern. The day the bastard cursed his beloved Taya. It took everything in Coletrane to stop Kojiro from taking command over his limbs and leaping at Cross' throat!

> *In his mind, there they were. Kojiro and Coletrane adrift on a dinghy. The fog surrounding them so thick that the sandy shore nearby could barely be seen. One moment, the two are peaceful and relaxed. The next, there is lightning and thunder in the sky. Kojiro reacts by looking at the shore -as if he sees something sinister, something he hates, something compelling him.*
>
> *"Don't," Coletrane says to him. But it's too late. Kojiro has already leapt into the water.*
>
> *At first he is fully submerged. And Coletrane panics because many moments go by, and Kojiro is yet to reemerge.*

"I've no doubt you know the story," Cross said. "But what of the legend?"

Coletrane decided to let Cross keep talking, lest responding distract from his hold on Kojiro.

Cross happily continued, sensing Coletrane's growing anger in the same way that Coletrane had sensed his.

"The grandchild of the sun goddess Amaterasu was born in the darkness of a cave, and so this blade was fashioned to balance his spirit. But the technique failed. Instead, it granted him superiority. It enabled him to transcend in the way that the Mayans did. The sword itself represents bravery. Fortitude."

> *At last, Kojiro came up out of the water, several yards away from the dinghy and approaching the shore. He walked not only against the water pushing him back, but also against random arms reaching out of the water and grabbing at him. He just kept pushing through those arms, the many grasping hands, with the sheer force of his will and mobility.*
>
> *Coletrane yelled at him from the boat, "NO! STOP!"*
>
> *But Kojiro didn't listen. He kept walking as more and more arms reached out in attempts to discourage him.*

Coletrane was slowly losing his hold on the spirit within, he stood up from the sofa and slowly approached Cross -their eyes locked in a silent, epic staring battle.

"Sounds revisionist to me," he argued, "because how can the blade of a Trickster be said to represent valor? Isn't treachery the opposite? Weakness. Cowardice."

> *Kojiro made it the shore, his bare feet making deep footprints in the sand with every step. In front of him was a vast fortification of cedar*

trees covering land much further out than the eye could see. But something hiding within it made the warrior even angrier, even more determined to enter the thicket.

But a hand on his shoulder stopped him. He turned to Coletrane, who shook his head.

"Don't do it, Kojiro. Not yet."

Kojiro, in a moment of impatient rage, grabbed Coletrane by the throat.

"Don't you see?!" he yelled. "This man was never your father's friend! He is a Trickster... He is the Tan'Mo!"

By the shock in Coletrane's face, Kojiro could tell that he did not, in fact, see.

"I will show you," he added. "Look close."

Then he pulled Coletrane closer to his face, hypnotizing Coletrane with the depth of his eyes. And in that bottomless pit, Coletrane sunk into the past. He was a boy again. And there his father, Vincent, was. Alive. Robust. A philanthropic captain of industry.

He saw Vincent at a charity event, toasting friends and colleagues. And there was Cross just outside of view, a contemptuous scowl on his face.

He saw Vincent again, on the night of he and Adaeze's murder; him and Cross talking and drinking in the trophy room. Laughing together. Smiling. But as soon as Vincent turns to refill Cross' drink, the hateful scowl returns.

Coletrane saw the two men together a third time, at the grand opening of Rain Forest Inc. It was Vincent himself who happily handed his "friend" the large pair of scissors to cut the red banner on the doors. They shook hands, but even then, when Vincent turned to face the crowd and the flashing cameras, there was that barely concealed look of hate just beneath the surface of Cross' fake grin.

"Long are the tales of the gutless," Coletrane said to Cross, hiding, barely, the anger presented by Kojiro's revelations of the past, now standing right in front of him, unafraid of the sword that Cross was still holding in his hand, " for the lies that exalt them will forever need refining."

The Inca Tan'Mo, invisible, was yet standing there watching the exchange between the two men. He could sense Kojiro as much as Kojiro could sense him, and he was silently transmitting his hatred and the urgency of it into his subject's mind, bones, intentions…

Another awkward moment passes between them, but then Cross ends it with a chuckle and then resting his free hand on Coletrane's shoulder.

"So cultured," he said in a way that seemed shrouded in insult, "Your father would be proud of you indeed."

———

A SIDE-EFFECT OF THE BRAIN DAMAGE was that sometimes Marcus would sit in a state of catatonia; unblinking, lost in thought, and as stiff as a corpse in rigor mortis.

Sitting sunken into a love seat on the first level of the duplex, early one morning, a Tuesday, he struck with this familiar condition. They'd become accustomed to it in the weeks since they broke him out of the facility, but Noa Kovács and Gordan Juric were still freaked out when he did it. They could unemotionally destroy the bodies of innocent people with automatic military-grade munitions, but a man sitting still made them squeamish.

Juric was standing in front of him, a steaming coffee in hand. He checked his watch. 6:05AM. Kovács was over by the kitchen using the single serving Moka pot to make a coffee of his own.

"Why do you think he does it?" Juric wondered out loud, looking at Marcus sideways.

"We've had this conversation already," Kovács, annoyed, replied. "One too many shots to the head. But he'll overcome it."

"You've been saying that for weeks."

"And you took months to overcome that Butalbital addiction."

"Eh. Not the same."

The Moka pot began its droning whistle. Kovács took it off the heat and poured the contents into a mug that read "MASTER COORDINATOR OF THE SHIT SHOW".

Juric leaned forward to get a closer look at Marcus' face.

"Come look at his eyes, buraz!"

"I'm not coming to look at his eyes."

"I'm serious. The pupils, they sink inward when he gets like this. I wonder where he goes."

Kovács walked over, blowing the steam off his black coffee.

"Where he needs to go. To fight his demons."

———

IT WAS JUST AFTER 2PM, HOUR OF THE sheep, when the remaining members of the Live Crew were making it into Honshu, not far from their destination in the mainland. Just seven members strong now, but strong enough, each one of the reasoned, for the challenges ahead. Their flanks were a fortification of muscle; the four largest and strongest among them, the two kanobo wielding Chinmoku Aki brothers Gorou and Ichiro, Otaku keeping himself satiated with the liquid courage housed in his sake gourd, and Jubei with his two split broad swords ever at the ready. At the back was Ittei with his wolf friend, and though Yoriko didn't technically count as a Live Crew member, she and four of her pack were among them. Tzukuba walked at the center, the perfect position to sustain the protective jutsu she casts to keep everyone's minds focused and guarded against the many predatory illusions that would otherwise besiege the group on the path ahead. And at the front was Kojiro and Kana, who lead the way with her precise navigations. She'd carved out a short cut to their final destination after they'd exited Chiyu's time loop forest. It required they hitch a ride on the back of The Chimera Kuni, a flying sentient city that held a village of the dead surrounded by timber badlands of trickery and preceded by the Graveyard of Hopes & Dreams. It was a dangerous passage indeed, wherein they faced phantoms of departed loved ones who sought to suffocate them with survival guilt, tangible illusions that took the shapes of their greatest fears (and tried to consume them like cannibal versions of themselves!), and echoing specters of regret that appeared to them as armored knights on horseback who attacked in eye-defying motions while leaving trailing afterimages of themselves as they moved.

Maintaining the close-knit phalanx structure, and staying within the confines of Tzukuba's defensive oasis, is how they all survived. And though both Jubei and Otaku protested Kana's pathfinding as usual, they both also knew that she was right to lead them into these dangers on the benefit of cutting near two weeks from their journey. This also meant avoiding another encounter with the Ashigaru, and not having to lose time on building a boat to cross the high tides of a forty mile river.

"Less than a day's walk from here," Kana told Kojiro, after the Crew had made it off of the Chimera and back onto stable ground. "In the forest ahead, we can rest and replenish on mangoes and papaya."

"You hear that, Otaku?" Kojiro said over his shoulder. "Food to quiet your ever cantankerous gullet."

Otaku laughed,

"Never enough, yuujin! I've an appetite for two men at least."

"Not four?" Kana joked, referencing his number of arms.

"Yeah, back atcha, Kana," he replied when she turned to look at him, with each of his four hands inserting the thumb between the first two fingers -the equivalent of *fuck you*. This captured everyone's amusement, even the Chinmoku brothers who couldn't hear but could read sign.

The laughter was faintly heard up ahead. It was within the forest that the Crew were heading towards, a high sun's warm rays beaming down between the fissures of shade from palmate maple and Green Cascades. There men were there that heard the laughter, hostiles that didn't have any friends among the Crew. Hostiles, in fact, that were waiting for them.

"Hear that?" the barrel chested brick-layer Omphalos said. He scratched around the scar over his one dead eye, a bad habit of his for when he sensed a fight. "Stop playing with your food and listen." Then he readied himself by putting on his Tekagi-shuko claws, an iron plated weapon that allowed him not only to strike like a tiger but to grab at and block against bladed assaults with his hands.

Jericho, the shape-shifter, stopped juggling the three yubari melons to listen.

The third man among them was leaned against a tree, chewing on a sugarcane straw. His posture was aloof, disinterested, and his hands were busy fiddling with a palm-like palmate leaf, tearing petal pieces off its delicate rachis.

This was Katsurou's way, always better in every regard when maintaining an incurious attitude.

The man known as The Prometheus looked up when, moments later, the Live Crew emerged from the thicket. Surprised to see the three, everyone stopped walking. The two life-long enemies locked eyes, and Katsurou grunted.

"You've grown a beard," Katsurou said to Kojiro. "Masculine at last. Maybe my boys and I will work up a sweat for this bounty."

Kojiro narrowed his eyes from across the clearing, his hand already on Hatsukoi's hilt.

This is where Marcus' initial memory of the event proved faulty. Before in his dawning memory, when the big fight broke out, he as Katsurou called the Pau'gukdoza Wraiths into the fray.

It went down differently in reality.

Yoriko snarled, but remained at Ittei's side despite her desire to pounce. Jubei and Otaku shared the *ready to pounce* sentiment, and so did Kana -who, in fact, was the most impulsive among them despite how well she hid this from the group. But it was Tzukuba, because of the spiritual sensitivity she experienced as a side effect of using her jutsu techniques, who could intuit the conflicts within both Kojiro and Katsurou alike. She was surprised to learn in this emotive revelation that the two had once upon a time been close, childhood friends. And they both held gauntlets for fathers that they believed they'd failed as men, this being the gouge by which their personalities were hewn -an enduring sense inadequacy compounded by every failure, every loss.

"What are you doing here, Katsurou?" Kojiro asked through his teeth.

"Satisfying a wager, old friend," he answered blithesomely, still leaning on the tree and fiddling with the leaf. "Omphalos here bet that you'd prove a child indeed, passing through here on the callow vagaries of a fool. Jericho, on the other hand, bet that none among you would have the courage even for that."

"I was sure of it, man," Jericho added, taking a bite out of one of the melons he'd broken in half. "Certain. I mean, look at this sad bunch! Amirite?!"

"Apparently not," Omphalos leaned back in a hearty guffaw.

Then Katsurou got off of the tree, dropped the leaf and pulled the bokken from his belt.

"Enough banter," he said, interrupting Omphalos' laughter. His eyes still locked with Kojiro's. "Time to pay up, Jerry. You owe us thirty **Yokeizo**."

Jericho stepped forward and shrugged, tossed his melon to the ground.

"A debt's a debt."

After saying this, the man's eyes began to glow bright cyan blue. This prompted Ichiro to step forward as well, his own eyes beginning to glow the color of amber, and his shinu shirt falling open to reveal the top of a full chest tattoo.

Kojiro drew Hatsukoi, and held out his left arm to hold Ichiro back.

"No. Not yet."

This made Jericho smirk, and then break out into a sprint towards the Crew.

Every warrior among them drew their weapons. Kana threw a wave of shuriken at Jericho. He lunged and flipped over them, tossing a black egg before him that exploded on the ground in a cloud of blue smoke. When he landed in that space, his body "shattered" in a splash of particles that became a fanning out army of **Yokeizo; armored *pra-ita*, a word meaning "gone forever" or zombie/ogre-like in Sanskrit, made of terra cotta and impervious to pain**. There were thirty of them in total, as Katsurou had mentioned. Their weapons were halberds, bayonets, daggers and spears, bronze swords and forearm mounted blades with double jagged edges. All of them yet were Jericho, so all of them shared those deathly blue eyes.

Kojiro's six outnumbered Crew members all engaged without hesitation, as well as the five ferocious wolves that were loyal to Ittei. The flute player, in fact, would write about this later.

I often wondered what to do with the rest of spring,
After the inviting winds would sweep away all traces of
ume, bara, tulips, and purple wisteria....

And on the final day that I see the mallards crying over
Lake Iware, I will yet remember the courage of my
brethren, and the battle-cry of our leader....

Gorou used the secret Chinmoku stills associated with his
deafness to anticipate the aggressors' attacks four moves ahead,
taking them out one by one with the heavy business end of his
kanobo. Kana engaged the steel clawed brute Omphalos, who
tripled her in both weight and girth. But her speed and the
distance she could maintain with the kusarigama quickly
frustrated the aggressive behemoth.

"Don't let me get my hands on you, little girl!" he warned.

"Wow,' she shot back, referring to his weapon, "you're an
angry kitty."

Otaku and Jubei against several terra cotta as they attempted
to swarm them.

Five spear wielders tried to all take on Ittei at once, but he
outclassed them with the naginata. And Kojiro, yelling, he ran
a zigzagging path through all of this, heading straight for
Katsurou -who happily met him halfway.

Despite all the skill of the Deadly Sakura and the
intimidating sharpness of Hatsukoi's blade, Katsurou was deft
enough with the bokken that he was able to connect with the
live sword only against the flat or unsharpened side. Katsurou's
talent for this precise aikido-like kenjutsu was near
supernatural, and he knew it! But he also knew the slim
likelihood of getting a blow in himself.

"The rumors I've heard then about your pitiful sword are
false," Katsurou taunted. "You can't even cut a piece of wood!"

Kojiro didn't reply. He knew what the bastard was doing, and wouldn't let him get away with it like he so often did when they were children.

It was as vivid as if it were happening right there and then, the two little nine year old boys practicing in the lake with their bokkens, balancing on the rocks in the shallow water as their fathers watched.

Little Katsurou, he was taller and stronger than Kojiro when they were boys.

Of this he took advantage and treated his friend like a little brother even though they were both the same age. When focused, the two were almost evenly matched in terms of balance on the rocks. And could flit from one to the next, crisscrossing each other, striking and parrying with impressive concinnity. But focus, here, is the operative term -and Katsurou was skilled in robbing Kojiro of his.

"Don't be afraid, Ko," he teased, "if you fall, it's just water! You're wet already in the crotch, after all."

"Shut up!"

And that was all he needed. Katsurou sidestepped a horizontal swing of Kojiro's clumsily committed to in anger, spun on a pivot and pegged Kojiro in the stomach with the butt of his bokken. Kojiro slipped backwards on the rock and, winded from the blow, tripped over his own foot and fell in the water.

Little Kat guffawed, a gesture of poor character that his father would later reprimand him for. Kojiro, after punching into the water, was so angry that tears welled up in his eyes. He was glad then for the cover of water. But later his own father would have words with him about allowing his anger to get the better of him.

Kojiro remembered that private talk while fighting Katsurou in those woods, thinking of the exact words relayed. *"Learn,"* wise Akimitsu said to his only son in private, *"to think deeper on the world than on the self. In this way attachments will not lay siege to you, disappointments will not suffocate, and no man will ever make use of your anger to set strings to your limbs."*

These words, Kojiro had failed so many times to heed them. But he wouldn't fail on this day.

He feigned anger in a way that he knew Katsurou would see, and attempted a strike that he knew Katsurou would roll off of -setting him up for a back elbow to the face. Katsurou stumbled backwards but quickly regained his footing. Kojiro crouched into a ready position, smirked at Katsurou -who wiped at the blood on his lip.

"Touché, runt," Katsurou said.

"Don't be afraid, Kat. It's just blood," Kojiro replied, then winked.

Omphalos was still frustrated with Kana, but he was studying her techniques with every cut she got on him with the kusarigama while avoiding killing strikes. He got some cuts in himself with the shuko claws, tattering her clothes and drawing blood from her legs, arms, torso... It was when she returned the serve by cutting a deep gash in his already scarred face that he lost his temper.

"Bitch!" he yelled. "I'm gonna break you like a twig!"

"You'll try!" she yelled back. But then he got hold of her sickle chain and yanked her towards him, then punched her in the stomach with enough force to launch her small body at a tree. He was on her again before she even got a chance to catch her breath, throwing a punch at her head meant to shatter it like one of Jericho's melons. But she ducked under it in the nick of time, pulling a dagger from her thigh holster and jamming it into his bicep before rolling out of the way.

"Ahhh!" he screamed, while turning and said, "you fucking bi-"

But was cut off by a shuriken thrown by her that lodged in his right cheek to match the gash she made earlier to the left.

"That'll fix your dirty mouth," she derided, smiling through her own bloodied teeth.

Ichiro wasn't wasting time with any particular Yokeizo. He instead was dashing from one to the next, engaging and disengaging, using his Chinmoku sense to try and sniff out which of them was the real Jericho.

His younger brother Gurou, who he usually fought with in synchronicity, was so sharp with his own talent of Chinmoku anticipation that Ichiro was confident to leave him to his devices while he searched for Jericho. But this was a miscalculation. At the same moment that he finally sensed where the real Jericho was, it dawned on him too late that the Chinmoku anticipatory technique could be undermined by a shape-shifter's stealth. He turned to his left, seeing Gurou going hard against a Yokeizo wielding two halberds. And while distracted, the real Jericho came up behind him and stabbed him in the back with a knife.

"NOOOO!" Ichiro yelled; the only word any member of the Crew had ever heard him speak. The sound of it drew Kojiro's attention, who was suddenly reminded of the vision that Xiao Xiao Chen showed him -of Jericho distracting him with doppelgangers of himself and then getting the drop on him with Vajra swords.

It was one of those same swords that Jericho used in this moment to remove Gurou's head from his shoulders.

Seeing this made Kojiro reflexively turn to Ichiro and call to him, renewing his earlier admonition,

"ICHIRO, DON'T!"

But it was too late. Seeing his last remaining brother die this way, it made Ichiro's eyes light up again. It made him fall to his knees and rip open his shirt, groaning at the pain of his now fully exposed tattoo of a Ningen sea monster begin to burn, bleed, and move involuntarily.

The ground under everyone's feet began to shake, and everything,, the trees, rocks, vegetation, all took on the amber glow of Ichiro's eyes as the ground started breaking into sections like the dry cracked surface a desert.

"What is your man doing, Kojiro?!" Katsurou called. And Kojiro, his berserker rage momentarily activated, draw a tanto from his hip and flung it over his shoulder at Katsurou.

"SHUT UP!" he commanded. The knife grazed Katsurou's cheek before lodging in the tree behind him. He grasped at the cut, but was more concerned with the moving ground than with retaliation.

More than twenty miles away, hovering high above the Isuzu river near where its waters passed through the Ise Grand Shrine to the sun goddess Amaterasu, was Astrid engaged in deep reflection. There was a question in her mind about Gods and Goddesses; she wondered if she were one herself and, if so, what place did she hold in the pantheon in relations to others such as Amaterasu.

Around her orbited psychic projections of the twenty seven moon stars, like an atomic nucleus of unanswered questions. She was the neutron to the protons and electrons represented by the glimmering spheres that were circling her. They all vanished however when her focus was interrupted the peristaltic wave of Ichiro's pain.

INSTEAD OF A BLUE-GRAY ARM LIKE Marcus initially envisioned, it was more of a white-gray arm that burst forth from the now liquified ground. Everyone took cover as the Ningen's full body came out to the torso in the flooding verdure, it's terrifying whale-like cranium, thin scaly arms, skeletal face with gills, no eyes, and three rows of shark-like teeth, scars and tooth-rake marks all over its barnacle laden skin, made for an arresting sight for all who bore witness. The barnacles were ever moving, and would jump off the Ningen to eat whole the unlucky before returning to crawl about the body of their host. A few of the Yokeizo were among the unlucky, and, to their surprise, the barnacles also attacked the Crew despite the monster being borne from Ichiro's magic.

Jubei toiled to fight them off, yelling,

"Control your creature, Ichiro!" But Ichiro, on his knees and holding his throbbing head while his chest bled, was completely lost in a prison of subconsciousness.

"He can't!" Kana warned, making a raft of a fallen tree, and pulling the drowning Otaku, who wouldn't swim, on top of it with her.

"My gourd," he cried, realizing he'd lost it in the commotion.

"Really?" Kana was nonplussed, "You're worried about sake right now?!"

Out of nowhere, Omphalos leapt from out of the swamp water, right behind Kana's perch on the makeshift raft. Her knife was still lodged in his bicep, but no matter -he was determined in this moment to drop down from behind and impale with the claw on his opposing hand. But Ittei at the same time leapt from a land patch, intercepting Omphalos in tackling move before he get his chance.

"Not so fast, you sonofabitch!"

Omphalos struggled to break free of Ittei's hold when the pacifist snatched the knife out of the brute's arm and stabbed him in the chest with it. A barnacle was approaching Ittei from behind while distracted with Omphalos, who seemed yet unphased by the blade in his chest, but one of Yoriko's pack dove in the way and was eaten by the barnacle instead.

"No!" said Ittei upon seeing this over his shoulder, leaving himself open to a vicious headbutt from Omphalos that knocked him unconscious. He sank then into the swamp. Yoriko dove into the water after him, taking his kimono collar into her mouth and swimming him back up to the surface.

Tzukuba used her Ninjutsu to dash across the surface of the water over to the patch of ground on which Ichiro toiled against his mind, grabbed him by the shoulders and attempted to shake him out of the trance so that the adrenaline-rushed Ningen would go away.

"Reel in your mind, Ichiro," she beckoned. "Reel it in!"

"He's in shock," a mocking voice said to her back. She turned to find Jericho standing at the edge of the ground patch.

Both his Vajra swords drawn, he smirked, "But can you blame him?"

Tzukuba stood and drew her onyx blade. Saying nothing, but telling him much with the hate in her eyes.

"The silent type then," he jeered. But again, Tzukuba said nothing and made no movement. It was a standoff; him making prowling feline steps back and forth and twirling the Vajra blades, her just standing there, the onyx at her side, still as a statue.

Another moment passed. Two. Three more…

Then he dashed at her, lightning speed. But still she didn't move until the last moment, to duck under a horizontal strike to the head and cut him across the right rib spinning on a pivot. He turned back in a backhand strike that Tzukuba blocked at the tricep with an elbow. He struck upward with opposite hand but Tzukuba's onyx, the blade turned down, met attempt with a loud *sheintz* and spark, spinning again on a pivot and flipping the onyx upward. She stepped back once and then forward, both hands on the tsuka. A series of glinting clashes of her blade versus his two, so fast that it happened in barely the space of two breaths; until she got an opening and cut off one of his hands at the forearm; the distraction of spurting blood cost him the other hand, and then his throat. Shock setting his eyes at maximum dilation, the last thing Jericho saw was the woman he underestimated kicking him into the swamp water.

And while the Ningen flailed and roared, Kojiro and Katsurou, as they did when they were children, leapt from rock to rock, ground patch to ground patch, engaging and disengaging to avoid being eaten by a barnacle or squashed by the blind, stampeding monster.

"You are a pestilence," Kojiro told him, "a crude distraction, an insufferable troll!"

"And you," Katsurou replied, "are a pigeon with no message to carry, KoKo! A soul wandering in search of a purpose he will never find! The weak cleave to you like flies to shit!"

"You talk too much!" now standing on the back of a barnacle, riding it like a wave. Looking at Katsurou ten yards across the unruly waters, standing on a plate of rock laden and muddy soil, the pupils of Kojiro's eyes split into the figure eights, he threw Hatsukoi across the way at his bitter opponent.

The way she twirled was epic, precise, like a pirouetting disk magnetized forth by powers unknown. And yet she zipped right past her target, Katsurou merely leaning to the left just outside of the blade's path.

He smiled. But then he noticed, too late, that Kojiro's right arm was still outstretched, the hand still open with the palm up. The Sakura closed his hand and yanked. When Katsurou looked over his shoulder, there was Hatsukoi flying back towards him -this time he didn't move fast enough. The business end of the golden blade sliced into Katsurou's left deltoid, spinning him back around by the force. What he saw when he turned was Kojiro in mid-air, having leapt across the water towards him, catching Hatsukoi at the tsuka. He landed right in front of Katsurou and slashed at an angle. Not even close enough to make direct contact with Katsurou's body, the force with which Kojiro swung sent a wave of energy across his chest so strong that it tore open Katsurou's shirt, burned into his flesh, and sent him hurling backwards into the water.

Katsurou sunk watching his blood trail upward, he sunk in disbelief. Then, several yards down into the depths of the impossible sea, he saw a glint of light shoot into the water like a comet across the sky. Then it vanished.

"I'm not dead, you runt!" he said in his mind, determined to swim back to the surface and engage Kojiro again. But before he could, two arms grabbed him from behind. One wrapped around his torso, the other went over his mouth. They were so strong that he was powerless to break free. Then he saw her hair going all over his face. He thought maybe it was a siren taking him into an aquatic death.

But no. It was Astrid.

———

MARCUS OPENED HIS EYES. HE WAS STILL in the chair. There was darkness all around him. Glancing to his right, at a window, he saw that it was dark outside as well. But even though he was in a state of catatonia before the vision snapped him from reality, he knew that it was the morning before consciousness left him. Now, night.

No matter. His memory was now fully restored. He'd made himself acquainted with his previous self, with Katsurou. He knew that Kovács and Juric were his fallen cohorts. But where were they?

He rose from the chair and stretched out, thawing his bones out of the deep sleep. When he walked, unconsciously, it was the gait of Katsurou -tentativeness replaced by confidence;

agency, urgency, poise, all stamping out every trace of consequential and bone-deep vacillation the result of years being treated like an invalid.

Thinking of the words he as Katsurou said to Kojiro upon seeing the beard, *"Masculine at last"*, Marcus chuckled to himself over the irony of it now applying to him simply for the way that he felt.

Like he mattered, like a **man**.

Marcus was wearing a white button up shirt. On a whim, he decided to unbutton it all the way. That's when he saw the scar from Hatsukoi across the length of his chest. His was a diagonal slant from the right, Coletrane's from the left. He ran his two middle fingers along the surface of the scar and recalled how he'd gotten it -overnight, in a *dream* about a phantom past. He recalled how the strike from Hatsukoi was so powerfully delivered that her golden blade didn't even have to touch his skin to cause the wound and throw him backwards. He also remembered the ferity of Kojiro's figure-eight eyes in the moment of contact, his gritted teeth and pointed maxillary canines.

"Berserker," he muttered under his breath, clenching his fists. "A dog to be put down."

Kovács and Juric shared a room on the second level of the duplex that was big enough for two beds and plenty of walk space in between. That's where Marcus stood, sipping a steaming coffee, when he said, loud enough to wake them both,

"Enough sleeping on the job, you peons. The devil finds work."

Kovács opened his eyes calmly. Juric started awake after being surprised by the boom of Marcus' voice. When Kovács sat up, he noticed that Marcus/Katsurou was drinking from his "MASTER COORDINATOR OF THE SHIT SHOW" mug. Didn't protest.

"Buraz," Juric said, excited, "is it you at last?"

"Of course, it's him," Kovács answered, getting up and walking over to Marcus. "Welcome, my liege."

Marcus smiled at Kovács, put his free hand on his shoulder. And giving him a sideways look, he said,

"I value your loyalty. A thing that has spanned over hundreds of years, across dimensions not only of time but of space and reality too. I value it, brother, …this gilded oddment of fealty. But…"

And then he slapped Kovács so hard that the man fell to the floor.

"…I can answer questions myself!"

Again, Kovács did not protest. He was surprised, yes, but seemed almost happy to have been slapped; happy for the stinging proof of Katsurou's full return.

Marcus looked over to Juric.

"It's me alright, Jerry," he said, calling him by Katsurou's nickname for Jericho. "And are you as dehydrated as I am for a sip of some revenge?"

"Parched!" was Juric's reply.

"Good. And you?" he asked Kovács, who was climbing to his feet.

"All the time."

"Well then, gentlemen," Marcus lifted the mug in cheers, "let's quench it."

"THE TEXT LEAPT FORWARD SEVENTY PAGES in just the last hour," Poole told Coletrane through the speaker in the rental Bentley. Immediately after leaving Cross' office, Coletrane was hurrying along the 101 to Van Nuys Airport. DeLoache had already been notified and was fueling up.

"I'm not surprised to hear that, Poole. Jeremiah Cross is the worst kind of villain. A crooked white industrialist who mistakes his avarice for philanthropy. Every minute with that bastard felt like a visit to Ashoka's Hell."

"It's still writing now," Patrick said, but mostly to Poole though Coletrane could hear him on the speaker. The two were in the library at the Marx Estate, Patrick leaned over the desk interpreting the blood-written passages as they filled blank pages in the magical book, and Poole, his shoulder bandaged, was pacing in front of the desk holding the speaker phone.

"What is it saying?" Coletrane asked.

Patrick took about a minute to read the new lines carefully, as they were now filling the pages much faster than he could readily translate.

"Dark omens," he read.

Then Poole, who still didn't quite like Patrick, said,

"You could suffer being more specific."

"Yeah, but that's the thing. It translates to basically that, over and over again. *Men in ivory towers who pray for rain will blame the destitute for the mud. And then pray some more until the mud reaches up to drown them as well."*

Coletrane gripped the steering wheel, his foot getting heavier on the gas.

"It's a warning,' he interpreted. "The destitute are entire populations living below the upper 1%. And the men in ivory towers are feckless billionaires like Cross. Whatever secret project he's developing that Global Dollar has been sniffing around is bad. Very bad."

"It is much worse than bad," Kojiro said in Coletrane's mind. *"You should have killed him there where he stood."*

Though he understood the urgency and conviction of the words, Coletrane did not immediately agree with the warrior living within him.

He would later regret it.

———

WHEN THE GROUND RETURNED TO NORMAL after the Ningen was sent back to rest, everyone still alive looked around to access the damage. When the waters settled back to its earthen form, it looked as though a natural disaster had occurred. A hurricane, earthquake, or both. Trees were toppled, canals and craggy hillocks had formed, a wealth of vegetative multeity had been replaced by a razed mess of herbaceous bedlam. Tzukuba, luckily, managed to wake Ichiro from his fugue before the monster and its supernatural deluge spread enough to destroy the entire forest or, worse, all of Honshu. He didn't remember losing control and consciousness, releasing the Ningen, but he did remember the death of his brother.

Gorou's body was gone. So were the bodies of most others lost, having been buried in the detritus. Some of the terra cotta, though they were clones of the shapeshifter Jericho, and at least two of Yoriko's pack, were sticking out of the ground by arm, leg, tail, snout, or head -a now permanent obelisk to strife.

The remaining Crew members were Tzukuba, Otaku, Ichiro, Kana, Jubei, Ittei, and Kojiro. Everyone else including the rest of their enemies were assumed to had been swallowed by the ground.

The Ningen? Gone. Just a tattoo again on Ichiro's chest.

Kojiro was on his knees, his open palms sunken into the mud as if he were trying to push his way through the solid surface. He balled his hands into fists, taking up dirt. This, he knew, was an act of futility against the outrage of loss; the crude, daily reminder that people, nay -all sentient beings, existed in a grievous, ineluctable state of vulnerability, subject at every moment to ruin or expulsion from life.

"Do not fret, yuujin," Jubei said, now standing over him.

"Do not fret?"

Kojiro rose to his feet, connecting not with the intent behind Jubei's words but with the callous implication of them.

"The entire point of our mission is to fret," Kojiro yelled. "Are we now to become like the gods -brazenly vilipending human life and calling it fortitude? Gorou was a father. So was Jirou and Aito. Will we tell their children to not fret?! I should not have let any of you journey with me!"

"Brother," Jubei grabbed Kojiro firmly by the arm, but with affection clearly displayed on his face, "I'm... I am sorry. That is not what I meant."

Then he looked over to Ichiro, who had already read the apology on his lips. They held each other's gaze for several moments of reflected empathy and understanding, before he turned his eyes to Ittei -who had lost his family's naginata in the battle along with, apparently, all his wolves.

"Ittei…"

"You needn't speak it," the flute player and poet said, stepping forward. "We all know in our hearts what you meant. That we must move on, so the sacrifices of those fallen will not been in vain."

"They already aren't," Kana chimed in. She was bleeding from wound to her arm, and her gait was slightly compromised by a bruised rib, but she walked up to a high ascension of ground to look out over yonder. She gestured for the others to join her. First was Kojiro. Then, Tzukuba, Jubei, Ittei, Ichiro and Otaku. They all saw and looked upon it with awe.

A modest archipelago of land masses separated by shallow interconnected streams. Beyond this was a wide open field of perennial cultivars, swaying variegated pampus and hakonechloa macra. Amid this beautiful display of verdure were hundreds - thousands (!) – of tsuka reaching up, slanted, from out of the ground -at the ends of long blades sheathed in elegant saya. Those sheathes were adorned by sageo stitching that matched the ito wrappings of their respective handles, making for a multicolored, field-long reliquary to warriors so great in number that they could never be individually named.

"At last," Ittei said.

"The bodhisattvas spoke truth," that was Otaku. "Just as they did of the Dragon Kings."

"We are here," Kana added. But it was Kojiro who gave voice to its name,

"The Valley of Swords."

———

COLETRANE MADE IT CLEAR THAT HE would waste no time getting back to Florida, having called DeLoach immediately after hanging up with Poole and Patrick and letting him know to make sure the plane was ready upon his arrival. For the good pilot's part, he was familiar enough with his employer's penchant for urgency so had already fueled up long before the call. He needed only gain clearance for takeoff and they'd be promptly on their way.

Not twenty minutes after Coletrane gave up the keys to the rental car, his private jet was in the air.

And neither was Jeremiah Cross one to procrastinate. After Coletrane left his office, a feeling came over him that he couldn't shake. As well as a whispery, influential, but near inaudible voice in his ear.

"He will interfere with your work if you let him live. He is yet one of the final heads you must collect anyway. Have him killed. Do it now."

Cross poured himself another Scotch and went to the window, looking out on the city. The unidentifiable feeling, it blossomed to suspicion and then to full blown apprehension.

The words, they played again:

"He will interfere with your work if you let him live. He is yet one of the final heads you must collect anyway. Have him killed. Do it now."

He recounted the conversation he'd had with Coletrane, carefully considering the subtext just under the surface of the words. Clearly, they both spoke almost entirely in veiled threats and affronts.

He thought of Coletrane's line of questioning. *"How can the blade of a Trickster be said to represent valor? Isn't treachery the opposite? Weakness. Cowardice."*

Who, Cross wondered, did this punk think he was?! To question the wisdom of his elder, such arrogance!

But what really made his blood boil was the other thing Coletrane said.

"Long are the tales of the gutless, for the lies that exalt them will forever need refining."

It is too bad, Cross continued in his silent rationalizations, that the brat's father didn't live to take him over the knee a few times before becoming a man. It is too bad that Vincent was against slapping the boy around to teach him lessons in the first place. Maybe then he'd know respect. Maybe then he'd have character. Maybe then... he'd be permitted to live.

"Your anger clouds your judgement," a familiar, more pronounced voice said to his back. But Cross remembered his own lessons, and did not turn to the sound. Though, he felt the presence drawing on him. He could hear the heavy, deliberate footsteps.

"It takes you, this anger, to a place far removed from where your mind needs to be. And this is a fault of all men. Especially men of considerable power, that they'd be so moved by the audacity of those they deem as lesser than them. Even the culture of idealism favors these lesser folk, the fantasy tales they grow up on leading every weaking to believe themselves a David in the great war against the Goliaths who keep the world turning on its axis. But the good news is this, Jeremiah. You are exactly where you need to be, and they, he, is exactly where you want him."

On that last word, the presence, the Tan'Mo, he came close enough to Cross to show up in his right peripheral. On a reflex, the billionaire flinched and moved a few paces away. Lest he anger the deity by setting eyes upon him.

But to his surprise, the shifty Trickster said,

"Unburden yourself, my loyal subject. And look upon me at last."

Though having heard the words, Cross still was reluctant. Not a man walking the earth had ever intimidated him. He'd been too shielded all the days of his life by the trappings of wealth and its pretentions, but the Inca Tan'Mo was no man.

Afraid yet, Cross ultimately regarded the words as less a sanction than a command. He turned, tentatively. And gasped at what he saw.

A gray suited being so tall that Cross had to look up to find his eyes, these soulless red orbs embedded in a fiendish effigy of dried, fractured enamel. Lean, chiseled features, a perpetual scowl, coal-black hair, a countenance of such disquieting influence that Cross near shivered with dread. But it wasn't this contradiction of macabre and rakish that confounded him.

It was that the demon bore the face of his long dead father.

"SO, WHAT ABOUT THE MYSTERIOUS Reynolds?," Cynthia posed the question to the study group. It was a Saturday afternoon on an unscheduled class day. Extra credit. Twelve students from her Tuesday and Thursday morning class were in attendance. Some because they were behind, the rest because they were industrious. And Cynthia, because she was married to her work and had no "friends" outside of Paulina.

They were all sitting on blankets, towels, or mats in the grass outside of the main library, under the shade of the oak trees and near the bed of blue, white, and purple flowers.

"Umm..,' one of the students, a Black male named Eugene, newly transferred from an out of state university and determined to make an impression, shuffled through his notes in formation of his reply. "Ok… yeah, Poe's Narrative of Arthur Gordon Pym of Nantucket."

"What about it, Eugene?" Cynthia challenged.

"Yeah, he, J.N. Reynolds, he was an explorer and completely wrong about the hollow earth theory, but was influential enough that he inspired Poe's…" Eugene checked his notes again, "… his 1838 novel. Reynolds inspired Melville's Moby-Dick too."

"*On that last night,*" another student, Yelonda, read from a book in her lap, "*as the shadows fell across him, it must have been the horrors of shipwreck, of thirst, and of drifting away into the unknown seas of darkness that troubled his last dreams, for, by some trick of his ruined brain, it was the scenes of Arthur Gordon Pym that rose in his imagination, and the man who was connected most intimately with them. 'Reynolds!' he called, 'Reynolds!, Oh,*

Reynolds!' The room sang with it. It echoed down the corridors hour
after hour all that Saturday night."

Across the way, entirely unbeknownst to Cynthia, another
student was sitting alone in the grass. Watching. Studying, much
more, the group than the mock study materials in front of her.

"Harvey Allen,' Cynthia replied. 'He wrote that of Poe in
'26. But Israfel is a fictional account of Poe's life, right? Based on
the already unreliable testimony of Dr. John Moran, the last
man to see Poe before his death. But it's unlikely that Poe ever
actually met the explorer. Why, then, would he be calling out
his name in the last hours before his passing?"

"Are we alluding to the possibility that Reynolds was a
tulpa?" a third student, Peter, questioned, "Wouldn't that kinda
break the rules since J.N. was an actual guy?"

"It would if J.N. is who Poe was calling out to. But then there
is question of doppelgangers, which could also be explained by
Theosophic theory. The study question is this: How far can the
human mind stretch, and to what extent can it create, the
boundaries of thought to soften the rough-hewn surface of its
existential predicament?"

Later, she and Paulina, who taught a Saturday morning
Achaemenid History course, were having lunch again at the
Mediterranean Bistro. Paulina was having the Souvlaki.
Cynthia, her usual, the Tabbouleh. They sat in their usual booth
by the window. They were nothing if not consistent.

What they were talking about was of little consequence and, anyway, could not be heard through the window and from across the street. The same person that was watching Cynthia earlier while pretending to study, she was watching her now while pretending to browse the audio book section in the mom and pop bookstore across the street. To keep up appearances and blend in, Qadr was wearing headphones at the audio station and actually listening to one of the readings. Cynthia and Paulina talked, laughed, ate, and sipped at their coffees, all while in Qadr's ears she heard the deep voiced narrator reading from Hemingway's *Green Hills of Africa*:

> *"A country, finally, erodes and the dust blows away, the people all die and none of them were of any importance permanently, except those who practiced the arts, and these now wish to cease their work because it is too lonely, too hard to do, and is not fashionable..."*

She continued to follow Cynthia throughout her day. Browsing stores in the local mall but buying nothing, taking a meditative walk through the Acadiana Park Nature Station, a 150 acre trail system in South Louisiana. There was a guided tour in progress that Cynthia declined to join, but the traffic of people was a perfect buffer for Qadr's reconnaissance. All the while, that narrator's voice continued playing in her mind:

> *"...A thousand years makes economics silly and a work of art endures forever, but it is very difficult to do... and the palm fronds of our victories, the worn light bulbs of our discoveries*

*and the empty condoms of our great loves float with no
significance against one single, lasting thing -the stream."*

That evening, Cynthia stopped at her mailbox before pulling
the white Kawasaki ZX6R into the driveway. The usual junk
mail; bills, ads, an Avon brochure. But with it all was an
envelope with familiar handwriting in the return address. A
letter from Brisa DeGruy, better known to Cynthia as *mom*.

After going inside and freshening up, Cynthia boiled a pot
of water for tea and sat at the kitchen counter to read the letter.
She never got to make the tea however, which was a lemon balm
and Magnolia bark blend to help her sleep. That letter set off a
restlessness in her that required sweat to subside. So, she let the
tea water cool, got dressed for exercise, then went out to the
garage. First, she opened the garage door to let in the evening
breeze. Then, she went to work on the heavy bag.

Her mother's voice, having leapt off the page of that letter,
haunted her still as she toiled to deafen its sound under the
loud, embittered thuds against the bag.

> *Dear Little Picknie,*
>
> *Forgive your old mother for still calling you that. I know that you
> hate it, but I miss you and you will always be my little girl. I was grading
> essays and a particularly industrious student reminded me of you. I didn't
> realize it until later, on a Sunday afternoon a few weeks ago, when I thought
> of how she broke a structural rule to describe the way the sun sets on the
> Seven Wonders of the World. This is a student who knew the rubrics well.
> And yet, here she was in an informative essay prompt switching out of the
> required 3rd person to use a 1st person reflective style to close out one of her
> main body paragraphs. I couldn't help but give the essay a high score,*

however. An A, for the audacity of it, the eloquent beauty in defiance of strict rules that suffocate personality.

This is what you always were; defiant beauty, eloquent rebellion. Making me, of course, with all my traditions, the superstitions I fought so hard to impose on you which only resulted in this rift between us, this gulf of misunderstandings, the hands of those strict rules bearing down on your throat.

I am sorry, daughter. My little picknie.

Eternally, I am sorry. And I love you. And I will always be your mother. And I am proud of you. So very proud of you.

-Mom

It wasn't until Cynthia stopped for breath, after a long sequence of kicks, knee and elbow strikes, punches to the bag, that the moisture on her face wasn't just from the sweat. There were tears as well, and she didn't know how to feel about them.

She didn't much know what to do with emotions at all, let alone her amorphous feelings for her mother. Maybe the migraines had something to do with this. Maybe the recurring fantasy she'd been having ever since her visit with Black Christopher, the idea of having been a warrior in a previous life, was the subconscious, watchful knight holding back every possibility for her to redress the pains of her heart.

It was nearly immediate that upon having this thought, she would also sense a dangerous presence nearby.

There, of course, was no one with her in the garage.

She stepped boldly out onto the carport, looked both left and right. There was nothing out of the ordinary. A car several houses down exiting the driveway and pulling out into the street. A couple of kids playing in their yard, as their mother calls to them from the porch to come inside -as the sun was at last completing its trade with the moon. The faint whistling of wind -cool, mellowing. Above, the first sign of stars readying to blink awake.

Cynthia sighed. She must have been imagining things. Much like her mother used to imagine excuses for God, she thought in jest; levity to dissipate the tension of the moment.

She went back inside and remote-closed the garage door.

The door inside the garage led into the house through the kitchen. Cynthia mixed a pineapple ginger smoothie from there instead of the tea. Then she entered the living-room dome of African tribal affectations, passing through there into the hallway leading to the bedroom and shower. She always glanced at the Maasai Laibon carvings when passing by the living room, if not going into it. A habit of sorts, or a reflexive indication that these were her favorite of her decorative collections. The reason suddenly occurred to her; they were a final gift from her father before he died, in fact, the impetus of this particular decorative aesthetic for her home.

Taking a big gulp of the smoothie on the way down the hallway, that feeling of apprehension came upon her again. And just in time.

Her body reacted before her eyes fully registered what they were seeing; a black-clad figure stepping out of the guestroom door to her right and swinging a sword horizontally in her direction. Her reflex effective, the sword made contact with the wall instead of lopping off her head. But the call was so close that the blade tip made a scratch on her neck. She pounced forward off the pivot and crashed Qadr over the head with the glass smoothie cup, then moved backwards again as Qadr yanked the sword out of the wall's grip. The pull segued on another slash attempt going right, a miss. Cynthia moved forward again on a pivot and grabbed Qadr's sword hand at the inner wrist, twisting around and elbowing her in the face with her left arm. Twice. This made Qadr let go of the blade again, which was now lodged in the opposite wall. She staggered backwards from the elbow strike, but the distance gave her room to tag Cynthia with a leaping spin-side kick to the abdomen. The force of which making Cynthia stumble back up the hall and fall down in the living room.

A distance now between them, in full light, Cynthia and Qadr locked eyes. The latter taking feline steps forward, the former, having quickly climbed to her feet, edging backwards more and more into the living room.

"Who are you?!" Cynthia yelled. "What are you doing in my house?! WHAT DO YOU WANT?!!"

Qadr, blood from the glass wound crawling down the right side of her face, offered no response.

"ANSWER ME!!" Cynthia demanded. But instead Qadr glanced at the sword. Deciding not to pick it back up, she pulled two curved-blade Jambiya Khanjar daggers from thigh sheaths. Tossed one to Cynthia, who caught it.

Before the incredulity in Cynthia could fully transition to understanding, Qadr rushed her and attacked. What happened for Nicolaou Steinitz, what happened for Lev Illsley Knopfler, happened in this moment for Cynthia. As Qadr knew would.

The spirit that resided in Cynthia, upon the threat of certain death, was awakened and assumed hold of her body's reflexes. So, she now fought for her life as the warrior she once was; Kana of the Live Crew.

Qadr, her sensitivity to this transition now fine-tuned, still did not know who Cynthia was or what their past relationship might be. So, she just fought without reservation, expecting some revelation to dawn on her. Their blades clashed and clashed, cuts got in on them both, furniture got destroyed, gashes were made in the walls, statues toppled, and though they were fighting to kill each other, Cynthia had never known this level of focus or peace. She couldn't remember the last time she was this free of her migraines. But then she took a horizontal cut to the stomach and fell over the sofa, dropping her dagger. Qadr leapt over the sofa to engage for a killing strike, but Cynthia grasped both her arms to push against the blade pressing down on her neck. It was now strength versus strength, determination against determination -an unstoppable force in competition with an immoveable object!

That's when the memory dawned on Qadr at last. It at the same time reached Cynthia as well, as vivid as a projection reel playing out in front of them.

Tzukuba in the field, fighting the large bodied Ashigaru. She knocks down one with a windmill kick, fights back the other with her katana until getting in a killing strike. Then the other having gotten back up, he is about to stab Tzukuba in the back with his sword! But instead he gets impaled in the head by

Kana's kusarigama. Then the two of them, Tzukuba and Kana, they lock eyes -forming an inseparable bond.

Qadr, recognizing her sister in blood, pulls back her blade from Cynthia's throat. They disengage, creating a space between one another. But both women remain on the floor. Hyperventilating, bleeding, looking at each other with disbelief. What now?

———

AT TWENTY THOUSAND, SEVEN HUNDRED and two feet, in the Cordillera Occidental of the Andes, the top most point of the Chimborazo mountain peak that sat right along the invisible line of the earth's equatorial bulge, there was a meeting in progress. They stood barefoot on the eternal snow, in the bed of one of the inactive volcano's many heavily glaciated craters. Discussing the fate of the world, and how each of them had broken their rule of intervening in human affairs.

"I made no attempt to turn away," Manthis said, "as an uneducated and downtrodden Florida man pointed his shotgun at me, yelling racial slurs and looking into my eyes -unaware that the act would doom him to certain, gruesome death. But why did I allow myself to be seen at all when I was only there to witness the rebirth of the makeshift goddess? This question has haunted me, suggesting that I have grown what humans identify as a subconscious. Another question arises. How necessary is this evolutionary event, and what does it imply for our station? If we can feel, then does it not stands to reason that we should also act?"

"Perhaps you did not allow anything," Clymene suggested, his beard now much longer, reaching past his torso, a physical representation of his growing wisdom, "like the DeGruy woman who saw me despite my invisibility, and made a moving effigy of me in her odyssey of memory. Perhaps, as you say, it is an evolutionary imperative that we, like humans, would arrive at some form of existential purpose. Agency... If not for this, then why do we exist? The implication of omnipresent knowledge is that humans ultimately do not succeed is self-annihilation."

"That," challenged Zhrontese, who had formed a Nexus with Qadr as a result of saving her from the bullet wound, and was still under the consequential, psychological influence of it, "..would require that we be products of human ideation. Or, at least, spawn from the same source of perennial sentience as they."

"Aren't we?" asked Clymene.

"If so, then where is the god of the Quagga? Or the Woolly mammoth? Where is the representative of the Pyrenean ibex? Where in the seas resides the ambassador of the Dunkeosteus?"

The two others considered this, looking into the cosmos of each other's eyes as they searched their immensity of knowledge for an appropriate answer. Finding none. Then, Manthis offered,

"In our visions as well as yet to be written in **The Qualekafilia**.."

"The Qualekafilia?" asked Clymene.

"It is the name that has come to him for the book in the Marx possession," Zhrontese answered, for Manthis, her hair like

Clymene's beard having grown dramatically in length in tandem with her now greater wealth in sensitivity, connection, and understanding. Greater in length, bustling with more vibrant color and ever-changing texture, and flowing aloft like a living cloud of sagacity.

And as the agreement between the three was shared in their collective intuition, so too did the book over two thousand miles away in Florida respond; still lying on the desk in the Marx library, the crest on its cover changed into a golden Roman Q. Poole, standing by a book shelf and reading a passage from Marcel Proust's In Search of Lost Time, was there to witness the metamorphosis.

"As it is to be written in this sacred, alchemical volume," Manthis restated, "man's desire to commodify the powers of gods will bring about the ruination of his race, and all sentient life that inhabit his world. If we are all that remains in the aftermath, as well as beings such as Astrid the Ghost Orchid, it will be left to us to re-seed the world with new intelligent life. And be seen by them, like the gods before us, as inert, arrogant, and indifferent."

"Setting the stage then," Zhrontese added, in her mind hearing the echoing sound of Qadr's scream, "for them to be formed in this dark, morose image, and for history to alas repeat itself."

———

"NO,' ASTRID'S VOICE ECHOED, A HEALING effect, "I am different. I care." And this is all that Joaquín could hear, or, rather, understand in the time that his body and all its cells rushed toward near combustion, and all he would remember of the trauma in its wake.

She rested him down gently on the asphalt and sat back, holding his hand. It occurred to Astrid that these curious behaviors were maternal in nature -which excited her! That she should feel as humans do, and that this level of awareness, astoundingly, was the key to harnessing her powers. Astrid folded Joaquín's hands over his chest, happy to see that, though unconscious, he was yet breathing. And then she looked at the palms of her own hands. Seeing patterns in the lines, seeing all the way through the layers of the earth -her extended body; past the composition of hundreds of thousands of lithospheric plates of solid rock and into the low resistance of flowing plastics amid the ductile asthenosphere, and then she saw all the way into the iron, the hot spherical bosom of geodynamic pressure of the core that communicated back to the beating heart in her chest. The story it told was of guilt for the people who had died in her transition from violent, unbridled energy to this current state of awakening and control. Guilt over those two police offers that she exploded as a consequence of trying to help her, guilt over the hunting party who were just trying to find their lost loved ones -who were trying to be heroes.

It would be several hours before the boy would stir, just before dawn. He was startled awake by a dream he was having, a dream of his own death. When Joaquín sat up and oriented to his surroundings, he saw Astrid sitting to his right. She was wrapped in her blanket, her arms hugging folded knees to her chest. Astrid smiled to see the boy moving, alive, still in one piece. But she kept her eyes turned down and he said,

"Why you never look at me?"

It's the last thing she expected he would say, let alone the first words to fall from his lips.

Still getting used to her own voice, she replied,

"You... you should know why that I can't."

He didn't understand, but on some level he must have remembered because just then Joaquín's body language shifted to fear. He shivered, flinched, and blinked. Then he settled again. When he moved to stand up, Astrid stopped him by reaching out her hand to touch his.

"No. Your body must still be weak. You have to be careful."

"I feel weird. And hungry."

This made Astrid chuckle. She appreciated this sensation, laughter.

"We'll have to get you some food then."

"You have a pretty voice."

"What?" Astrid, confused, wanted to know. She'd never been complimented before.

"You're voice. It's pretty. Different."

Another new sensation for Astrid, the feeling of being appreciated. Affection, friendship. It seemed also that Joaquín, in something so simple as a random compliment, was expressing a filial connection to her -or, at least, a need for such a connection. He'd never known his mother, and he'd lost all his brothers and, recently, his father, to violence.

Astrid, in the short time that they'd known each other, was filling a void for Joaquín. And she could feel herself sating that need for him when, without warning, he jolted and lurched -as if something were stuck in his throat. He sat all the way forward and began to vomit, a bit too fast to keep some of it from splashing onto his shirt. Astrid rushed over to him and laid supporting hands on his shoulders.

"Are you okay?!" she asked. "Joaquín?"

He couldn't yet answer. And since his back was to her, Astrid couldn't see that his eyes had gone completely white. And then... amber.

A consequence of Joaquín's near death experience was this, the triggering of not only subconscious memory but power. He'd had four brothers before, in another life. And rather than lose them to kidnappers, he'd watched all of them die. Violently. One by one... He realized suddenly that sound itself was a miraculous gift, which is why he talked so much in this life. And then he winced at a burning in his chest, excruciating pain.

"It hurts," he cried. "It hurts so much!"

At first, Astrid thought again that he was going to die. The dreadful image came to mind of that cop's chest blowing open when he made the fatal mistake of looking into her eyes.

She was going to scream, but then Joaquín tore open his shirt and lurched again. He shook free of Astrid's hold and fell to his back, convulsing as if experiencing an exorcism. Astrid could smell the burning flesh as smoke rose from Joaquín's chest. But he wasn't dying. Instead, branded skin-deep ink was manifesting like stigmata in the area of the burning.

Astrid recognized what was forming in the space. She recognized but only vaguely remembered the tattoo of the Ningen sea monster.

———

"IF I MAY,' POOLE SAID, 'YOU DON'T SEEM in any hurry to return to your life. Is it so empty and inconsequential?"

He and Patrick were sitting across from each other in the dining room, at opposite sides of the long, mahogany dinner table. A wealth of food was between them, as Poole tended to cook a lot when his nerves were bad. There was Niçoise salad complete with Dijon vinaigrette over seared ahi tuna, pouched eggs, green beans, potatoes, tomatoes, and olives. An appetizer of grilled scallop au vin in white wine and organic onion. The main course was prime rib au poivre.

Patrick would have sighed if his mouth weren't full of food. Instead, he shook his head and, after swallowing, said,

"Do you still hate me so much?"

"I never hated you, Mr. Elliot. I am protective of my ward. And it is the arrogant insouciance of your profession that offends me."

"Insouciance? Are you sure that's the word you're looking for?"

"I am indeed. How else has spectacle over substance become the standard of journalistic integrity?"

"Maybe since print media found itself waist deep in quicksand, relegated to a never-ending fight for survival in a world more concerned about some celebrity's dating rituals than starving children in Syria."

Poole grinned, lifting his wine glass,

"Touché, Mr. Elliot."

Patrick returned the gesture, and there was a silence while they both sipped.

"To answer your question though, I...," Patrick began, then stopped, having found the right words elusive.

"Yes?"

"Well, I guess there's some truth to it. The idea that my life before this was rather empty. My wife had recently left, so my home became a barren place. I'd also recently gone freelance so there was no regular employment for me beyond managing a glorified blog. And now, after all that has happened..."

"Hard to see purpose in returning to the drudgery of the mundane?"

"Yes! That exactly! You know, Poole, maybe there's work for you as an editor."

This made the dignified butler laugh.

"Perhaps."

Both men's attention was drawn away from the food and conversation when the lights in the room began to flicker. It happened only twice before going out, leaving them in total darkness. For the power in the entire mansion had been cut.

"What the hell?" said Patrick.

Poole's first instinctual response was suspicion, as the power in the mansion hadn't randomly gone out like that in over twenty years.

"Come with me," he promptly said.

Poole fished a flashlight out of a drawer, and the two of them left the kitchen in careful, prowling steps -following the scanning beam of light. Their eyes quickly adjusted to the darkness of their surroundings, and furniture and décor in this transition began to play about the shadows made by the light in tricky, menacing fashion.

Silence. Only their own footsteps could be heard. The shotgun and Ruger they used against the undead Akumeza were in a utility closet on the same floor, not far from the kitchen. They armed themselves and kept moving.

That's when Patrick saw, from his peripheral, movement cast from a shadow in a window to his left. He looked and saw a man standing outside the window wearing a black Hannya Kabuki Demon mask -staring.

"Poole!" Patrick said. Then the shotgun wielding butler looked too. When he saw him, this bold individual who continued to linger despite being seen, Poole moved past Patrick and lifted the shotgun in direction of the window.

There was a lightning strike, and the man vanished. A blink and there the man was again, inside, standing right next to Poole. When Poole reflexed and attempted to turn the barrel toward him, the black-clad demon masked assailant parried it and a shot went off -he struck Poole with three quick moves, knocking him down. Patrick turned the Ruger to him, having a clearer shot now that Poole was out of the way, fired three times and with each shot the man's impossibly fast dodging movements could be seen in the muzzle flares. Then, in an instant, he was gone again.

Patrick rushed over to Poole.

"I'm alright!" Poole assured, getting up and cocking the shotgun. "Where is he?! Where'd he go?! Did you hit him?"

"I don't know."

"Let's find out."

———

AN HOUR EARLIER, COLETRANE'S Learjet touched down on the runway. It was just after 7pm. As DeLoach was bringing it to a stop, a dark blue sedan was pulling onto the tarmac. It drove up right next to the jet when it made its stop. DeLoach, seeing it, assumed it was Coletrane's ride. Maybe Patrick.

He was wrong.

When he opened the entrance doors, it was already too late. A man with a leather satchel over his shoulder, dressed in a white suit and wearing a green Kabuki Demon mask with silver horns and teeth was standing at the bottom of the steps, pointing a silver Colt 1911 up at his face.

"Try to close these doors,' the man warned, 'catch a bullet in the cheek."

Coletrane emerged, heroically moving past his pilot and putting himself in the line of fire.

"Hello, Trane. Long time no see, brother."

The mask still covered his face, but Coletrane already knew who it was by the voice.

"Marcus," he said. It wasn't a question.

"Well,' his reply came with a matter-of-factly shrug of the shoulder, 'you're half right, runt."

———

CROSS STOOD IMPATIENTLY IN THE elevator chamber, waiting for the digital floor number to strike 42 and "ding". When it did, the doors opened on a long darkened corridor. His striding ingress was preceded by flanking rows of lights blinking on in the floor. As more and more of the cloister lit up, embedded lights in the surrounding machinery lit up as well to reveal an expansive hangar of futuristic technology. In the ceiling was a large orb resembling a crystal ball, filled with electrically charged clouds of swirling purple and violet, and its spherical surface crawling with molecular nanite spikes that never stopped moving. The orb was connected to a network of large interface cables going along the ceiling and heading toward the next room, which the lit up corridor also made a beeline to. That room was a glass encased laboratory with sliding doors, and full of more complicated networks of machinery. Along the back wall of the lab was the Trivium Motherboard; the nucleus Tri-Brain, and the twenty-four brain web that all-together bore the resemblance of a constellation of 27 stars. Minus two, since there were vacant hubs for the last brains that needed to be connected before the system could safely go online at full capacity.

Dr. Upadhyay was there with her clipboard. She was the only one there, besides Cross who was coming in through the automatic sliding doors. She turned to him.

"Mr. Cross."

"How's my baby, doctor?"

"The new um.. power units have synced perfectly with the rest of the network, Mr. Cross. Just two more and-"

"Turn it on. At 100 percent. The last two can be added later."

"Umm... theoretically... But unsafe practically. If I could coordinate with the rest of the team and recalibrate-"

"I said turn it on, Dr. Upadhyay. Now."

In this moment, looking into the threat behind his eyes, the good doctor had a decision to make. She was usually intimidated by Cross, but enough was enough.

"No,' she said at first, under her breath. And then she said it again with conviction. "No, Mr. Cross."

In response he steeled his jaw, again flabbergasted by the audacity of a plebeian.

"Is she the boss here?" the Tan'Mo said in his mind. "And should she be allowed to live in defiance of progress?"

"No,' Cross answered out loud. "No, she shouldn't."

"What?" she asked, her final inquiry before Cross, with the same hand he used to conjure the Lincoln pistol, grabbed her by the throat and lifted. With the limited Trivium power that he had access to through the brain chip, he was able to instantly intuit and transmit incredible strength into his hand. So much strength that crushing Dr. Upadhyay's windpipe was as easy as balling up a sheet of paper.

He dropped her lifeless body on the floor, but caught her electronic clipboard in the air as it fell. Then he put in the configuration to activate Trivium.

The orb in the next room responded by beaming with brighter light, and with a surge of more frantically moving nanite spikes. The Motherboard responded by backlighting the brain network. And Cross' cerebellum chip responded by shocking him with so much pain that he fell to his knees, his nose dropping blood on the floor in front of him as he braced for the gradual stabilization.

When he lifted his eyes, his face was stress-covered with veins. He looked to where the doctor's body lay, and with a blink of his eyes, her body and clothes all disintegrated into molecules that floated up from the floor and vanished.

Cross smiled.

"Let's redress your arrogance now, little Coletrane."

———

ALL WAS STILL WHILE THE SEVEN walked through the Valley of Swords, except that everyone could hear the whispering voices of fallen warriors reading their death poems. These voices were ferried on the filaments of fog drifting about as they made their passage. No one spoke of it, but everyone felt the tug and pull of consciousness against mortality.

Past the Valley was a shallow stream on which lie a winding S shaped bridge of serpentine sediment that led to the darkened, grotto-like ingress to the Tabernacle of the Thalatha. The seven remaining Crew members entered with caution. Each of them was hungry, tired, wounded and near crestfallen, but something about their surroundings edified their resolve. It was perhaps the coolness of the air or the contrast of nurturing shade from the irascible heat outside. Maybe it was the wide open eolian space that was bottle-shaped and bedded by a shallow pond giving off a turquoise glow reflective of the shiny, cylindrical stalactites that reached down from above.

There was the smell of wood in the air, a mild sunflower bouquet that tickled the nose. Kana could smell it vividly. So could Kojiro, remembering the way his father used to describe it.

You'd know it right away, son. Because it will take one weight from you and trade it for another.

He used to think it was poetry, these words. But he was wrong. Kojiro could feel his anxiety leaving him while attrition replaced it in the void of his chest.

"What is that?" Jubei gave voice to his thoughts. "Am I the only who feels it?"

"You are not," Kojiro confirmed, his eyes flitting back and forth, his right hand on Hatsukoi's tsuka.

"Your bodhisattvas,' Kana said, to Otaku, 'it say anything in there about this... place?"

"It does. But I didn't believe it."

"What?' Kana's voice made it sound like a quip, but her surprise was genuine. 'You believe the entries on invisible Dragon Kings but not about flower-smelling caves?"

"It is not flowers we smell. It is airborne anguish. I did not believe such a thing would travel this way."

As soon as Otaku said that, there was a disturbance of debris around all of them. Suddenly small rocks began to tremble and then hover just above ground, as if magnetized by an imperceptible force.

Ahead of the group, at the epicenter of the cave wall, a constellation of gray energy seeped out the pores of rock to form the shape of a person levitating, regal postured with their arms folded behind their back and wearing an emperor's sokutai kimono. The bright red outer robe had high, pointed shoulder pads decorated with green stencil-dyed patterns suggesting majesty. The gold and black damask trousers flowed like a gown, and the cap-shaped kammuri headdress was black lacquered silk with an upright pennon decorated with an imperial moth crest. Impossible to place whether man or woman, the figure's androgynous features looked upon the group not with pride but disinterest, through eyes that none would remember for their color and with intention that could be described as little more than placid curiosity.

The figure unfolded their arms and then brought their hands together in front of them, forming a violet energy spherule in the space between their palms. That's when six copies of themselves formed like echoes flanking both their left and right, twelve in total each standing slightly behind the other. This made them look like an arrow formation, with only the one in the center full of vibrancy and color while the rest were all gray and unmoving.

"The past, present, and future,' the Thalatha said, looking at no one in particular, 'are all wrapped in a circular consistency, happening at once and influencing one another at the same time. What then is the difference between seeking something, and finding it? What separates the creator from the created? Can any among you answer?"

The Crew members all regarded each other, incredulous. Only Kojiro stepped forward and said,

"We are not here to answer riddles."

"Ahh, but you are," then the Thalatha brought their right hand to their side while still holding the spherule up with their left. Opening the right hand, a long purple handle formed in the palm and out of it spawned the 36 inch curved blade of a lord's nodachi. "Or would you fight instead, like your dance with the Inca Tan'Mo, dooming more to despair, ruin, and death in the service of mortal arrogance?"

Kojiro narrowed his eyes, instinctively bringing his hand again to Hatsukoi's tsuka. But Jubei rested his own hand on Kojiro's shoulder, reminding the warrior of the importance of tact. Indeed, the Thalatha's own words reminding Kojiro of thus, while at the same time angering him for their damning truth.

He rested his shoulders then, calling back the urge for brash overreaction. But the Thalatha, observant, still replied in a somewhat taunting cadence,

"I see you are the wielder of Hatsukoi, *the seven body blade...* A remarkable ally, one with many legends surrounding her origin that even her master, I am sure, is unaware of. Thus is the dilemma of all sentient things, that the fires of mortal agency be ever counterbalanced by the icy implications of determinism, of ignorance, of the unknown."

On that, Kojiro removed any physical suggestion that he was present for a fight, steeled his resolve and walked a few paces closer.

"Perhaps you might disabuse us our ignorance, having journeyed so far and sacrificed so much to bid you an audience?"

"That depends, Sakura."

———

"NOW'S A GOOD TIME TO TAKE OFF the mask," Coletrane offered, the still mask wearing Marcus sitting across from him in the Lear Jet, the Colt 1911 still firmly held in hand and trained on Coletrane's gut.

"Not a fan? I thought you'd prefer it to looking into the eyes of the friend you betrayed."

"I never betrayed you, Marcus. I didn't put you in the ring. I didn't make you keep fighting beyond brain traumas."

"You in fact betrayed me in two lives."

"Marcus-"

"Call me Katsurou, runt," he demanded, finally taking off the mask. Coletrane recognized the battered face of his childhood friend. But not his eyes. The hatred in him had transformed them into something unrecognizable. But Kojiro, he recognized those eyes. "Your superior,' Marcus continued, 'in this life and the last."

"I see you haven't grown out of hubris."

"I see you haven't grown, period."

DeLoach refueled the jet, at Marcus' gun-point command, and cleared take off with air traffic control. Destination, back to Takayama. To return to the bridge leading to the Hanging Coffins of Shikakami.

"Where's that sword of yours?" Marcus/Katsurou asked. Even his voice, Coletrane noticed, was different. In the way that Coletrane and Kojiro shared consciousness, it seemed that Katsurou and Marcus had metamorphosed physically.

Careful to not take the gun off Coletrane, Marcus opened the duffle bag with his free hand to show his old friend its contents; two African Kondo swords.

"Cool, right? I was wondering if maybe we could do a comparison. Because for all of Hatsukoi's storied greatness, I remember you and her yet struggling against the bokken. A mere piece of glorified wood."

"Still insecure? That bokken was a Suburito, and its *mere* wood the strongest of reinforced loquat."

The jet finished making its ascend, stabilizing at 30 thousand feet.

"Those are nice blades though,' Coletrane continued to taunt. 'I wonder. Are you as inefficient with them as you were with the gloves in the ring?"

The magic phenomena of interpersonal intimacy between two men, especially that which spanned across multiple lives, is that a special talent for getting under the skin would be shared between them. It wasn't clear which of them, Katsurou or Marcus, was more affected by Coletrane's jab. It didn't matter. The distraction worked.

Coletrane leapt forward, slapped the gun out of Marcus' hand with his right while spinning to elbow him in the face with his left. When he recoiled to punch Marcus again head on with that same left hand, Marcus had recovered quickly enough from the elbow strike to deliver a right hand punch to Coletrane's solar plexus so strong that it sent him backwards over the leather seat.

Then Marcus pulled the two Kondo blades out the bag, while Coletrane regained his footing and drew Hatsukoi from a customized compartment built into one of the aisle seats.

He squared up in a Te Ura Gasumi fighting posture. Marcus stepped out into the aisle, one blade held at his side and the other pointed up at his opponent. Like Katsurou on the water when the two were boys, he was amused.

"Still always keep her near, I see. You're nothing if not predictable, old friend."

Coletrane's response to that was a tightened jaw, and his eyes taking on the figure-eights.

———

PATRICK MAINTAINED SHARP FOCUS with the flashlight and Ruger, drawing more on his past military munitions training than on his distant memory of wielding the naginata. Poole remained nearby; shotgun ready. The two of them were joined by the prowling, shadowy projection of Yoriko's spirit. Only her bright blue eyes could be seen in the darkness. They moved about the many halls of the large house, with nothing illumined besides that which the one flashlight beheld and the assistance of their adjusted vision. Now and again, the one masked man, who could clearly teleport, would appear just outside of their view to knock over something and then vanish again. Saying nothing, toying with them.

"Show yourself, you coward!" Poole yelled.

They were near the back of the bottom floor layout at this point, where behind them was a long hall through a series of unused rooms. At the end was a corner, beyond which was the chamber to a wine cellar and the hatch to an underground bunker. Out of that area stepped another man, also wearing black and disguised with an Oni mask. He was taller than his teleporting partner, and his demonic mask was red with horns and a matching white rope in its teeth that formed a noose knot under the chin.

He stepped out of the darkness, making no sound, and announced himself thus,

"Trifles,' he jeered, 'Trifles light as air."

Patrick turned the gun and light to the voice, began firing without warning. But after three bullets went right through the man and into the wall, it was clear that the man was an illusion. But was he? At first he was standing sideways, his right side not visible. But when he turned to face Patrick, it was shown that his right arm was outfitted with a silver, long-bladed Tekagi-shuko.

In that moment, Patrick experienced a flashed memory of himself as Ittei wrestling with Omphalos in the big forest fight. That moment when he snatched Kana's knife out of the big brute's arm and stabbed him in the chest. And as if the masked man, apparently Kovács, had experienced that memory as well, he on cue dashed forward. Running full speed toward Patrick, who fired the gun two more times to no effect. Kovács running at him, the Tekagi-shuko up and tearing through the wall like the worst sort of nails on a chalkboard, Patrick fired again, directly at his head, but also again, nothing. At the same time, the other masked man appeared next to Poole, grabbed him by the shoulders and hurled him across the room. It wasn't that high of a toss, but it was enough that Poole slammed into a glass curio before hitting the floor. He'd dropped the shotgun when grabbed, and Patrick, wasting no time, tossed aside the pistol and the flashlight and turned to pick up the shotgun. By now Kovács was upon him, and Patrick, calling on his dormant skills with the naginata, used the shotgun as a jo-like weapon to parry Kovács' strikes with the claw. The other man, Juric/Jericho, kept himself solid and was about to stab Poole in the back with a dagger he drew from his belt but this attempt was intercepted by the shadow of Yoriko, who took hold of his knife wielding arm with the devastating bear trap grip of his jaws!

Juric screamed, dropping the dagger. Poole, barely conscious and definitely hurt, saw the weapon land right next to him on the floor. And Patrick, he was engaged in a melee with Kovács; shotgun-jo versus shuko-claw!

———

THE TRIVIUM MOTHERBOARD BEHIND Cross was chaotic with rapidly flickering light, charges of electricity communicating between the interface cables, and violent vibrations each moment threatening to break the metal chassis holding it all together.

In the adjacent room, there was a similar response coming from the ceiling orb -that looked like a glass plasma ball ready to burst with electrostatic power. Cross stood directly underneath it, his eyes themselves full of this identical power as if possessed. Perhaps he was, being that the Tan'Mo stood with him in the room, directly in front of him, and gazing down on the man from his seven foot height with pride.

"Do you see it, son?" The Tan'Mo said, his voice now identical to the voice of Cross' father. This affectation, it made the otherwise stoic business man cry.

"I do. I see it."

"Two truths are told as happy prologues to the swelling act of your life's theme. To see the goodness in your deeds, to see the downfall of your enemies."

"My enemy is aloft in the skies, vulnerable and distracted, fighting his own friend. I see it as clearly as if I were there with them."

"Help them along," the Tan'Mo replied, hovering closer.

Cross' eyes lit up even more. So did the ceiling orb.

———

AS DID THE THALATHA'S SPHERULE, hovering just over the palm of their left hand as they in fact hovered as well. It glowed, the spherule, for everyone to see, communicating with their emotions and piquing their curiosity. There was a story being told by its light, and though unclear, that story heralded doom, destruction, death, destitution. But no one would inquire about any of these, yet having traveled so far and long for answers, for clarity. The human spirit at last proven committed more to staying in the dark and chasing the unknown than coming face to face with it, tackling it down, and creating in its space a greater pursuit.

"I can tell that each of you feel it," the Thalatha said, "the spirit of every question fighting to stay as thus, leaving chaos in its wake in lieu of answers."

"What if you are wrong?" Kojiro asked. "What if humans are so conditioned by not getting answers that they've become convinced that life itself is dependent upon nescience, upon not knowing, upon being ignorant? What if deep down we all fear that should we learn anything definitive about the human condition, we will all disintegrate and cease to exist?"

The Thalatha then let out a deep, almost paternal, pitying sigh, saying,

"Aaaaahhh, dear Sakura!.. But whoever ever suggested to you that this wasn't so?"

———

COLETRANE/KOJIRO AND MARCUS/Katsurou's fight continued to gain in momentum with as much fervency as the plane's jolting turbulence increases in perilousness. But none of them, not the fighters or DeLoach as he struggled to maintain control of the aircraft, knew that the external earthly assaults were coming from Cross himself. The Trivium power, realized and unstable. From him came the weather, the blinding fog, rain, lightning and thunder, the swarm of pterodactyl-like eagles, the impossible vultures forming together to become giant hands attempting to grab at the plane or mouths with ferocious jaws intent on biting it in half, all these deadly wonders spawn from the unhinged mind of a man who made his career on convincing millions of people of his artificial benevolence. Millions, billions(!), unaware of the ecological domino effects of these sort of selfish, sinister acts, who would yet not only consciously invest in this flavor of calamitous evil, but wield it themselves if (when?) it ever became available to them. This perhaps is why Cross openly made deals with notorious men, happily brushing it off as *means to an end* in the media spotlight. This perhaps is why he knew the Trivium would be a success, indeed, why the Inca Tan'Mo easily commanded so much influence behind the scenes. Because he, they, were right all along; because at the bottom of every heart, doomed, saved, privileged, frail, or strong, every man, woman, child, by nature, was essentially selfish. And yet, still Coletrane and Marcus struggled against one another in that small tossing cabin, blade versus blade, honor versus requital, all just a sliding exchange of sands cross the hourglass of self-delusion. And still came the three Interstices; Clymene, Zhrontese, Manthis, each and all flying, their robes flapping in back of them like capes, at breakneck speeds to cross hundreds of miles in minutes toward the ill-fated Leer Jet in order to break their rule of not intervening in the affairs of humans. To yet save them, people, from themselves, and to satisfy a wager made during their meeting on top of the Chimborazo: *What will be the consequences of their choice, and what by the most-high consciousness will be written in the Qualekafilia?*

In the cabin, both men battled, Tachi versus Konda. Coletrane sidestepped a stabbing attempt from Marcus and, hitting the blade near the hilt, managed to relieve Marcus of his weapon. The shellshocked boxer ducked under three of Coletrane's attempts to cut him with Hatsukoi. On the third he found an opening, catching him behind the wrist and hitting him in just the right place behind the elbow to make him drop the sword.

In the minds of both men, it was young Kojiro and Katsurou, fighting each other on the water and beneath the hot sun. Their fathers watching. Disarming Kojiro was something his taller, stronger friend was quite good at. But anger being both Kojiro's curse and strength, the boys would wind up wrestling in the stream.

Now in the rocking plane, all its emergency lights and alarms going off, both men unarmed, Marcus gained an advantage due to his professional hand-to-hand skills - especially in a tight space. And like Katsurou within him, he did not hesitate to exploit it.

Marcus threw a series of combinations at Coletrane, giving himself the upper hand. A right hook sent Coletrane over a seat and crashing against a window. Then Marcus was on him again. He used his knee to leverage his weight against the seat and press his forearm down on Coletrane's throat. The position put their faces close together, but the angle gave Coletrane a clear view of the chaos just outside of the plane. He recognized the giant eagles swarming outside the plane...

"I...,' Coletrane struggled to get the words out, Marcus' elbow pressed against his windpipe doing him no favors in this regard, "I.... am not ...your enemy."

Again, Marcus bore his bloodied teeth. But when he spoke, it was Katsurou's voice that came out.

"Too late for that."

In Coletrane's peripheral, in this exact moment, one of the white-tailed eagles came torpedoing toward the plane, slamming against the window that Coletrane was looking out of -causing a blazing eruption of wind and glass!

———

AT THE MANSION, THE FIGHT IN the darkness ensued. Juric/Jericho could not use his vanishing technique with

Yoriko's teeth sunken into his arm, and he found it quite the challenge to shake the beast off. Like a constrictor knot, the more he struggled the tighter her hold and the worse it hurt. Poole, in his own struggle to remain conscious, picked the knife up off the floor and used the frame of the now broken curio to pull himself up. Luckily for Patrick, his body in panic had drawn forth the full brunt of Ittei's naginata skills. Otherwise, his dance with Kovács/Omphalos would have already ended in his own brutal, bloody death. Instead, he held his own against the man who continued attacking with the claw, and without relent -sparks of clashing metals going on and off every time the Shuko made contact with the shotgun barrel.

The supernatural wolf's strength proved an outclassed match to Juric's mortal flesh. Even if Juric broke loose, flailing and flailing in complete desperation, he would not again use that arm at anywhere near 100% capacity.

Poole, seeing an opportunity, got himself up enough, and was close enough, to bury the knife into Juric's left hip. The man let out a blood curdling scream, and Yoriko let go of his now useless arm. Patrick, at the same time, got past Kovács' claw on a parry that provided him an opening to bludgeon Kovács across the face with the shotgun like a man at bat hitting a home run. Then he turned the gun to his left and fired one shot at Juric. The darkness made it unclear where he was hit, but the blast sent him backwards and spinning to his right before he vanished.

When Patrick turned the gun back to finish off the now downed Kovács, the man too had vanished.

———

"I DO NOT CARE ABOUT HOW WE EXIST or why," Kojiro said with conviction. The Thalatha he was talking to, went gray and stopped moving. And another of his after images to the right lit up with life, floating forward with prominence like a holy visitation. Kojiro turned to continue addressing that one, saying,

"I do not care which of you are real any more than I worry about returning to the dust from which I spawned. Do you think we came all this way to suffer riddles? Do you think any warrior true to him or herself would choose the path of the sword if not first fully resolved and complete in courage? We stand here before you today, Thalatha, for one reason and one reason only."

"Yes,' another one to his left said as the one he was talking to returned to the unmoving gray. And this new one holding the light became the center one as all the grays shifted to six on either side of them. "Yes," they said again, "I know. You've come all this way for the means to fight and kill gods."

"Not gods,' Kojiro corrected. 'Just one."

———

"AND WHAT PRICE WOULD YOU PAY?" the Tan'Mo asked Cross, the room now full of so much energy friction that all objects not bolted to the floor or embedded in the walls began to float and circulate around him and the ceiling orb. "What payment would you exact from the world in order to heap upon yourself the gifts befitting an atua among men, a true Olympian, a-"

"A God?" Cross cut him off, now looking away from the orb and into the Tan'Mo's eyes. Or, rather, through them -since all he saw now in the place of the being in front of him was the countenance of his father. A father who thought little of him in life, a father he could never please, that suddenly spoke to him with pride in his voice and a rare smile on his face.

"Isn't that what you want, son? To be an... Übermensch?"

"I would pay any price."

And then the Tan'Mo showed him a vision, briefly, of gray, dusty brume filling the air, pollution similar to the Great Smog of '52 that killed thousands in London, but much more powerful, unknown in origin, and quickly spreading over North and South America, over Canada, and across the seas to Greenland, Brazil, Africa, beyond.

Cross' features twitched, the brain chip responding with a brief jolt of electricity that corrupted the image, replacing it only with a vision of hubris -of greatness.

"Even that price?" the Tan'Mo challenged.

Cross didn't respond with words; his mind was occupied by the thought of easily and heroically handling a problem *so small as mere smoke*. Surely, he reasoned, he could prove to the world exactly how valuable the Trivium is by effortlessly brushing away a potentially extinction level event.

He smiled at the Tan'Mo, at his father, who in term smiled back. Sweat bubbled up on his forehead, along with a spiderweb a veins covering his entire face. The ceiling orb got brighter, busier with electricity, and so did Cross' eyes.

AFTER THE GIANT BIRD KAMIKAZIED against the plane, killing itself on impact, it badly dented the chassis along with shattering several windows -compromising cabin pressure and severely limiting DeLoach's ability to maintain control of the plane. Another vulture mouth formation this time got a bite out of the wing, making matters much worse. More birds sacrificed themselves by diving into the left turbofan engine, breaking it and causing the access cowl to burst open and catch aflame!

"PAN PAN PAN,' DeLoach yelled into his ATC radio, "MAYDAY!! An engine and a wing, lost! Spiraling more than 13000 kilometers off course! I have to try for an emergency landing!"

Another of the white pterodactyls flew fast enough to pass the plane and then turn back, intent on crashing directly into the cockpit window. DeLoach watched it coming, shellshocked and convinced that this was the end, but the giant bird was intercepted in the nick of time; tackled out of the way by Manthis.

The two of them tumbled until Manthis could get a hold of its throat and look into its eyes. The bird saw Manthis' glowing rhodium crystals looking back at him -and then, immediately, the bird imploded.

Manthis spun around to shake the beast's blood off his robe.

Clymene swooped in, positioning himself underneath the broken wing to stabilize the aircraft. And then came Zhrontese, coming up under the nosewheel doors to focus her energy on guiding the plane on its emergency course.

Manthis, after getting all the blood and entrails off his body, flew back into the fray; zigzagging like a laser beam trained on one vulture or pterodactyl at a time and destroying each one of them on impact!

They'd yet arrived too late, and none of them, despite the extent of their powers, possessed super strength or telekinesis. They'd also never before attempted the safe landing of a 45,000 pound object falling from over thirty thousand feet.

Inside, Coletrane and Marcus were still going at it, and in their heads, so were Kojiro and Katsurou still wrestling in the stream of their consciousnesses! One of the Khondo swords was still stuck in the wall, but the other one, as well as Hatsukoi, was still tumbling around as a sharp, airborne projectile while the two men fought by hand-to-hand.

"This plane is going down, Marcus!" Coletrane tried to reason. "We are going to die!!"

"We've died before!" was Marcus responded before side-kicking Coletrane in the chest. He caught view of the Khondo sliding in the aisle, picked it up and lunged at Coletrane. Marcus tried to kill him with it but Coletrane moved out of the way in time, then dove past Marcus and rolled. He got his hands on Hatsukoi just as Marcus, relentless, was back on him and attempting a cut to his back. But that cut attempt was met with Hatsukoi on Coletrane's turn and pivot, with so much force that both men recoiled backwards several feet!

"Stop this, Marcus!" Coletrane lifted Hatsukoi, pointing her tip at Marcus not only to hold the distance between them but to buy a few moments to make another attempt at reason. "You have never been evil! Not in this life or the one before it! You have never been a fool either!! You must see that there is a concern at hand much greater than us both!"

"You are just afraid to die, Train! Afraid to lose!"

"I AM NOT TALKING ABOUT DEATH! THIS IS WORSE THAN THAT!!"

And then there was a rumbling, an explosion, a loud noise that cut them off!

The plane lost its other wing, and the Interstices, like DeLoach, were losing control of its descend!

When the wing broke and the plane's weight violently shifted, Marcus and Coletrane were both flung -the latter backwards and the former forward.

Faster and faster, the plane was going down. DeLoach continued to pull back on the control wheel, teeth grit, muscles taut, sweat all over his face! The Interstices, they combined their efforts to help. But all these efforts were doing minuscule good!

The plane was going down, past Niger and the Cameroon, over Gabon and northern Angola...

The bushy tops of wenge trees and iroko, the fibrous shrubbery of raffia and sisal all rushing past the windows like a fast-forward reel, it was the last that anyone would see before ...the black.

———

A BLACK FERRARI 488 WAS ONE OF Coletrane's secondary vehicles. This is what Patrick grabbed the keys to. Poole's shoulder wound had been reopened in the fight, and he was also badly wounded by that throw into the curio.

Patrick helped him out to the car, putting the barely conscious old man in the passenger seat.

"You're gonna be alright, Poole," he assured, half convinced himself. "I'm getting you to a hospital."

"No,' Poole said weakly. "I am…. I'm fi-"

"We're not negotiating," Patrick turned over the engine and slammed his foot down on the accelerator. The car roared awake, her wheels kicking up dust and smoke while fishtailing to a start. And off they went!

———

THE CONSTELLATION OF THE THALATHA shifted once more, as the one previously talking went gray and another took on the light, all twelve afterimages collecting in a balance of six on their left and right.

The one now in color looked over the group; at Kojiro, Jubei, Kana, Otaku, Ittei, Kana, and Ichiro. They looked into the faces of these tired, browbeaten warriors, into their souls and the depths of their hearts, finding the truth of each one of them, and then said, holding up the spherule,

"Are all in agreement then, willing to pay the ultimate price for the ultimate answer, the ultimate skill, whatever its cost?"

Kojiro's six companions, they all regarded each other, nodding but saying nothing, their combined resolve solidified and unwavering. Kojiro himself, he never took his gaze off the Thalatha's face. And he didn't speak either, because he knew he didn't have to.

"Very well," said the Thalatha.

Then, one by one, the remaining Live Crew members faded, took on a translucence, and then vanished. Kojiro was the last to experience this, still staring into the eyes of the Thalatha, who added,

"We will meet again on the other side, Sakura. Perhaps.... We will spar."

Kojiro narrowed his eyes and smiled, and then was gone.

Hatsukoi dropped and the tip of her dragon decorated saya dug into the ground, the rest of her standing straight up with perfect balance.

DEEP WITHIN THE BELLY OF THE Congo Rainforest, exact location -unknown. Several dozen trees, toppled in the wake of a great crash. Debris, plane parts, scattered for miles. And somehow, miraculously, most of the Leer Jet executive cabin and cockpit were in one piece, dug into the earth where there used to be a small creek now destroyed by its unwelcome mechanical visitor. Residential animals, gorillas, chimpanzees, okapi, leopards, were hidden in plain sight among the still intact surrounding woods, looking upon the broken apart vessel.

Inside the cockpit, DeLoach's bleeding head was rested against the control panel. Somehow still alive, he was yet unconscious and badly wounded. It would not be discovered until later how many of his bones were broken.

A giant hole was torn out of the cabin wall, outside of which lay Coletrane in the grass -waking up and wondering how he was still in one piece, let alone alive at all.

He heard movement from inside of the plane, and so struggled to climb to his feet. Only to fall back down and discover that his left leg was broken, a piece of bone sticking out six inches below the knee. So he sat there, vulnerable and defenseless. Where, he wondered, was Hatsukoi?

Then as if on cue, the source of the noise was revealed as Marcus emerged from inside of the cabin -stepping out of the hole. There was blood on his face from a head wound, and he had to hold up his weight against the broken-open wall, but he could walk and appeared otherwise without injury.

Their eyes met. But then Marcus' attention was drawn to a presence behind his friend/enemy. Coletrane, fighting against the pain, turned to it as well.

And there they stood, in the grass, the three Interstices. All three had their heads down and their eyes closed, but then one by one they opened them and looked up. Their eyes, instead of deadly crystals that killed any animal on sight, had turned human-like in color and appearance. Therefore, Marcus and Coletrane could look at them without instantly, painfully, brutally dying.

Long moments passed before one of them, Zhrontese only, spoke.

"And now," she said, "it begins."

EPILOGUE

誕

THERE WAS A STORY ON A THEFT IN America so important that it made the evening news in Venice, Italy. At 10th St. NW, Washington, DC, the famous Ford's Theatre, time and date unknown, someone managed to break in, bypass all security measures, and steal an important object without leaving a shred of evidence. The theft, in fact, was only discovered by accident.

The reporter did not disclose what had been stolen, but Landau Kier, who was watching the news that night from a couch in his Paisiello apartment suite, knew what it was. The Deringer that killed president Abraham Lincoln. Up until this moment, he still believed that the gun in his possession was somehow a replica.

Not anymore.

Kier went out onto the balcony for some air, and to enjoy a cigarette. He stopped short of lighting it however when he looked up at the sky. There had been nothing in the news about a developing storm, yet he could see clouds forming over the Rialto Bridge on the horizon. They didn't look like clouds though. They looked more like... a body of living smoke.

———

AT A SMALL HOUSE IN LAFAYETTE, LOUISIANA, Qadr had just finished dressing Cynthia's wounds from the fight. And Cynthia hers...

They too went outside for some air, where there was a welcoming breeze and a calming stillness in the transition of night to morning. Also, however, a faint, burning scent. *Ash?*...

The moon was still visible, and it was splitting in two –*like a figure eight*.

"Do you see it, or is it just me? Am I... hallucinating?" Cynthia asked her would-be killer/friend from a previous life.

Qadr nodded.

Yes, she could see it, but then she turned her eyes to something happening west of the moon(s). Cynthia looked as well.

Clouds? No, smoke. A fog developing in the atmosphere that, now that they realized it, probably accounted for the strange smell in the air.

CPSIA information can be obtained
at www.ICGtesting.com
Printed in the USA
JSHW060206281222
34337JS00007B/8/J